© Kelly Campbell

About the Author

BERNARD CORNWELL is the author of the acclaimed and bestselling Saxon Tales, which include *The Last Kingdom*, *The Pale Horseman*, *Lords of the North*, and *Sword Song*; the Richard Sharpe novels; the Grail Quest series; the Nathaniel Starbuck Chronicles; the Warlord Chronicles; and many other novels, including *Stonehenge* and *Gallows Thief*. He lives with his wife on Cape Cod.

BOOKS BY BERNARD CORNWELL

The Saxon Tales

THE LAST KINGDOM
THE PALE HORSEMAN
LORDS OF THE NORTH
SWORD SONG

The Sharpe Novels (in chronological order)

SHARPE'S TIGER
Richard Sharpe and the Siege of Seringapatam, 1799

SHARPE'S TRIUMPH
Richard Sharpe and the Battle of Assaye, September 1803

SHARPE'S FORTRESS
Richard Sharpe and the Siege of Gawilghur, December 1803

SHARPE'S TRAFALGAR
Richard Sharpe and the Battle of Trafalgar, 21 October 1805

SHARPE'S PREY
Richard Sharpe and the Expedition to Copenhagen, 1807

SHARPE'S RIFLES
Richard Sharpe and the French Invasion of Galicia, January 1809

SHARPE'S HAVOC
Richard Sharpe and the Campaign in Northern Portugal, Spring 1809

SHARPE'S EAGLE
Richard Sharpe and the Talavera Campaign, July 1809

SHARPE'S GOLD
Richard Sharpe and the Destruction of Almeida, August 1810

SHARPE'S ESCAPE
Richard Sharpe and the Bussaco Campaign, 1810

SHARPE'S FURY
Richard Sharpe and the Battle of Barrosa, March 1811

SHARPE'S BATTLE
Richard Sharpe and the Battle of Fuentes de Onoro, May 1811

SHARPE'S COMPANY
Richard Sharpe and the Siege of Badajoz, January to April 1812

SHARPE'S SWORD
Richard Sharpe and the Salamanca Campaign, June and July 1812

SHARPE'S ENEMY
Richard Sharpe and the Defense of Portugal, Christmas 1812

SHARPE'S HONOUR
Richard Sharpe and the Vitoria Campaign, February to June 1813

SHARPE'S REGIMENT
Richard Sharpe and the Invasion of France, June to November 1813

SHARPE'S SIEGE
Richard Sharpe and the Winter Campaign, 1814

SHARPE'S REVENGE
Richard Sharpe and the Peace of 1814

SHARPE'S WATERLOO
Richard Sharpe and the Waterloo Campaign, 15 June to 18 June 1815

SHARPE'S DEVIL
Richard Sharpe and the Emperor, 1820–21

The Grail Quest Series

THE ARCHER'S TALE
VAGABOND
HERETIC

The Nathaniel Starbuck Chronicles

REBEL
COPPERHEAD
BATTLE FLAG
THE BLOODY GROUND

The Warlord Chronicles

THE WINTER KING
THE ENEMY OF GOD
EXCALIBUR

The Sailing Thrillers

STORMCHILD
SCOUNDREL

Other Novels

STONEHENGE, 2000 B.C.: A NOVEL
GALLOWS THIEF
A CROWNING MERCY
THE FALLEN ANGELS
REDCOAT

LORDS OF
THE NORTH

Bernard Cornwell

HARPER

NEW YORK ⋅ LONDON ⋅ TORONTO ⋅ SYDNEY

For Ed Breslin

HARPER

First published in a different form in the United Kingdom in 2006 by HarperCollins Publishers.

A hardcover edition of this book was published in 2007 by HarperCollins Publishers.

FIRST HARPER PAPERBACK PUBLISHED 2008.

Designed by Elliott Beard

The Library of Congress has catalogued the hardcover edition as follows:
Cornwell, Bernard.
    The lords of the North : a novel / Bernard Cornwell.—1st ed.
       p. cm. — (The Saxon novels)
    Sequel to: The pale horseman.
    ISBN-13: 978-0-06-088862-6
    ISBN-10: 0-06-088862-8
    1. Great Britain—History—Alfred, 871–899—Fiction. 2. Alfred, King of England, 849–899—Fiction. 3. Vikings—Fiction. I. Title.
    PS6053.075L67 2006
    823'.914—dc22   2006043627

ISBN: 978-0-06-114904-7 (pbk.)

22 23 24 25 26 LBC 32 31 30 29 28

... Com on wanre niht scriðan sceadugenga

From out of the wan night slides the shadow walker

—Beowulf

CONTENTS

PLACE-NAMES

The spelling of place-names in Anglo Saxon England was an uncertain business, with no consistency and no agreement even about the name itself. Thus London was variously rendered as Lundonia, Lundenberg, Lundenne, Lundene, Lundenwic, Lundenceaster and Lundres. Doubtless some readers will prefer other versions of the names listed below, but I have usually employed whichever spelling is cited in either the *Oxford Dictionary of English Place-Names* or the *Cambridge Dictionary of English Place-Names* for the years nearest or contained within Alfred's reign, A.D. 871–899, but even that solution is not foolproof. Hayling Island, in 956, was written as both Heilincigae and Hæglingaiggæ. Nor have I been consistent myself; I should spell England as Englaland, and have preferred the modern form Northumbria to Norðhymbralond to avoid the suggestion that the boundaries of the ancient kingdom coincide with those of the modern county. So this list, like the spellings themselves, is capricious.

Æthelingæg	Athelney, Somerset
Alclyt	Bishop Auckland, County Durham
Baðum (pronounced Bathum)	Bath, Avon
Bebbanburg	Bamburgh Castle, Northumberland

Berrocscire	Berkshire
Cair Ligualid	Carlisle, Cumbria
Cetreht	Catterick, Yorkshire
Cippanhamm	Chippenham, Wiltshire
Contwaraburg	Canterbury, Kent
Cumbraland	Cumbria
Cuncacester	Chester-le-Street, County Durham
Cynuit	Cynuit Hillfort, nr Cannington, Somerset
Defnascir	Devonshire
Dornwaraceaster	Dorchester, Dorset
Dunholm	Durham, County Durham
Dyflin	Dublin, Eire
Eoferwic	York
Ethandun	Edington, Wiltshire
Exanceaster	Exeter, Devon
Fifhidan	Fyfield, Wiltshire
Gleawecestre	Gloucester, Gloucestershire
Gyruum	Jarrow, County Durham
Hamptonscir	Hampshire
Haithabu	Hedeby, trading town in southern Denmark
Heagostealdes	Hexham, Northumberland
Hedene	River Eden, Cumbria
Hocchale	Houghall, County Durham
Horn	Hofn, Iceland
Hreapandune	Repton, Derbyshire
Kenet	River Kennet
Lindisfarena	Lindisfarne (Holy Island), Northumberland
Lundene	London
Onhripum	Ripon, Yorkshire

Pedredan	River Parrett
Readingum	Reading, Berkshire
Scireburnan	Sherborne, Dorset
Snotengaham	Nottingham, Nottinghamshire
Strath Clota	Strathclyde
Sumorsæte	Somerset
Suth Seaxa	Sussex (South Saxons)
Synningthwait	Swinithwaite, Yorkshire
Temes	River Thames
Thornsæta	Dorset
Thresk	Thirsk, Yorkshire
Tine	River Tyne
Tuede	River Tweed
Wiire	River Wear
Wiltun	Wilton, Wiltshire
Wiltunscir	Wiltshire
Wintanceaster	Winchester, Hampshire

PART ONE

THE SLAVE KING

I wanted darkness. There was a half-moon that summer night and it kept sliding from behind the clouds to make me nervous. I wanted darkness.

I had carried two leather bags to the small ridge which marked the northern boundary of my estate. My estate. Fifhaden, it was called, and it was King Alfred's reward for the service I had done him at Ethandun where, on the long green hill, we had destroyed a Danish army. It had been shield wall against shield wall, and at its end Alfred was king again and the Danes were beaten, and Wessex lived, and I daresay that I had done more than most men. My woman had died, my friend had died, I had taken a spear thrust in my right thigh, and my reward was Fifhaden.

Five hides. That was what the name meant. Five hides! Scarce enough land to support the four families of slaves who tilled the soil and sheared the sheep and trapped fish in the River Kenet. Other men had been given great estates and the church had been rewarded with rich woodlands and deep pastures, while I had been given five hides. I hated Alfred. He was a miserable, pious, tight-fisted king who distrusted me because I was no Christian, because I was a northerner, and because I had given him his kingdom back at Ethandun. And as reward he had given me Fifhaden. Bastard.

So I had carried the two bags to the low ridge that had been cropped by sheep and was littered with enormous gray boulders that glowed white when the moon escaped the wispy clouds. I crouched by one of the vast stones and Hild knelt beside me.

She was my woman then. She had been a nun in Cippanhamm, but the Danes had captured the town and they had whored her. Now she was with me. Sometimes, in the night, I would hear her praying and her prayers were all tears and despair, and I reckoned she would go back to her god in the end, but for the moment I was her refuge. "Why are we waiting?" she asked.

I touched a finger to my lips to silence her. She watched me. She had a long face, large eyes, and golden hair under a scrap of scarf. I reckoned she was wasted as a nun. Alfred, of course, wanted her back in the nunnery. That was why I let her stay. To annoy him. Bastard.

I was waiting to make certain that no one watched us. It was unlikely, for folk do not like to venture into the night when things of horror stalk the earth. Hild clutched at her crucifix, but I was comfortable in the dark. From the time I was a small child I had taught myself to love the night. I was a sceadugengan, a shadow-walker, one of the creatures other men feared.

I waited a long time until I was certain no one else was on the low ridge, then I drew Wasp-Sting, my short-sword, and I cut out a square of turf that I laid to one side. Then I dug into the ground, piling the soil onto my cloak. The blade kept striking chalk and flints and I knew Wasp-Sting's blade would be chipped, but I went on digging until I had made a hole large enough for a child's burial. We put the two bags into the earth. They were my hoard. My silver and gold, my wealth, and I did not wish to be burdened with it. I possessed five hides, two swords, a mail coat, a shield, a helmet, a horse, and a thin nun, but I had no men to protect a hoard and so I had to hide it instead. I kept only a few silver coins and the rest I put into the ground's keeping, and we covered the hoard over and stamped the soil down and then replaced the turf. I waited for the moon to sail out from behind a cloud and then I looked at the turf and reckoned no one would know it had been disturbed, and I memorized the place, marking it in my mind by the nearby boulders. One day, when I had the means to protect that treasure, I would return for it. Hild stared at the hoard's grave. "Alfred says you must stay here," she said.

"Alfred can piss down his own throat," I said, "and I hope the bastard chokes on it and dies." He would probably die soon enough for he was a sick man. He was only twenty-nine, eight years older than I was, yet he looked closer to fifty and I doubt any of us would have given him more than two or three years to live. He was forever griping about his belly pains or running to the shithole or shivering in a fever.

Hild touched the turf where the hoard was buried. "Does this mean we're coming back to Wessex?" she asked.

"It means," I said, "that no man travels among enemies with his hoard. It's safer here, and if we survive, we'll fetch it. And if I die, you fetch it." She said nothing, and we carried the earth that was left on the cloak back to the river and threw it into the water.

In the morning we took our horses and rode eastward. We were going to Lundene, for in Lundene all roads start. It was fate that drove me. It was the year 878, I was twenty-one years old and believed my swords could win me the whole world. I was Uhtred of Bebbanburg, the man who had killed Ubba Lothbrokson beside the sea and who had spilled Svein of the White Horse from his saddle at Ethandun. I was the man who had given Alfred his kingdom back and I hated him. So I would leave him. My path was the sword-path, and it would take me home. I would go north.

Lundene is the greatest city in all the island of Britain and I have always loved its ruined houses and feverish alleys, but Hild and I stayed there only two days, lodging in a Saxon tavern in the new town west of the decaying Roman walls. The place was a part of Mercia then and was garrisoned by the Danes. The alehouses were full of traders and foreigners and shipmasters, and it was a merchant called Thorkild who offered us passage to Northumbria. I told him my name was Ragnarson and he neither believed me nor questioned me and he gave us passage in return for two silver coins and my muscle on one of his oars. I was a Saxon, but I had been raised by the Danes so I spoke their tongue and Thorkild assumed I was Danish. My fine helmet, mail coat, and two swords told him I was a warrior and he must have suspected I was a fugitive from the defeated army, but what did he care? He needed oarsmen. Some traders used only slaves at their oars, but Thorkild reckoned they were trouble and employed free men.

We left on the ebb-tide, our hull filled with bolts of linen, oil from Frankia, beaver pelts, scores of fine saddles and leather sacks filled with precious cumin and mustard. Once away from the city and in the estuary of the Temes we were in East Anglia, but we saw little of that kingdom for on our first night a pernicious fog rolled in from the sea and it stayed for days. Some mornings we could not travel at all, and even when the weather was half good we never went far from shore. I had thought to sail home because it would be quicker than traveling by road, but instead we crept mile by foggy mile through a tangle of mudbanks, creeks, and treacherous currents. We stopped every night, finding some place to anchor or tie up, and spent a whole week in some godforsaken East Anglian marsh because a bow-strake sprang loose and the water could not be bailed fast enough, and so we were forced to haul the ship onto a muddy beach and make repairs. By the time the hull was caulked the weather had changed and the sun sparkled on a fogless sea and we rowed northward, still stopping every night. We saw a dozen other ships, all longer and narrower than Thorkild's craft. They were Danish warships and all were traveling northward. I assumed they were fugitives from Guthrum's defeated army and they were going home to Denmark or perhaps to Frisia or wherever there was easier plunder to be had than in Alfred's Wessex.

Thorkild was a tall, lugubrious man who thought he was thirty-five years old. He plaited his graying hair so that it hung in long ropes to his waist, and his arms were bare of the rings that showed a warrior's prowess. "I was never a fighter," he confessed to me. "I was raised as a trader and I've always been a trader and my son will trade when I'm dead."

"You live in Eoferwic?" I asked.

"Lundene. But I keep a storehouse in Eoferwic. It's a good place to buy fleeces."

"Does Ricsig still rule there?" I asked.

He shook his head. "Ricsig's been dead two years now. There's a man called Egbert on the throne now."

"There was a King Egbert in Eoferwic when I was a child."

"This is his son, or his grandson? Maybe his cousin? He's a Saxon, anyway."

"So who really rules in Northumbria?"

"We do, of course," he said, meaning the Danes. The Danes often put a tamed Saxon on the thrones of the countries they captured, and Egbert, whoever he was, was doubtless just such a leashed monarch. He gave a pretense of legality to the Danish occupiers, but the real ruler was Earl Ivarr, the Dane who owned most of the land about the city. "He's Ivarr Ivarson," Thorkild told me with a touch of pride in his voice, "and his father was Ivar Lothbrokson."

"I knew Ivar Lothbrokson," I said.

I doubt Thorkild believed me, but it was true. Ivar Lothbrokson had been a fearsome warlord, thin and skeletal, savage and ghastly, but he had been a friend to Earl Ragnar who raised me. His brother had been Ubba, the man I had killed by the sea. "Ivarr is the real power in Northumbria," Thorkild told me, "but not in the valley of the River Wiire. Kjartan rules there." Thorkild touched his hammer amulet when he spoke Kjartan's name. "He's called Kjartan the Cruel now," he said, "and his son is worse."

"Sven." I said the name sourly. I knew Kjartan and Sven. They were my enemies.

"Sven the One-Eyed," Thorkild said with a grimace and again touched his amulet as if to fend off the evil of the names he had just spoken. "And north of them," he went on, "the ruler is Ælfric of Bebbanburg."

I knew him too. Ælfric of Bebbanburg was my uncle and thief of my land, but I pretended not to know the name. "Ælfric?" I asked, "another Saxon?"

"A Saxon," Thorkild confirmed, "but his fortress is too powerful for us," he added by way of explanation why a Saxon lord was permitted to stay in Northumbria, "and he does nothing to offend us."

"A friend of the Danes?"

"He's no enemy," he said. "Those are the three great lords. Ivarr, Kjartan, and Ælfric, while beyond the hills in Cumbraland? No one knows what happens there." He meant the west coast of Northumbria which faced the Irish Sea. "There was a great Danish lord in Cumbraland," he went on. "Hardicnut, he was called, but I hear he was killed in a squabble. And now?" He shrugged.

So that was Northumbria, a kingdom of rival lords, none of whom had cause to love me and two of whom wanted me dead. Yet it was home, and I had a duty there and that is why I was following the sword-path.

It was the duty of the bloodfeud. The feud had started five years before when Kjartan and his men had come to Earl Ragnar's hall in the night. They had burned the hall and they had murdered the folk who tried to flee the flames. Ragnar had raised me, I had loved him like a father, and his murder was unavenged. He had a son, also called Ragnar, and he was my friend, but Ragnar the Younger could not take vengeance for he was now a hostage in Wessex. So I would go north and I would find Kjartan and I would kill him. And I would kill his son, Sven the One-Eyed, who had taken Ragnar's daughter prisoner. Did Thyra still live? I did not know. I only knew I had sworn to revenge Ragnar the Elder's death. It sometimes seemed to me, as I hauled on Thorkild's oar, that I was foolish to be going home because Northumbria was full of my enemies, but fate drove me, and there was a lump in my throat when at last we turned into the wide mouth of the Humber.

There was nothing to see other than a low muddy shore half glimpsed through rain, and withies in the shallows marking hidden creeks, and great mats of oarweed and bladderwrack heaving on the gray water, but this was the river that led into Northumbria and I knew, at that moment, that I had made the right decision. This was home. Not Wessex with its richer fields and gentler hills. Wessex was tamed, harnessed by king and church, but up here there were wilder skeins in the colder air.

"Is this where you live?" Hild asked as the banks closed on either side.

"My land is far to the north," I told her. "That's Mercia," I pointed to the river's southern shore, "and that's Northumbria," I pointed the other way, "and Northumbria stretches up into the barbarous lands."

"Barbarous?"

"Scots," I said, and spat over the side. Before the Danes came the Scots had been our chief enemies, ever raiding south into our land, but they, like us, had been assaulted by the Northmen and that had lessened their threat, though it had not ended it.

We rowed up the Ouse and our songs accompanied the oar strokes as we glided beneath willow and alder, past meadows and woods, and Thorkild, now that we had entered Northumbria, took the carved dog's head from his boat's prow so that the snarling beast would not scare the spirits of the land. And that evening, under a washed sky, we came to Eoferwic, the chief city of Northumbria and the place where my father had been slaughtered and where I had been orphaned and where I had met Ragnar the Elder who had raised me and given me my love of the Danes.

I was not rowing as we approached the city for I had pulled an oar all day and Thorkild had relieved me, and so I was standing in the bow, staring at the smoke sifting up from the city's roofs, and then I glanced down at the river and saw the first corpse. It was a boy, perhaps ten or eleven years old, and he was naked except for a rag about his waist. His throat had been cut, though the great wound was bloodless now because it had been washed clean by the Ouse. His long fair hair drifted like weed under water.

We saw two more floating bodies, then we were close enough to see men on the city's ramparts and there were too many men there, men with spears and shields, and there were more men by the river quays, men in mail, men watching us warily, men with drawn swords and Thorkild called an order and our oars lifted and water dripped from the motionless blades. The boat slewed in the current and I heard the screams from inside the city.

I had come home.

ONE

Thorkild let the boat drift downstream a hundred paces, then rammed her bows into the bank close to a willow. He jumped ashore, tied a sealhide line to tether the boat to the willow's trunk, and then, with a fearful glance at the armed men watching from higher up the bank, scrambled hurriedly back on board. "You," he pointed at me, "find out what's happening."

"Trouble's happening," I said. "You need to know more?"

"I need to know what's happened to my storehouse," he said, then nodded toward the armed men, "and I don't want to ask them. So you can instead."

He chose me because I was a warrior and because, if I died, he would not grieve. Most of his oarsmen were capable of fighting, but he avoided combat whenever he could because bloodshed and trading were bad partners. The armed men were advancing down the bank now. There were six of them, but they approached very hesitantly, for Thorkild had twice their number in his ship's bows and all those seamen were armed with axes and spears.

I pulled my mail over my head, unwrapped the glorious wolf-crested helmet I had captured from a Danish boat off the Welsh coast, buckled on Serpent-Breath and Wasp-Sting and, thus dressed for war, jumped clumsily ashore. I slipped on the steep bank, clutched at nettles for support and then, cursing because of the stings, clambered up to the path. I had been here before, for this was the wide riverside pasture where my father had led the attack on Eoferwic. I pulled on the helmet and shouted at Thorkild to throw me my shield. He did and, just as I was about to start walking toward the six men who were now standing and watching me with swords in their hands, Hild jumped after me. "You should have stayed on the boat," I told her.

"Not without you," she said. She was carrying our one leather bag in which was little more than a change of clothes, a knife and a whet-stone. "Who are they?" she asked, meaning the six men who were still fifty paces away and in no hurry to close the distance.

"Let's find out," I said, and drew Serpent-Breath.

The shadows were long and the smoke of the city's cooking fires was purple and gold in the twilight. Rooks flew toward their nests and in the distance I could see cows going to their evening milking. I walked toward the six men. I was in mail, I had a shield and two swords, I wore arm rings and a helmet that was worth the value of three fine mail coats and my appearance checked the six men, who huddled together and waited for me. They all had drawn swords, but I saw that two of them had crucifixes about their necks and that made me suppose they were Saxons. "When a man comes home," I called to them in English, "he does not expect to be met by swords."

Two of them were older men, perhaps in their thirties, both of them thick-bearded and wearing mail. The other four were in leather coats and were younger, just seventeen or eighteen, and the blades in their hands looked as unfamiliar to them as a plow handle would to me. They must have assumed I was a Dane because I had come from a Danish ship and they must have known that six of them could kill one Dane, but they also knew that one war-Dane, dressed in battle-splendor, was likely to kill at least two of them before he died and so they were relieved when I spoke to them in English. They were also puzzled. "Who are you?" one of the older men called.

I did not answer, but just kept walking toward them. If they had decided to attack me then I would have been forced to flee ignominiously or else die, but I walked confidently, my shield held low and with Serpent-Breath's tip brushing the long grass. They took my reluctance to answer for arrogance, when in truth it was confusion. I had thought to call myself by any name other than my own, for I did not want Kjartan or my traitorous uncle to know I had returned to Northumbria, but my name was also one to be reckoned with and I was foolishly tempted to use it to awe them, but inspiration came just in time. "I am Steapa of Defnascir," I announced, and just in case Steapa's name was unknown in Northumbria, I added a boast. "I am the man who put Svein of the White Horse into his long home in the earth."

The man who had demanded my name stepped a pace backward. "You are Steapa? The one who serves Alfred?"

"I am."

"Lord," he said, and lowered his blade. One of the younger men touched his crucifix and dropped to a knee. A third man sheathed his sword and the others, deciding that was prudent, did the same.

"Who are you?" I demanded.

"We serve King Egbert," one of the older men said.

"And the dead?" I asked, gesturing toward the river where another naked corpse circled slow in the current, "who are they?"

"Danes, lord."

"You're killing Danes?"

"It's God's will, lord," he said.

I gestured toward Thorkild's ship. "That man is a Dane and he is also a friend. Will you kill him?"

"We know Thorkild, lord," the man said, "and if he comes in peace he will live."

"And me?" I demanded, "what would you do with me?"

"The king would see you, lord. He would honor you for the great slaughter of the Danes."

"This slaughter?" I asked scornfully, pointing Serpent-Breath toward a corpse floating downriver.

"He would honor the victory over Guthrum, lord. Is it true?"

"It is true," I said, "I was there." I turned then, sheathed Serpent-Breath, and beckoned to Thorkild who untied his ship and rowed it upstream. I shouted to him across the water, telling him that Egbert's Saxons had risen against the Danes, but that these men promised they would leave him in peace if he came in friendship.

"What would you do in my place?" Thorkild called back. His men gave their oars small tugs to hold the ship against the river's flow.

"Go downstream," I shouted in Danish, "find sword-Danes and wait till you know what is happening."

"And you?" he asked.

"I stay here," I said.

He groped in a pouch and threw something toward me. It glittered in the fading light, then vanished among the buttercups that made the darkening pasture yellow. "That's for your advice," he called, "and may you live long, whoever you are."

He turned his ship which was a clumsy maneuver for the hull was almost as long as the Ouse was wide, but he managed it skillfully enough and the oars took him downstream and out of my life. I discovered later that his storehouse had been ransacked and the one-armed Dane who guarded it had been slaughtered and his daughter raped, so my advice was worth the silver coin Thorkild had thrown to me.

"You sent him away?" one of the bearded men asked me resentfully.

"I told you, he was a friend." I stooped and found the shilling in the long grass. "So how do you know of Alfred's victory?" I asked.

"A priest came, lord," he said, "and he told us."

"A priest?"

"From Wessex, lord. All the way from Wessex. He carried a message from King Alfred."

I should have known Alfred would want the news of his victory over Guthrum to spread throughout Saxon England, and it turned out that he had sent priests to wherever Saxons lived and those priests carried the message that Wessex was victorious and that God and his saints had given them the triumph. One such priest had been sent to King Egbert in Eoferwic, and that priest had reached the city just one day before me, and that was when the stupidity began.

The priest had traveled on horseback, his clerical frock wrapped in a bundle on the back of his saddle, and he had ridden from Saxon house to Saxon house through Danish-held Mercia. The Mercian Saxons had helped him on his way, providing fresh horses each day and escorting him past the larger Danish garrisons until he had come to Northumbria's capital to give King Egbert the good news that the West Saxons had defeated the Great Army of the Danes. Yet what appealed even more to the Northumbrian Saxons was the outrageous claim that Saint Cuthbert had appeared to Alfred in a dream and shown him how to gain the victory. The dream was supposed to have come to Alfred during the winter of defeat in Æthelingæg where a handful of fugitive Saxons hid from the conquering Danes, and the story of the dream was aimed at Egbert's Saxons like a huntsman's arrow, for there was no saint more revered north of the Humber than Cuthbert. Cuthbert was Northumbria's idol, the holiest Christian ever to live in the land, and there was not one pious Saxon household that did not pray to him daily. The idea that the north's own glorious saint had helped Wessex defeat the Danes drove the wits from King Egbert's skull like partridges fleeing the reapers. He had every right to be pleased at Alfred's victory, and he doubtless resented ruling on a Danish leash, but what he should have done was thank the priest who brought the news and then, to keep him quiet, shut him up like a dog in a kennel. Instead he had ordered Wulfhere, the city's archbishop, to hold a service of thanks in the city's largest church. Wulfhere, who was no fool, had immediately developed an ague and ridden into the country to recover, but a fool called Father Hrothweard took his place and Eoferwic's big church had resounded to a fiery sermon which claimed Saint Cuthbert had come from heaven to lead the West Saxons to victory, and that idiotic tale had persuaded Eoferwic's Saxons that God and Saint Cuthbert were about to deliver their own country from the Danes. And so the killing had started.

All this I learned as we went into the city. I learned too that there had been fewer than a hundred Danish warriors in Eoferwic because the rest had marched north under Earl Ivarr to confront a Scottish army that had crossed the border. There had been no such invasion in living memory, but the southern Scots had a new king who had sworn to make Eoferwic his new capital, and so Ivarr had taken his army north to teach the fellow a lesson.

Ivarr was the true ruler of southern Northumbria. If he had wanted to call himself the king then there was no one to stop him, but it was convenient to have a pliable Saxon on the throne to collect the taxes and to keep his fellow-Saxons quiet. Ivarr, meanwhile, could do what his family did best; make war. He was a Lothbrok and it was their boast that no male Lothbrok had ever died in bed. They died fighting with their swords in their hands. Ivarr's father and one uncle had died in Ireland, while Ubba, the third Lothbrok brother, had fallen to my sword at Cynuit. Now Ivarr, the latest sword-Dane from a war-besotted family, was marching against the Scots and had sworn to bring their king to Eoferwic in slave manacles.

I thought no Saxon in his right mind would rebel against Ivarr, who was reputed to be as ruthless as his father, but Alfred's victory and the claim that it was inspired by Saint Cuthbert had ignited the madness in Eoferwic. The flames were fed by Father Hrothweard's preaching. He bellowed that God, Saint Cuthbert, and an army of angels were coming to drive the Danes from Northumbria and my arrival only encouraged the insanity. "God has sent you," the men who had accosted me kept saying, and they shouted to folk that I was Svein's killer and by the time we reached the palace there was a small crowd following Hild and me as we pushed through narrow streets still stained with Danish blood.

I had been to Eoferwic's palace before. It was a Roman building of fine pale stone with vast pillars holding up a tiled roof that was now patched with blackened straw. The floor was also tiled, and those tiles had once formed pictures of the Roman gods, but they were all torn up now and those that were left were mostly covered by rushes that were stained by the previous day's blood. The big hall stank like a butcher's yard and was wreathed with smoke from the blazing torches that lit the cavernous space.

The new King Egbert turned out to be the old King Egbert's nephew and he had his uncle's shifty face and petulant mouth. He looked scared when he came onto the dais at the hall's end, and no wonder, for the mad Hrothweard had summoned up a whirlwind and Egbert must have known that Ivarr's Danes would be coming for revenge. Yet Egbert's followers were caught up in the excitement, sure that Alfred's victory foretold the final defeat of the Northmen, and my arrival was taken as another sign from heaven. I was pushed forward and the news of my coming was shouted at the king who looked confused, and was even more confused when another voice, a familiar voice, called out my name. "Uhtred! Uhtred!"

I looked for the speaker and saw it was Father Willibald.

"Uhtred!" he shouted again and looked delighted to see me. Egbert frowned at me, then looked at Willibald. "Uhtred!" the priest said, ignoring the king, and came forward to embrace me.

Father Willibald was a good friend and a good man. He was a West Saxon who had once been chaplain to Alfred's fleet, and fate had decreed that he would be the man sent north to carry the good news of Ethandun to the Northumbrian Saxons.

The clamor in the hall subsided. Egbert tried to take command. "Your name is," he said, then decided he did not know what my name was.

"Steapa!" one of the men who had escorted us into the city called out.

"Uhtred!" Willibald announced, his eyes bright with excitement.

"I am Uhtred of Bebbanburg," I confessed, unable to prolong my deception.

"The man who killed Ubba Lothbrokson!" Willibald announced and tried to hold up my right hand to show I was a champion. "And the man," he went on, "who toppled Svein of the White Horse at Ethandun!"

In two days, I thought, Kjartan the Cruel would know that I was in

Northumbria, and in three my uncle Ælfric would have learned of my
coming, and if I had possessed an ounce of sense I would have forced
my way out of that hall, taken Hild with me, and headed south as fast
as Archbishop Wulfhere had vanished from Eoferwic.

"You were at Ethandun?" Egbert asked me.

"I was, lord."

"What happened?"

They had already heard the tale of the battle from Willibald, but
his was a priest's version, heavy with prayers and miracles. I gave
them what they wanted which was a warrior's story of dead Danes
and sword-slaughter, and all the while a fierce-eyed priest with bristly
hair and an unruly beard interrupted me with shouts of hallelujah. I
gathered this was Father Hrothweard, the priest who had roused
Eoferwic to slaughter. He was young, scarce older than I was, but he
had a powerful voice and a natural authority that was given extra
force by his passion. Every hallelujah was accompanied by a shower
of spittle, and no sooner had I described the defeated Danes spilling
down the great slope from Ethandun's summit than Hrothweard
leaped forward and harangued the crowd. "This is Uhtred!" he
shouted, poking me in my mail-clad ribs, "Uhtred of Northumbria,
Uhtred of Bebbanburg, a killer of Danes, a warrior of God, a sword of
the Lord! And he has come to us, just as the blessed Saint Cuthbert
visited Alfred in his time of tribulation! These are signs from the
Almighty!" The crowd cheered, the king looked scared, and Hrothweard, ever ready to launch into a fiery sermon, began frothing at the
mouth as he described the coming slaughter of every Dane in
Northumbria.

I managed to sidle away from Hrothweard, making my way to the
back of the dais where I took Willibald by the scruff of his skinny neck
and forced him into a passage which led to the king's private chambers.
"You're an idiot," I growled at him, "you're an earsling. You're a witless
dribbling turd, that's what you are. I should slit your useless guts here
and now and feed them to the pigs."

Willibald opened his mouth, closed it, and looked helpless.

"The Danes will be back here," I promised him, "and there's going to be a massacre."

His mouth opened and closed again, and still no sound came.

"So what you're going to do," I said, "is cross the Ouse and go south as fast as your legs will carry you."

"But it's all true," he pleaded.

"What's all true?"

"That Saint Cuthbert gave us victory!"

"Of course it isn't true!" I snarled. "Alfred made it up. You think Cuthbert came to him in Æthelingæg? Then why didn't he tell us about the dream when it happened? Why does he wait till after the battle to tell us?" I paused and Willibald made a strangled noise. "He waited," I answered myself, "because it didn't happen."

"But . . ."

"He made it up!" I growled, "because he wants Northumbrians to look to Wessex for leadership against the Danes. He wants to be king of Northumbria, don't you understand that? And not just Northumbria. I've no doubt he's got fools like you telling the Mercians that one of their damned saints appeared to him in a dream."

"But he did," he interrupted me, and when I looked bemused, he explained further. "You're right! Saint Kenelm spoke to Alfred in Æthelingæg. He came to him in a dream and he told Alfred that he would win."

"No he did not," I said as patiently as I could.

"But it's true!" he insisted, "Alfred told me himself! It's God's doing, Uhtred, and wonderful to behold."

I took him by the shoulders, pressing him against the passage wall. "You've got a choice, father," I said. "You can get out of Eoferwic before the Danes come back, or you can tip your head to one side."

"I can do what?" he asked, puzzled.

"Tip your head," I said, "and I'll thump you on one ear so all the nonsense falls out of the other."

He would not be persuaded. God's glory, ignited by the bloodshed at Ethandun and fanned by the lie about Saint Cuthbert, was glowing

on Northumbria and poor Willibald was convinced he was present at
the beginning of great things.

There was a feast that night, a sorry business of salted herrings,
cheese, hard bread, and stale ale, and Father Hrothweard made
another impassioned speech in which he claimed that Alfred of Wessex had sent me, his greatest warrior, to lead the city's defense, and
that the fyrd of heaven would come to Eoferwic's protection.
Willibald kept shouting hallelujah, believing all the rubbish, and it
was only the next day when a gray rain and a sullen mist enveloped
the city that he began to doubt the imminent arrival of sword-angels.

Folk were leaving the city. There were rumors of Danish war-bands
gathering to the north. Hrothweard was still shrieking his nonsense,
and he led a procession of priests and monks about the city streets,
holding aloft relics and banners, but anyone with sense now understood that Ivarr was likely to return long before Saint Cuthbert turned
up with a heavenly host. King Egbert sent a messenger to find me,
and the man said the king would talk with me, but I reckoned Egbert
was doomed so I ignored the summons. Egbert would have to shift
for himself.

Just as I had to shift for myself, and what I wanted was to get far from
the city before Ivarr's wrath descended on it, and in the Crossed Swords
tavern, hard by the city's northern gate, I found my escape. He was a
Dane called Bolti and he had survived the massacre because he was married to a Saxon and his wife's family had sheltered him. He saw me in
the tavern and asked if I was Uhtred of Bebbanburg.

"I am."

He sat opposite me, bowed his head respectfully to Hild, then
snapped his fingers to summon a girl with ale. He was a plump man,
bald, with a pocked face, a broken nose and frightened eyes. His two
sons, both half Saxon, loitered behind him. I guessed one was about
twenty and the other five years younger, and both wore swords
though neither looked comfortable with the weapons. "I knew Earl
Ragnar the Elder," Bolti said.

"I knew him too," I said, "and I don't remember you."

"The last time he sailed in *Wind-Viper*," he said, "I sold him ropes and oar-looms."

"Did you cheat him?" I asked sarcastically.

"I liked him," he said fiercely.

"And I loved him," I said, "because he became my father."

"I know he did," he said, "and I remember you." He fell silent and glanced at Hild. "You were very young," he went on, looking back to me, "and you were with a small dark girl."

"You do remember me then," I said, and fell silent as the ale was brought. I noticed that Bolti, despite being a Dane, wore a cross about his neck and he saw me looking at it.

"In Eoferwic," he said, touching the cross, "a man must live." He pulled aside his coat and I saw Thor's hammer amulet had been hidden beneath it. "They mostly killed pagans," he explained.

I pulled my own hammer amulet out from beneath my jerkin. "Are many Danes Christians now?" I asked.

"A few," he said grudgingly, "you want food to go with that ale?"

"I want to know why you're talking with me," I said.

He wanted to leave the city. He wanted to take his Saxon wife, two sons and two daughters a long way from the vengeful massacre he suspected was coming, and he wanted swords to escort him, and he stared at me with pathetic, despairing eyes and did not know that what he wanted was just what I wanted. "So where will you go?" I asked.

"Not west," he said with a shudder. "There's killing in Cumbraland."

"There's always killing in Cumbraland," I said. Cumbraland was the part of Northumbria that lay across the hills and next to the Irish Sea, and it was raided by Scots from Strath Clota, by Norsemen from Ireland, and by Britons from north Wales. Some Danes had settled in Cumbraland, but not enough to keep the wild raids from ravaging the place.

"I'd go to Denmark," Bolti said, "but there are no warships." The only ships left at Eoferwic's quays were Saxon traders, and if any dared sail they would be snapped up by Danish ships that were doubtless gathering in the Humber.

"So?" I asked.

"So I want to go north," he said, "and meet Ivarr. I can pay you."

"And you think I can escort you through Kjartan's land?"

"I think I will do better with Ragnar's son beside me than on my own," he admitted, "and if men know you travel with me then they will join us."

So I let him pay me, and my price was sixteen shillings, two mares and a black stallion, and the price of the last made Bolti go pale. A man had been leading the stallion about the streets, offering it for sale, and Bolti bought the animal because his fear of being trapped in Eoferwic was worth forty shillings. The black horse was battle trained, which meant he was not startled at loud noises and he moved obediently to the pressure of a knee, which left a man free to hold shield and sword and still maneuver. The stallion had been plundered from one of the Danes massacred in the last few days for no one knew his name. I called him Witnere, which means Tormentor, and it was apt for he took a dislike to the two mares and kept snapping at them.

The mares were for Willibald and Hild. I told Father Willibald he should go south, but he was scared now and insisted on staying with me and so, the day after I had met Bolti, we all rode north along the Roman road. A dozen men came with us. Among them were three Danes and two Norsemen who had managed to hide from Hrothweard's massacre, and the rest were Saxons who wanted to escape Ivarr's revenge. All had weapons and Bolti gave me money to pay them. They did not get much in wages, just enough to buy food and ale, but their presence deterred any outlaws on the long road.

I was tempted to ride to Synningthwait which was where Ragnar and his followers had their land, but I knew there would be very few men there, for most had gone south with Ragnar. Some of those warriors had died at Ethandun and the rest were still with Guthrum, whose defeated army had stayed in Mercia. Guthrum and Alfred had made peace, and Guthrum had even been baptized, which Willibald said was a miracle. So there would be few warriors at Synningthwait. No place to find refuge against my uncle's murderous ambitions or Kjartan's hate. So, with no real plan for my future and content to let fate work its will, I kept faith with Bolti and escorted him north toward Kjartan's land which lay athwart our path like a dark cloud. To pass through that land meant paying a toll, and that toll would be steep, and only powerful men like Ivarr, whose warriors outnumbered Kjartan's followers, could cross the River Wiire without payment. "You can afford it," I teased Bolti. His two sons each led packhorses that I suspected were loaded with coins wrapped in cloth or fleece to stop them clinking.

"I can't afford it if he takes my daughters," Bolti said. He had twin daughters who were twelve or thirteen, ripe for marriage. They were short, plump, fair-haired, snub-nosed, and impossible to tell apart.

"Is that what Kjartan does?" I asked.

"He takes what he wants," Bolti said sourly, "and he likes young girls, though I suspect he'd prefer to take you."

"And why do you suspect that?" I asked him tonelessly.

"I know the tales," he said. "His son lost his eye because of you."

"His son lost his eye," I said, "because he stripped Earl Ragnar's daughter half naked."

"But he blames you."

"He does," I agreed. We had all been children then, but childhood injuries can fester and I did not doubt that Sven the One-Eyed would love to take both my eyes as revenge for his one.

So as we neared Dunholm we turned west into the hills to avoid Kjartan's men. It was summer, but a chill wind brought low clouds and a thin rain so that I was glad of my leather-lined mail coat. Hild had smeared the metal rings with lanolin squeezed out of newly-shorn fleeces, and it protected most of the metal from rust. She had put the grease on my helmet and sword-blades too.

We climbed, following the well-worn track, and a couple of miles behind us another group followed, and there were fresh hoofprints in

the damp earth betraying that others had passed this way not long
before. Such heavy use of the path should have made me think. Kjartan the Cruel and Sven the One-Eyed lived off the dues that travelers
paid them, and if a traveler did not pay then they were robbed, taken
as slaves or killed. Kjartan and his son had to be aware that folk were
trying to avoid them by using the hill paths, and I should have been
more wary. Bolti was unafraid, for he simply trusted me. He told me
tales of how Kjartan and Sven had become rich from slaves. "They
take anyone, Dane or Saxon," he said, "and sell them over the water.
If you're lucky you can sometimes ransom a slave back, but the price
will be high." He glanced at Father Willibald. "He kills all priests."

"He does?"

"He hates all Christian priests. He reckons they're sorcerers, so he
half buries them and lets his dogs eat them."

"What did he say?" Willibald asked me, pulling his mare aside
before Witnere could savage her.

"He said Kjartan will kill you if he captures you, father."

"Kill me?"

"He'll feed you to his hounds."

"Oh, dear God," Willibald said. He was unhappy, lost, far from
home, and nervous of the strange northern landscape. Hild, on the
other hand, seemed happier. She was nineteen years old, and filled
with patience for life's hardships. She had been born into a wealthy
West Saxon family, not noble, but possessed of enough land to live
well, but she had been the last of eight children and her father had
promised her to the church's service because her mother had nearly
died when Hild was born, and he ascribed his wife's survival to God's
benevolence. So, at eleven years old, Hild, whose proper name was
Sister Hildegyth, had been sent to the nuns in Cippanhamm and
there she had lived, shut away from the world, praying and spinning
yarn, spinning and praying, until the Danes had come and she had
been whored.

She still whimpered in her sleep and I knew she was remembering
her humiliations, but she was happy to be away from Wessex and

away from the folk who constantly told her she should return to
God's service. Willibald had chided her for abandoning her holy life,
but I had warned him that one more such comment would earn him
a new and larger belly button and ever since he had kept quiet. Now
Hild drank in every new sight with a child's sense of wonder. Her pale
face had taken on a golden glow to match her hair. She was a clever
woman, not the cleverest I have known, but full of a shrewd wisdom.
I have lived long now and have learned that some women are trouble, and some are easy companions, and Hild was among the easiest I
ever knew. Perhaps that was because we were friends. We were lovers
too, but never in love and she was assailed by guilt. She kept that to
herself and to her prayers, but in the daylight she had begun to laugh
again and to take pleasure from simple things, yet at times the darkness wrapped her and she would whimper and I would see her long
fingers fidget with her crucifix and I knew she was feeling God's claws
raking across her soul.

So we rode into the hills and I had been careless, and it was Hild
who saw the horsemen first. There were nineteen of them, most in
leather coats, but three in mail, and they were circling behind us, and
I knew then that we were being shepherded. Our track followed the
side of a hill and to our right was a steep drop to a rushing stream,
and though we could escape into the dale we would inevitably be
slower than the men who now joined the track behind us. They did
not try to approach. They could see we were armed and they did not
want a fight, they just wanted to make sure we kept plodding north
to whatever fate awaited us. "Can't you fight them off?" Bolti
demanded.

"Thirteen against nineteen?" I suggested. "Yes," I said, "if the thirteen will fight, but they won't." I gestured at the swordsmen Bolti was
paying to accompany us. "They're good enough to scare off bandits,"
I went on, "but they're not stupid enough to fight Kjartan's men. If I
ask them to fight they'll most likely join the enemy and share your
daughters."

"But . . ." he began, then fell silent for we could at last see what did await us. A slave fair was being held where the stream tumbled into a deeper dale and in that larger valley was a sizable village built where a bridge, nothing more than a giant stone slab, crossed a wider stream that I took to be the Wiire. There was a crowd in the village and I saw those folk were being guarded by more men. The riders who were following us came a little closer, but stopped when I stopped. I gazed down the hill. The village was too far away to tell whether Kjartan or Sven were there, but it seemed safe to assume the men in the valley had come from Dunholm and that one or other of Dunholm's two lords led them. Bolti was squeaking in alarm, but I ignored him.

Two other tracks led into the village from the south and I guessed that horsemen were guarding all such paths and had been intercepting travelers all day. They had been driving their prey toward the village and those who could not pay the toll were being taken captive. "What are you going to do?" Bolti asked, close to panic.

"I'm going to save your life," I said, and I turned to one of his twin daughters and demanded that she give me a black linen scarf that she wore as a belt. She unwound it and, with a trembling hand, gave it to me and I wrapped it around my head, covering my mouth, nose and forehead, then asked Hild to pin it into place. "What are you doing?" Bolti squawked again.

I did not bother to reply. Instead I crammed my helmet over the scarf. The cheek-pieces were fitted so that my face was now a mask of polished metal over a black skull. Only my eyes could be seen. I half drew Serpent-Breath to make sure she slid easily in her scabbard, then I urged Witnere a few paces forward. "I am now Thorkild the Leper," I told Bolti. The scarf made my voice thick and indistinct.

"You're who?" he asked, gaping at me.

"I am Thorkild the Leper," I said, "and you and I will now go and deal with them."

"Me?" he said faintly.

I waved everyone forward. The band that had circled to follow us had gone south again, presumably to find the next group trying to evade Kjartan's war-band.

"I hired you to protect me," Bolti said in desperation.

"And I am going to protect you," I said. His Saxon wife was wailing as though she were at someone's funeral and I snarled at her to be silent. Then, a couple of hundred paces from the village, I stopped and told everyone except Bolti to wait. "Just you and I now," I told Bolti.

"I think you should deal with them alone," he said, then squealed.

He squealed because I had slapped the rump of his horse so that it leaped forward. I caught up with him. "Remember," I said, "I'm Thorkild the Leper, and if you betray who I really am then I shall kill you, your wife, your sons and then I'll sell your daughters into whoredom. Who am I?"

"Thorkild," he stammered.

"Thorkild the Leper," I said. We were in the village now, a miserable place of low stone cottages roofed with turf, and there were at least thirty or forty folk being guarded at the village's center, but off to one side, close to the stone-slab bridge, a table and benches had been placed on a patch of grass. Two men sat behind the table with a jug of ale in front of them, and all that I saw, but in truth I really only noticed one thing.

My father's helmet.

It was on the table. The helmet had a closed face-piece which, like the crown, was inlaid with silver. A snarling mouth was carved into the metal, and I had seen that helmet so many times. I had even played with it as a small child, though if my father discovered me with it he would clout me hard about the skull. My father had worn that helmet on the day he died at Eoferwic, and Ragnar the Elder had bought it from the man who cut my father down, and now it belonged to one of the men who had murdered Ragnar.

It was Sven the One-Eyed. He stood as Bolti and I approached and I felt a savage shock of recognition. I had known Sven since he was a child, and now he was a man, but I instantly knew the flat, wide face with its one feral eye. The other eye was a wrinkled hole. He was tall and broad-shouldered, long-haired and full-bearded, a swaggering young man in a suit of richest mail and with two swords, a long and a short, hanging at his waist. "More guests," he announced our arrival, and he gestured to the bench on the far side of the table. "Sit," he ordered, "and we shall do business together."

"Sit with him," I growled softly to Bolti.

Bolti gave me a despairing glance, then dismounted and went to the table. The second man was dark-skinned, black-haired and much older than Sven. He wore a black gown so that he looked like a monk except that he had a silver hammer of Thor hanging at his neck. He also had a wooden tray in front of him and the tray was cunningly divided into separate compartments to hold the different coins that gleamed silver in the sunlight. Sven, sitting again beside the black-robed man, poured a beaker of ale and pushed it toward Bolti who glanced back at me, then sat as he had been commanded.

"And you are?" Sven asked him.

"Bolti Ericson," Bolti said. He had to say it twice because the first time he could not raise his voice enough to be heard.

"Bolti Ericson," Sven repeated, "and I am Sven Kjartanson and my father is lord of this land. You have heard of Kjartan?"

"Yes, lord."

Sven smiled. "I think you have been trying to evade our tolls, Bolti! Have you been trying to evade our tolls?"

"No, lord."

"So where have you come from?"

"Eoferwic."

"Ah! Another Eoferwic merchant, eh? You're the third today! And what do you carry on those packhorses?"

"Nothing, lord."

Sven leaned forward slightly, then grinned as he let out a huge fart. "Sorry, Bolti, I only heard thunder. Did you say you have nothing? But I see four women, and three are young enough." He smiled. "Are they your women?"

"My wife and daughters, lord," Bolti said.

"Wives and daughters, how we do love them," Sven said, then he looked up at me and though I knew my face was wrapped in black and that my eyes were deep-shadowed by the helmet, I felt my skin crawl under his gaze. "Who," Sven asked, "is that?"

He must have been curious for I looked like a king. My mail and helmet and weapons were of the very best, while my arm rings denoted a warrior of high status. Bolti threw me a terrified look, but said nothing. "I asked," Sven said, louder now, "who that is."

"His name," Bolti said, and his voice was a trembling squeak, "is Thorkild the Leper."

Sven made an involuntary grimace and clutched at the hammer amulet about his neck, for which I could not blame him. All men fear the gray, nerveless flesh of lepers, and most lepers are sent into the wilderness to live as they can and die as they must.

"What are you doing with a leper?" Sven challenged Bolti.

Bolti had no answer. "I am journeying north." I spoke for the first time, and my distorted voice seemed to boom inside my closed helmet.

"Why do you come north?" Sven asked.

"Because I am tired of the south," I said.

He heard the hostility in my slurred voice and dismissed it as impotent. He must have guessed that Bolti had hired me as an escort, but I was no threat, Sven had five men within a few paces, all of them armed with swords or spears, and he had at least forty other men inside the village.

Sven drank some ale. "I hear there was trouble in Eoferwic?" he asked Bolti.

Bolti nodded. I could see his right hand convulsively opening and closing beneath the table. "Some Danes were killed," he said.

Sven shook his head as though he found that news distressing. "Ivarr won't be happy."

"Where is Ivarr?" Bolti asked.

"I last heard he was in the Tuede valley," Sven said, "and Aed of Scotland was dancing around him." He seemed to be enjoying the customary exchange of news, as if his thefts and piracy were given a coating of respectability by sticking to the conventions. "So," he said, then paused to fart again, "so what do you trade in, Bolti?"

"Leather, fleeces, cloth, pottery," Bolti said, then his voice trailed away as he decided he was saying too much.

"And I trade in slaves," Sven said, "and this is Gelgill," he indicated the man beside him, "and he buys the slaves from us, and you have three young women I think might prove very profitable to him and to me. So what will you pay me for them? Pay me enough and you can keep them." He smiled as if to suggest he was being entirely reasonable.

Bolti seemed struck dumb, but he managed to bring a purse from beneath his coat and put some silver on the table. Sven watched the coins one by one and when Bolti faltered Sven just smiled and Bolti kept counting the silver until there were thirty-eight shillings on the table. "It is all I have, lord," he said humbly.

"All you have? I doubt that, Bolti Ericson," Sven said, "and if it is then I will let you keep one ear of one of your daughters. Just one ear as a keepsake. What do you think, Gelgill?"

It was a strange name, Gelgill, and I suspected the man had come from across the sea, for the most profitable slave markets were either in Dyflin or far off Frankia. He said something, too low for me to catch, and Sven nodded. "Bring the girls here," he said to his men, and Bolti shuddered. He looked at me again as if he expected me to stop what Sven planned, but I did nothing as the two guards walked to our waiting group.

Sven chatted of the prospects for the harvest as the guards ordered Hild and Bolti's daughters off their horses. The men Bolti had hired did nothing to stop them. Bolti's wife screamed a protest, then subsided into hysterical tears as her daughters and Hild were marched toward the table. Sven welcomed them with exaggerated politeness, then Gelgill stood and inspected the three. He ran his hands over their bodies as if he were buying horses. I saw Hild shiver as he pulled down her dress to probe her breasts, but he was less interested in her than in the two younger girls. "One hundred shillings each," he said after inspecting them, "but that one," he looked at Hild, "fifty." He spoke with a strange accent.

"But that one's pretty," Sven objected. "Those other two look like piglets."

"They're twins," Gelgill said. "I can get a lot of money for twins. And the tall girl is too old. She must be nineteen or twenty."

"Virginity is such a valuable thing," Sven said to Bolti, "don't you agree?"

Bolti was shaking. "I will pay you a hundred shillings for each of my daughters," he said desperately.

"Oh no," Sven said. "That's what Gelgill wants. I have to make some profit too. You can keep all three, Bolti, if you pay me six hundred shillings."

It was an outrageous price, and it was meant to be, but Bolti did not baulk at it. "Only two are mine, lord," he whined. "The third is his woman." He pointed at me.

"Yours?" Sven looked at me. "You have a woman, leper? So that bit hasn't dropped off yet?" He found that funny and the two men who had fetched the women laughed with him. "So, leper," Sven asked, "what will you pay me for your woman?"

"Nothing," I said.

He scratched his arse. His men were grinning. They were used to defiance, and used to defeating it, and they enjoyed watching Sven fleece travelers. Sven poured himself more ale. "You have some fine arm rings, leper," he said, "and I suspect that helmet won't be much use to you once you're dead, so in exchange for your woman I'll take your rings and your helmet and then you can go on your way."

I did not move, did not speak, but I gently pressed my legs against Witnere's flanks and I felt the big horse tremble. He was a fighting beast and he wanted me to release him, and perhaps it was Witnere's tension that Sven sensed. All he could see was my baleful helmet with its dark eye holes and its wolf's crest and he was becoming worried. He had flippantly raised the wager, but he could not back down if he wanted to keep his dignity. He had to play to win now. "Lost your tongue suddenly?" he sneered at me, then gestured at the two men who had fetched the women. "Egil! Atsur! Take the leper's helmet!"

Sven must have reckoned he was safe. He had at least a ship's crew of men in the village and I was by myself, and that convinced him that I was defeated even before his two men approached me. One had a spear, the other was drawing his sword, but the sword was not even halfway out of the scabbard before I had Serpent-Breath in my hand and Witnere moving. He had been desperate to attack, and he leaped with the speed of eight-legged Sleipnir, Odin's famed horse. I took the man on the right first, the man who was still drawing his sword, and Serpent-Breath came from the sky like a bolt of Thor's lightning and her edge went through his helmet as if it were made of parchment and Witnere, obedient to the pressure of my knee was already turning toward Sven as the spearman came for me. He should have thrust his blade into Witnere's chest or neck, but instead he tried to ram the spear up at my ribs and Witnere twisted to his right and snapped at the man's face with his big teeth and the man stumbled backward, just avoiding the bite, and he lost his footing to sprawl on the grass and I kept Witnere turning left. My right foot was already free of the stirrup and then I threw myself out of the saddle and dropped hard onto Sven. He was half tangled by the bench as he tried to stand, and I drove him down, thumping the wind from his belly, and then I found my feet, stood, and Serpent-Breath was at Sven's throat. "Egil!" Sven called to the spearman who had been driven back by Witnere, but Egil dared not attack me while my sword was at his master's gullet.

Bolti was whimpering. He had pissed himself. I could smell it and hear it dripping. Gelgill was standing very still, watching me, his narrow face expressionless. Hild was smiling. A half-dozen of Sven's other men were facing me, but none dared move because the tip of Serpent-Breath, her blade smeared with blood, was at Sven's throat. Witnere was beside me, teeth bared, one front hoof pawing at the ground and thumping very close to Sven's head. Sven was gazing up at me with his one eye that was filled with hate and fear, and I suddenly stepped away from him. "On your knees," I told him.

"Egil!" Sven pleaded again.

Egil, black-bearded and with gaping nostrils where the front of his nose had been chopped off in some fight, leveled his spear.

"He dies if you attack," I said to Egil, touching Sven with Serpent-Breath's tip. Egil, sensibly stepped backward, and I flicked Serpent-Breath across Sven's face, drawing blood. "On your knees," I said again, and when he was kneeling I leaned down and took his two swords from their scabbards and lay them beside my father's helmet on the table.

"You want to kill the slaver?" I called back to Hild, gesturing at the swords.

"No," she said.

"Iseult would have killed him," I said. Iseult had been my lover and Hild's friend.

"Thou shalt not kill," Hild said. It was a Christian commandment and about as futile, I thought, as commanding the sun to go backward.

"Bolti," I spoke in Danish now, "kill the slaver." I did not want Gelgill behind my back.

Bolti did not move. He was too scared to obey me, but, to my surprise, his two daughters came and fetched Sven's swords. Gelgill tried to run, but the table was in his way and one of the girls gave a wild swing that slashed across his skull and he fell sideways. Then they savaged him. I did not watch, because I was guarding Sven, but I heard the slaver's cries and Hild's gasp of surprise, and I could see the astonishment on the faces of the men in front of me. The twin girls grunted as they hacked. Gelgill took a long time to die and not one of Sven's men tried to save him, or to rescue their master. They all had weapons drawn and if just one of them had possessed any sense they would have realized that I dared not kill Sven, for his life was my life. If I took his soul they would have swamped me with blades, but they were scared of what Kjartan would do to them if his son died and so they did nothing and I pressed the blade harder against Sven's throat so that he gave a half-strangled yelp of fear.

Behind me Gelgill was at last hacked to death. I risked a glance and saw that Bolti's twin daughters were blood-drenched and grinning. "They are Hel's daughters," I told the watching men and I was proud of that sudden invention, for Hel is the corpse-goddess, rancid and terrible, who presides over the dead who do not die in battle. "And I am Thorkild!" I went on, "and I have filled Odin's hall with dead men." Sven was shaking beneath me. His men seemed to be holding their breath and suddenly my tale took wings and I made my voice as deep as I could. "I am Thorkild the Leper," I announced loudly, "and I died a long time ago, but Odin has sent me from the corpse-hall to take the souls of Kjartan and his son."

They believed me. I saw men touch amulets. One spearman even dropped to his knees. I wanted to kill Sven there and then, and perhaps I should have done, but it would only have taken one man to break the web of magical nonsense I had spun for them. What I needed at that moment was not Sven's soul, but our safety, and so I would trade the one for the other. "I shall let this worm go," I said, "to carry news of my coming to his father, but you will go first. All of you! Go back beyond the village and I shall release him. You will leave your captives here." They just stared at me and I twitched the blade so that Sven yelped again. "Go!" I shouted.

They went. They went fast, filled with dread. Bolti was gazing at his beloved daughters with awe. I told each girl they had done well, and that they should take a handful of coins from the table, and then they went back to their mother, both clutching silver and bloody blades. "They're good girls," I told Bolti and he said nothing, but hurried after them.

"I couldn't kill him," Hild said. She seemed ashamed of her squeamishness.

"Doesn't matter," I said. I kept the sword at Sven's throat until I was sure all his men had retreated a good distance eastward. The folk who had been their captives, mostly young boys and girls, stayed in the village, but none dared approach me.

I was tempted then to tell Sven the truth, to let him know that he had been humiliated by an old enemy, but the tale of Thorkild the Leper was too good to waste. I was also tempted to ask about Thyra, Ragnar's sister, but I feared that if she did live and that if I betrayed an interest in her, then she would not live much longer, and so I said nothing of her. Instead I gripped Sven's hair and pulled his head back so that he was staring up at me. "I have come to this middle earth," I told him, "to kill you and your father. I shall find you again, Sven Kjartanson, and I will kill you next time. I am Thorkild, I walk at night and I cannot be killed because I am already a corpse. So take my greetings to your father and tell him the dead swordsman has been sent for him and we shall all three sail in *Skidbladnir* back to Niflheim." Niflheim was the dreadful pit of the dishonored dead, and *Skidbladnir* was the ship of the gods that could be folded and concealed in a pouch. I let go of Sven then and kicked him hard in the back so he sprawled onto his face. He could have crawled away, but he dared not move. He was a whipped dog now, and though I still wanted to kill him I reckoned it would be better to let him carry my eerie tale to his father. Kjartan would doubtless learn that Uhtred of Bebbanburg had been seen in Eoferwic, but he would also hear of the corpse warrior come to kill him, and I wanted his dreams to be wreathed with terror.

Sven still did not move as I stooped to his belt and pulled away a heavy purse. Then I stripped him of his seven silver arm rings. Hild had cut off part of Gelgill's robe and was using it to make a bag to hold the coins in the slave-trader's tray. I gave her my father's helmet to carry, then climbed back into Witnere's saddle. I patted his neck and he tossed his head extravagantly as though he understood he had been a great fighting stallion that day.

I was about to leave when that weird day became stranger still. Some of the captives, as if realizing that they were truly freed, had started toward the bridge, while others were so confused or lost or despairing that they had followed the armed men eastward. Then, suddenly, there was a monkish chanting and out of one of the low, turf-roofed houses where they had been imprisoned, came a file of

monks and priests. There were seven of them, and they were the luck-
iest men that day, for I was to discover that Kjartan the Cruel did
indeed have a hatred of Christians and killed every priest or monk he
captured. These seven escaped him now, and with them was a young
man burdened with slave shackles. He was tall, well-built, very good-
looking, dressed in rags and about my age. His long curly hair was so
golden that it looked almost white and he had pale eyelashes and
very blue eyes and a sun-darkened skin unmarked by disease. His face
might have been carved from stone, so pronounced were his cheek-
bones, nose, and jaw, yet the hardness of the face was softened by a
cheerful expression that suggested he found life a constant surprise
and a continual amusement. When he saw Sven cowering beneath
my horse he left the chanting priests and shuffled toward us, stopping only to pick up the sword of the man I had killed. The young
man held the sword awkwardly, for his hands were joined by links of
chain, but he carried it to Sven and held it poised over Sven's neck.

"No," I said.

"No?" The young man smiled up at me and I instinctively liked
him. His face was open and guileless.

"I promised him his life," I said.

The young man thought about that for a heartbeat. "You did," he
said, "but I didn't." He spoke in Danish.

"But if you take his life," I said, "then I shall have to take yours."

He considered that bargain with amusement in his eyes. "Why?"
he asked, not in any alarm, but as if he genuinely wished to know.

"Because that is the law," I said.

"But Sven Kjartanson knows no law," he pointed out.

"It is my law," I said, "and I want him to take a message to his
father."

"What message?"

"That the dead swordsman has come for him."

The young man cocked his head thoughtfully as he considered the
message and he evidently approved of it for he tucked the sword
under an armpit and then clumsily untied the rope belt of his

breeches. "You can take a message from me too," he said to Sven, "and this is it." He pissed on Sven. "I baptize you," the young man said, "in the name of Thor and of Odin and of Loki."

The seven churchmen, three monks and four priests, solemnly watched the baptism, but none protested the implied blasphemy or tried to stop it. The young man pissed for a long time, aiming his stream so that it thoroughly soaked Sven's hair, and when at last he finished he retied the belt and offered me another of his dazzling smiles. "You're the dead swordsman?"

"I am," I said.

"Stop whimpering," the young man said to Sven, then smiled up at me again. "Then perhaps you will do me the honor of serving me?"

"Serve you?" I asked. It was my turn to be amused.

"I am Guthred," he said, as though that explained everything.

"Guthrum I have heard of," I said, "and I know a Guthwere and I have met two men named Guthlac, but I know of no Guthred."

"I am Guthred, son of Hardicnut," he said.

The name still meant nothing to me. "And why should I serve Guthred," I asked, "son of Hardicnut?"

"Because until you came I was a slave," he said, "but now, well, because you came, now I'm a king!" He spoke with such enthusiasm that he had trouble making the words come out as he wanted.

I smiled beneath the linen scarf. "You're a king," I said, "but of what?"

"Northumbria, of course," he said brightly.

"He is, lord, he is," one of the priests said earnestly.

And so the dead swordsman met the slave king, and Sven the One-Eyed crawled to his father, and the weirdness that infected Northumbria grew weirder still.

TWO

At sea, sometimes, if you take a ship too far from land and the wind rises and the tide sucks with a venomous force and the waves splinter white above the shield-pegs, you have no choice but to go where the gods will. The sail must be furled before it rips and the long oars would pull to no effect and so you lash the blades and bail the ship and say your prayers and watch the darkening sky and listen to the wind howl and suffer the rain's sting, and you hope that the tide and waves and wind will not drive you onto rocks.

That was how I felt in Northumbria. I had escaped Hrothweard's madness in Eoferwic, only to humiliate Sven who would now want nothing more than to kill me, if indeed he believed I could be killed. That meant I dared not stay in that middling part of Northumbria for my enemies in the region were far too numerous, nor could I go farther north for that would take me into Bebbanburg's territory, my own land, where it was my uncle's daily prayer that I should die and so leave him the legitimate holder of what he had stolen, and I did not wish to make it easy for that prayer to come true. So the winds of Kjartan's hatred and of Sven's revenge, and the tidal thrust of my uncle's enmity drove me westward into the wilds of Cumbraland.

We followed the Roman wall where it runs across the hills. That wall is an extraordinary thing which crosses the whole land from sea to sea. It is made of stone and it rises and falls with the hills and the valleys, never stopping, always remorseless and brutal. We met a shepherd who had not heard of the Romans and he told us that giants had built the wall in the old days and he claimed that when the world ends the wild men of the far north would flow across its rampart like a flood to bring death and horror. I thought of his prophecy that afternoon as I watched a she-wolf run along the wall's top, tongue lolling, and she gave us a glance, leaped down behind our horses, and ran off southward. These days the wall's masonry has crumbled, flowers blossom between the stones and turf lies thick along the rampart's wide top, but it is still an astonishing thing. We build a few churches and monasteries of stone, and I have seen a handful of stone-built halls, but I cannot imagine any man making such a wall today. And it was not just a wall. Beside it was a wide ditch, and behind that a stone road, and every mile or so there was a watchtower, and twice a day we would pass stone-built fortresses where the Roman soldiers had lived. The roofs of their barracks have long gone now and the buildings are homes for foxes and ravens, though in one such fort we discovered a naked man with hair down to his waist. He was ancient, claiming to be over seventy years old, and his gray beard was as long as his matted white hair. He was a filthy creature, nothing but skin, dirt, and bones, but Willibald and the seven churchmen I had released from Sven all knelt to him because he was a famous hermit.

"He was a bishop," Willibald told me in awed tones after he had received the scraggy man's blessing. "He had wealth, a wife, servants, and honor, and he gave them all up to worship God in solitude. He's a very holy man."

"Perhaps he's just a mad bastard," I suggested, "or else his wife was a vicious bitch who drove him out."

"He's a child of God," Willibald said reprovingly, "and in time he'll be called a saint."

Hild had dismounted and she looked at me as though seeking my permission to approach the hermit. She plainly wanted the hermit's blessing and so she appealed to me, but it was none of my business what she did, so I just shrugged and she knelt to the dirty creature. He leered at her and scratched his crotch and then made the sign of the cross on both her breasts, pushing hard with his fingers to feel her nipples and all the while pretending to bless her, and I was tempted to kick the old bastard into immediate martyrdom. But Hild was crying with emotion as he pawed at her hair and then dribbled some kind of prayer and afterward she looked grateful. He gave me the evil eye and held out a grubby paw as if expecting me to give him money, but instead I showed him Thor's hammer and he hissed a curse at me through his two yellow teeth and then we abandoned him to the moor and to the sky and to his prayers.

I had left Bolti. He was safe enough north of the wall, for he had entered Bebbanburg's territory where Ælfric's horsemen and the horsemen of the Danes who lived on my land would be patrolling the roads. We followed the wall westward and I now led Father Willibald, Hild, King Guthred, and the seven freed churchmen. I had managed to break the chain of Guthred's manacles so the slave king, who now rode Willibald's mare, wore two iron wristbands from which dangled short links of rusted chain. He chattered to me incessantly. "What we shall do," he told me on the second day of the journey, "is raise an army in Cumbraland and then we'll cross the hills and capture Eoferwic."

"What then?" I asked drily.

"Go north!" he said enthusiastically. "North! We shall have to take Dunholm, and after that we'll capture Bebbanburg. You want me to do that, don't you?"

I had told Guthred my name and that I was the rightful lord of Bebbanburg, and now I told him that Bebbanburg had never been captured.

"It's a tough place, eh?" Guthred responded. "Like Dunholm? Well, we shall see about Bebbanburg. But of course we'll have to finish off Ivarr first." He spoke as though destroying the most powerful Dane in Northumbria were a small matter. "So we'll deal with Ivarr," he said, then suddenly brightened. "Or perhaps Ivarr will accept me as king? He has a son and I've a sister who must be of marriageable age by now. They could make an alliance?"

"Unless your sister's already married," I interrupted.

"Can't think who'd want her," he said, "she's got a face like a horse."

"Horse-faced or not," I said, "she's Hardicnut's daughter. There must be an advantage for someone in marrying her."

"There might have been before my father died," Guthred said dubiously, "but now?"

"You're king now," I reminded him. I did not really believe he was a king, of course, but he believed it and so I indulged him.

"That's true!" he said. "So someone will want Gisela, won't they? Despite her face!"

"Does she really look like a horse?"

"Long face," he said, and grimaced, "but she's not completely ugly. And it's high time she married. She must be fifteen or sixteen! I think perhaps we should marry her to Ivarr's son. That'll make an alliance with Ivarr, and he'll help us deal with Kjartan, and then we'll have to make sure the Scots don't give us any trouble. And, of course, we'll have to keep those rascals in Strath Clota from being a nuisance."

"Of course we must," I said.

"They killed my father, see? And made me a slave!" He grinned.

Hardicnut, Guthred's father, had been a Danish earl who made his home at Cair Ligualid which was the chief town in Cumbraland. Hardicnut had called himself king of Northumbria, which was pretentious, but strange things happen west of the hills and a man there can claim to be king of the moon if he wants because no one outside of Cumbraland will take the slightest bit of notice. Hardicnut had posed no threat to the greater lords around Eoferwic, indeed he posed small threat to anyone, for Cumbraland was a sad and savage place, forever being raided by the Norsemen from Ireland or by the wild horrors from Strath Clota whose king, Eochaid, called himself king of Scotland, a title disputed by Aed who was now fighting Ivarr.

Of the insolence of the Scots, my father used to say, there is no end. He had cause to say that, for the Scots claimed much of Bebbanburg's land and until the Danes came our family was forever fighting against the northern tribes. I had been taught as a child that there were many tribes in Scotland, but the two tribes closest to Northumbria were the Scots themselves, of whom Aed was now king, and the savages of Strath Clota who lived on the western shore and never came near Bebbanburg. They raided Cumbraland instead and Hardicnut had decided to punish them and so led a small army north into their hills where Eochaid of Strath Clota ambushed him and then destroyed him. Guthred had marched with his father and had been captured and, for two years now, had been a slave.

"Why didn't they kill you?" I asked.

"Eochaid should have killed me," he admitted cheerfully, "but he didn't know who I was at first, and by the time he found out he wasn't really in a killing mood. So he kicked me a few times, then said I would be his slave. He liked to watch me empty his shit-pail. I was a household slave, see? It was another insult."

"Being a household slave?"

"Woman's work," Guthred explained, "but that meant I spent my time with the girls. I rather liked it."

"So how did you escape Eochaid?"

"I didn't. Gelgill bought me. He paid a lot for me!" He said this proudly.

"And Gelgill was going to sell you to Kjartan?" I asked.

"Oh no! He was going to sell me to the priests from Cair Ligualid!" he nodded toward the seven churchmen who had been rescued with him. "They'd agreed the price before, you see, but Gelgill wanted more money and then they all met Sven, and of course Sven wouldn't let the sale happen. He wanted me back in Dunholm and Gelgill would have done anything for Sven and his father, so we were all doomed until you came along."

Some of this made sense and, by talking to the seven churchmen and questioning Guthred further, I managed to piece the rest of the story together. Gelgill, known on both sides of the border as a slave-trader, had purchased Guthred from Eochaid and had paid a vast price, not because Guthred was worth it, but because the priests had hired Gelgill to make the trade. "Two hundred pieces of silver, eight bullocks, two sacks of malt, and a silver-mounted horn. That was my price," Guthred told me cheerfully.

"Gelgill paid that much?" I was astonished.

"He didn't. The priests did. Gelgill just negotiated the sale."

"The priests paid for you?"

"They must have emptied Cumbraland of silver," Guthred said proudly.

"And Eochaid agreed to sell you?"

"For that price? Of course he did! Why wouldn't he?"

"He killed your father. Your duty is to kill him. He knows that."

"He rather liked me," Guthred said, and I found that believable because Guthred was so very likable. He faced each day as though it would bring nothing but happiness, and in his company life somehow seemed brighter. "He still made me empty his shit-pail," Guthred admitted, continuing his story of Eochaid, "but he stopped kicking me every time I did it. And he liked to talk to me."

"About what?"

"Oh, about everything! The gods, the weather, fishing, how to make good cheese, women, everything. And he reckoned I wasn't a warrior, which I'm not really. Now I'm king, of course, so I have to be a warrior, but I don't much like it. Eochaid made me swear I'd never go to war against him."

"And you swore that?"

"Of course! I like him. I'll raid his cattle, of course, and kill any men he sends into Cumbraland, but that's not war, is it?"

So Eochaid had taken the church's silver and Gelgill had brought Guthred south into Northumbria, but instead of giving him to the priests he had taken him eastward, reckoning that he could make more money by selling Guthred to Kjartan than by honoring the contract he had made with the churchmen. The priests and monks followed, begging for Guthred's release, and it was then they had all met Sven who saw his own chance of profit in Guthred. The freed slave was Hardicnut's son, which

meant he was heir to land in Cumbraland, and that suggested he was
worth a largish bag of silver in ransom. Sven had planned to take Guthred
back to Dunholm where he would doubtless have killed all seven churchmen. Then I had arrived with my face wrapped in black linen and now
Gelgill was dead, Sven had stinking wet hair, and Guthred was free.

I understood all that, but what did not make sense was why seven
Saxon churchmen had come from Cair Ligualid to pay a fortune for
Guthred who was both a Dane and a pagan. "Because I'm their king,
of course," Guthred said, as though the answer were obvious, "though
I never thought I'd become king. Not after Eochaid took me captive,
but that's what the Christian god wants, so who am I to argue?"

"Their god wants you?" I asked, looking at the seven churchmen
who had traveled so far to free him.

"Their god wants me," Guthred said seriously, "because I'm the
chosen one. Do you think I should become a Christian?"

"No," I said.

"I think I should," he said, ignoring my answer, "just to show gratitude. The gods don't like ingratitude, do they?"

"What the gods like," I said, "is chaos."

The gods were happy.

Cair Ligualid was a sorry place. Norsemen had pillaged and burned it
two years before, just after Guthred's father had been killed by the Scots,
and the town had not even been half rebuilt. What was left of it stood
on the south bank of the River Hedene, and that was why the settlement existed, for it was built at the first crossing place of the river, a river
which offered some protection against marauding Scots. It had offered
no protection against the fleet of Vikings who had sailed up the Hedene,
stolen whatever they could, raped what they wanted, killed what they
did not want, and taken away the survivors as slaves. Those Vikings had
come from their settlements in Ireland and they were the enemy of the
Saxons, the Irish, the Scots and even, at times, of their cousins, the
Danes, and they had not spared the Danes living in Cair Ligualid. So we
rode through a broken gate in a broken wall into a broken town, and it

was dusk, and the day's rain had finally lifted and a shaft of red sunlight came from beneath the western clouds as we entered the ruined town. We rode straight into the light of that swollen sun which reflected from my helm that had the silver wolf on its crest and it shone from my mail coat and from my arm rings and from the hilts of my two swords, and someone shouted that I was the king. I looked like a king. I rode Witnere who tossed his great head and pawed at the ground and I was dressed in my shining war-glory.

Cair Ligualid was crowded. Here and there a house had been rebuilt, but most of the folk were camping in the scorched ruins, along with their livestock, and there were far too many of them to be the survivors of the old Norse raids. They were, instead, the people of Cumbraland who had been brought to Cair Ligualid by their priests or lords because they had been promised that their new king would come. And now, from the east, his mail reflecting the brilliance of the sinking sun, came a gleaming warrior on a great black horse.

"The king!" another voice shouted, and more voices took up the cry, and from the wrecked homes and the makeshift shelters folk scrambled to stare at me. Willibald was trying to hush them, but his West Saxon words were lost in the din. I thought Guthred would also protest, but instead he pulled his cloak's hood over his head so that he looked like one of the churchmen who struggled to keep up as the crowd pressed in on us. Folk knelt as we passed, then scrambled to their feet to follow us. Hild was laughing, and I took her hand so she rode beside me like a queen, and the growing crowd accompanied us up a long, low hill toward a new hall built on the summit. As we grew closer I saw it was not a hall, but a church, and that priests and monks were coming from its door to greet us.

There was a madness in Cair Ligualid. A different madness from that which had shed blood in Eoferwic, but madness just the same. Women were crying, men shouting, and children staring. Mothers held babies toward me as if my touch could heal them. "You must stop them!" Willibald had managed to reach my side and was clinging onto my right stirrup.

"Why?"

"Because they're mistaken, of course! Guthred is king!"

I smiled at him. "Maybe," I said slowly, as though the idea were just coming to me, "maybe I should be king instead?"

"Uhtred!" Willibald said, shocked.

"Why not?" I asked. "My ancestors were kings."

"Guthred is king!" Willibald protested. "The abbot named him!"

That was how Cair Ligualid's madness began. The town had been a haunt of foxes and birds when Abbot Eadred of Lindisfarena came across the hills. Lindisfarena, of course, is the monastery hard by Bebbanburg. It lies on Northumbria's eastern coast, while Cair Ligualid is on the western edge, but the abbot, driven from Lindisfarena by Danish raids, had come to Cair Ligualid and there built the new church to which we climbed. The abbot had also seen Guthred in his dreams. Nowadays, of course, every Northumbrian knows the story of how Saint Cuthbert revealed Guthred to Abbot Eadred, but back then, on the day of Guthred's arrival in Cair Ligualid, the tale seemed like just another insanity on top of the world's weltering madness. Folk were shouting at me, calling me king and Willibald turned and bellowed to Guthred. "Tell them to stop!"

"The people want a king," Guthred said, "and Uhtred looks like one. Let them have him for the moment."

A number of younger monks, armed with staves, kept the excited people away from the church doors. The crowd had been promised a miracle by Eadred and they had been waiting for days, expecting their king to come, and then I had ridden from the east in the glory of a warrior, which is what I am and always have been. All my life I have followed the path of the sword. Given a choice, and I have been given many choices, I would rather draw a blade than settle an argument with words, for that is what a warrior does, but most men and women are not fighters. They crave peace. They want nothing more than to watch their children grow, to plant their seeds and live to see the harvest, to worship their god, to love their family and to be left in peace. Yet it has been our fate to be born in a time when violence ruled us. The Danes appeared and our land was shattered, and all around our coasts the long ships with their beaked prows came to raid and enslave and steal and kill. In Cumbraland, which is the wildest part of all the Saxon lands, the Danes came and the Norsemen came and the Scots came, and no one could live in peace, and I think that when you break men's dreams, when you destroy their homes and ruin their harvests and rape their daughters and enslave their sons, you engender a madness. At the world's ending, when the gods will fight each other, all mankind will be stricken with a great frenzy and the rivers will flow with blood and the sky shall be filled with screaming and the great tree of life will fall with a crash that will be heard beyond the farthest star, but all that is yet to come. Back then, in 878 when I was young, there was just a smaller madness at Cair Ligualid. It was the madness of hope, the belief that a king, born in a churchman's dream, would end a people's suffering.

Abbot Eadred was waiting inside the cordon of monks and, as my horse came close, he raised his hands towards the sky. He was a tall man, old and white-haired, gaunt and fierce, with eyes like a falcon and, surprising in a priest, he had a sword strapped to his waist. He could not see my face at first because my cheek-pieces hid it, but even when I took off my helmet he still thought I was the king. He stared up at me, raised thin hands to heaven as if giving thanks for my arrival, then gave me a low bow. "Lord King," he said in a booming voice. The monks dropped to their knees and stared up at me. "Lord King," Abbot Eadred boomed again, "welcome!"

"Lord King," the monks echoed, "welcome."

Now that was an interesting moment. Eadred, remember, had selected Guthred to be the king because Saint Cuthbert had shown him Hardicnut's son in a dream. Yet now he thought that I was the king, which meant that either Cuthbert had shown him the wrong face or else that Eadred was a lying bastard. Or perhaps Saint Cuthbert was a lying bastard. But as a miracle, and Eadred's dream is always remembered as a miracle, it was decidedly suspicious. I told a priest that story once and he refused to believe me. He hissed at me, made the sign of the cross, and rushed off to say his prayers. The whole of Guthred's life was to be dominated by the simple fact that Saint Cuthbert revealed him to Eadred, and the truth is that Eadred did not recognize him, but these days no one believes me. Willibald, of course, was dancing around like a man with two wasps up his breeches, trying to correct Eadred's mistake, so I kicked him on the side of the skull to make him quiet then gestured toward Guthred who had taken the hood from his head. "This," I said to Eadred, "is your king."

For a heartbeat Eadred did not believe me, then he did and a look of intense anger crossed his face. It was a sudden contortion of utter fury because he understood, even if no one else did, that he was supposed to have recognized Guthred from his dream. The anger flared, then he mastered it and bowed to Guthred and repeated his greeting and Guthred returned it with his customary cheerfulness. Two monks hurried to take his horse and Guthred dismounted and was led into the church. The rest of us followed as best we could. I ordered some monks to hold Witnere and Hild's mare. They did not want to, they wanted to be inside the church, but I told them I would break their tonsured heads if the horses were lost, and they obeyed me.

It was dark in the church. There were rushlights burning on the altar, and more on the floor of the nave where a large group of monks bowed and chanted, but the small smoky lights hardly lifted the thick gloom. It was not much of a church. It was big, bigger even than the church Alfred was building in Wintanceaster, but it had been raised in a hurry and the walls were untrimmed logs and when my eyes became accustomed to the darkness I saw that the roof was ragged with rough thatch. There were probably fifty or sixty churchmen inside and half that number of thegns, if the men of Cumbraland aspired to that rank. They were the wealthier men of the region and they stood with their followers and I noted, with curiosity, that some wore the cross and others wore the hammer. There were Danes and Saxons in that church, mingled together, and they were not enemies. Instead they had gathered to support Eadred who had promised them a god-given king.

And there was Gisela.

I noticed her almost immediately. She was a tall girl, dark-haired, with a very long and very grave face. She was dressed in a gray cloak and shift so that at first I thought she was a nun, then I saw the silver bracelets and the heavy brooch holding the cloak at her neck. She had large eyes that shone, but that was because she was crying. They were tears of joy and, when Guthred saw her, he ran to her and they embraced. He held her tight, then he stepped away, holding her hands, and I saw she was half crying and half laughing, and he impulsively led her to me. "My sister," he introduced her, "Gisela." He still held her hands. "I am free," he told her, "because of Lord Uhtred."

"I thank you," she said to me, and I said nothing. I was conscious of Hild beside me, but even more conscious of Gisela. Fifteen? Sixteen? But unmarried, for her black hair was still unbound. What had her brother told me? That she had a face like a horse, but I thought it was a face of dreams, a face to set the sky on fire, a face to haunt a man. I still see that face so many years later. It was long, long nosed, with dark eyes that sometimes seemed far away and other times were mischievous and when she looked at me that first time I was lost. The spinners who make our lives had sent her and I knew nothing would be the same again.

"You're not married, are you?" Guthred asked her anxiously.

She touched her hair that still fell free like a girl's hair. When she married it would be bound up. "Of course not," she said, still looking at me, then turned to her brother, "are you?"

"No," he said.

Gisela looked at Hild, back to me, and just then Abbot Eadred came to hurry Guthred away and Gisela went back to the woman who was her guardian. She gave me a backward glance, and I can still see that look. The lowered eyelids and the small trip as she turned to give me a last smile.

"A pretty girl," Hild said.

"I would rather have a pretty woman," I said.

"You need to marry," Hild said.

"I am married," I reminded her, and that was true. I had a wife in Wessex, a wife who hated me, but Mildrith was now in a nunnery so whether she regarded herself as married to me or married to Christ I neither knew nor cared.

"You liked that girl," Hild said.

"I like all girls," I said evasively. I lost sight of Gisela as the crowd pressed forward to watch the ceremony which began when Abbot Eadred unstrapped the sword belt from his own waist and buckled it around Guthred's ragged clothes. Then he draped the new king in a fine green cloak, trimmed with fur, and put a bronze circlet on his fair hair. The monks chanted while this was being done, and kept chanting as Eadred led Guthred around the church so that everyone could see him. The abbot held the king's right hand aloft and no doubt many folk thought it odd that the new king was being acclaimed with slave chains hanging from his wrists. Men knelt to him. Guthred knew many of the Danes who had been his father's followers and he greeted them happily. He played the part of the king well, for he was an intelligent as well as a good-natured man, but I saw a look of amusement on his face. Did he really believe he was king then? I think he saw it all as an adventure, but one that was certainly preferable to emptying Eochaid's shit-pail.

Eadred gave a sermon that was blessedly short even though he spoke in both English and Danish. His Danish was not good, but it sufficed to tell Guthred's fellow-countrymen that God and Saint Cuthbert had chosen the new king, and here he was, and glory must inevitably follow. Then he led Guthred toward the rushlights burning in the center of the church and the monks who had been gathered about those smoky flames scrambled to make way for the new king and I saw they had been clustered around three chests which, in turn, were circled by the small lights.

"The royal oath will now be taken!" Eadred announced to the church. The Christians in the church went to their knees again and some of the pagan Danes clumsily followed their example.

It was supposed to be a solemn moment, but Guthred rather spoiled it by turning and looking for me. "Uhtred!" he called, "you should be here! Come!"

Eadred bridled, but Guthred wanted me beside him because the three chests worried him. They were gilded, and their lids were held by big metal clasps, and they were surrounded by the flickering rush-lights, and all that suggested to him that some Christian sorcery was about to take place and he wanted me to share the risk. Abbot Eadred glared at me. "Did he call you Uhtred?" he asked suspiciously.

"Lord Uhtred commands my household troops," Guthred said grandly. That made me the commander of nothing, but I kept a straight face. "And if there are oaths to be taken," Guthred continued, "then he must make them with me."

"Uhtred," Abbot Eadred said flatly. He knew the name, of course he did. He came from Lindisfarena where my family ruled and there was a sourness in his tone.

"I am Uhtred of Bebbanburg," I said loudly enough for everyone in the church to hear, and the announcement caused a hiss among the monks. Some crossed themselves and others just looked at me with apparent hatred.

"He's your companion?" Eadred demanded of Guthred.

"He rescued me," Guthred said, "and he is my friend."

Eadred made the sign of the cross. He had disliked me from the moment he mistook me for the dream-born king, but now he was fairly spitting malevolence at me. He hated me because our family was supposedly the guardians of Lindisfarena's monastery, but the monastery lay in ruins and Eadred, its abbot, had been driven into exile. "Did Ælfric send you?" he demanded.

"Ælfric," I spat the name, "is a usurper, a thief, a cuckoo, and one day I shall spill his rotting belly and send him to the tree where Corpse-Ripper will feed on him."

Eadred placed me then. "You're Lord Uhtred's son," he said, and he looked at my arm rings and my mail and at the workmanship of my swords and at the hammer about my neck. "You're the boy raised by the Danes."

"I am the boy," I said sarcastically, "who killed Ubba Lothbrokson beside a southern sea."

"He is my friend," Guthred insisted.

Abbot Eadred shuddered, then half bowed his head as if to show that he accepted me as Guthred's companion. "You will take an oath," he growled at me, "to serve King Guthred faithfully."

I took a half-step backward. Oath-taking is a serious matter. If I swore to serve this king who had been a slave then I would no longer be a free man. I would be Guthred's man, sworn to die for him, to obey him and serve him until death, and the thought galled me. Guthred saw my hesitation and smiled. "I shall free you," he whispered to me in Danish, and I understood that he, like me, saw this ceremony as a game.

"You swear it?" I asked him.

"On my life," he said lightly.

"The oaths will be taken!" Eadred announced, wanting to restore some dignity to the church that now murmured with talk. He glowered at the congregation until they went quiet, then he opened one of the two smaller chests. Inside was a book, its cover crusted with precious stones. "This is the great gospel book of Lindisfarena," Eadred said in awe. He lifted the book out of the chest and held it aloft so that the dim light glinted from its jewels. The monks all crossed themselves, then Eadred handed the heavy book to an attendant priest whose hands shook as he accepted the volume. Eadred stooped to the second of the small chests. He made the sign of the cross then opened the lid and there, facing me with closed eyes, was a severed head. Guthred could not suppress a grunt of distaste and, fearing sorcery, took my right arm. "That is the most holy Saint Oswald," Eadred said, "once king of Northumbria and now a saint most beloved of almighty God." His voice quivered with emotion.

Guthred took a half-pace backward, repelled by the head, but I shook off his grip and stepped forward to gaze down at Oswald. He had been the lord of Bebbanburg in his time, and he had been king of Northumbria too, but that had been two hundred years ago. He had died in battle against the Mercians who had hacked him to pieces, and I wondered how his head had been rescued from the charnel-house of defeat. The head, its cheeks shrunken and its skin dark, looked quite unscarred. His hair was long and tangled, while his neck had been hidden by a scrap of yellowed linen. A gilt-bronze circlet served as his crown. "Beloved Saint Oswald," Eadred said, making the sign of the cross, "protect us and guide us and pray for us." The king's lips had shrivelled so that three of his teeth showed. They were like yellow pegs. The monks kneeling closest to Oswald bobbed up and down in silent and fervent prayer. "Saint Oswald," Eadred announced, "is a warrior of God and with him on our side none can stand against us."

He stepped past the dead king's head to the last and biggest of the chests. The church was silent. The Christians, of course, were aware that by revealing the relics, Eadred was summoning the powers of heaven to witness the oaths, while the pagan Danes, even if they did not understand exactly what was happening, were awed by the magic they sensed in the big building. And they sensed that more and greater magic was about to happen, for the monks now prostrated themselves flat on the earthen floor as Eadred silently prayed beside the last box. He prayed for a long time, his hands clasped, his lips moving and with his eyes raised to the rafters where sparrows fluttered and then at last he unlatched the chest's two heavy bronze locks and lifted the big lid.

A corpse lay inside the big chest. The corpse was wrapped in a linen cloth, but I could see the body's shape clearly enough. Guthered had again taken my arm as if I could protect him against Eadred's sorcery. Eadred, meanwhile, gently unwrapped the linen and so revealed a dead bishop robed in white and with his face covered by a small white square of cloth that was hemmed with golden thread. The corpse had an embroidered scapular about its neck and a battered miter had fallen from its head. A cross of gold, decorated with garnets, lay half-hidden by his hands that were prayerfully clasped on his breast. A ruby ring shone on one shrunken finger. Some of the monks were gasping, as though they could not endure the holy power flowing from the corpse and even Eadred was subdued. He touched his forehead against the edge of the coffin, then straightened to look at me. "You know who this is?" he asked.

"No."

"In the name of the Father," he said, "and of the Son, and of the Holy Ghost," and he took the square of golden-hemmed linen away to reveal a yellowed face blotched with darker patches. "It is Saint Cuthbert," Eadred said with a tearful catch in his voice. "It is the most blessed, the most holy, the most beloved Cuthbert. Oh dear sweet God," he rocked backward and forward on his knees, "this is Saint Cuthbert himself."

Until the age of ten I had been raised on stories of Cuthbert. I learned how he had trained a choir of seals to sing psalms, and how the eagles had brought food to the small island off Bebbanburg where he lived in solitude for a time. He could calm storms by prayer and had rescued countless sailors from drowning. Angels came to talk with him. He had once rescued a family by commanding the flames that consumed their house to return to hell, and the fire had miraculously vanished. He would walk into the winter sea until the cold water reached his neck and he would stay there all night, praying, and when he came back to the beach in the dawn his monk's robes would be dry. He drew water from parched ground during a drought and when birds stole newly-sewn barley seed he commanded them to return it, which they did. Or so I was told. He was certainly the greatest saint of Northumbria, the holy man who watched over us and to whom we were supposed to direct our prayers so that he could whisper them into the ear of God, and here he was in a carved and gilded elm box, flat on his back, nostrils gaping, mouth slightly open, cheeks fallen in, and with five yellow-black teeth from which the gums had receded so they looked like fangs. One fang was broken. His eyes were shut. My stepmother had possessed Saint Cuthbert's comb and she had liked to tell me that she had found some of the saint's hair on the comb's teeth and that the hair had been the color of finest gold, but this corpse had hair black as pitch. It was long, lank, and brushed away from a high forehead and from his monkish tonsure. Eadred gently restored the miter, then leaned forward and kissed the ruby ring. "You will note," he said in a voice made hoarse by emotion, "that the holy flesh is uncorrupted," he paused to stroke one of the saint's bony hands, "and that miracle is a sure and certain sign of his sanctity." He leaned forward and this time kissed the saint full on the open, shriveled lips. "Oh most holy Cuthbert," he prayed aloud, "guide us and lead us and bring us to your glory in the name of Him who died for us and upon whose right hand you now sit in splendor everlasting, amen."

"Amen," the monks chimed. The closest monks had got up from the floor so they could see the uncorrupted saint and most of them cried as they gazed at the yellowing face.

Eadred looked up at me again. "In this church, young man," he said, "is the spiritual soul of Northumbria. Here, in these chests, are our miracles, our treasures, our glory, and the means by which we speak with God to seek his protection. While these precious and holy things are safe, we are safe, and once," he stood as he said that last word and his voice grew much harder, "once all these things were under the protection of the lords of Bebbanburg, but that protection failed! The pagans came, the monks were slaughtered, and the men of Bebbanburg cowered behind their walls rather than ride to slaughter the pagans. But our forefathers in Christ saved these things, and we have wandered ever since, wandered across the wild lands, and we keep these things still, but one day we shall make a great church and these relics will shine forth across a holy land. That holy land is where I lead these people!" He waved his hand to indicate the folk waiting outside the church. "God has sent me an army," he shouted, "and that army will triumph, but I am not the man to lead it. God and Saint Cuthbert sent me a dream in which they showed me the king who will take us all to our promised land. He showed me King Guthred!"

He stood and raised Guthred's arm aloft and the gesture provoked applause from the congregation. Guthred looked surprised rather than regal, and I just looked down at the dead saint.

Cuthbert had been the abbot and bishop of Lindisfarena, the island that lay just north of Bebbanburg, and for almost two hundred years his body had lain in a crypt on the island until the Viking raids became too threatening and, to save the saintly corpse, the monks had taken the dead man inland. They had been wandering Northumbria ever since.

Eadred disliked me because my family had failed to protect the holy relics, but the strength of Bebbanburg was its position on the sea-lashed crag, and only a fool would take its garrison beyond the walls to fight. If I had a choice between keeping Bebbanburg and abandoning a relic, then I would have surrendered the whole calendar of dead saints. Holy corpses are cheap, but fortresses like Bebbanburg are rare.

"Behold!" Eadred shouted, still holding Guthred's arm aloft, "the king of Haliwerfolkland!"

The king of what? I thought I had misheard, but I had not. Haliwerfolkland, Eadred had said, and it meant the Land of the Holy Man People. That was Eadred's name for Guthred's kingdom. Saint Cuthbert, of course, was the holy man, but whoever was king of his land would be a sheep among wolves. Ivarr, Kjartan, and my uncle were the wolves. They were the men who led proper forces of trained soldiers, while Eadred was hoping to make a kingdom on the back of a dream, and I had no doubts that his dream-born sheep would end up being savaged by the wolves. Still, for the moment, Cair Ligualid was my best refuge in Northumbria, because my enemies would need to cross the hills to find me and, besides, I had a taste for this kind of madness. In madness lies change, in change is opportunity, and in opportunity are riches.

"Now," Eadred let go of Guthred's hand and turned on me, "you will swear fealty to our king and his country."

Guthred actually winked at me then, and I obediently went on my knees and reached for his right hand, but Eadred knocked my hands away. "You swear to the saint," he hissed at me.

"To the saint?"

"Place your hands on Saint Cuthbert's most holy hands," Eadred ordered me, "and say the words."

I put my hands over Saint Cuthbert's fingers and I could feel the big ruby ring under my own fingers, and I gave the jewel a twitch just to see whether the stone was loose and would come free, but it seemed well fixed in its setting. "I swear to be your man," I said to the corpse, "and to serve you faithfully." I tried to shift the ring again, but the dead fingers were stiff and the ruby would not move.

"You swear by your life?" Eadred asked sternly.

I gave the ring another twitch, but it really was immovable. "I swear on my life," I said respectfully and never, in all that life, have I taken an oath so lightly. How can an oath to a dead man be binding?

"And you swear to serve King Guthred faithfully?"

"I do," I said.

"And to be an enemy to all his enemies?"

"I swear it," I said.

"And you will serve Saint Cuthbert even to the end of your life?"

"I will."

"Then you may kiss the most blessed Cuthbert," Eadred said. I leaned over the coffin's edge to kiss the folded hands. "No!" Eadred protested. "On the lips!" I shuffled on my knees, then bent and kissed the corpse on its dry, scratchy lips.

"Praise God," Eadred said. Then he made Guthred swear to serve Cuthbert and the church watched as the slave king knelt and kissed the corpse. The monks sang as the folk in the church were allowed to see Cuthbert for themselves. Hild shuddered when she came to the coffin and she fell to her knees, tears streaming down her face, and I had to lift her up and lead her away. Willibald was similarly overcome, but his face just glowed with happiness. Gisela, I noticed, did not bow to the corpse. She looked at it with curiosity, but it was plain it meant nothing to her and I deduced she was a pagan still. She stared at the dead man, then looked at me and smiled. Her eyes, I thought, were brighter than the ruby on the dead saint's finger.

And so Guthred came to Cair Ligualid. I thought then, and still think now, that it was all nonsense, but it was a magical nonsense, and the dead swordsman had made himself liege to a dead man and the slave had become a king. The gods were laughing.

Later, much later, I realized I was doing what Alfred would have wanted me to do. I was helping the Christians. There were two wars in those years. The obvious struggle was between Saxon and Dane, but there was also combat between pagans and Christians. Most

Danes were pagan and most Saxons were Christian, so the two wars appeared to be the same fight, but in Northumbria it all became confused, and that was Abbot Eadred's cleverness.

What Eadred did was to end the war between the Saxons and the Danes in Cumbraland, and he did it by choosing Guthred. Guthred, of course, was a Dane and that meant Cumbraland's Danes were ready to follow him and, because he had been proclaimed king by a Saxon abbot, the Saxons were equally prepared to support him. Thus the two biggest warring tribes of Cumbraland, the Danes and Saxons, were united, while the Britons, and a good many Britons still lived in Cumbraland, were also Christians and their priests told them to accept Eadred's choice and so they did.

It is one thing to proclaim a king and another for the king to rule, but Eadred had made a shrewd choice. Guthred was a good man, but he was also the son of Hardicnut who had called himself king of Northumbria, so Guthred had a claim to the crown, and none of Cumbraland's thegns was strong enough to challenge him. They needed a king because, for too long, they had squabbled among themselves and suffered from the Norse raids out of Ireland and from the savage incursions from Strath Clota. Guthred, by uniting Dane and Saxon, could now marshal stronger forces to face those enemies. There was one man who might have been a rival. Ulf, he was called, and he was a Dane who owned land south of Cair Ligualid and he had greater wealth than any other thegn in Cumbraland, but he was old and lame and without sons and so he offered fealty to Guthred, and Ulf's example persuaded the other Danes to accept Eadred's choice. They knelt to him one by one and he greeted them by name, raised them and embraced them.

"I really should become a Christian," he told me on the morning after our arrival.

"Why?"

"I told you why. To show gratitude. Aren't you supposed to call me lord?"

"Yes, lord."

"Does it hurt?"

"Calling you lord, lord?"

"No!" he laughed. "Becoming a Christian?"

"Why should it hurt?"

"I don't know. Don't they nail you to a cross?"

"Of course they don't," I said scornfully, "they just wash you."

"I wash myself anyway," he said, then frowned. "Why do Saxons not wash? Not you, you wash, but most Saxons don't. Not as much as Danes. Do they like being dirty?"

"You can catch cold by washing."

"I don't," he said. "So that's it? A wash?"

"Baptism, it's called."

"And you have to give up the other gods?"

"You're supposed to."

"And only have one wife?"

"Only one wife. They're strict about that."

He thought about it. "I still think I should do it," he said, "because Eadred's god does have power. Look at that dead man! It's a miracle that he hasn't rotted away!"

The Danes were fascinated by Eadred's relics. Most did not understand why a group of monks would carry a corpse, a dead king's head, and a jeweled book all over Northumbria, but they did understand that those things were sacred and they were impressed by that. Sacred things have power. They are a pathway from our world to the vaster worlds beyond, and even before Guthred arrived in Cair Ligualid some Danes had accepted baptism as a way of harnessing the power of the relics for themselves.

I am no Christian. These days it does no good to confess that, for the bishops and abbots have too much influence and it is easier to pretend to a faith than to fight angry ideas. I was raised a Christian, but at ten years old, when I was taken into Ragnar's family, I discovered the old Saxon gods who were also the gods of the Danes and of the Norsemen, and their worship has always made more sense to me than bowing down to a god who belongs to a country so far away that I have met no one who has ever been there. Thor and Odin walked our hills, slept in our valleys, loved our women and drank from our streams, and that makes them seem like neighbors. The other thing I like about our gods is that they are not obsessed with us. They have their own squabbles and love affairs and seem to ignore us much of the time, but the Christian god has nothing better to do than to make rules for us. He makes rules, more rules, prohibitions and commandments, and he needs hundreds of black-robed priests and monks to make sure we obey those laws. He strikes me as a very grumpy god, that one, even though his priests are forever claiming that he loves us. I have never been so stupid as to think that Thor or Odin or Hoder loved me, though I hope at times they have thought me worthy of them.

But Guthred wanted the power of the Christian holy relics to work for him and so, to Eadred's delight, he asked to be baptized. The ceremony was done in the open air, just outside the big church, where Guthred was immersed in a great barrel of river-water and all the monks waved their hands to heaven and said God's work was marvelous to behold. Guthred was then draped in a robe and Eadred crowned him a second time by placing the dead King Oswald's circlet of gilt bronze on his wet hair. Guthred's forehead was then smeared with cod oil, he was given a sword and shield, and asked to kiss both the Lindisfarena gospel book and the lips of Cuthbert's corpse that had been brought into the sunlight so that the whole crowd could see the saint. Guthred looked as though he enjoyed the whole ceremony, and Abbot Eadred was so moved that he took Saint Cuthbert's garnet-studded cross from the dead man's hands and hung it about the new king's neck. He did not leave it there for long, but returned it to the corpse after Guthred had been presented to his ragged people in Cair Ligualid's ruins.

That night there was a feast. There was little to eat, just smoked fish, stewed mutton, and hard bread, but there was plenty of ale, and next morning, with a throbbing head, I went to Guthred's first wita-negemot. Being a Dane, of course, he was not accustomed to such council meetings where every thegn and senior churchman was invited to offer advice, but Eadred insisted the Witan met, and Guthred presided.

The meeting took place in the big church. It had started to rain overnight and water dripped through the crude thatch so that men were forever trying to shift out of the way of the drops. There were not enough chairs or stools, so we sat on the rush-strewn floor in a big circle around Eadred and Guthred who were enthroned beside Saint Cuthbert's open coffin. There were forty-six men there, half of them clergy and the other half the biggest landowners of Cumbraland, both Danes and Saxons, but compared to a West Saxon witanegemot it was a paltry affair. There was no great wealth on display. Some of the Danes wore arm rings and a few of the Saxons had elaborate brooches, but in truth it looked more like a meeting of farmers than a council of state.

Eadred, though, had visions of greatness. He began by telling us news from the rest of Northumbria. He knew what happened because he received reports from churchmen all across the land, and those reports said that Ivarr was still in the valley of the River Tuede, where he was fighting a bitter war of small skirmishes against King Aed of Scotland. "Kjartan the Cruel lurks in his stronghold," Eadred said, "and won't emerge to fight. Which leaves Egbert of Eoferwic, and he is weak."

"What about Ælfric?" I intervened.

"Ælfric of Bebbanburg is sworn to protect Saint Cuthbert," Eadred said, "and he will do nothing to offend the saint."

Maybe that was true, but my uncle would doubtless demand my skull as a reward for keeping the corpse undefiled. I said nothing more, but just listened as Eadred proposed that we formed an army and marched it across the hills to capture Eoferwic. That caused some astonishment. Men glanced at each other, but such was Eadred's forceful confidence that at first no one dared question him. They had expected to be told that they should have their men ready to fight against the Norse Vikings from Ireland or to fend off another assault by Eochaid of Strath Clota, but instead they were being asked to go far afield to depose King Egbert.

Ulf, the wealthiest Dane of Cumbraland, finally intervened. He was elderly, perhaps forty years old, and he had been lamed and scarred in Cumbraland's frequent quarrels, but he could still bring forty or fifty trained warriors to Guthred. That was not many by the standards of most parts of Britain, but it was a substantial force in Cumbraland. Now he demanded to know why he should lead those men across the hills. "We have no enemies in Eoferwic," he declared, "but there are many foes who will attack our lands when we're gone." Most of the other Danes murmured their agreement.

But Eadred knew his audience. "There is great wealth in Eoferwic," he said.

Ulf liked that idea, but was still cautious. "Wealth?" he asked.

"Silver," Eadred said, "and gold, and jewels."

"Women?" a man asked.

"Eoferwic is a sink of corruption," Eadred announced, "it is a haunt of devils and a place of lascivious women. It is a city of evil that needs to be scoured by a holy army." Most of the Danes cheered up at the prospect of lascivious women, and none made any more protest at the thought of attacking Eoferwic.

Once the city was captured, a feat Eadred took for granted, we were to march north and the men of Eoferwic, he claimed, would swell our ranks. "Kjartan the Cruel will not face us," Eadred declared, "because he is a coward. He will go to his fastness like a spider scuttling to his web and he will stay there and we shall let him rot until the time comes to strike him down. Ælfric of Bebbanburg will not fight us, for he is a Christian."

"He's an untrustworthy bastard," I growled, and was ignored.

"And we shall defeat Ivarr," Eadred said, and I wondered how our rabble was supposed to beat Ivarr's shield wall, but Eadred had no doubts. "God and Saint Cuthbert will fight for us," he said, "and then we shall be masters of Northumbria and almighty God will have established Haliwerfolkland and we shall build a shrine to Saint Cuthbert that will astonish all the world."

That was what Eadred really wanted, a shrine. That was what the whole madness was about, a shrine to a dead saint, and to that end

Eadred had made Guthred king and would now go to war with all Northumbria. And next day the eight dark horsemen came.

We had three hundred and fifty-four men of fighting age, and of those fewer than twenty possessed mail, and only about a hundred had decent leather armor. The men with leather or mail mostly possessed helmets and had proper weapons, swords or spears, while the rest were armed with axes, adzes, sickles, or sharpened hoes. Eadred grandly called it the Army of the Holy Man, but if I had been the holy man I would have bolted back to heaven and waited for something better to come along.

A third of our army was Danish, the rest was mostly Saxon though there were a few Britons armed with long hunting bows, and those can be fearful weapons, so I called the Britons the Guard of the Holy Man and said they were to stay with the corpse of Saint Cuthbert who would evidently accompany us on our march of conquest. Not that we could start our conquering just yet because we had to amass food for the men and fodder for the horses, of which we had only eighty-seven.

Which made the arrival of the dark horsemen welcome. There were eight of them, all on black or brown horses and leading four spare mounts, and four of them wore mail and the rest had good leather armor and all had black cloaks and black painted shields, and they rode into Cair Ligualid from the east, following the Roman wall that led to the far bank of the river and there they crossed by the ford because the old bridge had been pulled down by the Norsemen.

The eight horsemen were not the only newcomers. Men trickled in every hour. Many of them were monks, but some were fighters coming from the hills and they usually came with an ax or a quarterstaff. Few came with armor or a horse, but the eight dark riders arrived with full war-gear. They were Danes and told Guthred they were from the steading of Hergist who had land at a place called Heagostealdes. Hergist was old, they told Guthred, and could not come himself, but he had sent the best men he had. Their leader was named Tekil and he looked to be a useful warrior for he boasted four arm rings, had a long sword and a hard, confident face. He appeared to be around thirty years old, as were most of his men, though one was much younger, just a boy, and he was the only one without arm rings. "Why," Guthred demanded of Tekil, "would Hergist send men from Heagostealdes?"

"We're too close to Dunholm, lord," Tekil answered, "and Hergist wishes you to destroy that nest of wasps."

"Then you are welcome," Guthred said, and he allowed the eight men to kneel to him and swear him fealty. "You should bring Tekil's men into my household troops," he said to me later. We were in a field to the south of Cair Ligualid where I was practicing those household troops. I had picked thirty young men, more or less at random, and made sure that half were Danes and half were Saxons, and I insisted they made a shield wall in which every Dane had a Saxon neighbor, and now I was teaching them how to fight and praying to my gods that they never had to, for they knew next to nothing. The Danes were better, because the Danes are raised to sword and shield, but none had yet been taught the discipline of the shield wall.

"Your shields have to touch!" I shouted at them, "otherwise you're dead. You want to be dead? You want your guts spooling around your feet? Touch the shields. Not that way, you earsling! The right side of your shield goes in front of the left side of his shield. Understand?" I said it again in Danish then glanced at Guthred. "I don't want Tekil's men in the bodyguard."

"Why not?"

"Because I don't know them."

"You don't know these men," Guthred said, gesturing at his household troops.

"I know they're idiots," I said, "and I know their mothers should have kept their knees together. What are you doing, Clapa?" I shouted at a hulking young Dane. I had forgotten his real name, but everyone called him Clapa, which meant clumsy. He was a huge farm boy, as strong as two other men, but not the cleverest of mortals. He stared at me with dumb eyes as I stalked toward the line. "What are you supposed to do, Clapa?"

"Stay close to the king, lord," he said with a puzzled look.

"Good!" I said, because that was the first and most important lesson that had to be thumped into the thirty young men. They were the king's household troops so they must always stay with the king, but that was not the answer I wanted from Clapa. "In the shield wall, idiot," I said, thumping his muscled chest, "what are you supposed to do in the shield wall?"

He thought for a while, then brightened. "Keep the shield up, lord."

"That's right," I said, dragging his shield up from his ankles. "You don't dangle it around your toes! What are you grinning at, Rypere?" Rypere was a Saxon, skinny where Clapa was solid, and clever as a weasel. Rypere was a nickname which meant thief, for that was what Rypere was and if there had been any justice he would have been branded and whipped, but I liked the cunning in his young eyes and reckoned he would prove a killer. "You know what you are, Rypere?" I said, thumping his shield back into his chest, "you're an earsling. What's an earsling, Clapa?"

"A turd, lord."

"Right, turds! Shields up! Up!" I screamed the last word. "You want folk to laugh at you?" I pointed at other groups of men fighting mock battles in the big meadow. Tekil's warriors were also present, but they were sitting in the shade, just watching, implying that they did not need to practice. I went back to Guthred. "You can't have all the best men in your household troops," I told him.

"Why not?"

"Because you'll end up surrounded when everyone else has run away. Then you die. It isn't pretty."

"That's what happened when my father fought Eochaid," he admitted.

"So that's why you don't have all your best men in the household guard," I said. "We'll put Tekil on one flank and Ulf and his men on the other." Ulf, inspired by a dream of unlimited silver and lasciviously evil women, was now eager to march on Eoferwic. He was not at Cair Ligualid when the dark horsemen arrived, but had taken his men to collect forage and food.

I divided the household troops into two groups and made them fight, though first I ordered them to wrap their swords in cloth so they wouldn't end up slaughtering each other. They were eager but hopeless. I broke through both shield walls in the time it took to blink, but they would learn how to fight eventually unless they met Ivarr's troops first, in which case they would die. After a while, when they were weary and the sweat was streaming down their faces, I told them to rest. I noticed that the Danes sat with the other Danes, and the Saxons with the Saxons, but that was only to be expected and in time, I thought, they would learn trust. They could more or less speak to each other because I had noticed that in Northumbria the Danish and Saxon tongues were becoming muddled. The two languages were similar anyway, and most Danes could be understood by Saxons if they shouted loud enough, but now the two tongues grew ever more alike. Instead of talking about their swordcraft the Saxon earslings in Guthred's household troops boasted of their "skill" with a sword, though they had none, and they ate eggs instead of eating eyren. The Danes, meanwhile, called a horse a horse instead of a hros and sometimes it was hard to know whether a man was a Dane or a Saxon. Often they were both, the son of a Danish father and Saxon mother, though never the other way around. "I should marry a Saxon," Guthred told me. We had wandered to the edge of the field where a group of women were chopping straw and mixing the scraps with oats. We would carry the mixture to feed our horses as we crossed the hills.

"Why marry a Saxon?" I asked.

"To show that Haliwerfolkland is for both tribes," he said.

"Northumbria," I said bad-temperedly.

"Northumbria?"

"It's called Northumbria," I said, "not Haliwerfolkland."

He shrugged as if the name did not matter. "I should still marry a Saxon," he said, "and I'd like it to be a pretty one. Pretty as Hild, maybe? Except she's too old."

"Too old?"

"I need one about thirteen, fourteen maybe? Ready to pup some babies." He clambered across a low fence and edged down a steep bank toward a small stream that flowed north toward the Hedene. "There must be some pretty Saxons in Eoferwic?"

"But you want a virgin, don't you?"

"Probably," he said, then nodded, "yes."

"Might be one or two left in Eoferwic," I said.

"Pity about Hild," he said vaguely.

"What do you mean?"

"If you weren't with her," he said vigorously, "you might make a husband for Gisela."

"Hild and I are friends," I said, "just friends," which was true. We had been lovers, but ever since Hild had seen the body of Saint Cuthbert she had withdrawn into a contemplative mood. She was feeling the tug of her god, I knew, and I had asked her if she wanted to put on the robes of a nun again, but she had shaken her head and said she was not ready.

"But I should probably marry Gisela to a king," Guthred said, ignoring my words. "Maybe Aed of Scotland? Keep him quiet with a bride? Or maybe it's better if she marries Ivarr's son. Do you think she's pretty enough?"

"Of course she is!"

"Horseface!" he said, then laughed at the old nickname. "The two of us used to catch sticklebacks here," he went on, then tugged off his boots, left them on the bank, and began wading upstream. I followed him, staying on the bank where I pushed under alders and through the rank grass. Flies buzzed around me. It was a warm day.

"You want sticklebacks?" I asked, still thinking of Gisela.

"I'm looking for an island," he said.

"Can't be a very big island," I said. The stream could be crossed in two paces and it never rose above Guthred's calves.

"It was big enough when I was thirteen," he said.

"Big enough for what?" I asked, then slapped at a horsefly, crushing it against my mail. It was hot enough to make me wish I had not worn the mail, but I had long learned that a man must be accustomed to the heavy armor or else, in battle, it becomes cumbersome and so I wore it most days just so that it became like a second skin. When I took the mail off it was as though the gods had given me winged feet.

"It was big enough for me and a Saxon called Edith," he said, grinning at me, "and she was my first. She was a sweet thing."

"Probably still is."

He shook his head. "She was gored by a bull and died." He waded on, passing some rocks where ferns grew and, fifty or so paces beyond he gave a happy cry as he discovered his island and I felt sorry for Edith for it was nothing more than a bank of stones that must have been sharp as razors on her scrawny backside.

Guthred sat and began flicking pebbles into the water. "Can we win?" he asked me.

"We can probably take Eoferwic," I said, "so long as Ivarr hasn't returned."

"And if he has?"

"Then you're dead, lord."

He frowned at that. "We can negotiate with Ivarr," he suggested.

"That's what Alfred would do," I said.

"Good!" Guthred cheered up. "And I can offer him Gisela for his son!"

I ignored that. "But Ivarr won't negotiate with you," I said instead. "He'll fight. He's a Lothbrok. He doesn't negotiate except to gain time. He believes in the sword, the spear, the shield, the war ax and the death of his enemies. You won't negotiate with Ivarr, you'll have to fight him and we don't have the army to do that."

"But if we take Eoferwic," he said energetically, "folk there will join us. The army will grow."

"You call this an army?" I asked, then shook my head. "Ivarr leads war-hardened Danes. When we meet them, lord, most of our Danes will join him."

He looked up at me, puzzlement on his honest face. "But they took oaths to me!"

"They'll still join him," I said grimly.

"So what do we do?"

"We take Eoferwic," I said, "we plunder it and we come back here. Ivarr won't follow you. He doesn't care about Cumbraland. So rule here and eventually Ivarr will forget about you."

"Eadred wouldn't like that."

"What does he want?"

"His shrine."

"He can build it here."

Guthred shook his head. "He wants it on the east coast because that's where most folk live."

What Eadred wanted, I suppose, was a shrine that would attract thousands of pilgrims who would shower his church with coins. He could build his shrine here in Cair Ligualid, but it was a remote place and the pilgrims would not come in their thousands. "But you're the king," I said, "so you give the orders. Not Eadred."

"True," he said wryly and tossed another pebble. Then he frowned at me. "What makes Alfred a good king?"

"Who says he's good?"

"Everyone. Father Willibald says he's the greatest king since Charlemagne."

"That's because Willibald is an addled earsling."

"You don't like Alfred?"

"I hate the bastard."

"But he's a warrior, a lawgiver . . ."

"He's no warrior!" I interrupted scornfully, "he hates fighting! He has to do it, but he doesn't like it, and he's far too sick to stand in a shield wall. But he is a lawgiver. He loves laws. He thinks if he invents enough laws he'll make heaven on earth."

"But why do men say he's good?" Guthred asked, puzzled.

I stared up at an eagle sliding across the sky's blue vault. "What Alfred is," I said, trying to be honest, "is fair. He deals properly with folk, or most of them. You can trust his word."

"That's good," Guthred said.

"But he's a pious, disapproving, worried bastard," I said, "that's what he really is."

"I shall be fair," Guthred said. "I shall make men like me."

"They already like you," I said, "but they also have to fear you."

"Fear me?" He did not like that idea.

"You're a king."

"I shall be a good king," he said vehemently, and just then Tekil and his men attacked us.

I should have guessed. Eight well-armed men do not cross a wilderness to join a rabble. They had been sent, and not by some Dane called Hergild in Heagostealdes. They had come from Kjartan the Cruel who, infuriated by his son's humiliation, had sent men to track the dead swordsman, and it had not taken them long to discover that we had followed the Roman wall, and now Guthred and I had wandered away on a warm day and were at the bottom of a small valley as the eight men swarmed down the banks with drawn swords.

I managed to draw Serpent-Breath, but she was knocked aside by Tekil's blade and then two men hit me, driving me back into the stream. I fought them, but my sword arm was pinned, a man was kneeling on my chest, and another was holding my head under the stream and I felt the gagging horror as the water choked in my throat. The world went dark. I wanted to shout, but no sound came, and then Serpent-Breath was taken from my hand and I lost consciousness.

I recovered on the shingle island where the eight men stood around Guthred and me, their swords at our bellies and throats. Tekil, grinning, kicked away the blade that was prodding my gullet and knelt beside me. "Uhtred Ragnarson," he greeted me, "and I do believe you met Sven the One-Eyed not long ago. He sends you greetings." I said nothing. Tekil smiled. "You have *Skidbladnir* in your pouch, perhaps? You'll sail away from us? Back to Niflheim?"

I still said nothing. The breath was rasping in my throat and I kept coughing up water. I wanted to fight, but a sword point was hard against my belly. Tekil sent two of his men to fetch the horses, but that still left six warriors guarding us. "It's a pity," Tekil said, "that we didn't catch your whore. Kjartan wanted her." I tried to summon all my strength to heave up, but the man holding his blade at my belly prodded and Tekil just laughed at me, then unbuckled my sword belt and dragged it out from beneath me. He felt the pouch and grinned when he heard the coins chink. "We have a long journey, Uhtred Ragnarson, and we don't want you to escape us. Sihtric!"

The boy, the only one without arm rings, came close. He looked nervous. "Lord?" he said to Tekil.

"Shackles," Tekil said, and Sihtric fumbled with a leather bag and brought out two sets of slave manacles.

"You can leave him here," I said, jerking my head at Guthred.

"Kjartan wants to meet him too," Tekil said, "but not as much as he wants to renew your acquaintance." He smiled then, as if at a private jest, and drew a knife from his belt. It was a thin-bladed knife and so sharp that its edges looked serrated. "He told me to hamstring you, Uhtred Ragnarson, for a man without legs can't escape, can he? So we'll cut your strings and then we'll take an eye. Sven said I should leave you one eye for him to play with, but that if I wanted I could take the other if it would make you more biddable, and I do want you to be biddable. So which eye would you like me to take, Uhtred Ragnarson? The left eye or the right eye?"

I said nothing again and I do not mind confessing that I was scared. I again tried to heave myself away from him, but he had one knee on my right arm and another man was holding my left, and then the knife blade touched the skin just beneath my left eye and Tekil smiled. "Say good-bye to your eye, Uhtred Ragnarson," he said.

The sun was shining, reflecting off the blade so that my left eye was filled with its brilliance, and I can still see that dazzling brightness now, years later.

And I can still hear the scream.

THREE

It was Clapa who screamed. It was a high-pitched shriek like a young boar being gelded. It sounded more like a scream of terror than a challenge, and that was not surprising for Clapa had never fought before. He had no idea that he was screaming as he came down the slope. The rest of Guthred's household troops followed him, but it was Clapa who led, all clumsiness and savagery. He had forgotten to untie the scrap of torn blanket that protected the edge of his sword, but he was so big and strong that the cloth-wrapped sword acted like a club. There were only five men with Tekil, and the thirty young men came down the steep bank in a rush and I felt Tekil's knife slice across my cheekbone as he rolled away. I tried to seize his knife hand, but he was too quick, then Clapa hit him across the skull and he stumbled, then I saw Rypere about to plunge his sword into Tekil's throat and I shouted that I wanted them alive. "Alive! Keep them alive!"

Two of Tekil's men died despite my shout. One had been stabbed and torn by at least a dozen blades and he twisted and jerked in the stream that ran red with his blood. Clapa had abandoned his sword and wrestled Tekil onto the shingle bank where he held him down by brute strength. "Well done, Clapa," I said, thumping him on the shoulder, and he grinned at me as I took away Tekil's knife and sword. Rypere finished off the man thrashing in the water. One of my boys had received a sword thrust in his thigh, but the rest were uninjured and now they stood grinning in the stream, wanting praise like puppies that had run down their first fox. "You did well," I told them, and so they had, for we now held Tekil and three of his men prisoner. Sihtric, the youngster, was one of the captives and he was still holding the slave shackles and, in my anger, I snatched them from him and whipped them across his skull. "I want the other two men," I told Rypere.

"What other men, lord?"

"He sent two men to fetch their horses," I said, "find them." I gave Sihtric another hard blow, wanting to hear him cry out, but he kept silent even though blood was trickling from his temple.

Guthred was still sitting on the shingle, a look of astonishment on his handsome face. "I've lost my boots," he said. It seemed to worry him far more than his narrow escape.

"You left them upstream," I told him.

"My boots?"

"They're upstream," I said and kicked Tekil, hurting my foot more than I hurt his mail-clad ribs, but I was angry. I had been a fool, and felt humiliated. I strapped on my swords, then knelt and took Tekil's four arm rings. He looked up at me and must have known his fate, but his face showed nothing.

The prisoners were taken back to the town and meanwhile we discovered that the two men who had been sent to fetch Tekil's horses must have heard the commotion for they had ridden away eastward. It took us far too much time to saddle our own horses and set off in pursuit and I was cursing because I did not want the two men to take news of me back to Kjartan. If the fugitives had been sensible they would have crossed the river and ridden hard along the wall, but they must have reckoned it was risky to ride through Cair Ligualid and safer to go south and east. They also should have abandoned the riderless horses, but they were greedy and took them all and that meant their tracks were easy to follow even though the ground was dry. The two men were in unfamiliar country, and they veered too far to the south and so gave us a chance to block the eastward tracks. By evening we had more than sixty men hunting them and in the dusk we found them gone to ground in a stand of hornbeam.

The older man came out fighting. He knew he had small time left to live and he was determined to go to Odin's corpse-hall rather than to the horrors of Niflheim and he charged from the trees on his tired horse, shouting a challenge, and I touched my heels to Witnere's flanks, but Guthred headed me off. "Mine," Guthred said and he drew his sword and his horse leaped away, mainly because Witnere, offended at being blocked, had bitten the smaller stallion in the rump.

Guthred was behaving like a king. He never enjoyed fighting, and he was far less experienced in battle than I, but he knew he had to make this killing himself or else men would say he sheltered behind my sword. He managed it well enough. His horse stumbled just before he met Kjartan's man, but that was an advantage for the stumble veered him away from the enemy whose wild blow swept harmlessly past Guthred's waist while Guthred's own desperate hack struck the man's wrist, breaking it, and after that it was a simple matter to ride the enemy down and chop him to death. Guthred did not enjoy it, but knew he had to do it, and in time the killing became part of his legend. Songs were sung how Guthred of Northumbria slew six evildoers in combat, but it had been only one man and Guthred was lucky that his horse had tripped. But that is good in a king. Kings need to be lucky. Later, when we got back to Cair Ligualid, I gave him my father's old helmet as a reward for his bravery and he was pleased.

I ordered Rypere to kill the second man which he did with an encouraging relish. It was not hard for Rypere because the second man was a coward and only wanted to surrender. He threw away his sword and knelt, shivering, calling out that he yielded, but I had other plans for him. "Kill him!" I told Rypere who gave a wolfish grin and chopped down hard.

We took the twelve horses, stripped the two men of their armor and weapons and left their corpses for the beasts, but first I told Clapa to use his sword to cut off their heads. Clapa stared at me with ox-eyes. "Their heads, lord?" he asked.

"Chop them off, Clapa," I said, "and these are for you." I gave him two of Tekil's arm rings.

He gazed at the silver rings as though he had never seen such wonders before. "For me, lord?"

"You saved our lives, Clapa."

"It was Rypere who brought us," he admitted. "He said we shouldn't leave the king's side and you'd gone away so we had to follow."

So I gave Rypere the other two rings, and then Clapa chopped at the dead men and learned how hard it is to cut through a neck, but once the deed was done we carried the bloody heads back to Cair Ligualid and when we reached the ruined town I had the first two corpses pulled from the stream and decapitated.

Abbot Eadred wanted to hang the four remaining prisoners, but I persuaded him to give me Tekil, at least for a night, and I had him brought to me in the ruins of an old building which I think must have been made by the Romans. The tall walls were made of dressed stone and were broken by three high windows. There was no roof. The floor was made of tiny black and white tiles that had once made a pattern, but the pattern had long been broken. I made a fire on the biggest remaining patch of tile and the flames threw a lurid flicker on the old walls. A wan light came through the windows when clouds slid away from the moon. Rypere and Clapa brought Tekil to me, and they wanted to stay and watch whatever I did to him, but I sent them away.

Tekil had lost his armor and was now dressed in a grubby jerkin. His face was bruised and his wrists and ankles were joined by the slave manacles he had intended for me. He sat at the far end of the old room and I sat across the fire from him and he just stared at me. He had a good face, a strong face, and I thought that I might have liked Tekil if we had been comrades instead of enemies. He seemed amused by my inspection of him. "You were the dead swordsman," he said after a while.

"Was I?"

"I know the dead swordsman wore a helmet with a silver wolf on the crown, and I saw the same helmet on you," he shrugged, "or perhaps he lends you his helmet?"

"Perhaps he does," I said.

He half smiled. "The dead swordsman scared Kjartan and his son halfway to death, but that's what you intended, isn't it?"

"That's what the swordsman intended," I said.

"Now," he said, "you've cut off the heads of four of my men and you're going to give those heads back to Kjartan, aren't you?"

"Yes."

"Because you want to frighten him even more?"

"Yes," I said.

"But there have to be eight heads," he said. "Isn't that so?"

"Yes," I said again.

He grimaced at that, then leaned against the wall and gazed up at the clouds drifting beside the crescent moon. Dogs howled in the ruins and Tekil turned his head to listen to the noise. "Kjartan likes dogs," he said. "He keeps a pack of them. Vicious things. They have to fight each other and he only keeps the strongest. He kennels them in a hall at Dunholm and he uses them for two things." He stopped then and looked at me quizzically. "That's what you want, isn't it? For me to tell you all about Dunholm? Its strengths, its weaknesses, how many men are there and how you can break the place?"

"All that," I said, "and more."

"Because this is your bloodfeud, isn't it? Kjartan's life in revenge for Earl Ragnar's death?"

"Earl Ragnar raised me," I said, "and I loved him like a father."

"What about his son?"

"Alfred kept him as a hostage."

"So you'll do a son's duty?" he asked, then shrugged as if my answer would be obvious. "You'll find it hard," he said, "and harder still if you have to fight Kjartan's dogs. He keeps them in their own hall. They live like lords, and under the hall's floor is Kjartan's treasure. So much gold and silver. A hoard that he never looks at. But it's all there, buried in the earth beneath the dogs."

"Who guards it?" I asked.

"That's one of their jobs," Tekil said, "but the second is to kill people. It's how he'll kill you. He'll take your eyes first, then you'll be torn to pieces by his hounds. Or perhaps he'll take the skin off you inch by inch. I've seen him do that."

"Kjartan the Cruel," I said.

"He's not called that for nothing," Tekil said.

"So why do you serve him?"

"He's generous," Tekil said. "There are four things Kjartan loves. Dogs, treasure, women, and his son. I like two of those, and Kjartan is generous with both."

"And the two you don't like?" I asked.

"I hate his dogs," he admitted, "and his son is a coward."

"Sven?" I was surprised. "He wasn't a coward as a child."

Tekil stretched out a leg, then grimaced when the slave shackles checked his foot. "When Odin lost an eye," he said, "he gained wisdom, but when Sven lost an eye he learned fear. He's courageous enough when he's fighting the weak, but he doesn't like facing the strong. But his father, now, he's no coward."

"I remember Kjartan was brave," I said.

"Brave, cruel, and brutal," Tekil said, "and now you've also learned that he has a lordly hall filled with hounds that will tear you to bloody scraps. And that, Uhtred Ragnarson, is all that I will tell you."

I shook my head. "You will tell me more," I said.

He watched as I put a log on the fire. "Why will I tell you more?" he asked.

"Because I have something you want," I told him.

"My life?"

"The manner of your death," I said.

He understood that and gave a half-smile. "I hear the monks want to hang me?"

"They do," I said, "because they have no imagination. But I won't let them hang you."

"So what will you do instead? Give me to those boys you call soldiers? Let them practice on me?"

"If you don't talk," I said, "that's just what I'll do because they need the practice. But I'll make it easy for them. You won't have a sword."

Without a sword he would not go to the corpse-hall and that was threat enough to make Tekil talk. Kjartan, he told me, had three crews of men at Dunholm, which amounted to about a hundred and fifty warriors, but there were others in steadings close to the stronghold who would fight for him if they were summoned so that if Kjartan wished he could lead four hundred well-trained warriors. "And they're loyal to him," Tekil warned me.

"Because he's generous to them?"

"We never lack for silver or women. What more can a warrior want?"

"To go to the corpse-hall," I said and Tekil nodded at that truth. "So where do the slaves come from?" I asked.

"From traders like the one you killed. Or we find them for ourselves."

"You keep them at Dunholm?"

Tekil shook his head. "Only the young girls go there, the rest go to Gyruum. We've got two crews at Gyruum." That made sense. I had been to Gyruum, a place where there had once been a famous monastery before Ragnar the Elder destroyed it. It was a small town on the south bank of the River Tine, very close to the sea, which made it a convenient place to ship slaves across the water. There was an old Roman fort on Gyruum's headland, but the fort was not nearly so defensible as Dunholm, which scarcely mattered because if trouble loomed the Gyruum garrison would have time to march south to the larger fortress and find refuge there, taking their slaves with them. "And Dunholm," Tekil told me, "cannot be taken."

"Cannot?" I asked skeptically.

"I'm thirsty," Tekil said.

"Rypere!" I shouted. "I know you're out there! Bring some ale!"

I gave Tekil a pot of ale, some bread, and cold goat-meat, and while he ate he talked of Dunholm and assured me it was truly impregnable.

"A large enough army could take it," I suggested.

He scoffed at that idea. "You can only approach from the north," he said, "and that approach is steep and narrow, so if you have the greatest army in the world you can still only lead a few men against the defenses."

"Has anyone tried?"

"Ivarr came to look at us, stayed four days, and marched away. Before that Earl Ragnar's son came and he didn't even stay that long. You could starve the place, I suppose, but that will take you a year, and how many men can afford to keep a besieging force in food for a year?" He shook his head. "Dunholm is like Bebbanburg, it's impregnable."

Yet my fate was leading me to both places. I sat in silence, thinking, until Tekil heaved at his slave shackles as if to see whether he could snap them. He could not. "So tell me the manner of my death," he said.

"I have one more question."

He shrugged. "Ask it."

"Thyra Ragnarsdottir."

That surprised him and he was silent for a while, then he realized that of course I had known Thyra as a child. "The lovely Thyra," he said sarcastically.

"She lives?"

"She was supposed to be Sven's wife," Tekil said.

"And is she?"

He laughed at that. "She was forced to his bed, what do you think? But he doesn't touch her now. He fears her. So she's locked away and Kjartan listens to her dreams."

"Her dreams?"

"The gods talk through her. That's what Kjartan thinks."

"And you think?"

"I think the bitch is mad."

I stared at him through the flames. "But she lives?"

"If you can call it living," he said drily.

"Mad?"

"She cuts herself," Tekil said, drawing the edge of a hand across his arm. "She wails, cuts her flesh, and makes curses. Kjartan is frightened of her."

"And Sven?"

Tekil grimaced. "He's terrified of her. He wants her dead."

"So why isn't she dead?"

"Because the dogs won't touch her," Tekil said, "and because Kjartan believes she has the gift of prophecy. She told him the dead swordsman would kill him, and he half believes her."

"The dead swordsman will kill Kjartan," I said, "and tomorrow he will kill you."

He accepted that fate. "The hazel rods?"

"Yes."

"And a sword in my hand?"

"In both hands, if you want," I said, "because the dead swordsman will kill you all the same."

He nodded, then closed his eyes and leaned against the wall again. "Sihtric," he told me, "is Kjartan's son."

Sihtric was the boy who had been captured with Tekil. "He's Sven's brother?" I asked.

"His half-brother. Sihtric's mother was a Saxon slave girl. Kjartan gave her to the dogs when he believed she tried to poison him. Maybe she did or maybe he just had a pain in his belly. But whatever it was he fed her to his dogs and she died. He let Sihtric live because he's my servant and I pleaded for him. He's a good boy. You'd do well to let him live."

"But I need eight heads," I reminded him.

"Yes," he said tiredly, "you do." Fate is inexorable.

Abbot Eadred wanted the four men hanged. Or drowned. Or strangled. He wanted them dead, dishonored, and forgotten. "They
assaulted our king!" he declared vehemently. "And they must suffer a
vile death, a vile death!" He kept repeating those words with a rare
relish, and I just shrugged and said I had promised Tekil an honorable
death, one that would send him to Valhalla instead of to Niflheim,
and Eadred stared at my hammer amulet and screeched that in Haliwerfolkland there could be no mercy for men who attacked Cuthbert's chosen one.

We were arguing on the slope just beneath the new church and the
four prisoners, all in shackles or ropes, were sitting on the ground,
guarded by Guthred's household troops, and many of the folk from
the town were there, waiting for Guthred's decision. Eadred was
haranguing the king, saying that a show of weakness would under-
mine Guthred's authority. The churchmen agreed with the abbot,
which was no surprise, and chief amongst his supporters were two
newly-arrived monks who had walked across the hills from eastern
Northumbria. They were named Jænberht and Ida, both were in their
twenties and both owed obedience to Eadred. They had evidently
been across the hills on some mission for the abbot, but now they
were back in Cair Ligualid and they were vehement that the prisoners
should die ignominiously and painfully. "Burn them!" Jænberht
urged, "as the pagans burned so many of the holy saints! Roast them
over the flames of hell!"

"Hang them!" Abbot Eadred insisted.

I could sense, even if Eadred could not, that the Cumbraland
Danes who had joined Guthred were taking offense at the priests'
vehemence, so I took the king aside. "You think you can stay king
without the Danes?" I asked him.

"Of course not."

"But if you torture fellow Danes to death they'll not like it. They'll
think you favor the Saxons over them."

Guthred looked troubled. He owed his throne to Eadred and would not keep it if the abbot deserted him, but nor would he keep it if he lost the support of Cumbraland's Danes. "What would Alfred do?" he asked me.

"He'd pray," I said, "and he'd have all his monks and priests praying, but in the end he would do whatever is necessary to keep his kingdom intact." Guthred just stared at me. "Whatever is necessary," I repeated slowly.

Guthred nodded, then, frowning, he walked back to Eadred. "In a day or two," Guthred said loudly enough for most of the crowd to hear him, "we shall march eastward. We shall cross the hills and carry our blessed saint to a new home in a holy land. We shall overcome our enemies, whoever they are, and we shall establish a new kingdom." He was speaking in Danish, but his words were being translated into English by three or four folk. "This will happen," he said, speaking more strongly now, "because my friend Abbot Eadred was given a dream sent by God and by the holy Saint Cuthbert, and when we leave here to cross the hills we shall go with God's blessing and with Saint Cuthbert's aid, and we shall make a better kingdom, a hallowed kingdom which will be guarded by the magic of Christianity." Eadred frowned at the word magic, but did not protest. Guthred's grasp of his new religion was still sketchy, but he was mostly saying what Eadred wanted to hear. "And we shall have a kingdom of justice!" Guthred said very loudly. "A kingdom in which all men will have faith in God and the king, but in which not every man worships the same god." They were all listening now, listening closely, and Jænberht and Ida half reared as if to protest Guthred's last proposal, but Guthred kept speaking, "and I will not be king of a land in which I force on men the customs of other men, and it is the custom of these men," he gestured at Tekil and his companions, "to die with a sword in their hands, and so they shall. And God will have mercy on their souls."

There was silence. Guthred turned to Eadred and spoke much lower. "There are some folk," he said in English, "who do not think we can beat the Danes in a fight. So let them see it done now."

Eadred stiffened, then forced himself to nod. "As you command, lord King," he said.

And so the hazel branches were fetched.

The Danes understand the rules of a fight inside an area marked by stripped branches of hazel. It is a fight from which only one man can emerge alive, and if either man flees the hazel-marked space then he can be killed by anyone. He has become a nothing. Guthred wanted to fight Tekil himself, but I sensed he was only making the suggestion because it was expected of him and he did not really want to face a seasoned warrior. Besides, I was in no mood to be denied. "I'll do them all," I said, and he did not argue.

I am old now. So old. I lose count of how old sometimes, but it must be eighty years since my mother died giving birth to me, and few men live that long, and very few who stand in the shield wall live half that many years. I see folk watching me, expecting me to die, and doubtless I will oblige them soon. They drop their voices when they are near me in case they disturb me, and that is an annoyance for I do not hear as well as I did, and I do not see as well as I did, and I piss all night and my bones are stiff and my old wounds ache and each dusk, when I lie down, I make certain that Serpent-Breath or another of my swords is beside the bed so that I can grip the hilt if death comes for me. And in the darkness, as I listen to the sea beat on the sand and the wind fret at the thatch, I remember what it was like to be young and tall and strong and fast. And arrogant.

I was all those things. I was Uhtred, killer of Ubba, and in 878, the year that Alfred defeated Guthrum and the year in which Guthred came to the throne of Northumbria, I was just twenty-one and my name was known wherever men sharpened swords. I was a warrior. A sword warrior, and I was proud of it. Tekil knew it. He was good, he had fought a score of battles, but when he stepped across the hazel branch he knew he was dead.

I will not say I was not nervous. Men have looked at me on battle-fields across the island of Britain and they wondered that I had no fear, but of course I had fear. We all have fear. It crawls inside you like a beast, it claws at your guts, it weakens your muscles, it tries to loosen your bowels, and it wants you to cringe and weep, but fear must be thrust away and craft must be loosed, and savagery will see you through, and though many men have tried to kill me and so earn the boast that they killed Uhtred, so far that savagery has let me survive and now, I think, I am too old to die in battle and so will dribble away to nothingness instead. Wyrd bið ful aræd, we say, and it is true. Fate is inexorable.

Tekil's fate was to die. He fought with sword and shield, and I had given him back his mail and, so that no man would say I had an advantage over him, I fought without any armor at all. No shield either. I was arrogant, and I was conscious that Gisela was watching, and in my head I dedicated Tekil's death to her. It took scarcely a moment, despite my limp. I have had that slight limp ever since the spear thrust into my right thigh at Ethandun, but the limp did not slow me. Tekil came at me in a rush, hoping to beat me down with his shield and then hack me with his sword, but I turned him neatly and then I kept moving. That is the secret of winning a sword fight. Keep moving. Dance. In the shield wall a man cannot move, only lunge and beat and hack and keep the shield high, but inside the hazel boughs litheness means life. Make the other man respond and keep him off balance, and Tekil was slow because he was in mail and I was unarmored, but even in armor I was fast and he had no chance of matching my speed. He came at me again, and I let him pass me by, then made his death swift. He was turning to face me, but I moved faster and Serpent-Breath took the back of his neck, just above the edge of his mail and, because he had no helmet, the blade broke through his spine and he collapsed in the dust. I killed him quickly and he went to the corpse-hall where one day he will greet me.

The crowd applauded. I think the Saxons among them might have preferred to see the prisoners burned or drowned or trampled by horses, but enough of them appreciated sword work and they clapped me. Gisela was grinning at me. Hild was not watching. She was at the edge of the crowd with Father Willibald. The two spent long hours talking and I knew it was Christian matters they discussed, but that was not my business.

The next two prisoners were terrified. Tekil had been their leader, and a man leads other men because he is the best fighter, and in Tekil's sudden death they saw their own, and neither put up any real fight. Instead of attacking me they tried to defend themselves, and the second had enough skill to parry me again and again, until I lunged high, his shield went up and I kicked his ankle out from beneath him and the crowd cheered as he died.

That left Sihtric, the boy. The monks, who had wanted to hang these Danes, but who now took an unholy glee in their honorable deaths, pushed him into the hazel ring and I could see that Sihtric did not know how to hold the sword and that his shield was nothing but a burden. His death was a heartbeat away, no more trouble to me than swatting a fly. He knew that too and was weeping.

I needed eight heads. I had seven. I stared at the boy and he could not meet my gaze, but looked away instead and he saw the bloody scrapes in the earth where the first three bodies had been dragged away and he fell to his knees. The crowd jeered. The monks were shouting at me to kill him. Instead I waited to see what Sihtric would do and I saw him conquer his fear. I saw the effort he made to stop blubbering, to control his breath, to force his shaking legs to obey him so that he managed to stand. He hefted the shield, sniffed, then looked me in the eye. I gestured at his sword and he obediently raised it so that he would die like a man. There were bloody scabs on his forehead where I had hit him with the slave shackles.

"What was your mother's name?" I asked him. He stared at me and seemed incapable of speaking. The monks were shouting for his death. "What was your mother's name?" I asked him again.

"Elflæd," he stammered, but so softly I could not hear him. I frowned at him, waited, and he repeated the name. "Elflæd."

"Elflæd, lord," I corrected him.

"She was called Elflæd, lord," he said.

"She was Saxon?"

"Yes, lord."

"And did she try to poison your father?"

He paused, then realized that no harm could come from telling the truth now. "Yes, lord."

"How?" I had to raise my voice over the noise of the crowd.

"The black berries, lord."

"Nightshade?"

"Yes, lord."

"How old are you?"

"I don't know, lord."

Fourteen, I guessed. "Does your father love you?" I asked.

That question puzzled him. "Love me?"

"Kjartan. He's your father, isn't he?"

"I hardly know him, lord," Sihtric said, and that was probably true. Kjartan must have whelped a hundred pups in Dunholm.

"And your mother?" I asked.

"I loved her, lord," Sihtric said, and he was close to tears again.

I went a pace closer to him and his sword arm faltered, but he tried to brace himself. "On your knees, boy," I said.

He looked defiant then. "I would die properly," he said in a voice made squeaky by fear.

"On your knees!" I snarled, and the tone of my voice terrified him and he dropped to his knees and he seemed unable to move as I came toward him. He flinched when I reversed Serpent-Breath, expecting me to hit him with the heavy pommel, but then disbelief showed in his eyes as I held the sword's hilt to him. "Clasp it," I said, "and say the words." He still stared up at me, then managed to drop his shield and sword and put his hands on Serpent-Breath's hilt. I put my hands over his. "Say the words," I told him again.

"I will be your man, lord," he said, looking up at me, "and I will serve you till death."

"And beyond," I said.

"And beyond, lord. I swear it."

Jænberht and Ida led the protest. The two monks stepped across the hazel branches and shouted that the boy had to die, that it was God's will that he died, and Sihtric flinched as I tore Serpent-Breath from his hands and whipped her around. The blade, all newly-bloodied and nicked, swept toward the monks and then I held her motionless with her tip at Jænberht's neck. The fury came then, the battle-fury, the bloodlust, the joy of slaughter, and it was all I could do not to let Serpent-Breath take another life. She wanted it, I could feel her trembling in my hand. "Sihtric is my man," I said to the monk, "and if anyone harms him then they will be my enemy, and I would kill you, monk, if you harm him, I would kill you without a thought." I was shouting now, forcing him back. I was nothing but anger and red-haze, wanting his soul. "Does anyone here," I shouted, at last managing to take Serpent-Breath's tip away from Jænberht's throat and whirling the sword around to embrace the crowd, "deny that Sihtric is my man? Anyone?"

No one spoke. The wind gusted across Cair Ligualid and they could all smell death in that breeze and no one spoke, but their silence did not satisfy my anger. "Anyone?" I shouted, desperately eager for someone to meet my challenge. "Because you can kill him now. You can kill him there, on his knees, but first you must kill me."

Jænberht watched me. He had a narrow, dark face and clever eyes. His mouth was twisted, perhaps from some boyhood accident, and it gave him a sneering look. I wanted to tear his rotten soul out of his thin body. He wanted my soul, but he dared not move. No one moved until Guthred stepped across the hazel branches and held his hand to Sihtric. "Welcome," he said to the boy.

Father Willibald, who had come running when he first heard my furious challenge, also stepped over the hazel branches. "You can sheathe your sword, lord," he said gently. He was too frightened to come close, but brave enough to stand in front of me and gently push Serpent-Breath aside. "You can sheathe the sword," he repeated.

"The boy lives!" I snarled at him.

"Yes, lord," Willibald said softly, "the boy lives."

Gisela was watching me, eyes as bright as when she had welcomed her brother back from slavery. Hild was watching Gisela.

And I was still lacking one severed head.

We left at dawn, an army going to war.

Ulf's men were the vanguard, then came the horde of churchmen carrying Abbot Eadred's three precious boxes, and behind them Guthred rode a white mare. Gisela walked beside her brother and I walked close behind while Hild led Witnere, though when she was tired I insisted she climb into the stallion's saddle.

Hild looked like a nun. She had plaited her long golden hair and then twisted the plaits about her skull, and over it she wore a pale gray hood. Her cloak was of the same pale gray and around her neck hung a plain wooden cross that she fingered as she rode. "They've been pestering you, haven't they?" I said.

"Who?"

"The priests," I said. "Father Willibald. They've been telling you to go back to the nunnery."

"God has been pestering me," she said. I looked up at her and she smiled as if to reassure me that she would not burden me with her dilemma. "I prayed to Saint Cuthbert," she said.

"Did he answer?"

She fingered her cross. "I just prayed," she said calmly, "and that's a beginning."

"Don't you like being free?" I asked her harshly.

Hild laughed at that. "I'm a woman," she said, "how can I be free?" I said nothing and she smiled at me. "I'm like mistletoe," she said, "I need a branch to grow on. Without the branch, I'm nothing." She spoke without bitterness, as if she merely stated an obvious truth. And it was true. She was a woman of good family and if she had not been given to the church then, like little Æthelflaed, she would have been given to a man. That is woman's fate. In time I knew a woman who defied it, but Hild was like the ox that missed its yoke on a feast day.

"You're free now," I said.

"No," she said, "I'm dependant on you." She looked at Gisela who was laughing at something her brother had just said. "And you are taking good care, Uhtred, not to shame me." She meant I was not humiliating her by abandoning her to pursue Gisela, and that was true, but only just true. She saw my expression and laughed. "In many ways," she said, "you're a good Christian."

"I am?"

"You try to do the right thing, don't you?" She laughed at my shocked expression. "I want you to make me a promise," she said.

"If I can," I said cautiously.

"Promise me you won't steal Saint Oswald's head to make up the eight."

I laughed, relieved that the promise did not involve Gisela. "I was thinking about it," I admitted.

"I know you were," she said, "but it won't work. It's too old. And you'll make Eadred unhappy."

"What's wrong with that?"

She ignored that question. "Seven heads are enough," she insisted.

"Eight would be better."

"Greedy Uhtred," she said.

The seven heads were now sewn into a sack which Sihtric had put on a donkey that he led by a rope. Flies buzzed around the sack, which stank so that Sihtric walked alone.

We were a strange army. Not counting churchmen, we numbered three hundred and eighteen men, and with us marched at least that many women and children and the usual scores of dogs. There were sixty or seventy priests and monks and I would have exchanged every one of them for more horses or more warriors. Of the three hundred and eighteen men I doubted that even a hundred were worth putting in a shield wall. In truth we were not an army, but a rabble.

The monks chanted as they walked. I suppose they chanted in Latin, for I did not understand the words. They had draped Saint Cuthbert's coffin with a fine green cloth embroidered with crosses and that morning a raven had spattered the cloth with shit. At first I took this to be a bad omen, then decided that as the raven was Odin's bird he was merely showing his displeasure with the dead Christian and so I applauded the god's joke, thus getting a malignant look from Brothers Ida and Jænberht.

"What do we do," Hild asked me, "if we get to Eoferwic and find that Ivarr has returned?"

"We run away, of course."

She laughed. "You're happy, aren't you?" she said.

"Yes."

"Why?"

"Because I'm away from Alfred," I said, and I realized that was true.

"Alfred is a good man," Hild chided me.

"He is," I answered, "but do you ever look forward to his company? Do you brew special ale for him? Do you remember a joke to tell him? Does anyone ever sit by a fire and try him with riddles? Do we sing with him? All he ever does is worry about what his god wants, and he makes rules to please his god, and if you do something for him it's never enough because his wretched god just wants more."

Hild gave me her customary patient smile when I insulted her god. "Alfred wants you back," she said.

"He wants my sword," I said, "not me."

"Will you go back?"

"No," I said firmly, and I tried to see into the future to test that answer, but I did not know what the spinners who make our fate planned for me. Somehow, with this rabble of men, I hoped to destroy Kjartan and capture Bebbanburg, and hard sense told me it could not be done, but hard sense would never have imagined that a freed slave would be accepted as king by Saxon and Dane alike.

"You'll never go back?" Hild asked, skeptical of my first answer.

"Never," I said, and I could hear the spinners laughing at me and I feared that fate had tied me to Alfred and I resented that because it suggested I was not my own master. Perhaps I was mistletoe too, except I had a duty. I had a bloodfeud to finish.

We followed the Roman roads across the hills. It took us five days, slow going, but we could go no faster than the monks carrying the saint's corpse on their shoulders. Every night they said prayers, and every day new folk joined us so that as we marched on the last day across the flat plain toward Eoferwic we numbered close to five hundred men. Ulf, who now called himself Earl Ulf, led the march under his banner of an eagle's head. He had come to like Guthred, and Ulf and I were the king's closest advisers. Eadred was also close, of course, but Eadred had little to say about matters of war. Like most churchmen he assumed his god would bring us victory, and that was all he had to contribute. Ulf and I, on the other hand, had plenty to say and the gist of it was that five hundred half-trained men were not nearly enough to capture Eoferwic if Egbert had a mind to defend it.

But Egbert was in despair. There is a tale in a Christian holy book about a king who saw some writing on the wall. I have heard the story a few times, but cannot remember the details, except that it was a king and there were words on his wall and they frightened him. I think the Christian god wrote the words, but I am not even sure about that. I could send for my wife's priest, for I allow her to employ such a creature these days, and I could ask him for the details, but he would only grovel at my feet and beg that I increase his family's allowance of fish, ale, and firewood, which I do not wish to do, so the details do not matter now. There was a king, his wall had words on it and they frightened him.

It was Willibald who put that story into my head. He was crying as we entered the city, crying tears of joy, and when he learned that Egbert would not resist us, he began shouting that the king had seen the writing on the wall. Over and over he shouted it, and it made no sense to me at the time, but now I know what he meant. He meant that Egbert knew he had lost before he had even begun to fight.

Eoferwic had been expecting Ivarr's return and many of its citizens, fearing the Dane's revenge, had left. Egbert had a bodyguard, of course, but most had deserted him so that now his household troops only numbered twenty-eight men and not one of them wanted to die for a king with writing on his wall, and the remaining citizens were in no mood to barricade the gates or man the wall, and so Guthred's army marched in without meeting any resistance. We were welcomed. I think the folk of Eoferwic thought we had come to defend them against Ivarr rather than take the crown from Egbert, but even when they learned that they had a new king they seemed happy enough. What cheered them most, of course, was the presence of Saint Cuthbert, and Eadred propped the saint's coffin in the archbishop's church, opened the lid, and the folk crowded in to see the dead man and say prayers to him.

Wulfhere, the archbishop, was not in the city, but Father Hrothweard was still there and still preaching madness, and he sided instantly with Eadred. I suppose he had seen the writing on the wall too, but the only writing I saw were crosses scratched on doorways. These were supposed to indicate that Christians lived inside, but most of the surviving Danes also displayed the cross as a protection against plunderers, and Guthred's men wanted plunder. Eadred had promised them lascivious women and heaps of silver, but now the abbot strove mightily to protect the city's Christians from Guthred's Danes. There was some trouble, but not much. Folk had the good sense to offer coins, food, and ale rather than be robbed, and Guthred discovered chests of silver inside the palace and he distributed the money to his army and there was plenty of ale in the taverns, so for the moment the men of Cumbraland were happy enough.

"What would Alfred do?" Guthred asked me on that first evening in Eoferwic. It was a question I was getting used to, for somehow Guthred had convinced himself that Alfred was a king worth emulating. This time he asked me the question about Egbert who had been discovered in his bedchamber. Egbert had been dragged to the big hall where he went on his knees to Guthred and swore fealty. It was a strange sight, one king kneeling to another, and the old Roman hall lit by braziers that filled the upper part with smoke, and behind Egbert were his courtiers and servants who also knelt and shuffled forward to promise loyalty to Guthred. Egbert looked old, ill, and unhappy while Guthred was a shining young monarch. I had found Egbert's mail and given it to Guthred who wore the armor because it made him look regal. He was cheerful with the deposed king, raising him from his knees and kissing him on both cheeks, then courteously inviting him to sit beside him.

"Kill the old bastard," Ulf said.

"I am minded to be merciful," Guthred said regally.

"You're minded to be an idiot," Ulf retorted. He was in a gloomy mood for Eoferwic had not yielded a quarter of the plunder he had expected, but he had found twin girls who pleased him and they kept him from making too many complaints.

When the ceremonies were over, and after Eadred had bellowed an interminable prayer, Guthred walked with me through the city. I think he wanted to show off his new armor, or perhaps he just wanted to clear his head from the smoke fumes in the palace. He drank ale in every tavern, joking with his men in English and Danish, and he kissed at least fifty girls, but then he led me on to the ramparts and we walked for a time in silence until we came to the city's eastern side where I stopped and looked across the field to where the river lay like a sheet of beaten silver under a half-moon. "This is where my father died," I said.

"Sword in hand?"

"Yes."

"That's good," he said, forgetting for a moment that he was a Christian. "But a sad day for you."

"It was a good day," I said, "I met Earl Ragnar. And I never much liked my father."

"You didn't?" he sounded surprised. "Why not?"

"He was a grim beast," I said. "Men wanted his approval, and it was grudging."

"Like you, then," he said, and it was my turn to be surprised.

"Me?"

"My grim Uhtred," he said, "all anger and threat. So tell me what I do about Egbert?"

"What Ulf suggests," I said, "of course."

"Ulf would kill everyone," Guthred said, "because then he'd have no problems. What would Alfred do?"

"It doesn't matter what Alfred would do."

"Yes it does," he insisted patiently, "so tell me."

There was something about Guthred that always made me tell the truth to him, or mostly tell the truth, and I was tempted to answer that Alfred would drag the old king out to the marketplace and lop off his head, but I knew that was not true. Alfred had spared his traitorous cousin's life after Ethandun and he had permitted his nephew, Æthelwold, to live when that nephew had a better claim to the throne than Alfred himself. So I sighed. "He'd let him live," I said, "but Alfred's a pious fool."

"No he's not," Guthred said.

"He's terrified of God's disapproval," I said.

"That's a sensible thing to be frightened of," Guthred said.

"Kill Egbert, lord," I said vehemently. "If you don't kill him then he'll try to get the kingdom back. He's got estates south of here. He can raise men. You let him live and he'll take those men to Ivarr, and Ivarr will want him back on the throne. Egbert's an enemy!"

"He's an old man, and he's not well and he's frightened," Guthred said patiently.

"So put the bastard out of his misery," I urged him. "I'll do it for you. I've never killed a king."

"And you'd like to?"

"I'll kill this one for you," I said. "He let his Saxons massacre Danes! He's not as pathetic as you think."

Guthred gave me a reproachful look. "I know you, Uhtred," he said fondly. "You want to boast that you're the man who killed Ubba beside the sea and unhorsed Svein of the White Horse and sent King Egbert of Eoferwic to his cold grave."

"And killed Kjartan the Cruel," I said, "and slaughtered Ælfric, usurper of Bebbanburg."

"I'm glad I'm not your enemy," he said lightly, then grimaced. "The ale is sour here."

"They make it differently," I explained. "What does Abbot Eadred tell you to do?"

"The same as you and Ulf, of course. Kill Egbert."

"For once Eadred's right."

"But Alfred would not kill him," he said firmly.

"Alfred is king of Wessex," I said, "and he's not facing Ivarr, and he doesn't have a rival like Egbert."

"But Alfred's a good king," Guthred insisted.

I kicked the palisade in my frustration. "Why would you let Egbert live?" I demanded, "so that folk will like you?"

"I want men to like me," he said.

"They should fear you," I said vehemently. "You're a king! You have to be ruthless. You have to be feared."

"Is Alfred feared?"

"Yes," I said, and was surprised to realize I had spoken the truth.

"Because he's ruthless?"

I shook my head. "Men fear his displeasure." I had never realized that before, but it was suddenly clear to me. Alfred was not ruthless. He was given to mercy, but he was still feared. I think men recognized that Alfred was under discipline, just as they were under his rule. Alfred's discipline was fear of his god's displeasure. He could never escape that. He could never be as good as he wanted, but he never stopped trying. Me, I had long accepted that I was fallible, but Alfred would never accept that of himself.

"I would like men to fear my displeasure," Guthred said mildly.

"Then let me kill Egbert," I said, and could have saved my breath.

Guthred, inspired by his reverence for Alfred, spared Egbert's life, and in the end he was proved right. He made the old king go to live in a monastery south of the river and he charged the monks to keep Egbert confined to the monastery's walls, which they did, and within a year Egbert died of some disease that wasted him away to a pain-racked scrap of bone and sinew. He was buried in the big church at Eoferwic, though I saw none of that.

It was high summer by now and every day I feared to see Ivarr's men coming south, but instead there came a rumor of a great battle between Ivarr and the Scots. There were always such rumors, and most are untrue, so I gave it no credence, but Guthred decided to believe the story and he gave his permission for most of his army to go back to Cumbraland to gather their harvest. That left us very few troops to garrison Eoferwic. Guthred's household troops stayed and every morning I made them practice with swords, shields and spears, and every afternoon made them work to repair Eoferwic's wall that was falling down in too many places. I thought Guthred a fool to let most of his men go, but he said that without a harvest his people would starve, and he was quite certain they would return. And again he was right. They did return. Ulf led them back from Cumbraland and demanded to know how the gathering army would be employed.

"We march north to settle Kjartan," Guthred said.

"And Ælfric," I insisted.

"Of course," Guthred said.

"How much plunder does Kjartan have?" Ulf wanted to know.

"Vast plunder," I said, remembering Tekil's tales. I said nothing of the feral dogs that guarded the silver and gold. "Kjartan is rich beyond dreams."

"Time to sharpen our swords," Ulf said.

"And Ælfric has an even bigger hoard," I added, though I had no idea whether I spoke the truth.

But I truly believed we could capture Bebbanburg. It had never been taken by an enemy, but that did not mean it could not be taken. It all depended on Ivarr. If he could be defeated then Guthred would be the most powerful man in Northumbria and Guthred was my friend and he, I believed, would not only help me kill Kjartan and so revenge Ragnar the Elder, but then return me to my lands and to my fortress beside the sea. Those were my dreams that summer. I thought the future was golden if only I could secure the kingdom for Guthred, but I had forgotten the malevolence of the three spinners at the world's root.

Father Willibald wanted to return to Wessex, for which I did not blame him. He was a West Saxon and he disliked Northumbria. I remember one night when we ate a dish of elder, which is cow's udder pressed and cooked, and I was devouring it and saying that I had not eaten so well since I was a child, and poor Willibald could not finish a mouthful. He looked as though he wanted to be sick, and I mocked him for being a weak-spined southerner. Sihtric, who was my servant now, brought him bread and cheese instead and Hild and I divided his elder between us. She was a southerner too, but not so choosy as Willibald. It was that night, as he grimaced at the food, that he told us he wanted to go back to Alfred.

We had heard little news of Wessex, except that it was at peace. Guthrum, of course, had been defeated and had accepted baptism as part of the peace treaty he made with Alfred. He had taken the baptismal name of Æthelstan, which meant "noble stone', and Alfred was his godfather, and reports from the south said that Guthrum or whatever he was now called was keeping the peace. Alfred lived, and that was about all we knew.

Guthred decided he would send an embassy to Alfred. He chose four Danes and four Saxons to ride south, reckoning that such a group could ride safely through Danish or Saxon territory, and he chose Willibald to carry his message. Willibald wrote it down, his quill scratching on a piece of newly scraped parchment. "By God's help," Guthred dictated, "I have taken the kingdom of Northumbria . . ."

"Which is called Haliwerfolkland," Eadred interrupted.

Guthred waved courteously, as if to suggest that Willibald could decide for himself whether to add that phrase. "And I am determined," Guthred went on, "by God's grace to rule this land in peace and justice . . ."

"Not so fast, lord," Willibald said.

"And to teach them how to brew proper ale," Guthred continued.

"And to teach them . . ." Willibald said under his breath.

Guthred laughed. "No, no, father! You don't write that!"

Poor Willibald. That letter was so long that another lambskin had to be stretched, scraped, and trimmed. The message went on and on about the holy Saint Cuthbert and how he had brought the army of the holy folk to Eoferwic, and how Guthred would make a shrine to the saint. The letter did mention that there were still enemies who might spoil that ambition, but it made light of them, as though Ivarr and Kjartan and Ælfric were minor obstacles. It asked for King Alfred's prayers and assured the king of Wessex that prayers were being said for him each day by the Christians of Haliwerfolkland. "I should send Alfred a present," Guthred said, "what would he like?"

"A relic," I suggested sourly.

That was a good suggestion for there was nothing Alfred loved so dearly as a holy relic, but there was nothing much to be had in Eoferwic. The archbishop's church possessed many treasures, including the sponge on which Jesus had been given wine to drink as he died and it also had the halter from Balaam's ass, though who Balaam was I did not know, and why his ass was holy was even more of a mystery. The church possessed a dozen such things, but the archbishop had carried them away with him and no one was certain where Wulfhere was. I assumed he had joined Ivarr. Hrothweard said he had a seed from a sycamore tree mentioned in the gospel book, but when we opened the silver box in which the seed was kept there was nothing but dust. In the end I suggested that we draw two of Saint Oswald's three teeth. Eadred bridled at that, then decided that the idea was not so bad after all, so pliers were fetched and the small chest opened and one of the monks tugged out two of the dead king's yellow peg-like teeth and they were placed in a beautiful silver pot that Egbert had used to store smoked oysters.

The embassy left on a late August morning. Guthred took Willibald aside and gave him a last message for Alfred, assuring Alfred that though he, Guthred, was a Dane he was also a Christian, and begging that should Northumbria be threatened by enemies that Alfred should send warriors to fight for God's land. That was pissing into the wind, I thought, for Wessex had enemies enough without worrying about Northumbria's fate.

I also took Willibald aside. I was sorry he was going, for I liked him, and he was a good man, but I could see he was impatient to see Wessex again. "You will do something for me, father," I said.

"If it is possible," he said cautiously.

"Give the king my greetings," I said.

Willibald looked relieved as if he had expected my favor to be a great deal more burdensome, which it was, as he would find out. "The king will want to know when you will return, lord," he said.

"In good time," I answered, though the only reason I now had for visiting Wessex was to retrieve the hoard I had hidden at Fifhaden. I regretted burying that treasure now, for in truth I never wanted to see Wessex again. "I want you to find Earl Ragnar," I told Willibald.

His eyes widened. "The hostage?" he asked.

"Find him," I said, "and give him a message from me."

"If I can," he said, still cautious.

I gripped his shoulders to make him pay attention and he grimaced from the strength of my hands. "You will find him," I said threateningly, "and you will give him a message. Tell him I am going north to kill Kjartan. And tell him his sister lives. Tell him I will do all I can to find her and keep her safe. Tell him I swear that on my life. And tell him to come here as soon as he is freed." I made him repeat it, and I made him swear on his crucifix that he would deliver the message and he was reluctant to make such an oath, but he was frightened of my anger and so he gripped the little cross and made the solemn promise.

And then he went.

And we had an army again, for the harvest was gathered, and it was time to strike north.

Guthred went north for three reasons. The first was Ivarr who had to be defeated, and the second was Kjartan whose presence in Northumbria was like a foul wound and the third was Ælfric who had to submit to Guthred's authority. Ivarr was the most dangerous and he would surely defeat us if he brought his army south. Kjartan was less dangerous, but he had to be destroyed for there could be no peace in Northumbria while he lived. Ælfric was the least dangerous. "Your uncle is king in Bebbanburg," Guthred told me as we marched north.

"Does he call himself that?" I asked, angry.

"No, no! He's got too much sense. But in effect that's what he is. Kjartan's land is a barrier, isn't it? So Eoferwic's rule doesn't stretch past Dunholm."

"We used to be kings in Bebbanburg," I said.

"You did?" Guthred was surprised. "Kings of Northumbria?"

"Of Bernicia," I said. Guthred had never heard the name. "It was all of northern Northumbria," I said, "and everything around Eoferwic was the kingdom of Deira."

"They joined together?" Guthred asked.

"We killed their last king," I said, "but that was years ago. Back before Christianity came."

"So you have a claim to the kingship here?" he asked and, to my astonishment, there was suspicion in his voice. I stared at him and he blushed. "But you do?" he said, trying to sound as if he did not care what I answered.

I laughed at him. "Lord King," I said, "if you restore me to Bebbanburg I shall kneel to you and swear you and your heirs lifelong fealty."

"Heirs!" he said brightly. "Have you seen Osburh?"

"I've seen Osburh," I said. She was Egbert's niece, a Saxon girl, and she had been living in the palace when we took Eoferwic. She was fourteen, dark-haired and had a plump, pretty face.

"If I marry her," Guthred asked me, "will Hild be her companion?"

"Ask her," I said, jerking my head to where Hild followed us. I had thought Hild might return to Wessex with Father Willibald, but she had said she was not ready to face Alfred yet and I could not blame her for that and so I had not pressed her. "I think she'd be honored to be your wife's companion," I told Guthred.

We camped that first night at Onhripum where a small monastery gave Guthred, Eadred, and the host of clergymen shelter. Our army was close to six hundred men now, and almost half of them were mounted, and our campfires lit the fields all about the monastery. As commander of the household troops I camped closest to the buildings and my young men, who now numbered forty, and most of whom possessed mail coats plundered from Eoferwic, slept close to the monastery's gate.

I stood guard with Clapa and two Saxons for the first part of the night. Sihtric was with me. I called him my servant, but he was learning to use a sword and shield and I reckoned he would make a useful soldier in a year or two. "You have the heads safe?" I asked him.

"You can smell them!" Clapa protested.

"No worse than you smell, Clapa," I retorted.

"They're safe, lord," Sihtric said.

"I should have eight heads," I said, and put my fingers around Sihtric's throat. "Pretty skinny neck, Sihtric."

"But it's a tough neck, lord," he said.

Just then the monastery door opened and Gisela, cloaked in black, slipped through. "You should be asleep, lady," I chided her.

"I can't sleep. I want to walk." She stared defiantly at me. Her lips were slightly apart and the firelight glinted off her teeth and reflected from her wide eyes.

"Where do you want to walk?" I asked.

She shrugged, still looking at me, and I thought of Hild sleeping in the monastery.

"I'll leave you in charge, Clapa," I said, "and if Ivarr comes, kill the bastard."

"Yes, lord."

I heard the guards sniggering as we walked away. I quietened them with a growl, then led Gisela toward the trees east of the monastery for it was dark there. She reached out and took my hand. She said nothing, content to walk close beside me. "Aren't you frightened of the night?" I asked her.

"Not with you."

"When I was a child," I said, "I made myself into a sceadugengan."

"What's a sceadugengan?" The word was Saxon and unfamiliar to her.

"A shadow-walker," I told her. "A creature that stalks the dark." An owl hooted quite close by and her fingers instinctively tightened on mine.

We stopped under some wind-rustled beech trees. Some small light came through the leaves, cast by the campfires, and I tilted her face up and looked down at her. She was tall, but still a head shorter than me. She let herself be examined, then closed her eyes as I drew a gentle finger down her long nose. "I . . ." I said, then stopped.

"Yes," she said, as if she knew what I had been about to say.

I made myself turn away from her. "I cannot make Hild unhappy."

"She told me," Gisela said, "that she would have gone back to Wessex with Father Willibald, but she wants to see if you capture Dunholm. She says she's prayed for that and it will be a sign from her god if you succeed."

"She said that?"

"She said it would be a sign that she must go back to her convent. She told me that tonight."

I suspected that was true. I stroked Gisela's face. "Then we should wait till after Dunholm is taken," I said, and it was not what I wanted to say.

"My brother says I have to be a peace cow," she said bitterly. A peace cow was a woman married to a rival family in an attempt to bring friendship, and doubtless Guthred had in mind Ivarr's son or else a Scottish husband. "But I won't be a peace cow," she said harshly. "I cast the runesticks and learned my fate."

"What did you learn?"

"I am to have two sons and a daughter."

"Good," I said.

"They will be your sons," she said defiantly, "and your daughter."

For a moment I did not speak. The night suddenly seemed fragile. "The runesticks told you that?" I managed to say after a few heartbeats.

"They have never lied," she said calmly. "When Guthred was taken captive the runesticks told me he would come back, and they told me my husband would arrive with him. And you came."

"But he wants you to be a peace cow," I said.

"Then you must carry me off," she said, "in the old way." The old Danish way of taking a bride was to kidnap her, to raid her household and snatch her from her family and carry her off to marriage. It is still done occasionally, but in these softer days the raid usually follows formal negotiations and the bride has time to pack her belongings before the horsemen come.

"I will carry you off," I promised her, and I knew I was making trouble, and that Hild had done nothing to deserve the trouble, and that Guthred would feel betrayed, but even so I tipped Gisela's face up and kissed her.

She clung to me and then the shouting started. I held Gisela tight and listened. The shouts were from the camp and I could see, through the trees, folk running past fires toward the road. "Trouble," I said, and I seized her hand and ran with her to the monastery where Clapa and the guards had drawn swords. I pushed Gisela toward the door and drew Serpent-Breath.

But there was no trouble. Not for us. The newcomers, attracted by the light of our campfires, were three men, one of them badly wounded, and they brought news. Within an hour the monastery's small church blazed with fire and the priests and monks were singing God's praises, and the message the three men had brought from the north went all through our camp so that newly-woken folk came to the monastery to hear the news again and to be assured that it was true.

"God works miracles!" Hrothweard shouted at the crowd. He had used a ladder to climb onto the monastery roof. It was dark, but some people had brought flaming torches and in their light Hrothweard looked huge. He raised his arms so that the crowd fell silent. He let them wait as he stared down at their upturned faces, and from behind him came the solemn chanting of the monks, and somewhere in the night an owl called, and Hrothweard clenched his fists and reached higher still as though he could touch heaven in the moonlight. "Ivarr is defeated!" he finally shouted. "Praise God and the saints, the tyrant Ivarr Ivarson is defeated! He has lost his army!"

And the people of Haliwerfolkland, who had feared to fight the mighty Ivarr, cheered themselves hoarse because the biggest obstacle to Guthred's rule in Northumbria had been swept away. He could truly call himself king at last and so he was. King Guthred.

FOUR

There had been a battle, we heard, a slaughter battle, a fight of horror in which a dale had reeked of blood, and Ivarr Ivarson, the most powerful Dane of Northumbria, had been defeated by Aed of Scotland.

The killing on both sides had been awesome. We heard more about the fight next morning when nearly sixty new survivors arrived. They had traveled in a band large enough to be spared Kjartan's attention, and they were still reeling from the butcher's work they had endured. Ivarr, we learned, had been lured across a river and into a valley where he believed Aed had taken refuge, but it was a trap. The hills on either side of the valley were thick with tribesmen who came howling through the mist and heather to hack into the Danish shield walls. "There were thousands of them," one man said and he was still shaking as he spoke.

Ivarr's shield wall held, but I could imagine the ferocity of that battle. My father had fought the Scots many times and he had always described them as devils. Mad devils, he said, sword devils, howling devils, and Ivarr's Danes told us how they had rallied from that first assault, and used sword and spear to cut the devils down, and still the shrieking hordes came, climbing over their own dead, their wild hair red with blood, their swords hissing, and Ivarr tried to climb north out of the dale to reach the high ground. That meant cutting and slashing a path through flesh, and he failed. Aed had then led his household troops against Ivarr's best men and the shields clashed and the blades rang and one by one the warriors died. Ivarr, the survivors said, fought like a fiend, but he took a sword thrust to the chest and a spear cut in his leg and his household troops dragged him back from the shield wall. He raved at them, demanding to die in the face of his enemies, but his men held him back and fought off the devils and by then night was falling.

The rearmost part of the Danish column still held, and the survivors, almost all of them bleeding, dragged their leader south toward the river. Ivarr's son, Ivar, just sixteen years old, assembled the least wounded warriors and they made a charge and broke through the encircling Scots, but scores more died as they tried to cross the river in the dark. Some, weighed down by their mail, drowned. Others were butchered in the shallows, but perhaps a sixth of Ivarr's army made it through the water and they huddled on the southern bank where they listened to the cries of the dying and the howling of the Scots. In the dawn they made a shield wall, expecting the Scots to cross the river and complete the slaughter, but Aed's men were almost as bloodied and wearied as the defeated Danes. "We killed hundreds," a man said bleakly, and later we heard that was true and that Aed had limped back north to lick his wounds.

Earl Ivarr lived. He was wounded, but he lived. He was said to be hiding in the hills, fearful of being captured by Kjartan, and Guthred sent a hundred horsemen north to find him and they discovered that Kjartan's troops were also scouring the hills. Ivarr must have known he would be found, and he preferred being Guthred's captive to being Kjartan's prisoner, and so he surrendered to a troop of Ulf's men who brought the injured earl back to our camp just after midday. Ivarr could not ride a horse so he was being carried on a shield. He was accompanied by his son, Ivar, and by thirty other survivors, some of them as badly wounded as their leader, but when Ivarr realized he must confront the man who had usurped Northumbria's throne he insisted that he do so on his own two feet. He walked. I do not know how he did it for he must have been in agony, but he forced himself to limp and every few steps he paused to lean on the spear he used as a crutch. I could see the pain, but I could also see the pride that would not let him be carried into Guthred's presence.

So he walked to us. He flinched with every step, but he was defiant and angry. I had never met him before because he had been raised in Ireland, but he looked just like his father. He had Ivar the Boneless's skeletal appearance. He had the same skull-like face with its sunken eyes, the same yellow hair drawn back to the nape of his neck and the same sullen malevolence. He had the same power.

Guthred waited at the monastery entrance and his household troops made two lines through which Ivarr had to walk. Guthred was flanked by his chief men and attended by Abbot Eadred, Father Hrothweard and all the other churchmen. When Ivarr was a dozen paces away he stopped, leaned on the spear and gave us all a scathing look. He mistook me for the king, perhaps because my mail and helmet were so much finer than Guthred's. "Are you the boy who calls himself king?" he demanded.

"I'm the boy who killed Ubba Lothbrokson," I answered. Ubba had been Ivarr's uncle, and the taunt made Ivarr jerk up his face and I saw a strange green glint in his eyes. They were serpent's eyes in a skull face. He might have been wounded and he might have had his power broken, but all he wanted at that moment was to kill me.

"And you are?" he demanded of me.

"You know who I am," I said scornfully. Arrogance is all in a young warrior.

Guthred gripped my arm as if to tell me to be quiet, then stepped forward. "Lord Ivarr," he said, "I am sorry to see you wounded."

Ivarr sneered at that. "You should be glad," he said, "and only sorry I am not dead. You're Guthred?"

"I grieve you are wounded, lord," Guthred said, "and I grieve for the men you have lost and I rejoice in the enemies you have killed. We owe you thanks." He stepped back and looked past Ivarr to where our army had gathered about the road. "We owe Ivarr Ivarson thanks!" Guthred shouted. "He has removed a threat to our north! King Aed has limped home to weep over his losses and to console the widows of Scotland!"

The truth, of course, was that Ivarr was limping and Aed was victorious, but Guthred's words prompted cheers, and those cheers astonished Ivarr. He must have expected that Guthred would kill him, which is exactly what Guthred should have done, but instead Ivarr was being treated with honor.

"Kill the bastard," I muttered to Guthred.

He gave me a look of utter astonishment, as if such a thing had never occurred to him. "Why?" he asked quietly.

"Just kill him now," I said urgently, "and that rat of a son."

"You're obsessed with killing," Guthred said, amused, and I saw Ivarr watching and he must have known what I had been saying. "You are truly welcome, Lord Ivarr," Guthred turned away from me and smiled at Ivarr. "Northumbria has need of great warriors," he went on, "and you, lord, are in need of rest."

I was watching those serpent eyes and I saw Ivarr's amazement, but I also saw that he thought Guthred a fool, but it was at that moment I understood Guthred's fate was golden. Wyrd biƌ ful aræd. When I had rescued Guthred from Sven and he had claimed to be a king I had thought him a joke, and when he was made a king in Cair Ligualid I still thought the jest was rich, and even in Eoferwic I could not see the laughter lasting more than a few weeks for Ivarr was the great brutal overlord of Northumbria, but now Aed had done our work for us. Ivarr had lost most of his men, he had been wounded, and there were now just three great lords in Northumbria. There was Ælfric, clinging to his stolen land at Bebbanburg, Kjartan, who was the dark spider lord in his fastness by the river, and there was King Guthred, lord of the north, and the only Dane in Britain who led willing Saxons as well as Danes.

We stayed at Onhripum. We had not planned to do that, but Guthred insisted that we wait while Ivarr was treated for his wounds. The monks tended him and Guthred waited on the wounded earl, taking him food and ale. Most of Ivarr's survivors were wounded, and Hild washed wounds and found clean cloths for bandages. "They need food," she told me, but we had little enough food already and every day I had to lead forage parties farther away to find grain or livestock. I urged Guthred to march again, to take us into country where supplies might be more plentiful, but he was entranced by Ivarr. "I like him!" he told me, "and we can't leave him here."

"We can bury him here," I suggested.

"He's our ally!" Guthred insisted, and he believed it. Ivarr was heaping praises on him and Guthred trusted every treacherous word.

The monks did their work well, for Ivarr recovered swiftly. I had hoped he would die of his wounds, but within three days he was riding a horse. He still hurt. That was obvious. The pain must have been terrible, but he forced himself to walk and to mount a horse, just as he forced himself to offer fealty to Guthred.

He had little choice in that. Ivarr now led fewer than a hundred men, many of whom were injured, and he was no longer the great warlord he had been, so he and his son knelt to Guthred and clasped his hands and swore their loyalty. The son, sixteen-year-old Ivar, looked like his father and grandfather, lean and dangerous. I distrusted them both, but Guthred would not listen to me. It was right, he said, that a king should be generous, and in showing mercy to Ivarr he believed he was binding the man to him for ever. "It's what Alfred would have done," he told me.

"Alfred would have taken the son hostage and sent the father away," I said.

"He has taken an oath," Guthred insisted.

"He'll raise new men," I warned him.

"Good!" He offered me his infectious grin. "We need men who can fight."

"He'll want his son to be king."

"He didn't want to be king himself, so why should he want it for his son? You see enemies everywhere, Uhtred. Young Ivar's a good-looking fellow, don't you think?"

"He looks like a half-starved rat."

"He's the right age for Gisela! Horseface and the rat, eh?" he said, grinning at me and I wanted to strike the grin off his face with my fist. "It's an idea, isn't it?" he went on. "It's time she married and it would bind Ivarr to me."

"Why not bind me to you?" I asked.

"You and I are friends already," he said, still grinning, "and I thank God for that."

We marched northward when Ivarr was sufficiently recovered. Ivarr was certain others of his men had survived the Scottish slaughter and so Brothers Jænberht and Ida rode ahead with an escort of fifty men. The two monks, Guthred assured me, knew the country about the River Tuede and could guide the searchers who looked for Ivarr's missing men.

Guthred rode with Ivarr for much of the journey. He had been flattered by Ivarr's oath which he ascribed to Christian magic and when Ivarr dropped behind to ride with his own men Guthred summoned Father Hrothweard and questioned the wild-bearded priest about Cuthbert, Oswald, and the Trinity. Guthred wanted to know how to work the magic for himself and was frustrated by Hrothweard's explanations. "The son is not the father," Hrothweard tried again, "and the father is not the spirit, and the spirit is not the son, but father, son and spirit are one, indivisible, and eternal."

"So they're three gods?" Guthred asked.

"One god!" Hrothweard said angrily.

"Do you understand it, Uhtred?" Guthred called back to me.

"I never have, lord," I said. "To me it's all nonsense."

"It is not nonsense!" Hrothweard hissed at me. "Think of it as the clover leaf, lord," he said to Guthred, "three leaves, separate, but one plant."

"It is a mystery, lord," Hild put in.

"Mystery?"

"God is mysterious, lord," she said, ignoring Hrothweard's malevolent glance, "and in his mystery we can discover wonder. You don't need to understand it, just be astonished by it."

Guthred twisted in his saddle to look at Hild. "So will you be my wife's companion?" he asked her cheerfully.

"Marry her first, lord," Hild said, "and then I'll decide."

He grinned and turned away.

"I thought you'd decided to go back to a nunnery," I said quietly.

"Gisela told you that?"

"She did."

"I'm looking for a sign from God," Hild said.

"The fall of Dunholm?"

She frowned. "Maybe. It's an evil place. If Guthred takes it under the banner of Saint Cuthbert then it will show God's power. Perhaps that's the sign I want."

"It sounds to me," I said, "as though you have your sign already."

She moved her mare away from Witnere who was giving it the evil eye. "Father Willibald wanted me to go back to Wessex with him," she said, "but I said no. I told him that if I retire from the world again then first I want to know what the world is." She rode in silence for a few paces, then spoke very softly. "I would have liked children."

"You can have children," I said.

She shook her head dismissively. "No," she said, "it is not my fate." She glanced at me. "You know Guthred wants to marry Gisela to Ivarr's son?" she asked.

I was startled by her sudden question. "I know he's thinking about it," I said cautiously.

"Ivarr said yes. Last night."

My heart sank, but I tried to show nothing. "How do you know?" I asked.

"Gisela told me. But there is a bride-price."

"There's always a bride-price," I said harshly.

"Ivarr wants Dunholm," she said.

It took me a moment to understand, then I saw the whole monstrous bargain. Ivarr had lost most of his power when his army was massacred by Aed, but if he were to be given Dunholm and Dunholm's lands, then he would be strong again. The men who now followed Kjartan would become his men and in a stroke Ivarr would regain his strength. "And has Guthred accepted?" I asked.

"Not yet."

"He can't be that stupid," I said angrily.

"Of the stupidity of men," Hild said tartly, "there seems no end. But do you remember, before we left Wessex, how you told me Northumbria was full of enemies?"

"I remember."

"More full, I think, than you realize," she said, "so I will stay till I know that you will survive." She reached out and touched my arm. "I think, sometimes, I am the only friend you have here. So let me stay till I know you're safe."

I smiled at her and touched Serpent-Breath's hilt. "I'm safe," I said.

"Your arrogance," she said, "blinds folk to your kindness." She said it reprovingly, then looked at the road ahead. "So what will you do?" she asked.

"Finish my bloodfeud," I said. "That's why I'm here." And that was true. That was why I rode north, to kill Kjartan and to free Thyra, but if I achieved those things then Dunholm would belong to Ivarr, and Gisela would belong to Ivarr's son. I felt betrayed, though in truth there was no betrayal, for Gisela had never been promised to me. Guthred was free to marry her to whoever he wished. "Or maybe we should just ride away," I said bitterly.

"Ride where?"

"Anywhere."

Hild smiled. "Back to Wessex?"

"No!"

"Then where?"

Nowhere. I had ridden away from Wessex and would not ride back except to fetch my hoard when I had a safe place to bring it. Fate had me in its grip and fate had given me enemies. Everywhere.

We forded the River Wiire well west of Dunholm and then marched the army to a place the locals called Cuncacester which lay athwart the Roman road five miles north of Dunholm. The Romans had built a fort at Cuncacester, and the walls were still there, though by now they were little more than worn-down banks in green fields. Guthred announced the army would stay close to the decrepit fort, and I said the army should keep marching south until it reached Dunholm, and we had our first argument, because he would not change his mind. "What is the purpose, lord," I asked, "of keeping an army two hours' march from its enemy?"

"Eadred says we must stop here."

"Abbot Eadred? He knows how to take fortresses?"

"He had a dream," Guthred said.

"A dream?"

"Saint Cuthbert wants his shrine here," Guthred said. "Right there," he pointed to a small hill where the coffined saint was surrounded by praying monks.

It made no sense to me. The place was undistinguished, except for the remnants of the fort. There were hills, fields, a couple of farms, and a small river, altogether a pleasant enough spot, though why it was the right place for the saint's shrine was quite beyond my understanding. "Our job, lord," I said, "is to capture Dunholm. We don't do that by building a church here."

"But Eadred's dreams have always been right," Guthred said earnestly, "and Saint Cuthbert has never failed me."

I argued and I lost. Even Ivarr supported me, telling Guthred that we had to take the army closer to Dunholm, but Abbot Eadred's dream meant that we camped at Cuncacester and the monks immediately began working on their church. The hilltop was leveled, trees were felled, and Abbot Eadred planted stakes to show where the walls should go. He wanted stone for its foundations, and that meant searching for a quarry, or better still an old Roman building that could be pulled down, but it would have to be a large building because the church he planned was bigger than the halls of most kings.

And next day, a late summer's day, under high scattered clouds, we rode south to Dunholm. We rode to confront Kjartan and to explore the fortress's strength.

One hundred and fifty men made the short journey. Ivarr and his son flanked Guthred, Ulf and I followed, and only the churchmen stayed at Cuncacester. We were Danes and Saxons, sword-warriors and spearmen, and we rode under Guthred's new banner that showed Saint Cuthbert with one hand raised in blessing and the other hand holding the jeweled gospel book of Lindisfarena. It was not an inspiring banner, at least not to me, and I wished I had thought to ask Hild to make me a banner, one showing the wolf's head of Bebbanburg. Earl Ulf had his banner of the eagle's head, Guthred had his flag, and Ivarr rode under a ragged banner showing two ravens that he had somehow rescued from his defeat in Scotland, but I rode without any standard.

Earl Ulf cursed when we came in sight of Dunholm for it was the first time he had ever seen the strength of that high rock girdled by a loop of the River Wiire. The rock was not sheer, for hornbeams and sycamore grew thick on its steep slopes, but the summit had been cleared and we could see a stout wooden palisade protecting the height where three or four halls had been built. The entrance to the fort was a high gatehouse, surmounted by a rampart where a triangular banner flew. The flag showed a serpent-headed ship, a reminder that Kjartan had once been a shipmaster, and beneath the banner were men with spears, and hanging on the palisade were rows of shields.

Ulf stared at the fortress. Guthred and Ivarr joined him and none of us spoke, for there was nothing to say. It looked impregnable. It looked terrible. There was a path up to the fortress, but it was steep and it was narrow, and very few men would be needed to hold that track as it twisted up through tree stumps and past boulders to the high gate. We could throw all our army up that path, but in places the way was so constricted that twenty men could hold off that army, and all the while spears and rocks would rain down on our heads. Guthred, who plainly believed Dunholm could not be taken, threw me a mute look of pleading.

"Sihtric!" I called, and the boy hurried to my side. "That wall," I said, "does it go all the way around the summit?"

"Yes, lord," he said, then hesitated, "except . . ."

"Except where?"

"There's a small place on the southern side, lord, where there's a crag. No wall there. It's where they throw the shit."

"A crag?" I asked, and he made a gesture with his right hand to show that it was a sheer slab of rock. "Can the crag be climbed?" I asked him.

"No, lord."

"What about water?" I asked him. "Is there a well?"

"Two wells, lord, both outside the palisade. There's one to the west which they don't often use, and the other's on the eastern side. But that one's high up the slope where the trees grow."

"It's outside the wall?"

"It's outside, lord, but it has its own wall."

I tossed him a coin as reward, though his answers had not cheered me. I had thought that if Kjartan's men took their water from the river then we might post archers to stop them, but no archer could pierce trees and a wall to stop them reaching the well.

"So what do we do?" Guthred asked me, and a flicker of annoyance tempted me to ask him why he didn't consult his priests who had insisted on making the army's camp so inconveniently far away. I managed to stifle that response. "You can offer him terms, lord," I said, "and when he refuses you'll have to starve him out."

"The harvest is in," Guthred pointed out.

"So it will take a year," I retorted. "Build a wall across the neck of land. Trap him. Let him see we won't go away. Let him see starvation coming for him. If you build the wall," I said, warming to the idea, "you won't have to leave an army here. Even sixty men should be enough."

"Sixty?" Guthred asked.

"Sixty men could defend a wall here," I said. The great mass of rock on which Dunholm stood was shaped like a pear, its lower narrow end forming the neck of land from where we stared at the high walls. The river ran to our right, swept about the great bulge of stone, then reappeared to our left, and just here the distance between the river banks was a little less than three hundred paces. It would take us a week to clear those three hundred paces of trees, and another week to dig a ditch and throw up a palisade, and a third week to strengthen that palisade so that sixty men would be sufficient to defend it. The neck was not a flat strip of land, but an uneven hump of rock, so the palisade would have to climb across the hump. Sixty men could never defend three hundred paces of wall, but much of the neck was impassable because of stone bluffs where no attack could ever come, so in truth the sixty would only have to defend the palisade in three or four places.

"Sixty," Ivarr had been silent, but now spat that word like a curse. "You'll need more than sixty. The men will have to be relieved at night. Other men have to fetch water, herd cattle, and patrol the river's bank. Sixty men might hold the wall, but you'll need two hundred more to hold those sixty men in place." He gave me a scathing look. He was right, of course. And if two to three hundred men were occupied at Dunholm, then that was two to three hundred men who could not guard Eoferwic or patrol the frontiers or grow crops.

"But a wall here," Guthred said, "would defeat Dunholm."

"It would," Ivarr agreed, though he sounded dubious.

"So I just need men," Guthred said. "I need more men."

I walked Witnere to the east as if I were exploring where the wall might be made. I could see men on Dunholm's high gate watching us. "Maybe it won't take a year," I called back to Guthred. "Come and look at this."

He urged his horse toward me and I thought I had never seen him so out of spirits. Till now everything had come easily to Guthred, the throne, Eoferwic, and Ivarr's homage, but Dunholm was a great raw block of brute power that defied his optimism. "What are you showing me?" he asked, puzzled that I had brought him away from the path.

I glanced back, making sure that Ivarr and his son were out of earshot, then I pointed to the river as if I were discussing the lie of the land. "We can capture Dunholm," I told Guthred quietly, "but I won't help you if you give it as a reward to Ivarr." He bridled at that, then I saw a flicker of guile on his face and knew he was tempted to deny he had ever considered giving Dunholm to Ivarr. "Ivarr is weak," I told him, "and so long as Ivarr is weak he will be your friend. Strengthen him and you make an enemy."

"What use is a weak friend?" he asked.

"More use than a strong enemy, lord."

"Ivarr doesn't want to be king," he said, "so why should he be my enemy?"

"What Ivarr wants," I said, "is to control the king like a puppy on his leash. Is that what you want? To be Ivarr's puppy?"

He stared up at the high gate. "Someone has to hold Dunholm," he said weakly.

"Then give it to me," I said, "because I'm your friend. Do you doubt that?"

"No, Uhtred," he said, "I do not doubt it." He reached over and touched my elbow. Ivarr was watching us with his snake-like eyes. "I have made no promises," Guthred went on, but he looked troubled as he said it. Then he forced a smile. "Can you capture the place?"

"I think we can get Kjartan out of there, lord."

"How?" he asked.

"I work sorcery tonight, lord," I told him, "and tomorrow you talk with him. Tell him that if he stays here then you will destroy him. Tell him you'll start by firing his steadings and burning his slave pens at Gyruum. Promise that you'll impoverish him. Let Kjartan understand that nothing but death, fire, and misery wait for him so long as he stays here. Then you offer him a way out. Let him go across the seas." That was not what I wanted, I wanted Kjartan the Cruel writhing under Serpent-Breath, but my revenge was not so important as getting Kjartan out of Dunholm.

"So work your sorcery," Guthred told me.

"And if it works, lord, you promise you won't give the place to Ivarr?"

He hesitated, then held his hand to me. "If it works, my friend," he said, "then I promise I will give it to you."

"Thank you, lord," I said, and Guthred rewarded me with his infectious smile.

Kjartan's watching men must have been puzzled when we rode away late in the afternoon. We did not go far, but made a camp on a hillside north of the fortress and we lit fires to let Kjartan know that we were still close. Then, in the darkness, I rode back to Dunholm with Sihtric. I went to work my sorcery, to scare Kjartan, and to do that I needed to be a sceadugengan, a shadow-walker. The sceadugengan walk at night, when honest men fear to leave their houses. The night is when strange things stalk the earth, when shape-shifters, ghosts, wild men, elves, and beasts roam the land.

But I had ever been comfortable with the night. From a child I had practiced shadow-walking until I had become one of the creatures men fear, and that night I took Sihtric up the path toward Dunholm's high gate. Sihtric led our horses and they, like him, were scared. I had trouble keeping to the path for the moon was hidden by newly arrived clouds, so I felt my way, using Serpent-Breath as a stick to find bushes and rocks. We went slowly with Sihtric holding onto my cloak so that he did not lose me. It became easier as we went higher, for there were fires inside the fortress and the glow of their flames above the palisade acted as a beacon. I could see the shadowed outlines of sentries on the high gate, but they could not see us as we reached a shelf of land where the path dropped a few feet before climbing the last long stretch to the gate. The whole slope between the brief shelf and the palisade had been cleared of trees so that no enemy could creep unseen to the defenses and attempt a sudden assault.

"Stay here," I told Sihtric. I needed him to guard the horses and to carry my shield, helmet, and the bag of severed heads which I now took from him. I told him to hide behind the trees and wait there.

I placed the heads on the path, the closest less than fifty paces from the gate, the last very near to the trees which grew at the lip of the shelf. I could feel maggots squirming under my hands as I lifted the heads from the sack. I made the dead eyes look toward the fortress, positioning the rotting skulls by feel so that my hands were slimy when at last I was finished. No one heard me, no one saw me. The dark wrapped about me and the wind sighed across the hill and the river ran noisily over the rocks below. I found Sihtric, who was shivering, and he gave me the black scarf that I wrapped about my face, knotting it at the nape of my neck, and then I forced my helmet over the linen and took my shield. Then I waited.

The light comes slowly in a clouded dawn. First there is just a shiver of grayness that touches the sky's eastern rim, and for a time there is neither light nor dark, nor any shadows, just the cold gray filling the world as the bats, the shadow-fliers, skitter home. The trees turn black as the sky pales the horizon, and then the first sunlight skims the world with color. Birds sang. Not as many as sing in spring and early summer, but I could hear wrens, chiff-chaffs, and robins greeting the day's coming, and below me in the trees a woodpecker rattled at a trunk. The black trees were dark green now and I could see the bright red berries of a rowan bush not far away. And it was then that the guards saw the heads. I heard them shout, saw more men come to the rampart, and I waited. The banner was raised over the high gate, and still more men came to the wall and then the gate opened and two men crept out. The gate closed behind them and I heard a dull thud as its great locking bar was dropped into place. The two men looked hesitant. I was hidden in the trees, Serpent-Breath drawn, my cheek-pieces open so that the black linen filled the space between the helmet's edges. I wore a black cloak over my mail that Hild had brightened by scrubbing it with river-sand. I wore high black boots. I was the dead swordsman again and I watched as the two men came cautiously down the path toward the line of heads. They reached the first blood-matted head and one of them shouted up to the fortress that it was one of Tekil's men. Then he asked what he should do.

Kjartan answered. I was sure it was him, though I could not see his face, but his voice was a roar. "Kick them away!" he shouted, and the two men obeyed, kicking the heads off the path so that they rolled down into the long grass where the trees had been felled.

They came closer until there was only one of the seven heads left and, just as they reached it, I stepped from the trees.

They saw a shadow-faced warrior, gleaming and tall, with sword and shield in hand. They saw the dead swordsman, and I just stood there, ten paces from them, and I did not move and I did not speak, and they gazed at me and one made a sound like a kitten mewing and then, without another word, they fled.

I stood there as the sun rose. Kjartan and his men stared at me and in that early light I was dark-faced death in shining armor, death in a bright helmet, and then, before they decided to send the dogs to discover I was not a specter, but flesh and blood, I turned back into the shadows and rejoined Sihtric.

I had done my best to terrify Kjartan. Now Guthred had to talk him into surrender, and then, I dared hope, the great fort on its rock would become mine, and Gisela with it, and I dared hope those things because Guthred was my friend. I saw my future as golden as Guthred's. I saw the bloodfeud won, I saw my men raiding Bebbanburg's land to weaken my uncle, and I saw Ragnar returning to Northumbria to fight at my side. In short I forgot the gods and spun my own bright fate, while at the root of life the three spinners laughed.

Thirty horsemen rode back to Dunholm in midmorning. Clapa went ahead of us with a leafy branch to show we came in peace. We were all in mail, though I had left my good helmet with Sihtric. I had thought of dressing as the dead swordsman, but he had done his sorcery and now we would discover if it had worked.

We came to the place where I had stood and watched the two men kick the seven heads off the path and there we waited. Clapa waved the branch energetically and Guthred fidgeted as he watched the gate. "How long will it take us to reach Gyruum tomorrow?" he asked.

"Gyruum?" I asked.

"I thought we'd ride there tomorrow," he said, "and burn the slave pens. We can take hawks. Go hunting."

"If we leave at dawn," Ivarr answered, "we'll be there by noon."

I looked to the west where there were ominous dark clouds. "There's bad weather coming," I said.

Ivarr slapped at a horsefly on his stallion's neck, then frowned at the high gate. "Bastard doesn't want to speak to us."

"I'd like to go tomorrow," Guthred said mildly.

"There's nothing there," I said.

"Kjartan's slave pens are there," Guthred said, "and you told me we have to destroy them. Besides, I have a mind to see the old monastery. I hear it was a great building."

"Then go when the bad weather's passed," I suggested.

Guthred said nothing because, in response to Clapa's waving branch, a horn had suddenly sounded from the high gate. We fell silent as the gates were pushed open and a score of men rode toward us.

Kjartan led them, mounted on a tall, brindled horse. He was a big man, wide-faced, with a huge beard and small suspicious eyes, and he carried a great war ax as though it weighed nothing. He wore a helmet on which a pair of raven wings had been fixed and had a dirty white cloak hanging from his broad shoulders. He stopped a few paces away and for a time he said nothing, but just stared at us, and I tried to find some fear in his eyes, but he just looked belligerent, though when he broke the silence his voice was subdued. "Lord Ivarr," he said, "I am sorry you did not kill Aed."

"I lived," Ivarr said drily.

"I am glad of it," Kjartan said, then he gave me a long look. I was standing apart from the others, off to one side of the path and slightly above them where the track rose to the tree-covered knob before dropping to the neck. Kjartan must have recognized me, known I was Ragnar's adopted son who had cost his own son an eye, but he decided to ignore me, looking back to Ivarr. "What you needed to defeat Aed," he said, "was a sorcerer."

"A sorcerer?" Ivarr sounded amused.

"Aed fears the old magic," Kjartan said. "He would never fight against a man who could take heads by sorcery."

Ivarr said nothing. Instead he just turned and stared at me, and thus he betrayed the dead swordsman and reassured Kjartan that he did not face sorcery, but an old enemy, and I saw the relief on Kjartan's face. He laughed suddenly, a brief bark of scorn, but he still ignored me. He turned on Guthred instead. "Who are you?" he demanded.

"I am your king," Guthred said.

Kjartan laughed again. He was relaxed now, certain that he faced no dark magic. "This is Dunholm, pup," he said, "and we have no king."

"Yet here I am," Guthred said, unmoved by the insult, "and here I stay until your bones have bleached in Dunholm's sun."

Kjartan was amused at that. "You think you can starve me out? You and your priests? You think I'll die of hunger because you're here? Listen, pup. There are fish in the river and birds in the sky and Dunholm will not starve. You can wait here till chaos shrouds the world and I'll be better fed than you. Why didn't you tell him that, Lord Ivarr?" Ivarr just shrugged as though Guthred's ambitions were no concern of his. "So," Kjartan rested the ax on his shoulder as if to suggest it would not be needed, "what are you here to offer me, pup?"

"You can take your men to Gyruum," Guthred said, "and we shall provide ships and you can sail away. Your folk can go with you, except those who wish to stay in Northumbria."

"You play at being a king, boy," Kjartan said, then looked at Ivarr again. "And you're allied to him?"

"I am allied to him," Ivarr said tonelessly.

Kjartan looked back to Guthred. "I like it here, pup. I like Dunholm. I ask for nothing more than to be left in peace. I don't want your throne, I don't want your land, though I might want your woman if you have one and if she's pretty enough. So I shall make you an offer. You leave me in peace and I shall forget that you exist."

"You disturb my peace," Guthred said.

"I'll shit all over your peace, pup, if you don't leave here," Kjartan snarled, and there was a force in his voice that startled Guthred.

"So you refuse my offer?" Guthred asked. He had lost this confrontation and knew it.

Kjartan shook his head as if he found the world a sadder place than he had expected. "You call that a king?" he demanded of Ivarr. "If you need a king, find a man."

"I hear this king was man enough to piss all over your son," I spoke for the first time, "and I hear Sven crawled away weeping. You bred a coward, Kjartan."

Kjartan pointed the ax at me. "I have business with you," he said, "but this is not the day to make you scream like a woman. But that day will come." He spat at me, then wrenched his horse's head about and spurred back toward the high gate without another word. His men followed.

Guthred watched him go. I stared at Ivarr, who had deliberately betrayed the sorcery, and I guessed that he had been told I was to hold Dunholm if it fell and so he had made certain it did not fall. He glanced at me, said something to his son, and they both laughed.

"In two days," Guthred spoke to me, "you start work on the wall. I'll give you two hundred men to make it."

"Why not start tomorrow?" I asked.

"Because we're going to Gyruum, that's why. We're going to hunt!"

I shrugged. Kings have whims and this king wanted to hunt.

We rode back to Cuncacester where we discovered that Jænberht and Ida, the two monks, had returned from their search for more of Ivarr's survivors. "Did you find anyone?" I asked them as we dismounted.

Jænberht just stared at me, as if the question puzzled him, then Ida shook his head hurriedly. "We found no one," he said.

"So you wasted your time," I said.

Jænberht smirked at that, or perhaps it was just his twisted mouth that made me think he smirked, then both men were summoned to tell Guthred of their journey and I went to Hild and asked her if Christians pronounced curses, and if they did then she was to make a score of curses against Ivarr. "Put your devil onto him," I said.

That night Guthred tried to restore our spirits by giving a feast. He had taken a farm in the valley below the hill where Abbot Eadred was laying out his church, and he invited all the men who had confronted Kjartan that morning and served us seethed mutton and fresh trout, ale, and good bread. A harpist played after the meal and then I told the tale of Alfred going into Cippanhamm disguised as a harpist. I made them laugh when I described how a Dane had thumped him because he was such a bad musician.

Abbot Eadred was another of the guests and, when Ivarr left, the abbot offered to say evening prayers. The Christians gathered at one side of the fire, and that left Gisela with me beside the farm's door. She had a lambskin pouch at her belt and, as Eadred chanted his words, she opened the pouch and took out a bundle of runesticks bound with a woolen thread. The sticks were slender and white. She looked at me as if to ask whether she should cast them and I nodded. She held them above the ground, closed her eyes, then let them go.

The sticks fell in their usual disarray. Gisela knelt beside them, her face sharply shadowed by the fire's dying flames. She stared at the tangled sticks a long time, once or twice looking up at me, and then, quite suddenly, she began to cry. I touched her shoulder. "What is it?" I asked.

Then she screamed. She raised her head to the smoky rafters and wailed. "No!" she called, startling Eadred into silence, "no!" Hild came hurrying around the hearth and put an arm about the weeping girl, but Gisela tore herself free and stooped over the runesticks again. "No!" she shouted a third time.

"Gisela!" Her brother crouched beside her. "Gisela!"

She turned on him and slapped him once, slapped him hard about the face, and then she began gasping as if she could not find breath enough to live, and Guthred, his cheek red, scooped up the sticks.

"They are a pagan sorcery, lord," Eadred said, "they are an abomination."

"Take her away," Guthred said to Hild, "take her to her hut," and Hild pulled Gisela away, helped by two serving women who had been attracted by her wailing.

"The devil is punishing her for sorcery," Eadred insisted.

"What did she see?" Guthred asked me.

"She didn't say."

He kept looking at me and I thought for a heartbeat that there were tears in his eyes, then he abruptly turned away and dropped the runesticks onto the fire. They crackled fiercely and a searing flame leaped toward the roof-tree, then they dulled into blackened squiggles. "What do you prefer," Guthred asked me, "falcon or hawk?" I stared at him, puzzled. "When we hunt tomorrow," he explained, "what do you prefer?"

"Falcon," I said.

"Then tomorrow you can hunt with Swiftness," he said, naming one of his birds.

"Gisela's ill," Hild told me later that night, "she has a fever. She shouldn't have eaten meat."

Next morning I bought a set of runesticks from one of Ulf's men. They were black sticks, longer than the burned white ones, and I paid well for them. I took them to Gisela's hut, but one of her women said Gisela was sick with a woman's sickness and could not see me. I left the sticks for her. They told the future and I would have done better, much better, to have cast them myself. Instead I went hunting.

It was a hot day. There were still dark clouds heaped in the west, but they seemed to be no nearer, and the sun burned fiercely so that only the score of troops who rode to guard us wore mail. We did not expect to meet enemies. Guthred led us, and Ivarr and his son rode, and Ulf was there, and so were the two monks, Jænberht and Ida, who came to say prayers for the monks who had once been massacred at Gyruum. I did not tell them that I had been present at the massacre that had been the work of Ragnar the Elder. He had cause. The monks had murdered Danes and Ragnar had punished them, though these days the story is always told that the monks were innocently at prayer and died as spotless martyrs. In truth they were malevolent killers of women and children, but what chance does truth have when priests tell tales?

Guthred was feverishly happy that day. He talked incessantly, laughed at his own jests, and even tried to stir a smile on Ivarr's skull face. Ivarr said little except to give his son advice on hawking. Guthred had given me his falcon to fly, but at first we rode through wooded country where a falcon could not hunt, so his goshawk had an advantage and brought down two rooks among the branches. He whooped with each kill. It was not till we reached the open ground by the river that my falcon could fly high and stoop fast to strike at a duck, but the falcon missed and the duck flew into the safety of a grove of alders. "Not your lucky day," Guthred told me.

"We might all be unlucky soon," I said, and pointed westward to where the clouds were gathering. "There's going to be a storm."

"Maybe tonight," he said dismissively, "but not till after dark." He had given his goshawk to a servant and I handed the falcon to another. The river was on our left now and the scorched stone buildings of Gyruum's monastery were ahead, built on the riverbank where the ground rose above the long salt-marshes. It was low tide and wicker fish traps stretched into the river that met the sea a short distance eastward.

"Gisela has a fever," Guthred told me.

"I heard."

"Eadred says he'll touch her with the cloth that covers Cuthbert's face. He says it will cure her."

"I hope it does," I said dutifully. Ahead of us Ivarr and his son rode with a dozen of their followers in mail. If they turned now, I thought, they could slaughter Guthred and me, so I leaned over and checked his horse so that Ulf and his men could catch up with us.

Guthred let me do that, but was amused. "He's no enemy, Uhtred."

"One day," I said, "you will have to kill him. On that day, lord, you'll be safe."

"I'm not safe now?"

"You have a small army, an untrained army," I said, "and Ivarr will raise men again. He'll hire sword-Danes, shield-Danes and spear-Danes until he is lord of Northumbria again. He's weak now, but he won't always be weak. That's why he wants Dunholm, because it will make him strong again."

"I know," Guthred said patiently. "I know all that."

"And if you marry Gisela to Ivarr's son," I said, "how many men will that bring you?"

He looked at me sharply. "How many men can you bring me?" he asked, but did not wait for my answer. Instead he put spurs to his horse and hurried up the slope to the ruined monastery that Kjartan's men had used as their hall. They had made a thatched roof between the stone walls, and beneath it was a hearth and a dozen sleeping platforms. The men who had lived here must have gone back to Dunholm before we ever crossed the river on our way north for the hall had long been deserted. The hearth was cold. Beyond the hill, in the wide valley between the monastery and the old Roman fort on its headland, were slave pens that were just wattle hurdles staked into enclosures. All were deserted. Some folk lived up at the old fort and they tended a high beacon which they were supposed to light if raiders came to the river. I doubted if the beacon was ever used for no Dane would raid Kjartan's land, but there was a single ship beneath the beacon's hill, anchored where the River Tine made its turn toward the sea. "We'll see what business he has," Guthred said grimly, as if he resented the ship's presence, then he ordered his household troops to pull down the wattle fences and burn them with the thatch roof. "Burn it all!" he ordered. He watched as the work began, then grinned at me. "Shall we see what ship that is?"

"It's a trader," I said. It was a Danish ship, for no other kind sailed this coast, but she was plainly no warship for her hull was shorter and her beam wider than any warrior's boat.

"Then let's tell him there's no trade here any more," Guthred said, "at least none in slaves."

He and I rode eastward. A dozen men came with us. Ulf was one, Ivarr and his son came too, and tagging behind them was Jænberht who kept urging Guthred to start rebuilding the monastery.

"We must finish Saint Cuthbert's church first," Guthred told Jænberht.

"But the house here must be remade," Jænberht insisted, "it's a sacred place. The most holy and blessed Bede lived here."

"It will be rebuilt," Guthred promised, then he curbed his horse beside a stone cross that had been toppled from its pedestal and now lay half buried in the soil and overgrown with grass and weeds. It was a fine piece of carving, writhing with beasts, plants, and saints. "And this cross shall stand again," he said and then looked around the wide river bend. "A good place," he said.

"It is," I agreed.

"If the monks come back," he said, "then we can make it prosperous again. Fish, salt, crops, cattle. How does Alfred raise money?"

"Taxes," I said.

"He taxes the church too?"

"He doesn't like taxing the church," I said, "but he does when things are hard. They have to pay to be protected, after all."

"He mints his own money?"

"Yes, lord."

He laughed. "It's complicated, being a king. Maybe I should visit Alfred. Ask his advice."

"He'd like that," I said.

"He'd welcome me?" He sounded wary.

"He would."

"Though I'm a Dane?"

"Because you're a Christian," I said.

He thought about that, then rode on to where the path twisted through a marsh and crossed a small shallow stream where two ceorls were setting eel traps. They knelt as we passed and Guthred acknowledged them with a smile which neither of them saw because their heads were bowed so low. Four men were wading ashore from the moored ship and none of them had weapons and I supposed they were merely coming to greet us and assure us that they meant no harm. "Tell me," Guthred said suddenly, "is Alfred different because he's a Christian?"

"Yes," I said.

"In what way?"

"He's determined to be good, lord," I said.

"Our religion," he said, momentarily forgetting that he had been baptized, "doesn't do that, does it?"

"It doesn't?"

"Odin and Thor want us to be brave," he said, "and they want us to respect them, but they don't make us good."

"No," I agreed.

"So Christianity is different," he insisted, then curbed his horse where the path ended in a low ridge of sand and shingle. The four men waited a hundred paces away at the shingle's far end. "Give me your sword," Guthred said suddenly.

"My sword?"

He smiled patiently. "Those sailors are not armed, Uhtred, and I want you to go and talk to them, so give me your sword."

I was only armed with Serpent-Breath. "I hate being unarmed, lord," I said in mild protest.

"It is a courtesy, Uhtred," Guthred insisted, and held out his hand.

I did not move. No courtesy I had ever heard of suggested that a lord should take off his sword before talking to common seamen. I stared at Guthred and behind me I heard blades hissing from scabbards.

"Give me the sword," Guthred said, "then walk to the men. I'll hold your horse."

I remember looking around me and seeing the marsh behind and the shingle ridge in front and I was thinking that I only had to dig my spurs in and I could gallop away, but Guthred reached over and gripped my reins. "Greet them for me," he said in a forced voice.

I could still have galloped away, tearing the reins from his hand,
but then Ivarr and his son crowded me. Both men had drawn swords
and Ivarr's stallion blocked Witnere who snapped in irritation. I
calmed the horse. "What have you done, lord?" I asked Guthred.

For a heartbeat he did not speak. Indeed he seemed incapable of
looking at me, but then he made himself answer. "You told me," he
said, "that Alfred would do whatever is necessary to preserve his kingdom. That is what I'm doing."

"And what is that?"

He had the grace to look embarrassed. "Ælfric of Bebbanburg is bring-
ing troops to help capture Dunholm," he said. I just stared at him. "He
is coming," Guthred went on, "to give me an oath of loyalty."

"I gave you that oath," I said bitterly.

"And I promised I would free you from it," he said, "which now I do."

"So you're giving me to my uncle?" I asked.

He shook his head. "Your uncle's price was your life, but I refused
it. You are to go away, Uhtred. That is all. You are to go far away. And
in exchange for your exile I gain an ally with many warriors. You
were right. I need warriors. Ælfric of Bebbanburg can provide them."

"And why must an exile go unarmed?" I asked, touching Serpent-
Breath's hilt.

"Give me the sword," Guthred said. Two of Ivarr's men were
behind me, also with drawn swords.

"Why must I go unarmed?" I asked again.

Guthred glanced at the ship, then back to me. He forced himself
to say what needed to be said. "You will go unarmed," he told me,
"because what I was, you must be. That is the price of Dunholm."

For a heartbeat I could neither breathe nor speak and it took me a
moment to convince myself that he meant what I knew he meant.
"You're selling me into slavery?" I asked.

"On the contrary," he said, "I paid to have you enslaved. So go
with God, Uhtred."

I hated Guthred then, though a small part of me recognized that he
was being ruthless and that is part of kingship. I could provide him

with two swords, nothing more, but my uncle Ælfric could bring him three hundred swords and spears, and Guthred had made his choice. It was, I suppose, the right choice and I was stupid not to have seen it coming.

"Go," Guthred said more harshly and I vowed revenge and rammed my heels back and Witnere lunged forward, but was immediately knocked off balance by Ivarr's horse so that he stumbled onto his foreknees and I was pitched onto his neck. "Don't kill him!" Guthred shouted, and Ivarr's son slapped the flat of his sword-blade against my head so that I fell off and, by the time I had regained my feet, Witnere was safe in Ivarr's grasp and Ivarr's men were above me with their sword-blades at my neck.

Guthred had not moved. He just watched me, but behind him with a smile on his crooked face, was Jænberht and I understood then. "Did that bastard arrange this?" I asked Guthred.

"Brother Jænberht and Brother Ida are from your uncle's household," Guthred admitted.

I knew then what a fool I had been. The two monks had come to Cair Ligualid and ever since they had been negotiating my fate and I had been oblivious of it.

I dusted off my leather jerkin. "Grant me a favor, lord?" I said.

"If I can."

"Give my sword and my horse to Hild. Give her everything of mine and tell her to keep them for me."

He paused. "You will not be coming back, Uhtred," he said gently.

"Grant me that favor, lord," I insisted.

"I shall do all that," Guthred promised, "but give me the sword first."

I unbuckled Serpent-Breath. I thought of drawing her and laying about me with her good blade, but I would have died in an eyeblink and so I kissed her hilt and then handed her up to Guthred. Then I slid off my arm rings, those marks of a warrior, and I held those to him. "Give these to Hild," I asked him.

"I will," he said, taking the rings, then he looked at the four men who waited for me. "Earl Ulf found these men," Guthred said, nodding at the waiting slavers, "and they do not know who you are, only that they are to take you away." That anonymity was a gift, of sorts. If the slavers had known how badly Ælfric wanted me, or how much Kjartan the Cruel would pay for my eyes, then I would not have lived a week. "Now go," Guthred commanded me.

"You could have just sent me away," I told him bitterly.

"Your uncle has a price," Guthred said, "and this is it. He wanted your death, but accepted this instead."

I looked beyond him to where the black clouds heaped in the west like mountains. They were much closer and darker, and a freshening wind was chilling the air. "You must go too, lord," I said, "for a storm is coming."

He said nothing and I walked away. Fate is inexorable. At the root of life's tree the three spinners had decided that the thread of gold that made my life fortunate had come to its end. I remember my boots crunching on the shingle and remember the white gulls flying free.

I had been wrong about the four men. They were armed, not with swords or spears, but with short cudgels. They watched me approach as Guthred and Ivarr watched me walk away, and I knew what was to happen and I did not try to resist. I walked to the four men and one of them stepped forward and struck me in the belly to drive all the breath from my body, and another hit me on the side of the head so that I fell onto the shingle and then I was hit again and knew nothing more. I was a lord of Northumbria, a sword-warrior, the man who had killed Ubba Lothbrokson beside the sea and who had brought down Svein of the White Horse, and now I was a slave.

PART TWO

THE RED SHIP

FIVE

The shipmaster, my master, was called Sverri Ravnson and had been one of the four men who greeted me with blows. He was a head shorter than me, ten years older, and twice as wide. He had a face flat as an oar-blade, a nose that had been broken to a pulp, a black beard shot through with wiry gray strands, three teeth, and no neck. He was one of the strongest man I ever knew. He did not speak much.

He was a trader and his ship was called *Trader*. She was a tough craft, well built and strongly rigged, with benches for sixteen oarsmen, though when I joined Sverri's crew he only had eleven rowers so he was glad to have me to balance the numbers. The rowers were all slaves. The five free crew members never touched an oar, but were there to relieve Sverri on the steering oar, to make certain we worked, to ensure we did not escape, and to throw our bodies overboard if we died. Two, like Sverri, were Norsemen, two were Danes and the fifth was a Frisian called Hakka and it was Hakka who riveted the slave manacles onto my ankles. They first stripped me of my fine clothes, leaving only my shirt. They tossed me a pair of louse-ridden breeches. Hakka, having chained my ankles, tore the shirt open at the left shoulder and carved a big S in the flesh of my upper arm with a short knife. The blood poured down to my elbow where it was diluted by the first few specks of rain gusting from the west. "I should burn your skin," Hakka said, "but a ship's no place for a fire." He scooped filth from the bilge and rubbed it into the newly opened cut. It turned foul, that wound, and wept pus and gave me a fever, but when it healed I was left with Sverri's mark on my arm. I have it to this day.

The slave mark almost had no time to heal, for we all came near death that first night. The wind suddenly blew hard, turning the river into a welter of small, hurrying whitecaps, and *Trader* jerked at her anchor line, and the wind rose and the rain was being driven horizontally. The ship was bucking and shuddering, the tide was ebbing so that wind and current were trying to drive us ashore, and the anchor, that was probably nothing more than a big stone ring that held the ship by weight alone, began to drag. "Oars!" Sverri shouted and I thought he wanted us to row against the pressure of wind and tide, but instead he slashed through the quivering hide rope that tied us to the anchor and *Trader* leaped away. "Row, you bastards!" Sverri shouted, "row!"

"Row!" Hakka echoed and slashed at us with his whip. "Row!"

"You want to live?" Sverri bellowed over the wind, "row!"

He took us to sea. If we had stayed in the river we would have been driven ashore, but we would have been safe because the tide was dropping and the next high tide would have floated us off, but Sverri had a hold full of cargo and he feared that if he were stranded he would be pillaged by the sullen folk who lived in Gyruum's hovels. He reckoned it was better to risk death at sea than to be murdered ashore, and so he took us into a gray chaos of wind, darkness, and water. He wanted to turn north at the river mouth and take shelter by the coast and that was not such a bad idea, for we might have lain in the lee of the land and ridden out the storm, but he had not reckoned with the force of the tide and, row as we might, and despite the lashes put onto our shoulders, we could not haul the boat back. Instead we were swept to sea and within moments we had to stop rowing, plug the oar-holes and start bailing the boat. All night we scooped water from the bilge and chucked it overboard and I remember the weariness of it, the bone-aching tiredness, and the fear of those vast unseen seas as they lifted us and roared beneath us. Sometimes we turned broadside onto the waves and I thought we must capsize and I remember clinging to a bench as the oars clattered across the hull and water churned about my thighs, but somehow *Trader* staggered upward and we hurled water over the side, and why she did not sink I will never know.

Dawn found us half waterlogged in an angry, but no longer vicious sea. No land was in sight. My ankles were bloody for the manacles had bitten into the skin during the night, but I was still bailing. No one else moved. The other slaves, I had not even learned their names yet, were slumped on the benches and the crew was huddled under the steering platform where Sverri was clinging to the steering oar and I felt his dark eyes watching me as I scooped up buckets of water and poured them back to the ocean. I wanted to stop. I was bleeding, bruised, and exhausted, but I would not show weakness. I hurled bucket after bucket, and my arms were aching and my belly was sour and my eyes stung from the salt and I was miserable, but I would not stop. There was vomit slopping in the bilge, but it was not mine.

Sverri stopped me in the end. He came down the boat and struck me across the shoulders with a short whip and I collapsed onto a bench, and a moment later two of his men brought us stale bread soaked in seawater and a skin of sour ale. No one spoke. The wind slapped the leather halliards against the short mast and the waves hissed down the hull and the wind was bitter and rain pitted the sea. I clutched the hammer amulet. They had left me that, for it was a poor thing of carved oxbone and had no value. I prayed to all the gods. I prayed to Njord to let me live in his angry sea, and I prayed to the other gods for revenge. I thought Sverri and his men must sleep and when they slept I would kill them, but I fell asleep before they did and we all slept as the wind lost its fury, and some time later we slaves were kicked awake and we hauled the sail up the mast and ran before the rain toward the gray-edged east.

Four of the rowers were Saxons, three were Norsemen, three were

Danes and the last man was Irish. He was on the bench across from me
and I did not know he was Irish at first for he rarely spoke. He was wiry,
dark-skinned, black-haired and, though only a year or so older than
me, he bore the battle scars of an old warrior. I noted how Sverri's men
watched him, fearing he was trouble and when, later that day, the wind
went southerly and we were ordered to row, the Irishman pulled his oar
with an angry expression. That was when I asked him his name and
Hakka came storming down the boat and struck me across the face
with a leather knout. Blood ran from my nostrils. Hakka laughed, then
became angry because I showed no sign of pain and so hit me again.
"You do not speak," he told me, "you are nothing. What are you?" I did
not answer, so he hit me again, harder. "What are you?" he demanded.

"Nothing," I grunted.

"You spoke!" he snarled, and hit me again. "You mustn't speak!"
he screamed into my face and slashed me around the scalp with his
knout. He laughed, having tricked me into breaking the rules, and
went back to the prow. So we rowed in silence, and we slept through
the dark, though before we slept they chained our manacles together.
They always did that and one man always had an arrow on a bow in
case any of us tried to fight as the man threading the chain bent in
front of us.

Sverri knew how to run a slave ship. In those first days I looked for
a chance to fight and had none. The manacles never came off. When
we made port we were ordered into the space beneath the steering
platform and it would be closed up by planks that were nailed into
place. We could talk there and that is how I learned something of the
other slaves. The four Saxons had all been sold into slavery by Kjartan. They had been farmers and they cursed the Christian god for
their predicament. The Norsemen and Danes were thieves, con-
demned to slavery by their own people, and all of them were sullen
brutes. I learned little of Finan, the Irishman, for he was tight-lipped,
silent, and watchful. He was the smallest of us, but strong, with a
sharp face behind his black beard. Like the Saxons he was a Christian,
or at least he had the splintered remnants of a wooden cross hanging

on a leather thong, and sometimes he would kiss the wood and hold it to his lips as he silently prayed. He might not have spoken much, but he listened intently as the other slaves spoke of women, food, and the lives they had left behind, and I daresay they lied about all three. I kept quiet, just as Finan kept quiet, though sometimes, if the others were sleeping, he would sing a sad song in his own language.

We would be let out of the dark prison to load cargo that went into the deep hold in the center of the ship just aft of the mast. The crew sometimes got drunk in port, but two of them were always sober and those two guarded us. Sometimes, if we anchored offshore, Sverri would let us stay on deck, but he chained our manacles together so none of us could attempt an escape.

My first voyage on *Trader* was from the storm-racked coast of Northumbria to Frisia where we threaded a strange seascape of low islands, sandbanks, running tides, and glistening mudflats. We called at some miserable harbor where four other ships were loading cargoes and all four ships were crewed by slaves. We filled *Trader*'s hold with eelskins, smoked fish, and otter pelts.

From Frisia we ran south to a port in Frankia. I learned it was Frankia because Sverri went ashore and came back in a black mood. "If a Frank is your friend," he snarled to his crew, "you can be sure he's not your neighbor." He saw me looking at him and lashed out with his hand, cutting my forehead with a silver and amber ring he wore. "Bastard Franks," he said, "bastard Franks! Tight-moneyed misbegotten bastard Franks." That evening he cast the runesticks on the steering platform. Like all sailors, Sverri was a superstitious man and he kept a sheaf of black runesticks in a leather bag and, locked away beneath the platform, I heard the thin sticks clatter on the deck above. He must have peered at the pattern the fallen sticks made and found some hope in their array, for he decided we would stay with the tight-moneyed misbegotten bastard Franks, and at the end of three days he had bargained successfully for we loaded a cargo of sword-blades, spear-heads, scythes, mail coats, yew logs, and fleeces. We took that north, far north, into the lands of the Danes and the

Svear where he sold the cargo. Frankish blades were much prized, while the yew logs would be cut into plow blades, and with the money he earned Sverri filled the boat with iron-ore that we carried back south again.

Sverri was good at managing slaves and very good at making money. The coins fairly flowed into the ship, all of them stored in a vast wooden box kept in the cargo hold. "You'd like to get your hands on that, wouldn't you?" he sneered at us one day as we sailed up some nameless coast. "You sea-turds!" The thought of us robbing him had made him voluble. "You think you can cheat me? I'll kill you first. I'll drown you. I'll push seal shit down your throats till you choke." We said nothing as he raved.

Winter was coming by then. I did not know where we were, except we were in the north and somewhere in the sea that lies about Denmark. After delivering our last cargo we rowed the unladen ship beside a desolate sandy shore until Sverri finally steered us up a tidal creek edged with reeds and there he ran *Trader* ashore on a muddy bank. It was high tide and the ship was stranded at the beginning of the ebb. There was no village at the creek, just a long low house thatched with moss-covered reeds. Smoke drifted from the roof hole. Gulls called. A woman emerged from the house and, as soon as Sverri jumped down from the ship, she ran to him with cries of joy and he took her in his arms and swept her about in a circle. Then three children came running and he gave each a handful of silver and tickled them and threw them in the air and hugged them.

This was evidently where Sverri planned to winter *Trader* and he made us empty her of her stone ballast, strip her sail, mast, and rigging, and then haul her on log rollers so she stood clear of the highest tides. She was a heavy boat and Sverri called on a neighbor from across the marsh to help haul her with a pair of oxen. His eldest child, a son aged about ten, delighted in pricking us with the ox goad. There was a slave hut behind the house. It was made of heavy logs, even the roof was of logs, and we slept there in our manacles. By day we worked, cleaning *Trader's* hull, scraping away the filth and weeds and barnacles. We cleaned the muck from her bilge, spread the sail to be washed by rain, and watched hungrily as Sverri's woman repaired the cloth with a bone needle and catgut. She was a stocky woman with short legs, heavy thighs, and a round face pockmarked by some disease. Her hands and arms were red and raw. She was anything but beautiful, but we were starved of women and gazed at her. That amused Sverri. He hauled down her dress once to show us a plump white breast and then laughed at our wide-eyed stares. I dreamed of Gisela. I tried to summon her face to my dreams, but it would not come, and dreaming of her was no consolation.

Sverri's men fed us gruel and eel soup and rough bread and fish stew, and when the snow came they threw us mud-clotted fleeces and we huddled in the slave hut and listened to the wind and watched the snow through the chinks between the logs. It was cold, so cold, and one of the Saxons died. He had been feverish and after five days he just died and two of Sverri's men carried his body to the creek and threw him beyond the ice so that his body floated away on the next tide. There were woods not far away and every few days we would be taken to the trees, given axes and told to make firewood. The manacles were deliberately made too short so that a man could not take a full stride, and when we had axes they guarded us with bows and with spears, and I knew I would die before I could reach one of the guards with the ax, but I was tempted to try. One of the Danes tried before I did, turning and screaming, running clumsily, and an arrow took him in the belly and he doubled over and Sverri's men killed him slowly. He screamed for every long moment. His blood stained the snow for yards around and he died so very slowly as a lesson to the rest of us, and so I just chopped at trees, trimmed the trunks, split the trunks with a maul and wedges, chopped again and went back to the slave hut.

"If the little bastard children would just come close," Finan said next day, "I'd strangle the filthy wee creatures, so I would."

I was astonished for it was the longest statement I had ever heard him make. "Better to take them hostage," I suggested.

"But they know better than to come close," he said, ignoring my suggestion. He spoke Danish in a strange accent. "You were a warrior," he said.

"I am a warrior," I said. The two of us were sitting outside the hut on a patch of grass where the snow had melted and we were gutting herrings with blunt knives. The gulls screamed about us. One of Sverri's men watched us from outside the long-house. He had a bow across his knees and a sword at his side. I wondered how Finan had guessed I was a warrior, for I had never talked of my life. Nor had I revealed my true name, preferring them to think that I was called Osbert. Osbert had once been my real name, the name I was given at birth, but I had been renamed Uhtred when my elder brother died because my father insisted his eldest son must be called Uhtred. But I did not use the name Uhtred on board *Trader*. Uhtred was a proud name, a warrior's name, and I would keep it a secret until I had escaped slavery. "How did you know I'm a warrior?" I asked Finan.

"Because you never stop watching the bastards," he said. "You never stop thinking about how to kill them."

"You're the same," I said.

"Finan the Agile, they called me," he said, "because I would dance around enemies. I would dance and kill. Dance and kill." He slit another fish's belly and flicked the offal into the snow where two gulls fought for it. "There was a time," he went on angrily, "when I owned five spears, six horses, two swords, a coat of bright mail, a shield, and a helmet that shone like fire. I had a woman with hair that fell to her waist and with a smile that could dim the noonday sun. Now I gut herrings." He slashed with the knife. "And one day I shall come back here and I shall kill Sverri, hump his woman, strangle his bastard children, and steal his money." He gave a harsh chuckle. "He keeps it all here. All that money. Buried it is."

"You know that for sure?"

"What else does he do with it? He can't eat it because he doesn't shit silver, does he? No, it's here."

"Wherever here is," I said.

"Jutland," he said. "The woman's a Dane. We come here every winter."

"How many winters?"

"This is my third," Finan said.

"How did he capture you?"

He flipped another cleaned fish into the rush basket. "There was a fight. Us against the Norsemen and the bastards beat us. I was taken prisoner and the bastards sold me to Sverri. And you?"

"Betrayed by my lord."

"So that's another bastard to kill, eh? My lord betrayed me too."

"How?"

"He wouldn't ransom me. He wanted my woman, see? So he let me go, in return for which favor I pray he may die and that his wives get lockjaw and that his cattle get the staggers and that his children rot in their own shit and that his crops wither and his hounds choke." He shuddered as if his anger was too much to contain.

Sleet came instead of snow and the ice slowly melted in the creek. We made new oars from seasoned spruce cut the previous winter, and by the time the oars had been shaped the ice was gone. Gray fogs cloaked the land and the first flowers showed at the edges of the reeds. Herons stalked the shallows as the sun melted the morning frosts. Spring was coming and so we caulked *Trader* with cattle hair, tar, and moss. We cleaned her and launched her, returned the ballast to her bilge, rigged the mast and bent the cleaned and mended sail onto her yard. Sverri embraced his woman, kissed his children, and waded out to us. Two of his crew hauled him aboard and we gripped the oars.

"Row, you bastards!" he shouted, "row!"

We rowed.

Anger can keep you alive, but only just. There were times when I was sick, when I felt too weak to pull the oar, but pull it I did for if I faltered then I would be tossed overboard. I pulled as I vomited, pulled

as I sweated, pulled as I shivered, and pulled as I hurt in every muscle.
I pulled through rain and sun and wind and sleet. I remember having
a fever and thinking I was going to die. I even wanted to die, but
Finan cursed me under his breath. "You're a feeble Saxon," he goaded
me, "you're weak. You're pathetic, you Saxon scum." I grunted some
response, and he snarled at me again, louder this time so that Hakka
heard from the bows. "They want you to die, you bastard," Finan
said, "so prove them wrong. Pull, you feeble Saxon bastard, pull."
Hakka hit him for speaking. Another time I did the same for Finan. I
remember cradling him in my arms and putting gruel into his mouth
with my fingers. "Live, you bastard," I told him, "don't let these
earslings beat us. Live!" He lived.

We went north that next summer, pulling into a river that twisted
through a landscape of moss and birch, a place so far north that rills
of snow still showed in shadowed places. We bought reindeer hides
from a village among the birches and carried them back to the sea,
and exchanged them for walrus tusks and whalebone, which in turn
we traded for amber and eider feathers. We carried malt and sealskin,
furs and salt meat, iron-ore and fleeces. In one rock-circled cove we
spent two days loading slates that would be turned into whetstones,
and Sverri traded the slates for combs made from deer antlers and for
big coils of sealskin rope and a dozen heavy ingots of bronze, and we
took all those back to Jutland, going into Haithabu which was a big
trading port, so big that there was a slave compound and we were
taken there and released inside where we were guarded by spearmen
and high walls.

Finan found some fellow Irishmen in the compound and I discovered a Saxon who had been captured by a Dane from the coast of East
Anglia. King Guthrum, the Saxon said, had returned to East Anglia
where he called himself Æthelstan and was building churches. Alfred,
so far as he knew, was still alive. The East Anglian Danes had not tried
to attack Wessex, but even so he had heard that Alfred was making
forts about his frontier. He knew nothing about Alfred's Danish
hostages, so could not tell me whether Ragnar had been released, nor

had the man heard any news of Guthred or Northumbria, so I stood in the compound's center and shouted a question. "Is anyone here from Northumbria?" Men stared at me dully. "Northumbria?" I shouted again, and this time a woman called from the far side of the palisade which divided the men's compound from the women's. Men were crowded at the palisade, peering through its chinks at the women, but I pushed two aside. "You're from Northumbria?" I asked the woman who had called to me.

"From Onhripum," she told me. She was a Saxon, fifteen years old and a tanner's daughter. Her father had owed money to Earl Ivarr and, to settle the debt, Ivarr had taken the girl and sold her to Kjartan.

At first I thought I must have misheard. "To Kjartan?" I asked her.

"To Kjartan," she said dully, "who raped me, then sold me to these bastards."

"Kjartan's alive?" I asked, astonished.

"He lives," she said.

"But he was being besieged," I protested.

"Not while I was there," she said.

"And Sven? His son?"

"He raped me too," she said.

Later, much later, I pieced the whole tale together. Guthred and Ivarr, joined by my uncle Ælfric, had tried to starve Kjartan into submission, but the winter was hard, their armies had been struck by disease, and Kjartan had offered to pay tribute to all three and they had accepted his silver. Guthred had also extracted a promise that Kjartan would stop attacking churchmen, and for a time that promise was kept, but the church was too wealthy and Kjartan too greedy, and within a year the promise had been broken and some monks were killed or enslaved. The annual tribute of silver that Kjartan was supposed to give to Guthred, Ælfric, and Ivarr had been paid once, and never paid again. So nothing had changed. Kjartan had been humbled for a few months, then he had judged the strength of his enemies and found it feeble. The tanner's daughter from Onhripum knew nothing of Gisela, had never even heard of her, and I thought

perhaps she had died and that night I knew despair. I wept. I remembered Hild and I wondered what had happened to her, and I feared
for her, and I remembered that one night with Gisela when I had
kissed her beneath the beech trees and I thought of all my dreams
that were now hopeless and so I wept.

I had married a wife in Wessex and I knew nothing of her and, if
the truth were known, I cared nothing. I had lost my baby son to
death. I had lost Iseult to death. I had lost Hild, I had lost all chance
of Gisela, and that night I felt a swamping pity for myself and I sat in
the hut and tears rolled down my cheeks and Finan saw me and he
began weeping too and I knew he had been reminded of home. I tried
to rekindle my anger because it is only anger that will keep you alive,
but the anger would not come. I just wept instead. I could not stop. It
was the darkness of despair, of the knowledge that my fate was to pull
an oar until I was broken and then I would go overboard. I wept.

"You and me," Finan said, and paused. It was dark. It was a cold
night, though it was summer.

"You and me?" I asked, my eyes closed in an attempt to stop the
tears.

"Swords in hand, my friend," he said, "you and me. It will happen." He meant we would be free and we would have our revenge.

"Dreams," I said.

"No!" Finan said angrily. He crawled to my side and took my hand
in both his. "Don't give up," he snarled at me. "We're warriors, you and
I, we're warriors!" I had been a warrior, I thought. There had been a
time when I shone in mail and helmet, but now I was lice-ridden,
filthy, weak, and tearful. "Here," Finan said, and he pushed something
into my hand. It was one of the antler-combs we had carried as cargo
and somehow he had managed to steal it and secrete it in his rags.
"Never give up," he told me, and I used the comb to disentangle my
hair that now grew almost to my waist. I combed it out, tearing knots
free, pulling lice from the teeth, and next morning Finan plaited my
straight hair and I did the same for him. "It's how warriors dress their
hair in my tribe," he explained, "and you and I are warriors. We're not

slaves, we're warriors!" We were thin, dirty, and ragged, but the despair had passed like a squall at sea and I let the anger give me resolve.

Next day we loaded *Trader* with ingots of copper, bronze, and iron. We rolled barrels of ale into her stern and filled the remaining cargo space with salt meat, rings of hard bread, and tubs of salted cod. Sverri laughed at our plaited hair. "You two think you'll find women, do you?" he mocked us. "Or are you pretending to be women?" Neither of us answered and Sverri just grinned. He was in a good mood, one of unusual excitement. He liked seafaring and from the amount of provisions we stowed I guessed he planned a long voyage and so it proved. He cast his runesticks time after time and they must have told him he would prosper for he bought three new slaves, all of them Frisians. He wanted to be well-manned for the voyage ahead, a voyage that began badly, for, as we left Haithabu, we were pursued by another ship. A pirate, Hakka announced sourly, and we ran north under sail and oars and the other ship slowly overhauled us for she was longer, leaner, and faster, and it was only the coming of night that let us escape, but it was a nervous night. We stowed the oars and lowered the sail so that *Trader* would make no noise, and in the dark I heard the oar-splashes of our pursuer and Sverri and his men were crouching near us, swords in hand, ready to kill us if we made a noise. I was tempted, and Finan wanted to thump on the ship's side to bring the pursuers to us, but Sverri would have slaughtered us instantly and so we kept silent and the strange ship passed us in the darkness and when dawn came she had vanished.

Such threats were rare. Wolf does not eat wolf, and the falcon does not stoop on another falcon, and so the Northmen rarely preyed on each other, though some men, desperate, would risk attacking a fellow Dane or Norseman. Such pirates were reviled as outcasts, as nothings, but they were feared. Usually they were hunted down and the crews were killed or enslaved, but still some men risked being outcasts, knowing that if they could just capture one rich ship like *Trader* they could make a fortune that would give them status, power, and acceptance. But we escaped that night, and next day we sailed farther north and still farther north, and we did not put into land that night, nor for many nights. Then one morning I saw a black coast of terrible cliffs and the sea was shattering white against those grim rocks, and I thought we had come to our journey's end, but we did not seek land. Instead we sailed on, going west now, and then briefly south to put into the bay of an island where we anchored.

At first Finan thought it was Ireland, but the folk who came to *Trader* in a small skin boat did not speak his language. There are islands all about the northern coast of Britain and this, I think was one of them. Savages live on those islands and Sverri did not go ashore, but traded a few paltry coins with the savages and received in return some gulls' eggs, dried fish and goat-meat. And next morning we rowed into a brisk wind and we rowed all day and I knew we were heading into the western wastes of the wilderness sea. Ragnar the Elder had warned me of those seas, saying that there were lands beyond them, but that most men who sought the far lands never came back. Those western lands, he told me, were inhabited by the souls of dead sailors. They were gray places, fog-shrouded and storm-battered, but that was where we were going and Sverri stood at the steering oar with a look of happiness on his flat face and I remembered that same happiness. I remembered the joy of a good ship and the pulse of its life in the loom of the steering oar.

For two weeks we voyaged. This was the whale path, and the monsters of the sea rolled to look at us or spouted water, and the air became colder and the sky was forever clouded, and I knew Sverri's crewmen were nervous. They thought we were lost, and I thought the same, and I believed my life would end at the sea's edge where great whirlpools drag ships down to their deaths. Seabirds circled us, their cries forlorn in the white cold, and the great whales plunged beneath us, and we rowed until our backs were sore. The seas were gray and mountainous, unending and cold, scummed with white foam, and we had only one day of friendly wind when we could travel under sail with the big gray seas hissing along our hull.

And so we came to Horn in the land of fire that some men call

Thule. Mountains smoked and we heard tales of magical pools of hot water, though I saw none. And it was not just a land of fire, but a haunt of ice. There were mountains of ice, rivers of ice, and shelves of ice in the sky. There were codfish longer than a man is tall and we ate well there and Sverri was happy. Men feared to make the voyage we had just made, and he had achieved it, and in Thule his cargo was worth three times what he would have received in Denmark or Frankia, though of course he had to yield some of the precious cargo as tribute to the local lord. But he sold the rest of the ingots and took on board whalebones and walrus tusks and walrus hides and sealskin, and he knew he would make much money if he could take those things home. He was in such a good mood that he even allowed us ashore and we drank sour birch wine in a long-house that stank of whale flesh. We were all shackled, not just with our ordinary manacles, but with neck chains too, and Sverri had hired local men to guard us. Three of those sentinels were armed with the long heavy spears that the men of Thule use to kill whales while the other four had flensing knives. Sverri was safe with them watching us, and he knew it, and for the only time in all the months I was with him he deigned to speak with us. He boasted of the voyage we had made and even praised our skill at the oars. "But you two hate me," he said, looking at Finan and then at me.

I said nothing.

"The birch wine is good," Finan said, "thank you for it."

"The birch wine is walrus piss," Sverri said, then belched. He was drunk. "You hate me," he said, amused by our hatred. "I watch you two and you hate me. The others now, they're whipped, but you two would kill me before I could sneeze. I should kill you both, shouldn't I? I should sacrifice you to the sea." Neither of us spoke. A birch log cracked in the fire and spewed sparks. "But you row well," Sverri said. "I did free a slave once," he went on, "I released him because I liked him. I trusted him. I even let him steer *Trader*, but he tried to kill me. You know what I did with him? I nailed his filthy corpse to the prow and let him rot there. And I learned my lesson. You're there to row.

Nothing else. You row and you work and you die." He fell asleep shortly after, and so did we, and next morning we were back on board *Trader* and, under a spitting rain, left that strange land of ice and flame.

It took much less time to go back east because we ran before a friendly wind and so wintered in Jutland again. We shivered in the slave hut and listened to Sverri grunting in his woman's bed at night. The snow came, ice locked the creek, and it became the year 880 and I had lived twenty-three years and I knew my future was to die in shackles because Sverri was watchful, clever, and ruthless.

And then the red ship came.

She was not truly red. Most ships are built of oak that darkens as the ship lives, but this ship had been made from pine and when the morning or evening light lanced low across the sea's edge she seemed to be the color of darkening blood.

She looked a livid red when we first saw her. That was on the evening of the day we had launched and the red ship was long and low and lean. She coursed from the eastern horizon, coming toward us at an angle, and her sail was a dirty gray, criss-crossed by the ropes that strengthen the cloth, and Sverri saw the beast-head at her prow and decided she was a pirate and so we struck inshore to waters he knew well. They were shallow waters and the red ship hesitated to follow. We rowed through narrow creeks, scattering wildfowl, and the red ship stayed within sight, but out beyond the dunes, and then the night fell and we reversed our course and let the ebb-tide take us out to sea and Sverri's men whipped us to make us row hard to escape the coast. The dawn came cold and misty, but as the mist lifted we saw that the red ship was gone.

We were going to Haithabu to find the first cargo of the season, but as we approached the port Sverri saw the red ship again and she turned toward us and Sverri cursed her. We were upwind of her, which made escaping easy, but even so she tried to catch us. She used her oars and, because she had at least twenty benches, she was much faster than *Trader*, but she could not close the wind's gap and by the following morning we were again alone on an empty sea. Sverri cursed her all the same. He cast his runesticks and they persuaded him to abandon the idea of Haithabu and so we crossed to the land of the Svear where we loaded beaver hides and dung-encrusted fleeces.

We exchanged that cargo for fine candles of rolled wax. We shipped iron-ore again and so the spring passed and the summer came and we did not see the red ship. We had forgotten her. Sverri reckoned it was safe to visit Haithabu so we took a cargo of reindeer skins to the port, and there he learned that the red ship had not forgotten him. He came back aboard in a hurry, not bothering to load a cargo, and I heard him talking to his crewmen. The red ship, he said, was prowling the coasts in search of *Trader*. She was a Dane, he thought, and she was crewed by warriors.

"Who?" Hakka asked.

"No one knows."

"Why?"

"How would I know?" Sverri growled, but he was worried enough to throw his runesticks on the deck and they instructed him to leave Haithabu at once. Sverri had made an enemy and he did not know who, and so he took *Trader* to a place near his winter home and there he carried gifts ashore. Sverri had a lord. Almost all men have a lord who offers protection, and this lord was called Hyring and he owned much land, and Sverri would pay him silver each winter and in return Hyring would offer protection to Sverri and his family. But there was little Hyring could do to protect Sverri on the sea, though he must have promised to discover who sailed the red ship and to learn why that man wanted Sverri. In the meantime Sverri decided to go far away and so we went into the North Sea and down the coast and made some money with salted herrings. We crossed to Britain for the first time since I had been a slave. We landed in an East Anglian river, and I never did learn what river it was, and we loaded thick fleeces that we took back to Frankia and there bought a cargo of iron ingots. That was a rich cargo because Frankish iron is the best in the world, and we also purchased a hundred of their prized sword-blades. Sverri, as ever, cursed the Franks for their hard-headedness, but in truth Sverri's head was as hard as any Frank's and, though he paid well for the iron and sword-blades, he knew that they would bring him a great profit in the northern lands.

So we headed north and the summer was ending and the geese were flying south above us in great skeins and, two days after we had loaded the cargo, we saw the red ship waiting for us off the Frisian coast. It had been weeks since we had seen her and Sverri must have hoped that Hyring had ended her threat, but she was lying just off-shore and this time the red ship had the wind's advantage and so we turned inshore and Sverri's men whipped us desperately. I grunted with every stroke, making it look as though I hauled the oar-loom with all my strength, but in truth I was trying to lessen the force of the blade in the water so that the red ship could catch us. I could see her clearly. I could see her oar-wings rising and falling and see the white bone of water snapping at her bows. She was much longer than *Trader*, and much faster, but she also drew more water which is why Sverri had taken us inshore to the coast of Frisia which all shipmasters fear.

It is not rockbound like so many northern coasts. There are no cliffs against which a good ship can be broken in pieces. Instead it is a tangle of reeds, islands, creeks, and mudflats. For mile after mile there is nothing but dangerous shallows. Passages are marked through those shallows with withies rammed into the mud, and those frail signals offer a safe way through the tangle, but the Frisians are pirates too. They like to mark false channels that lead only to a mudbank where a falling tide can strand a ship, and then the folk, who live in mud huts on their mud islands, will swarm like water-rats to kill and pillage.

But Sverri had traded here and, like all good shipmasters, he carried memories of good and bad water. The red ship was catching us, but Sverri did not panic. I would watch him as I rowed, and I could see his eyes darting left and right to decide which passage to take, then he would make a swift push on the steering oar and we would turn into his chosen channel. He sought the shallowest places, the most twisted creeks, and the gods were with him for, though our oars sometimes struck a mudbank, *Trader* never grounded. The red ship, being larger, and presumably because her master did not know the coast as Sverri did, was traveling much more cautiously and we were leaving her behind.

She began to overhaul us again when we had to cross a wide stretch of open water, but Sverri found another channel at the far side, and here, for the first time, he slowed our oar-beats. He put Hakka in the bows and Hakka kept throwing a lead-weighted line into the water and calling the depth. We were crawling into a maze of mud and water, working our slow way north and east, and I looked across to the east and saw that Sverri had at last made a mistake. A line of withies marked the channel we threaded, but beyond them and beyond a low muddy island thick with birds, larger withies marked a deep water channel that cut inshore of our course and would allow the red ship to head us off, and the red ship saw the opportunity and took that larger channel. Her oar-blades beat at the water, she ran at full speed, she was overtaking us fast, and then she ran aground in a tangle of clashing oars.

Sverri laughed. He had known the larger withies marked a false channel and the red ship had fallen into the trap. I could see her clearly now, a ship laden with armed men, men in mail, sword-Danes and spear-warriors, but she was stranded.

"Your mothers are goats!" Sverri shouted across the mud, though I doubt his voice carried to the grounded ship, "you are turds! Learn to master a ship, you useless bastards!"

We took another channel, leaving the red ship behind, and Hakka was still in *Trader's* bows where he constantly threw the line weighted with its lump of lead. He would shout back how deep the water was. This channel was unmarked, and we had to go perilously slowly for Sverri dared not run aground. Behind us, far behind now, I could see the crew of the red ship laboring to free her. The warriors had discarded their mail and were in the water, heaving at the long hull, and as night fell I saw her slip free and resume her pursuit, but we were far ahead now and the darkness cloaked us.

We spent that night in a reed-fringed bay. Sverri would not go ashore. There were folk on the nearby island, and their fires sparked in the night. We could see no other lights, which surely meant that the island was the only settlement for miles, and I knew Sverri was worried because the fires would attract the red ship and so he kicked us awake in the very first glimmerings of the dawn and we pulled the anchor and Sverri took us north into a passage marked by withies. The passage seemed to wriggle about the island's coast to the open sea where the waves broke white, and it offered a way out of the tangled shore. Hakka again called the depths as we eased our way past reeds and mudbanks. The creek was shallow, so shallow that our oar-blades constantly struck bottom to kick up swirls of mud, yet pace by pace we followed the frail channel marks, and then Hakka shouted that the red ship was behind us.

She was a long way behind us. As Sverri had feared she had been attracted by the settlement's fires, but she had ended up south of the island, and between us and her was the mystery of mudbanks and creeks. She could not go west into the open sea, for the waves broke continuously on a long half-sunken beach there, so she could either pursue us or else try to loop far around us to the east and discover another way to the ocean.

She decided to follow us and we watched as she groped her way along the island's southern coast, looking for a channel into the harbor where we had anchored. We kept creeping north, but then, suddenly, there was a soft grating sound beneath our keel and *Trader* gave a gentle shudder and went ominously still. "Back oars!" Sverri bellowed.

We backed oars, but she had grounded. The red ship was lost in the half-light and in the tenuous mist that drifted across the islands. The tide was low. It was the slack water between ebb and flood and Sverri stared hard at the creek, praying that he could see the tide flowing inward to float us off, but the water lay still and cold.

"Overboard!" he shouted. "Push her!"

We tried. Or the others tried, while Finan and I merely pretended to push, but *Trader* was stuck hard. She had gone aground so softly, so quietly, yet she would not move and Sverri, still standing on the steering platform, could see the islanders coming toward us across the reed-beds and, more worrying, he could see the red ship crossing the wide bay where we had anchored. He could see death coming.

"Empty her," he shouted.

That was a hard decision for Sverri to take, but it was better than death, and so we threw all the ingots overboard. Finan and I could no longer shirk, for Sverri could see how much work we were doing, and he lashed at us with a stick and so we destroyed the profits of a year's trading. Even the sword-blades went, and all the time the red ship crept closer, coming up the channel, and she was only a quarter-mile behind us when the last ingots splashed over the side and *Trader* gave a slight lurch. The tide was flooding now, swirling past and around the jettisoned ingots.

"Row!" Sverri shouted. The islanders were watching us. They had not dared approach for fear of the armed men on the red ship, and now they watched as we slid away northward, and we fought the incoming tide and our oars pulled on mud as often as they bit water, but Sverri screamed at us to row harder. He would risk a further grounding to get clear, and the gods were with him, for we shot out of the passage's mouth and *Trader* reared to the incoming waves and suddenly we were at sea again with the water breaking white on our bows and Sverri hoisted the sail and we ran northward and the red ship seemed to have grounded where we had been stranded. She had run onto the pile of ingots and, because her hull was deeper than *Trader*'s, it took her a long time to escape and by the time she was free of the channel we were already hidden by rain squalls that crashed from the west and pounded the ship as they passed.

Sverri kissed his hammer amulet. He had lost a fortune, but he was a wealthy man and could afford it. Yet he had to stay wealthy and he knew that the red ship was pursuing him and that it would stay on the coast until it found us and so, as dark fell, he dropped the sail and ordered us to the oars.

We went northward. The red ship was still behind us, but far behind, and the rain squalls hid us from time to time and when a bigger squall came Sverri dropped the sail, turned the ship westward into the wind and his men whipped us to work. Two of his men even took oars themselves so that we could escape across the darkening horizon before the red ship saw that we had changed course. It was brutally hard work. We were thumping into the wind and seas, and every stroke burned the muscles until I thought I would drop from exhaustion. Deep night ended the work. Sverri could no longer see the big waves hissing from the west and so he let us ship the oars and plug the oar-holes and we lay like dead men as the ship heaved and wallowed in the dark and churning sea.

Dawn found us alone. Wind and rain whipped from the south, and that meant we did not have to row, but instead could hoist the sail and let the wind carry us across the gray waters. I looked aft, searching for the red ship and she was not to be seen. There were only the waves and the clouds and the squalls hurtling across our wake and the wild birds flying like white scraps in the bitter wind, and *Trader* bent to that wind so that the water rushed past us and Sverri leaned on the steering oar and sang to celebrate his escape from the mysterious enemy. I could have wept again. I did not know what the red ship was, or who sailed her, but I knew she was Sverri's enemy and that any enemy of Sverri was my friend. But she was gone. We had escaped her.

And so we came back to Britain. Sverri had not intended to go there, and he had no cargo to sell though he did have coins hidden aboard to buy goods, but the coins would also have to be expended in survival. He had evaded the red ship, but he knew that if he went home he would find her lurking off Jutland and I do not doubt he was thinking of some other place he might spend the winter in safety. That meant discovering a lord who would shelter him while *Trader* was hauled ashore, cleaned, repaired, and re-caulked, and that lord would require silver. We oarsmen heard snatches of conversation and gathered that Sverri reckoned he should pick up one last cargo, take it to Denmark, sell it, then find some port where he could shelter and from where he could travel overland to his home to collect more silver to fund the next year's trading.

We were off the British coast. I did not recognize where we were. I knew it was not East Anglia for there were bluffs and hills. "Nothing to buy here," Sverri complained.

"Fleeces?" Hakka suggested.

"What price will they fetch at this time of year?" Sverri demanded angrily. "All we'll get is whatever they couldn't sell in the spring. Nothing but rubbish matted with sheep shit. I'd rather carry charcoal."

We sheltered one night in a river mouth and armed horsemen rode to the shore to stare at us, but they did not use any of the small fishing craft which were hauled on the beach to come out to us, suggesting that if we left them alone then they would leave us alone. Just as dark fell another trading boat came into the river and anchored near us, and its Danish shipmaster used a small craft to row across to us and he and Sverri squatted in the space beneath the steering platform and exchanged news. We heard none of it. We just saw the two men drinking ale and talking. The stranger left before darkness hid his ship and Sverri seemed pleased with the conversation, for in the morning he shouted his thanks to the other boat and ordered us to haul the anchor and take the oars. It was a windless day, the sea was calm, and we rowed northward beside the shore. I stared inland and saw smoke rising from settlements and thought that freedom lay there.

I dreamed of freedom, but now I did not think it would ever come. I thought I would die at that oar as so many others had died under Sverri's lash. Of the eleven oarsmen who had been aboard when I was given to Sverri only four still lived, of whom Finan was one. We now had fourteen oarsmen, for Sverri had replaced the dead and, ever since the red ship had come to haunt his existence, he had paid for more slaves to man his oars. Some shipmasters used free men to row their boats, reckoning they worked more willingly, but such men expected a share in the silver and Sverri was a miserly man.

Late that morning we came to a river's mouth and I gazed up at the headland on the southern bank and saw a high beacon waiting to be lit to warn the inland folk that raiders came, and I had seen that beacon before. It was like a hundred others, yet I recognized it, and I knew it stood in the ruins of the Roman fort at the place where my slavery had begun. We had come back to the River Tine.

"Slaves!" Sverri announced to us. "That's what we're buying. Slaves, just like you bastards. Except they're not like you, because they're women and children. Scots. Anyone here speak their bastard language?" None of us answered. Not that we needed to speak the Scottish language, for Sverri had whips that spoke loudly enough.

He disliked carrying slaves as cargo for they needed constant watching and feeding, but the other trader had told him of women and children newly captured in one of the endless border raids between Northumbria and Scotland, and those slaves offered the best prospect of any profit. If any of the women and children were pretty then they would sell high in Jutland's slave markets, and Sverri needed to make a good trade, and so we rowed into the Tine on a rising tide. We were going to Gyruum, and Sverri waited until the water had almost reached the high-tide mark of sea-wrack and flotsam, and then he beached *Trader*. He did not often beach her, but he wanted us to scrape her hull before going back to Denmark, and a beached ship made it easier to load human cargo, and so we ran her ashore and I saw that the slave pens had been rebuilt and that the ruined monastery had a thatched roof again. All was as it was.

Sverri made us wear slave collars that were chained together so we could not escape and then, while he crossed the salt-marsh and climbed to the monastery, we scraped the exposed hull with stones. Finan sang in his native Irish as he worked, but sometimes he would throw me a crooked grin. "Tear the caulking out, Osbert," he suggested.

"So we sink?"

"Aye, but Sverri sinks with us."

"Let him live so we can kill him," I said.

"And we will kill him," Finan said.

"Never give up hope, eh?"

"I dreamed it," Finan said. "I've dreamed it three times since the red ship came."

"But the red ship's gone," I said.

"We'll kill him. I promise you. I'll dance in his guts, I will."

The tide had been at its height at midday so all afternoon it fell until *Trader* was stranded high above the fretting waves, and she could not be refloated until long after dark. Sverri was always uneasy when his ship was ashore and I knew he would want to load his cargo that same day and then refloat the ship on the night's tide. He had an anchor ready so that, in the dark, we could push off from the beach and moor in the river's center and be ready to leave the river at first light.

He purchased thirty-three slaves. The youngest were five or six years old, the oldest were perhaps seventeen or eighteen, and they were all women and children, not a man among them. We had finished cleaning the hull and were squatting on the beach when they arrived, and we stared at the women with the hungry eyes of men denied partners. The slaves were weeping, so it was hard to tell if any were pretty. They were weeping because they were slaves, and because they had been stolen from their own land, and because they feared the sea, and because they feared us. A dozen armed men rode behind them. I recognized none of them. Sverri walked down the manacled line, examining the children's teeth and pulling down the women's dresses to examine their breasts. "The red-haired one will fetch a good price," one of the armed men called to Sverri.

"So will they all."

"I humped her last night," the man said, "so perhaps she's carrying my baby, eh? You'll get two slaves for the price of one, you lucky bastard."

The slaves were already shackled and Sverri had been forced to pay for those manacles and chains, just as he had to buy food and ale to keep the thirty-three Scots alive on their voyage to Jutland. We had to fetch those provisions from the monastery and so Sverri led us back across the salt-marsh, over the stream, and up to the fallen stone cross where a wagon and six mounted men waited. The wagon had barrels of ale, tubs of salt herring and smoked eels, and a sack of apples. Sverri bit into an apple, made a wry face, and spat out the mouthful. "Worm-ridden," he complained and tossed the remnants to us, and I managed to snatch it out of the air despite everyone else reaching for it. I broke it in half and gave one portion to Finan. "They'll fight over a wormy apple," Sverri jeered, then spilled a bag of coins onto the wagon bed. "Kneel, you bastards," he snarled at us as a seventh horseman rode toward the wagon.

We knelt in obeisance to the newcomer. "We must test the coins," the newcomer said and I recognized the voice and looked up and saw Sven the One-Eyed.

And he looked at me.

I dropped my gaze and bit into the apple.

"Frankish deniers," Sverri said proudly, offering some of the silver coins to Sven.

Sven did not take them. He was staring at me. "Who is that?" he demanded.

Sverri looked at me. "Osbert," he said. He selected some more coins. "These are Alfred's pennies," he said, holding them out to Sven.

"Osbert?" Sven said. He still gazed at me. I did not look like Uhtred of Bebbanburg. My face had new scars, my nose was broken, my uncombed hair was a great tangled thatch, my beard was ragged, and my skin was as dark as pickled wood, but still he stared at me. "Come here, Osbert," he said.

I could not go far, because the neck chain held me close to the other oarsmen, but I stood and shuffled towards him and knelt again because I was a slave and he was a lord.

"Look at me," he snarled.

I obeyed, staring into his one eye, and I saw he was dressed in fine mail and had a fine cloak and was mounted on a fine horse. I made my right cheek quiver and I dribbled as if I were halfway mad and I grinned as though I were pleased to see him and I bobbed my head compulsively and he must have decided I was just another ruined half-mad slave and he waved me away and took the coins from Sverri. They haggled, but at last enough coins were accepted as good silver, and we oarsmen were ordered to carry the barrels and tubs down to the ship.

Sverri clouted me over the shoulders as we walked. "What were you doing?"

"Doing, master?"

"Shaking like an idiot. Dribbling."

"I think I'm falling ill, master."

"Did you know that man?"

"No, lord."

Sverri was suspicious of me, but he could learn nothing, and he left me alone as we heaved the barrels onto *Trader* that was still half stranded on the beach. But I did not shake or dribble as we stowed the provisions, and Sverri knew something was amiss and he thought about it further and then hit me again as the answer came to him. "You came from here, didn't you?"

"Did I, lord?"

He hit me again, harder, and the other slaves watched. They knew a wounded animal when they saw one and only Finan had any sympathy for me, but he was helpless. "You came from here," Sverri said. "How could I have forgotten that? This is where you were given to me." He pointed toward Sven who was across the marsh on the ruin-crowned hill. "What's Sven the One-Eyed to you?"

"Nothing," I said. "I've never seen him before."

"You lying turd," he said. He had a merchant's instinct for profit and so he ordered me released from the other oarsmen though he made sure my ankles were still shackled and that I still wore the neck chain. Sverri took its end, meaning to lead me back to the monastery, but we got no farther than the shingle bank because Sven had also been having second thoughts. My face haunted his bad dreams and, in the twitching idiot visage of Osbert, he had seen his nightmares and now he was galloping toward us, followed by six horsemen.

"Kneel," Sverri ordered me.

I knelt.

Sven's horse skidded to a halt on the shingle bank. "Look at me," he ordered a second time, and I looked up and spittle hung from my mouth into my beard. I twitched, and Sverri struck me hard. "Who is he?" Sven demanded.

"He told me his name was Osbert, lord," Sverri said.

"He told you?"

"I was given him here, lord, in this place," Sverri said, "and he told me he was called Osbert."

Sven smiled then. He dismounted and walked to me, tipping my chin up so he could stare into my face. "You got him here?" he asked Sverri.

"King Guthred gave him to me, lord."

Sven knew me then and his one-eyed face was contorted with a strange mix of triumph and hatred. He hit me across the skull, hit me so hard that my mind went dark for an instant and I fell to one side. "Uhtred!" he proclaimed triumphantly, "you're Uhtred!"

"Lord!" Sverri was standing over me, protecting me. Not because he liked me, but because I represented a windfall profit.

"He's mine," Sven said, and his long sword whispered out of its fleece-lined scabbard.

"He's mine to sell, lord, and yours to buy," Sverri said humbly, but firmly.

"To take him," Sven said, "I will kill you, Sverri, and all your men. So the price for this man is your life."

Sverri knew he was beaten then. He bowed, released my neck chain and stepped back, and I seized the neck chain and whipped its loose end at Sven and it whistled close to him, driving him back, and then

I ran. The leg shackles hobbled me and I had no choice but to run into the river. I stumbled through the small waves and turned, ready to use the chain as a weapon and I knew I was dead because Sven's horsemen were coming for me and I backed deeper into the water. It was better to drown, I thought, than to suffer Sven's tortures.

Then the horsemen stopped. Sven pushed past them and then he too checked and I was up to my chest in the river and the chain was awkward in my hand and I was readying to throw myself backward to black death in the river when Sven himself stepped away. Then he went back another pace, turned, and ran for his horse. There had been fear on his face and I risked turning to see what had frightened him.

And there, coming from the sea, driven by twin oar-banks and by the swiftly flooding tide, was the red ship.

SIX

The red ship was close and was coming fast. Her bows were crowned with a black-toothed dragon's head and filled with armed men in mail and helmets. She came in a gale of noise; the splash of oar-blades, the shouts of her warriors and the seethe of white water around the great red breast of her high prow. I had to stagger to one side to avoid her, for she did not slow as she neared the beach, but kept coming, and the oars gave one last heave and the bows grated on the shore and the dragon's head reared up and the great ship's keel crashed up the beach in a thunder of scattering shingle. The dark hull loomed above me, then an oar-shaft struck me in the back, throwing me under the waves and when I managed to stagger upright I saw the ship had shuddered to a halt and a dozen mail-clad men had jumped from the prow with spears, swords, axes and shields. The first men onto the beach bellowed defiance as the rowers dropped their oars, plucked up weapons, and followed. This was no trading ship, but a Viking come to her kill.

Sven fled. He scrambled into his saddle and spurred across the marsh while his six men, much braver, rode their horses at the invading Vikings, but the beasts were axed down screaming and the unsaddled riders were butchered on the strand, their blood trickling to the small waves where I stood, mouth open, hardly believing what I saw. Sverri was on his knees with his hands spread wide to show he had no weapons.

The red ship's master, glorious in a helmet crested with eagle wings, took his men to the marsh path and led them toward the monastery buildings. He left a half-dozen warriors on the beach and one of those was a huge man, tall as a tree and broad as a barrel, who carried a great war ax that was stained with blood. He dragged off his helmet and grinned at me. He said something, but I did not hear him. I was just staring in disbelief and he grinned wider.

It was Steapa.

Steapa Snotor. Steapa the Clever, that meant, which was a joke because he was not the brightest of men, but he was a great warrior who had once been my sworn enemy and had since become my friend. Now he grinned at me from the water's edge and I did not understand why a West Saxon warrior was traveling in a Viking ship, and then I began to cry. I cried because I was free and because Steapa's broad, scarred, baleful face was the most beautiful thing I had seen since I had last been on this beach.

I waded out of the water and I embraced him, and he patted my back awkwardly and he could not stop grinning because he was happy. "They did that to you?" he said, pointing at my leg shackles.

"I've worn them for more than two years," I said.

"Put your legs apart, lord," he said.

"Lord?" Sverri had heard Steapa and he understood that one Saxon word. He got up from his knees and took a faltering step toward us. "Is that what he called you?" he asked me, "lord?"

I just stared at Sverri and he went on his knees again. "Who are you?" he asked, frightened.

"You want me to kill him?" Steapa growled.

"Not yet," I said.

"I kept you alive," Sverri said, "I fed you."

I pointed at him. "Be silent," I said and he was.

"Put your legs apart, lord," Steapa said again. "Stretch that chain for me."

I did as he ordered. "Be careful," I said.

"Be careful!" he mocked, then he swung the ax and the big blade whistled past my groin and crashed into the chain and my ankles were twitched inward by the massive blow so that I staggered. "Be still," Steapa ordered me, and he swung again and this time the chain snapped. "You can walk now, lord," Steapa said, and I could, though the links of broken chain dragged behind my ankles.

I walked to the dead men and selected two swords. "Free that man," I told Steapa, pointing at Finan, and Steapa chopped through more chains and Finan ran to me, grinning, and we stared at each other, eyes bright with tears of joy, and then I held a sword to him. He looked at the blade for a moment as though he did not believe what he was seeing, then he gripped the hilt and bayed like a wolf at the darkening sky. Then he threw his arms around my neck. He was weeping. "You're free," I told him.

"And I am a warrior again," he said. "I am Finan the Agile!"

"And I am Uhtred," I said, using that name for the first time since I had last been on this beach. "My name is Uhtred," I said again, but louder this time, "and I am the lord of Bebbanburg." I turned on Sverri, my anger welling up. "I am Lord Uhtred," I told him, "the man who killed Ubba Lothbrokson beside the sea and sent Svein of the White Horse to the corpse-hall. I am Uhtred." I was in a red rage now. I stalked to Sverri and tipped his face up with the sword-blade. "I am Uhtred," I said, "and you call me lord."

"Yes, lord," he said.

"And he is Finan of Ireland," I said, "and you call him lord."

Sverri looked at Finan, could not meet his gaze and lowered his eyes. "Lord," he said to Finan.

I wanted to kill him, but I had a notion that Sverri's usefulness on this earth was not quite finished and so I contented myself with taking Steapa's knife and slitting open Sverri's tunic to bare his arm. He was shaking, expecting his throat to be cut, but instead I carved the letter S into his flesh, then rubbed sand into the wound. "So tell me, slave," I said, "how you undo these rivets?" I tapped my ankle chains with the knife.

"I need a blacksmith's tools, lord," Sverri said.

"If you want to live, Sverri, pray that we find them."

There had to be tools up at the ruined monastery, for that was where Kjartan's men manacled their slaves, and so Steapa sent two men to search for the means to strike off our chains and Finan amused himself by butchering Hakka because I would not let him slaughter Sverri. The Scottish slaves watched in awe as the blood swilled into the sea beside the stranded *Trader*. Finan danced with joy afterward and chanted one of his wild songs, then he killed the rest of Sverri's crew.

"Why are you here?" I asked Steapa.

"I was sent, lord," he said proudly.

"Sent? Who sent you?"

"The king, of course," he said.

"Guthred sent you?"

"Guthred?" Steapa asked, puzzled by the name, then shook his head. "No, lord. It was King Alfred, of course."

"Alfred sent you?" I asked, then gaped at him. "Alfred?"

"Alfred sent us," he confirmed.

"But these are Danes," I gestured at the crewmen who had been left on the beach with Steapa.

"Some are Danes," Steapa said, "but we're mostly West Saxons. Alfred sent us."

"Alfred sent you?" I asked again, knowing I sounded like an incoherent fool, but I could scarcely believe what I was hearing. "Alfred sent Danes?"

"A dozen of them, lord," Steapa said, "and they're only here because they follow him." He pointed to the shipmaster in his winged helmet who was striding back to the beach. "He's the hostage," Steapa said as though that explained everything, "and Alfred sent me to keep him honest. I guard him."

The hostage? Then I remembered whose badge was the eagle wing and I stumbled toward the red ship's master, inhibited by the ragged chains dragging from my ankles, and the approaching warrior took off his winged helmet and I could scarcely see his face because of my tears. But I still shouted his name. "Ragnar!" I shouted. "Ragnar!"

He was laughing when we met. He embraced me, whirled me about, embraced me a second time, and then pushed me away. "You stink," he said, "you're the ugliest, hairiest, smelliest bastard I've ever laid eyes on. I should throw you to the crabs, except why would a good crab want anything as revolting as you?"

I was laughing and I was crying. "Alfred sent you?"

"He did, but I wouldn't have come if I'd known what a filthy turd you've become," he said. He smiled broadly and that smile reminded me of his father, all good humor and strength. He embraced me again. "It is good to see you, Uhtred Ragnarson," he said.

Ragnar's men had driven Sven's remaining troops away. Sven himself had escaped on horseback, fleeing toward Dunholm. We burned the slave pens, freed the slaves, and that night, by the light of the burning wattle hurdles, my shackles were struck off and for the next few days I raised my feet ludicrously high when I walked for I had grown so accustomed to the weight of the iron bonds.

I washed. The red-haired Scottish slave cut my hair, watched by Finan. "Her name's Ethne," he told me. He spoke her language, or at least they could understand one another, though I guessed, from the way they looked at each other, that different languages would not have been a barrier. Ethne had found two of the men who had raped her among Sven's dead and she had borrowed Finan's sword to mutilate their corpses and Finan had watched her proudly. Now she used shears to cut my hair and trim my beard, and afterward I dressed in a leather jerkin and in clean hose and proper shoes. And then we ate in the ruined monastery church and I sat with Ragnar, my friend, and heard the tale of my rescue.

"We've been following you all summer," he said.

"We saw you."

"Couldn't miss us, could you, not with that hull? Isn't she a horror? I hate pine-built hulls. She's called *Dragon-Fire*, but I call her

Worm-Breath. It took me a month to get her ready for sea. She belonged to a man who was killed at Ethandun and she was just rotting away on the Temes when Alfred gave her to us."

"Why would Alfred do that?"

"Because he said you won him his throne at Ethandun," Ragnar said and grinned. "Alfred was exaggerating," he went on, "I'm sure he was. I imagine you just stumbled about the battlefield and made a bit of noise, but you did enough to fool Alfred."

"I did enough," I said softly, remembering the long green hill. "But I thought Alfred didn't notice."

"He noticed," Ragnar said, "but he didn't do this just for you. He gained a nunnery as well."

"He did what?"

"Got himself a nunnery. God knows why he'd want one. Me, I might have exchanged you for a whorehouse, but Alfred got a nunnery and he seemed well enough pleased with that bargain."

And that was when the story emerged. I did not hear the whole tale that night, but later I pieced it all together and I shall tell it here. It had all started with Hild.

Guthred kept his last promise to me and treated her honorably. He gave her my sword and my helmet, he let her keep my mail and my arm rings, and he asked her to be the companion of his new wife, Queen Osburh, the Saxon niece of the dethroned king in Eoferwic. But Hild blamed herself for my betrayal. She decided that she had offended her god by resisting her calling as a nun and so she begged Guthred to give her leave to go back to Wessex and rejoin her order. He had wanted her to stay in Northumbria, but she pleaded with him to let her go and she told him that God and Saint Cuthbert demanded it of her, and Guthred was ever open to Cuthbert's persuasion. And so he allowed her to accompany messengers he was sending to Alfred and thus Hild returned to Wessex and once there she found Steapa, who had always been fond of her.

"She took me to Fifhaden," Steapa told me that night when the hurdles burned beneath the ruined walls of Gyruum's monastery.

"To Fifhaden?"

"And we dug up your hoard," Steapa said. "Hild showed me where it was and I dug it up. Then we carried it to Alfred. All of it. We poured it on the floor and he just stared at it."

That hoard was Hild's weapon. She told Alfred the story of Guthred and how he had betrayed me, and she promised Alfred that if he sent men to find me then she would use all that gold and silver on his hall's floor to build a house of God and that she would repent of her sins and live the rest of her life as a bride of Christ. She would wear the church's manacles so that my iron chains could be struck off.

"She became a nun again?" I asked.

"She said she wanted that," Steapa said. "She said God wanted it. And Alfred did. He said yes to her."

"So Alfred released you?" I asked Ragnar.

"I hope he will," Ragnar said, "when I take you back home. I'm still a hostage, but Alfred said I could search for you if I promised to return to him. And we'll all be released soon enough. Guthrum's making no trouble. King Æthelstan, he's called now."

"He's in East Anglia?"

"He's in East Anglia," Ragnar confirmed, "and he's building churches and monasteries."

"So he really did become a Christian?"

"The poor bastard's as pious as Alfred," Ragnar said gloomily. "Guthrum always was a credulous fool. But Alfred sent for me. Told me I could search for you. He let me take the men who served me in exile and the rest are crewmen that Steapa found. They're Saxons, of course, but the bastards can row well enough."

"Steapa said he was here to guard you," I said.

"Steapa!" Ragnar looked across the fire we had lit in the nave of the monastery's ruined church, "you foul scrap of stinking stoat-shit. Did you say you were here to guard me?"

"But I am, lord," Steapa said.

"You're a piece of shit. But you fight well." Ragnar grinned and looked back to me. "And I'm to take you back to Alfred."

I stared into the fire where strips of burning wattle glowed a brilliant red. "Thyra is at Dunholm," I said, "and Kjartan still lives."

"And I go to Dunholm when Alfred releases me," Ragnar said, "but first I have to take you to Wessex. I swore an oath on it. I swore I would not break Northumbria's peace, but only fetch you. And Alfred kept Brida, of course." Brida was his woman.

"He kept her?"

"As a hostage for me, I suppose. But he'll release her and I shall raise money and I shall assemble men and then I shall scrape Dunholm off the face of the earth."

"You have no money?"

"Not enough."

So I told him about Sverri's home in Jutland and how there was money there, or at least we believed there was money there, and Ragnar thought about that and I thought about Alfred.

Alfred did not like me. He had never liked me. At times he hated me, but I had done him service. I had done him great service, and he had been less than generous in rewarding that service. Five hides, he had given me, while I had given him a kingdom. Yet now I owed my freedom to him, and I did not understand why he had done it. Except, of course, that Hild had given him a house of prayer, and he would have wanted that, and he would have welcomed her repentance, and both those things made a twisted kind of sense. Yet he had still rescued me. He had reached out and plucked me from slavery and I decided he was generous after all. But I also knew there would be a price to pay. Alfred would want more than Hild's soul and a new convent. He would want me. "I hoped I'd never see Wessex again," I said.

"Well you're going to see it," Ragnar said, "because I swore to take you back. Besides, we can't stay here."

"No," I agreed.

"Kjartan will have a hundred men here in the morning," Ragnar said.

"Two hundred," I said.

"So we must go," he said, then looked wistful. "There's a hoard in Jutland?"

"A great hoard," Finan said.

"We think it's buried in a reed hut," I added, "and guarded by a woman and three children."

Ragnar stared through the door to where a few sparks of fire showed among the hovels built by the old Roman fort. "I can't go to Jutland," he said softly. "I swore an oath that I would take you back as soon as I found you."

"So someone else can go," I suggested. "You have two ships now. And Sverri will reveal where his hoard is if he's frightened enough."

So next morning Ragnar ordered his twelve Danes to take *Trader* across the sea. The command of the ship was given to Rollo, Ragnar's best steersman, and Finan begged to go with Rollo's crew, and the Scottish girl Ethne went with Finan who now wore mail and a helmet and had a long sword buckled at his waist. Sverri was chained to one of *Trader*'s oar-benches and, as she left the shore, I saw Finan whipping him with the lash that had scarred our backs for so many months.

Trader left and we then carried the Scottish slaves across the river in the red ship and released them on the northern bank. They were frightened and did not know what to do, so we gave them a handful of the coins we had taken from Sverri's strongbox and told them to keep walking with the sea always on their right hand and, with a little luck, they might reach home. They would more likely be captured by Bebbanburg's garrison and sold back into slavery, but we could not help that. We left them, pushed the red ship away from the shore, and turned for the sea.

Behind us, where Gyruum's hilltop smoked from the remnants of our fires, horsemen in mail and helmets appeared. They lined the crest, and a column of them galloped across the salt-marsh to clatter onto the shingle bank, but they were much too late. We were riding the ebb-tide toward the open sea and I looked behind and saw Kjartan's men and I knew I would see them again and then the *Dragon-*

Fire rounded the river's bend and the oars bit the water and the sun glittered like sharpened spear-points on the small waves and an osprey flew overhead and I raised my eyes to the wind and wept.

Pure tears of joy.

It took us three weeks to voyage to Lundene where we paid silver to the Danes who exacted a toll from every ship that rowed upriver, and then it was another two days to Readingum where we beached *Dragon-Fire* and purchased horses with Sverri's money. It was autumn in Wessex, a time of mists and fallow fields. The peregrine falcons had returned from wherever they voyage in the high sky during the summer months and the oak leaves were turning a wind-shivered bronze.

We rode to Wintanceaster for we were told that was where Alfred was holding court, but the day we arrived he had ridden to one of his estates and was not expected to return that night and so, as the sun lowered over the scaffolding of the big church Alfred was building, I left Ragnar in the Two Cranes tavern and walked to the northern edge of the town. I had to ask directions and was pointed down a long alley that was choked with muddy ruts. Two pigs rooted in the alley that was bordered on one side by the town's high palisade and on the other by a wooden wall in which there was a low door marked by a cross. A score of beggars were crouched in the mud and dung outside the door. They were in rags. Some had lost arms or legs, most were covered in sores, while a blind woman held a scarred child. They all shuffled nervously aside as I approached.

I knocked and waited. I was about to knock again when a small hatch was slid aside in the door and I explained my business, then the hatch snapped shut and I waited again. The scarred child cried and the blind woman held a begging bowl toward me. A cat walked along the wall's top and a cloud of starlings flew westward. Two women with huge loads of firewood strapped on their backs passed me and behind them a man drove a cow. He bobbed his head in deference to me for I looked like a lord again. I was dressed in leather and had a sword at my side, though the sword was not Serpent-

Breath. My black cloak was held at my throat with a heavy brooch of silver and amber that I had taken from one of Sverri's dead crewmen, and that brooch was my only jewel for I had no arm rings.

Then the low door was unbolted and pulled inward on its leather hinges and a small woman beckoned me inside. I ducked through, she closed the door and led me across a patch of grass, pausing there to let me scrape the street dung off my boots before taking me to a church. She ushered me inside, then paused again to genuflect toward the altar. She muttered a prayer, then gestured that I should go through another door into a bare room with walls made of mud and wattle. Two stools were the only furniture and she told me I might sit on one of them, and then she opened a shutter so that the late sun could illuminate the room. A mouse scuttled in the floor rushes and the small woman tutted and then left me alone.

I waited again. A rook cawed on the roof. From some place nearby I could hear the rhythmic squirt of milk going into a pail. Another cow, its udder full, waited patiently just beyond the open shutter. The rook cawed again and then the door opened and three nuns came into the room. Two of them stood against the far wall, while the third just gazed at me and began to weep silently. "Hild," I said, and I stood to embrace her, but she held a hand out to keep me from touching her. She went on weeping, but she was smiling too, and then she put both her hands over her face and stayed that way for a long while.

"God has forgiven me," she finally spoke through her fingers.

"I am glad of it," I said.

She sniffed, took her hands from her face and indicated that I should sit again, and she sat opposite me and for a time we just looked at each other and I thought how I had missed her, not as a lover, but as a friend. I wanted to embrace her, and perhaps she sensed that for she sat straighter and spoke very formally. "I am now the Abbess Hildegyth," she said.

"I had forgotten your proper name is Hildegyth," I said.

"And it does my heart good to see you," she said primly. She was dressed in a coarse gray robe that matched the gowns of her two companions, both of whom were older women. The robes were belted with hemp-rope and had heavy hoods hiding their hair. A plain wooden cross hung at Hild's neck and she fingered it compulsively. "I have prayed for you," she went on.

"It seems your prayers worked," I said awkwardly.

"And I stole all your money," she said with a touch of her old mischief.

"I give it to you," I said, "willingly."

She told me about the nunnery. She had built it with the money from Fifhaden's hoard and now it housed sixteen sisters and eight laywomen. "Our lives," she said, "are dedicated to Christ and to Saint Hedda. You know who Hedda was?"

"I've never heard of her," I said.

The two older nuns, who had been looking at me with stern disapproval, suddenly broke into giggles. Hild smiled. "Hedda was a man," she told me gently, "and he was born in Northumbria and he was the first bishop of Wintanceaster. He is remembered as a most holy and good man, and I chose him because you are from Northumbria and it was your unwitting generosity that let us build this house in the town where Saint Hedda preached. We vowed to pray to him every day until you returned, and now we shall pray to him every day to thank him for answering our prayers."

I said nothing for I did not know what to say. I remember thinking that Hild's voice was forced as if she were persuading herself as well as me that she was happy, and I was wrong about that. It was forced because my presence brought her unpleasant memories, and in time I learned she truly was happy. She was useful. She had made her peace with her god and after she died she was remembered as a saint. Not so very long ago a bishop told me all about the most holy and blessed Saint Hildegyth and how she had been a shining example of Christian chastity and charity, and I was sorely tempted to tell him that I had once spread-eagled the saint among the buttercups, but managed to restrain myself. He was certainly right about her charity. Hild told me that the purpose of Saint Hedda's nunnery was not just to pray for me, its benefactor, but to heal the sick. "We are busy all day," she said, "and all night. We take the poor and we tend them. I've no doubt there are some waiting outside our gate right now."

"There are," I said.

"Then those poor folk are our purpose," she said, "and we are their servants." She gave me a brisk smile. "Now tell me what I have prayed to hear. Tell me your tales."

So I told her and I did not tell her all of what had happened, but made light of slavery, saying only that I had been chained so I could not escape. I told her of the voyages, of the strange places and of the people I had seen. I spoke of the land of ice and fire, of watching the great whales breach in the endless sea, and I told her of the long river that twisted into a land of birch trees and lingering snow, and I finished by saying that I was glad to be a free man again and grateful to her for making me so.

Hild was silent when I finished. The milk still spurted into the pail outside. A sparrow perched on the window ledge, preened itself and flew away. Hild had been staring at me, as if testing the veracity of my words. "Was it bad?" she asked after a while.

I hesitated, tempted to lie, then shrugged. "Yes," I said shortly.

"But now you are the Lord Uhtred again," she said, "and I have your possessions." She signaled to one of the nuns, who left the room. "We kept everything for you," Hild said brightly.

"Everything?" I asked.

"Except your horse," she said ruefully. "I couldn't bring the horse. What was he called? Witnere?"

"Witnere," I said.

"I fear he was stolen."

"Stolen?"

"The Lord Ivarr took him."

I said nothing because the nun had come back into the room with a cumbersome armful of weapons and mail. She had my helmet, my heavy coat of leather and mail, she had my arm rings and she had Wasp-Sting and Serpent-Breath, and she dropped them all at my feet and there were tears in my eyes as I leaned forward and touched Serpent-Breath's hilt. "The mail coat was damaged," Hild said, "so we had one of the king's armorers repair it."

"Thank you," I said.

"I have prayed," Hild said, "that you will not take revenge on King Guthred."

"He enslaved me," I said harshly. I could not take my hand from the sword. There had been so many moments of despair in the last two years, moments when I thought I would never touch a sword again, let alone Serpent-Breath, yet here she was, and my hand slowly closed about the hilt.

"Guthred did what he felt was best for his kingdom," Hild said sternly, "and he is a Christian."

"He enslaved me," I said again.

"And you must forgive him," Hild said forcefully, "as I have forgiven the men who wronged me and as God has forgiven me. I was a sinner," she went on, "a great sinner, but God has touched me and poured his grace into me and so forgiven me. So swear to me that you will spare Guthred."

"I will make no oaths," I said harshly, still holding Serpent-Breath.

"You are not an unkind man," Hild said. "I know that. You were kinder to me than I ever deserved. So be kind to Guthred. He's a good man."

"I will remember that when I meet him," I said evasively.

"And remember that he regretted what he did," Hild said, "and that he did it because he believed it would preserve his kingdom. And remember too that he has given this house money as a penance. We have much need of silver. There is no shortage of poor, sick folk, but there is ever a shortage of alms."

I smiled at her. Then I stood and I unbuckled the sword I had taken from one of Sven's men at Gyruum and I unpinned the brooch at my neck, and I dropped cloak, brooch, and sword onto the rushes. "Those you can sell," I said. Then, grunting with the effort, I pulled on my old mail coat and I buckled on my old swords and I picked up my wolf-crested helmet. The coat felt monstrously heavy because it had been so long since I had worn mail. It was also too big for me for I had become thinner in those years of pulling Sverri's oar. I slipped the arm rings over my hands, then looked at Hild. "I will give you one oath, Abbess Hildegyth," I said. She looked up at me and she was seeing the old Uhtred, the shining lord and sword-warrior. "I will support your house," I promised, "and you will have money from me and you will thrive and you will always have my protection."

She smiled at that, then reached into a purse that hung at her belt and held out a small silver cross. "And that is my gift to you," she said, "and I pray that you will revere it as I do and learn its lesson. Our Lord died on that cross for the evil we all do, and I have no doubt, Lord Uhtred, that some of the pain he felt at his death was for your sins."

She gave me the cross and our fingers touched and I looked into her eyes and she snatched her hand away. She blushed, though, and she looked up at me through half-lowered lids. For a heartbeat I saw the old Hild, the fragile, beautiful Hild, but then she composed her face and tried to look stern. "Now you can go to Gisela," she said.

I had not mentioned Gisela and now I pretended the name meant little. "She will be married by now," I said carelessly, "if she even lives."

"She lived when I left Northumbria," Hild said, "though that was eighteen months ago. She would not speak to her brother then, not after what he did to you. I spent hours comforting her. She was full of tears and anger. A strong girl, that one."

"And marriageable," I said harshly.

Hild smiled gently. "She swore to wait for you."

I touched Serpent-Breath's hilt. I was so full of hope and so racked by dread. Gisela. In my head I knew she could not match a slave's feverish dreams, but I could not rid my head of her.

"And perhaps she does wait for you," Hild said, then she stepped back, brusque suddenly. "Now we have prayers to say, folk to feed, and bodies to heal."

And so I was dismissed and I ducked out of the door in the convent wall to stand in the muddy alleyway. The beggars were allowed inside, leaving me leaning against the wooden wall with tears in my eyes. Folk edged by on the alley's far side, fearful of me for I was dressed for war with my two swords.

Gisela, I thought, Gisela. Maybe she did wait, but I doubted it for she was too valuable as a peace cow, but I knew I would go back north as soon as I could. I would go for Gisela. I gripped the silver cross until I could feel its edges hurting through the great callouses that Sverri's oar had made on my hand. Then I drew Serpent-Breath and I saw that Hild had looked after the blade well. It shone with a light coating of lard or lanolin that had prevented the patterned steel from rusting. I raised the sword to my lips and kissed her long blade. "You have men to kill," I told her, "and revenge to take."

And so she had.

I found a swordsmith the next day and he told me he was too busy and could not do my work for many days and I told him that he would do my work that day or else he would do no work ever again, and in the end we came to an agreement. He agreed to do my work that day.

Serpent-Breath is a lovely weapon. She was made by Ealdwulf the Smith in Northumbria and her blade is a magical thing, flexible and strong, and when she had been made I had wanted her plain iron hilt decorated with silver or gilt-bronze, but Ealdwulf had refused. "It's a tool," he had told me, "just a tool. Something to make your work easier."

She had handles of ash wood, one either side of the sword's tang, and over the years the twin handles had become polished and smooth. Such worn handles are dangerous. In battle they can slip in the hand, especially when blood is splashed on them, and so I told the swordsmith that I wanted new handles riveted onto the hilt, and that the handles must give a good grip, and that the small silver cross that Hild had given me must be embedded in the hilt's pommel.

"I shall do it, lord," he said.

"Today."

"I shall try, lord," he said weakly.

"You will succeed," I said, "and the work will be well done." I drew Serpent-Breath and her blade was bright in the shadowed room as I held her toward the smith's furnace and in the red firelight I saw the patterns on her steel. She had been forged by beating three smooth and four twisted rods into one metal blade. She had been heated and hammered, heated and hammered, and when she was done, and when the seven rods had become one single savage streak of shining steel, the twists in the four rods were left in the blade as ghostly patterns. That was how she got her name, for the patterns looked like the swirling breath of a dragon.

"She is a fine blade, lord," the swordsmith said.

"She is the blade that killed Ubba by the sea," I said, stroking the steel.

"Yes, lord," he said. He was terrified of me now.

"And you will do the work today," I stressed, and I put sword and scabbard on his fire-scarred bench. I laid Hild's cross on the hilt, then added a silver coin. I was no longer wealthy, but nor was I poor, and with the help of Serpent-Breath and Wasp-Sting I knew I would be rich again.

It was a lovely autumn day. The sun shone, making the new wood of Alfred's church glow like gold. Ragnar and I were waiting for the king and we sat on the newly-scythed grass in a courtyard and Ragnar watched a monk carrying a pile of parchments to the royal scriptorium. "Everything's written down here," he said, "everything! Can you read?"

"I can read and write."

He was impressed by that. "Is it useful?"

"It's never been useful for me," I admitted.

"So why do they do it?" he wondered.

"Their religion is written down," I said, "ours isn't."

"A written religion?" He was puzzled by that.

"They've got a book," I said, "and it's all in there."

"Why do they need it written down?"

"I don't know. They just do. And, of course, they write down the laws. Alfred loves making new laws, and they all have to be written in books."

"If a man can't remember the laws," Ragnar said, "then he's got too many of them."

The shouts of children interrupted us, or rather the offended screech of one small boy and the mocking laughter of a girl, and a heartbeat later the girl ran around the corner. She looked nine or ten years old, had golden hair as bright as the sun, and was carrying a carved wooden horse that was plainly the property of the small boy who followed her. The girl, brandishing the carved horse like a trophy, ran across the grass. She was coltish, thin and happy, while the boy, three or four years younger, was built more solidly and looked thoroughly miserable. He had no chance of catching the girl for she was much too quick, but she saw me and her eyes widened and she stopped in front of us. The boy caught up with her, but was too overawed by Ragnar and me to try to retrieve his wooden horse. A nurse, red-faced and panting, appeared around the corner and shouted the children's names. "Edward! Æthelflaed!"

"It's you!" Æthelflaed said, staring at me with a look of delight.

"It's me," I said, and I stood because Æthelflaed was the daughter of a king and Edward was the ætheling, the prince who might well rule Wessex when Alfred, his father, died.

"Where have you been?" Æthelflaed demanded, as if she had only missed me for a week or two.

"I have been in the land of giants," I said, "and places where fire runs like water and where the mountains are made of ice and where sisters are never, ever unkind to their little brothers."

"Never?" she asked, grinning.

"I want my horse!" Edward insisted and tried to snatch it from her, but Æthelflaed held it out of reach.

"Never use force to get from a girl," Ragnar said to Edward, "what you can take by guile."

"Guile?" Edward frowned, evidently unfamiliar with the word.

Ragnar frowned at Æthelflaed. "Is the horse hungry?"

"No." She knew he was playing a game and she wanted to see if she could win.

"But suppose I use magic," Ragnar suggested, "and make it eat grass?"

"You can't."

"How do you know?" he asked. "I have been to places where the wooden horses go to pasture every morning, and every night the grass grows to touch the sky and every day the wooden horses eat it back to nothing again."

"No they don't," she said, grinning.

"And if I say the magic words," Ragnar said, "your horse will eat the grass."

"It's my horse," Edward insisted.

"Magic words?" Æthelflaed was interested now.

"You have to put the horse on the grass," Ragnar said.

She looked at me, wanting reassurance, but I just shrugged, and so she looked back at Ragnar who was being very serious, and she decided she wanted to see some magic and so she carefully placed the wooden horse beside a swathe of cut grass. "Now?" she asked expectantly.

"You have to shut your eyes," Ragnar said, "turn around three times very fast, then shout Havacar very loudly."

"Havacar?"

"Careful!" he warned her, looking alarmed. "You can't say magic words carelessly."

So she shut her eyes, turned around three times, and while she did Ragnar pointed at the horse and nodded to Edward who snatched it up and ran off to the nurse, and by the time Æthelflaed, staggering slightly from dizziness, had shouted her magic word the horse was gone.

"You cheated!" she accused Ragnar.

"But you learned a lesson," I said, squatting beside her as if I were going to tell her a secret. I leaned forward and whispered in her ear, "Never trust a Dane."

She smiled at that. She had known me well during the long wet winter when her family had been fugitives in the marshes of Sumorsæte and in those dismal months she had learned to like me and I had come to like her. She reached out now and touched my nose. "How did that happen?"

"A man broke my nose," I said. It had been Hakka, striking me in *Trader* because he thought I was shirking at the oar.

"It's crooked," she said.

"It lets me smell crooked smells."

"What happened to the man who broke it?"

"He's dead," I said.

"Good," she said. "I'm going to be married."

"You are?" I asked.

"To Æthelred of Mercia," she said proudly, then frowned because a flicker of distaste had crossed my face.

"To my cousin?" I asked, trying to look pleased.

"Is Æthelred your cousin?" she asked.

"Yes."

"I'm to be his wife," she said, "and live in Mercia. Have you been to Mercia?"

"Yes."

"Is it nice?"

"You will like it," I said, though I doubted she would, not married to my snotty-nosed, pompous cousin, but I could hardly say that.

She frowned. "Does Æthelred pick his nose?"

"I don't think so," I said.

"Edward does," she said, "and then he eats it. Ugh." She leaned forward, gave me an impulsive kiss on my broken nose, then ran off to the nurse.

"A pretty girl," Ragnar said.

"Who is to be wasted on my cousin," I said.

"Wasted?"

"He's a bumptious little shit called Æthelred," I said. He had brought men to Ethandun, only a few, but enough to loft him into

Alfred's good graces. "The idea is," I went on, "that he'll be Ealdor-man of Mercia when his father dies and Alfred's daughter will be his wife, and that will bind Mercia to Wessex."

Ragnar shook his head. "There are too many Danes in Mercia. The Saxons won't ever rule there again."

"Alfred wouldn't waste his daughter on Mercia," I said, "unless he thought there was something to gain."

"To gain things," Ragnar said, "you have to be bold. You can't write things down and win, you have to take risks. Alfred's too cautious."

I half smiled. "You really think he's cautious?"

"Of course he is," Ragnar said scornfully.

"Not always," I said, then paused, wondering if I should say what I was thinking.

My hesitation provoked Ragnar. He knew I was hiding something. "What?" he demanded.

I still hesitated, then decided no harm could come from an old tale. "Do you remember that winter night in Cippanhamm?" I asked him. "When Guthrum was there and you all believed Wessex had fallen, and you and I drank in the church?"

"Of course I remember it, yes."

It had been the winter when Guthrum had invaded Wessex and it had seemed that Guthrum must have won the war, for the West Saxon army was scattered. Some thegns fled abroad, many made their own peace with Guthrum, while Alfred had been driven into hiding on the marshes of Sumorsæte. Yet Alfred, though he was defeated, was not broken, and he had insisted on disguising himself as a harpist and going secretly to Cippanhamm to spy on the Danes. That had almost ended in disaster, for Alfred did not possess the cunning to be a spy. I had rescued him that night, the same night that I had found Ragnar in the royal church. "And do you remember," I went on, "that I had a servant with me and he sat at the back of the church with a hood over his head and I ordered him to be silent?"

Ragnar frowned, trying to recall that winter night, then he nod-ded. "You did, that's right."

"He was no servant," I said, "that was Alfred."

Ragnar stared at me. In his head he was working things out, realizing that I had lied to him on that distant night, and he was understanding that if he had only known that the hooded servant had been Alfred then he could have won all Wessex for the Danes that same night. For a moment I regretted telling him, because I thought he would be angry with me, but then he laughed. "That was Alfred? Truly?"

"He went to spy on you," I said, "and I went to rescue him."

"It was Alfred? In Guthrum's camp?"

"He takes risks," I said, reverting to our talk of Mercia.

But Ragnar was still thinking of that far-off cold night. "Why didn't you tell me?" he demanded.

"Because I'd given him my oath."

"We would have made you richer than the richest king," Ragnar said. "We would have given you ships, men, horses, silver, women, anything! All you had to do was speak."

"I had given him my oath," I said again, and I remembered how close I had come to betraying Alfred. I had been so tempted to blurt out the truth. That night, with a handful of words, I could have ensured that no Saxon ever ruled in England again. I could have made Wessex into a Danish kingdom. I could have done all that by betraying a man I did not much like to a man I loved as a brother, and yet I had kept silent. I had given an oath and honor binds us to paths we might not choose. "Wyrd bið ful aræd," I said.

Fate is inexorable. It grips us like a harness. I thought I had escaped Wessex and escaped Alfred, yet here I was, back in his palace, and he returned that afternoon in a clatter of hooves and a noisy rush of servants, monks, and priests. Two men carried the king's bedding back to his chamber while a monk wheeled a barrow piled with documents which Alfred had evidently needed during his single day's absence. A priest hurried by with an altar cloth and a crucifix, while two more brought home the relics that accompanied Alfred on all his travels. Then came a group of the king's bodyguards, the only men allowed to

carry weapons in the royal precincts, and then more priests, all talking, among whom was Alfred himself. He had not changed. He still
had a clerk's look about him, lean and pale and scholarly. A priest was
talking urgently to him and he nodded his head as he listened. He was
dressed simply, his black cloak making him look like a cleric. He wore
no royal circlet, just a woolen cap. He was holding Æthelflaed's hand
and Æthelflaed, I noticed, was once again holding her brother's horse.
She was hopping on one leg rather than walking which meant that she
kept tugging her father away from the priest, but Alfred indulged her
for he was ever fond of his children. Then she tugged him purposely,
trying to draw him onto the grass where Ragnar and I had stood to
welcome him and he yielded to her, letting her bring him to us.

Ragnar and I knelt. I kept my head bowed.

"Uhtred has a broken nose," Æthelflaed told her father, "and the
man who did it is dead now."

A royal hand tipped my head up and I stared into that pale, narrow
face with its clever eyes. He looked drawn. I supposed that he was suffering another bout of the bowel cramps that made his life perpetual
agony. He was looking at me with his customary sternness, but then
he managed a half-smile. "I thought never to see you again, Lord
Uhtred."

"I owe you thanks, lord," I said humbly, "so I thank you."

"Stand," he said, and we both stood and Alfred looked at Ragnar. "I
shall free you soon, Lord Ragnar."

"Thank you, lord."

"But in a week's time we shall be holding a celebration here. We shall
rejoice that our new church is finished, and we shall formally betroth
this young lady to Lord Æthelred. I have summoned the Witan, and I
would ask you both to stay until our deliberations are over."

"Yes, lord," I said. In truth all I wanted was to go to Northumbria,
but I was beholden to Alfred and could wait a week or two.

"And at that time," he went on, "I may have matters," he paused,
as if fearing that he spoke too much, "matters," he said vaguely, "in
which you might be of service to me."

"Yes, lord," I repeated, then he nodded and walked away.

And so we waited. The town, anticipating the celebrations, filled with folk. It was a time of reunions. All the men who had led Alfred's army at Ethandun were there, and they greeted me with pleasure. Wiglaf of Sumorsæte and Harald of Defnascir and Osric of Wiltunscir and Arnulf of Suth Seaxa all came to Wintanceaster. They were the powerful men of the kingdom now, the great lords, the men who had stood by their king when he had seemed doomed. But Alfred did not punish those who had fled Wessex. Wilfrith was still Ealdorman of Hamptonscir, even though he had run to Frankia to escape Guthrum's attack, and Alfred treated Wilfrith with exaggerated courtesy, but there was still an unspoken divide between those who had stayed to fight and those who had run away.

The town also filled with entertainers. There were the usual jugglers and stilt-walkers, story-tellers and musicians, but the most successful was a dour Mercian called Offa who traveled with a pack of performing dogs. They were only terriers, the kind most men use to hunt rats, but Offa could make them dance, walk on their hind legs, and jump through hoops. One of the dogs even rode a pony, holding the reins in its teeth, and the other dogs followed with small leather pails to collect the crowd's pennies. To my surprise Offa was invited to the palace. I was surprised because Alfred was not fond of frivolity. His idea of a good time was to discuss theology, but he commanded the dogs be brought to the palace and I assumed it was because he thought they would amuse his children. Ragnar and I both went to the performance, and Father Beocca found me there.

Poor Beocca. He was in tears because I lived. His hair, which had always been red, was heavily touched by gray now. He was over forty, an old man, and his wandering eye had gone milky. He limped and had a palsied left hand, for which afflictions men mocked him, though none did in my presence. Beocca had known me since I was a child, for he had been my father's mass-priest and my early tutor, and he veered between loving me and detesting me, though he was ever my friend. He was also a good priest, a clever man, and one of Alfred's chaplains, and he was happy in the king's service. He was delirious now, beaming at me with tears in his eyes. "You live," he said, giving me a clumsy embrace.

"I'm a hard man to kill, father."

"So you are, so you are," he said, "but you were a weakly child."

"Me?"

"The runt of the litter, your father always said. Then you began to grow."

"Haven't stopped, have I?"

"Isn't that clever!" Beocca said, watching two dogs walk on their hind legs. "I do like dogs," he went on, "and you should talk to Offa."

"To Offa?" I asked, glancing at the Mercian who controlled his dogs by clicking his fingers or whistling.

"He was in Bebbanburg this summer," Beocca said. "He tells me your uncle has rebuilt the hall. It's bigger than it was. And Gytha is dead. Poor Gytha," he made the sign of the cross, "she was a good woman."

Gytha was my stepmother and, after my father was killed at Eofer-wic, she married my uncle and so was complicit in his usurpation of Bebbanburg. I said nothing of her death, but after the performance, when Offa and his two women assistants were packing up the hoops and leashing the dogs, I sought the Mercian out and said I would talk with him.

He was a strange man. He was tall like me, lugubrious, knowing, and, oddest of all, a Christian priest. He was really Father Offa. "But I was bored with the church," he told me in the Two Cranes where I had bought him a pot of ale, "and bored with my wife. I became very bored with her."

"So you walked away?"

"I danced away," he said, "I skipped away. I would have flown away if God had given me wings."

He had been traveling for a dozen years now, ranging throughout the Saxon and Danish lands in Britain and welcome everywhere because he provided laughter, though in conversation he was a gloomy man. But Beocca had been right. Offa had been in Northumbria and it was clear that he had kept a very sharp eye on all that he saw. So sharp that I understood why Alfred had invited his dogs to the palace. Offa was plainly one of the spies who brought news of Britain to the West Saxon court. "So tell me what happens in Northumbria," I invited him.

He grimaced and stared up at the ceiling beams. It was the pleasure of the Two Cranes for a man to cut a notch in the beam every time he hired one of the tavern's whores and Offa seemed to be counting the cuts, a job that might take a lifetime, then he glanced at me sourly. "News, lord," he said, "is a commodity like ale or hides or the service of whores. It is bought and sold." He waited until I laid a coin on the table between us, then all he did was look at the coin and yawn, so I laid another shilling beside the first. "Where do you wish me to begin?" he asked.

"The north."

Scotland was quiet, he said. King Aed had a fistula and that distracted him, though of course there were frequent cattle raids into Northumbria where my uncle, Ælfric the Usurper, now called himself the Lord of Bernicia.

"He wants to be king of Bernicia?" I asked.

"He wants to be left in peace," Offa said. "He offends no one, he amasses money, he acknowledges Guthred as king, and he keeps his swords sharp. He is no fool. He welcomes Danish settlers because they offer protection against the Scots, but he allows no Danes to enter Bebbanburg unless he trusts them. He keeps that fortress safe."

"But he wants to be king?" I insisted.

"I know what he does," Offa said tartly, "but what he wants is between Ælfric and his god."

"His son lives?"

"He has two sons now, both young, but his wife died."

"I heard."

"His eldest son liked my dogs and wanted his father to buy them. I said no."

He had little other news of Bebbanburg, other than that the hall had been enlarged and, more ominously, the outer wall and the low gate rebuilt higher and stronger. I asked if he and his dogs were welcome at Dunholm and he gave me a very sharp look and made the sign of the cross. "No man goes to Dunholm willingly," Offa said. "Your uncle gave me an escort through Kjartan's land and I was glad of it."

"So Kjartan thrives?" I asked bitterly.

"He spreads like a green bay tree," Offa said and, when he saw my puzzlement, enlarged the answer. "He thrives and steals and rapes and kills and he lurks in Dunholm. But his influence is wider, much wider. He has money and he uses it to buy friends. If a Dane complains about Guthred then you can be sure he has taken Kjartan's money."

"I thought Kjartan agreed to pay a tribute to Guthred?"

"It was paid for one year. Since then Good King Guthred has learned to do without."

"Good King Guthred?" I asked.

"That is how he is known in Eoferwic," Offa said, "but only to the Christians. The Danes consider him a gullible fool."

"Because he's a Christian?"

"Is he a Christian?" Offa asked himself. "He claims to be, and he goes to church, but I suspect he still half believes in the old gods. No, the Danes dislike him because he favors the Christians. He tried to levy a church tax on the Danes. It was not a clever idea."

"So how long does Good King Guthred have?" I asked.

"I charge more for prophecy," Offa said, "on the grounds that what is worthless must be made expensive."

I kept my money in its purse. "What of Ivarr?" I asked.

"What of him?"

"Does he still acknowledge Guthred as king?"

"For the moment," Offa said carefully, "but the Earl Ivarr is once again the strongest man in Northumbria. He took money from Kjartan, I hear, and used it to raise men."

"Why raise men?"

"Why do you think?" Offa asked sarcastically.

"To put his own man on the throne?"

"It would seem likely," Offa said, "but Guthred has an army too."

"A Saxon army?"

"A Christian army. Mostly Saxon."

"So civil war is brewing?"

"In Northumbria," Offa said, "civil war is always brewing."

"And Ivarr will win," I said, "because he's ruthless."

"He's more cautious than he was," Offa said. "Aed taught him that three years ago. But in time, yes, he will attack. When he's sure he can win."

"So Guthred," I said, "must kill Ivarr and Kjartan."

"What kings must do, lord, is beyond my humble competence. I teach dogs to dance, not men to rule. You wish to know about Mercia?"

"I wish to know about Guthred's sister."

Offa half smiled. "That one! She's a nun."

"Gisela!" I was shocked. "A nun? She's become a Christian?"

"I doubt she's a Christian," Offa said, "but going into a nunnery protected her."

"From whom?"

"Kjartan. He wanted the girl as a bride for his son."

That did surprise me. "But Kjartan hates Guthred," I said.

"But even so Kjartan decided Guthred's sister would be a suitable bride for his one-eyed son," Offa said. "I suspect he wants the son to be king in Eoferwic one day, and marrying Guthred's sister would help that ambition. Whatever, he sent men to Eoferwic and offered Guthred money, peace, and a promise to stop molesting Christians and I think Guthred was half tempted."

"How could he be?"

"Because a desperate man needs allies. Perhaps, for a day or two, Guthred dreamed of separating Ivarr and Kjartan. He certainly needs money, and Guthred has the fatal mind of a man who always believes the best in other people. His sister isn't so burdened with charitable ideas, and she would have none of it. She fled to a nunnery."

"When was this?"

"Last year. Kjartan took her rejection as another insult and has threatened to let his men rape her one by one."

"She's still in the nunnery?"

"She was when I left Eoferwic. She's safe from marriage there, isn't she? Perhaps she doesn't like men. Lots of nuns don't. But I doubt her brother will leave her there for very much longer. She's too useful as a peace cow."

"To marry Kjartan's son?" I asked scornfully.

"That won't happen," Offa said. He poured himself more ale. "Father Hrothweard, you know who he is?"

"A nasty man," I said, remembering how Hrothweard had raised the mob in Eoferwic to murder the Danes.

"Hrothweard is an exceedingly unpleasant creature," Offa agreed with rare enthusiasm. "He was the one who suggested the church tax on the Danes. He's also suggested that Guthred's sister become your uncle's new wife, and that notion probably does have some appeal to Guthred. Ælfric needs a wife, and if he were willing to send his spearmen south then it would hugely increase Guthred's strength."

"It would leave Bebbanburg unprotected," I said.

"Sixty men can hold Bebbanburg till Judgment Day," Offa said dismissively. "Guthred needs a larger army, and two hundred men from Bebbanburg would be a Godsend, and certainly worth a sister. Mind you, Ivarr would do anything to stop that marriage. He doesn't want the Saxons of northern Northumbria uniting with the Christians of Eoferwic. So, lord," he pushed his bench back as if to suggest that his survey was finished, "Britain is at peace, except for Northumbria, where Guthred is in trouble."

"No trouble in Mercia?" I asked.

He shook his head. "Nothing unusual."

"East Anglia?"

He paused. "No trouble there," he said after the hesitation, but I knew the pause had been deliberate, a bait on a hook, and so I waited. Offa just looked innocently at me and so I sighed, took another coin from my purse and placed it on the table. He rang it to make sure the silver was good. "King Æthelstan," he said, "Guthrum as was, negotiates with Alfred. Alfred doesn't think I know, but I do. Together they will divide England."

"They?" I asked. "Divide England? It's not theirs to divide!"

"The Danes will be given Northumbria, East Anglia, and the northeastern parts of Mercia. Wessex will gain the southwestern part of Mercia."

I stared at him. "Alfred won't agree to that," I said.

"He will."

"He wants all England," I protested.

"He wants Wessex to be safe," Offa said, spinning the coin on the table.

"So he'll agree to give up half England?" I asked in disbelief.

Offa smiled. "Think of it this way, lord," he said. "In Wessex there are no Danes, but where the Danes rule there are many Saxons. If the Danes agree not to attack Alfred then he can feel safe. But how can the Danes ever feel safe? Even if Alfred agrees not to attack them, they still have thousands of Saxons on their land and those Saxons could rise against them at any time, especially if they receive encouragement from Wessex. King Æthelstan will make his treaty with Alfred, but it won't be worth the parchment it's scribbled on."

"You mean Alfred will break the treaty?"

"Not openly, no. But he will encourage Saxon revolt, he will support Christians, he will foment trouble, and all the time he will say his prayers and swear eternal friendship with the enemy. You all think of Alfred as a pious scholar, but his ambition embraces all the land between here and Scotland. You see him praying, I see him dreaming. He will send missionaries to the Danes and you will think that's all he does, but whenever a Saxon kills a Dane then Alfred will have supplied the blade."

"No," I said, "not Alfred. His god won't let him be treacherous."

"What do you know of Alfred's god?" Offa asked scornfully, then closed his eyes. "'Then the Lord our God delivered the enemy to us,'" he intoned, "'and we struck him, and his sons, and all his tribe. We took all his cities and utterly destroyed the men, and the women, and the little children.'" He opened his eyes. "Those are the actions of Alfred's god, Lord Uhtred. You want more from the holy scriptures? "'The Lord thy God shall deliver all thy enemies to thee and thou shalt smite them and utterly destroy them.'" Offa grimaced. "Alfred believes in God's promises, and he dreams of a land free of pagans, a land where the enemy is utterly destroyed and where only godly Christians live. If there is one man in the island of Britain to fear, Lord Uhtred, that man is King Alfred." He stood. "I must make sure those stupid women have fed my dogs."

I watched him go and I thought he was a clever man who had misunderstood Alfred.

Which was, of course, what Alfred wanted me to think.

SEVEN

The Witan was the royal council, formed by the leading men of the kingdom, and it assembled for the dedication of Alfred's new church and to celebrate Æthelflaed's betrothal to my cousin. Ragnar and I had no business in their discussions so we drank in the town's taverns while they talked. Brida had been allowed to join us and Ragnar was the happier for it. She was an East Anglian Saxon and had once been my lover, but that had been years before when we were both children. Now she was a woman and more Danish than the Danes. She and Ragnar had never formally married, but she was his friend, lover, adviser, and sorceress. He was fair and she was dark, he ate like a boar while she picked at her food, he was raucous and she was quietly wise, but together they were happiness. I spent hours telling her about Gisela, and Brida listened patiently. "You really think she's waited for you?" she asked me.

"I hope so," I said and touched Thor's hammer.

"Poor girl," Brida said, smiling. "So you're in love?"

"Yes."

"Again," she said.

The three of us were in the Two Cranes on the day before Æthelflaed's formal betrothal and Father Beocca found us there. His hands were filthy with ink. "You've been writing again," I accused him.

"We are making lists of the shire fyrds," he explained. "Every man between twelve and sixty has to take an oath to serve the king now. I'm compiling the lists, but we've run out of ink."

"No wonder," I said, "it's all on you."

"They're mixing a new pot," he said, ignoring me, "and that will take time, so I thought you'd like to see the new church."

"I've been dreaming of little else," I said.

He insisted on taking us and the church was, indeed, a thing of utter splendor. It was bigger than any hall I had ever seen. It soared to a great height, its roof held up by massive oak beams that had been carved with saints and kings. The carvings had been painted, while the crowns of the kings and the halos and wings of the saints glinted with gold leaf that Beocca said had been applied by craftsmen brought from Frankia. The floor was stone-flagged, all of it, so that no rushes were needed and dogs were confused where to piss. Alfred had made a rule that no dogs were allowed in the church, but they got in anyway, so he had appointed a warden who was given a whip and charged with driving the animals out of the big nave, but the warden had lost a leg to a Danish war ax at Ethandun and he could only move slowly, so the dogs had no trouble avoiding him. The lower part of the church's walls were built of dressed stone, but the upper parts and the roof were of timber, and just below the roof were high windows that were filled with scraped horn so the rain could not come in. Every scrap of the walls was covered with stretched leather panels painted with pictures of heaven and hell. Heaven was populated with Saxons while hell seemed to be the abode of Danes, though I noticed, with surprise, that a couple of priests seemed to have tumbled down to the devil's flames. "There are bad priests," Beocca assured me earnestly. "Not many, of course."

"And there are good priests," I said, pleasing Beocca, "talking of which, do you hear anything of Father Pyrlig?" Pyrlig was a Briton who had fought beside me at Ethandun and I was fond of him. He spoke Danish and had been sent to be one of Guthrum's priests in East Anglia.

"He does the Lord's work," Beocca said enthusiastically. "He says the Danes are being baptized in great numbers! I truly believe we are seeing the conversion of the pagans."

"Not this pagan," Ragnar said.

Beocca shook his head. "Christ will come to you one day, Lord Ragnar, and you will be astonished by his grace."

Ragnar said nothing. I could see, though, that he was as impressed as I was by Alfred's new church. The tomb of Saint Swithun was railed in silver and lay in front of the high altar that was covered with a red cloth as big as a dragon-boat's sail. On the altar were a dozen fine wax candles in silver holders that flanked a big silver cross inlaid with gold that Ragnar muttered would be worth a month's voyaging to capture. Either side of the cross were reliquaries; boxes and flasks of silver and gold, all studded with jewels, and some had small crystal windows through which the relics could be glimpsed. Mary Magdalene's toe ring was there, and what remained of the feather from the dove that Noah had released from the ark. There was Saint Kenelm's horn spoon, a flask of dust from Saint Hedda's tomb, and a hoof from the donkey that Jesus rode into Jerusalem. The cloth with which Mary Magdalene had washed Jesus's feet was encased in a great golden chest and next to it, and quite dwarfed by the gold's splendor, were Saint Oswald's teeth, the gift from Guthred. The two teeth were still encased in their silver oyster pot which looked very shabby compared to the other vessels. Beocca showed us all the holy treasures, but was most proud of a scrap of bone displayed behind a shard of milky crystal. "I found this one," he said, "and it's most exciting!" He lifted the lid of the box and took out the bone, which looked like something left over from a bad stew. "It's Saint Cedd's aestel!" Beocca said with awe in his voice. He made the sign of the cross and peered at the yellowed bone sliver with his one good eye as if the arrow-head shaped relic had just dropped from heaven.

"Saint Cedd's what?" I asked.

"His aestel."

"What's an aestel?" Ragnar asked. His English, after years of being a hostage, was good, but some words still confused him.

"An aestel is a device to help reading," Beocca said. "You use it to follow the lines. It's a pointer."

"What's wrong with a finger?" Ragnar wanted to know.

"It can smear the ink. An aestel is clean."

"And that one really belonged to Saint Cedd?" I asked, pretending to be amazed.

"It did, it did," Beocca said, almost delirious with wonder, "the holy Cedd's very own aestel. I discovered it! It was in a little church in Dornwaraceaster and the priest there was an ignorant fellow and had no idea what it was. It was in a horn box and Saint Cedd's name was scratched on the box and the priest couldn't even read the writing! A priest! Illiterate! So I confiscated it."

"You mean you stole it?"

"I took it into safekeeping!" he said, offended.

"And when you're a saint," I said, "someone will put one of those smelly shoes of yours into a golden box and worship it."

Beocca blushed. "You tease me, Uhtred, you tease me." He laughed, but I saw from his blush that I had touched on his secret ambition. He wanted to be declared a saint, and why not? He was a good man, far better than many I have known who are now revered as saints.

Brida and I visited Hild that afternoon and I gave her nunnery thirty shillings, almost all the money I had, but Ragnar was blithely confident that Sverri's fortune would come from Jutland and that Ragnar would share with me, and in that belief I pressed the money on Hild who was delighted by the silver cross in Serpent-Breath's hilt. "You must use the sword wisely from now on," she told me sternly.

"I always use it wisely."

"You have harnessed the power of God to the blade," she said, "and it must do nothing evil."

I doubted I would obey that command, but it was good to see Hild. Alfred had given her a gift of some of the dust from Saint Hedda's tomb and she told me that mixed with curds it made a miraculous medicine that had prompted at least a dozen cures among the nunnery's sick. "If you are ever ill," she said, "you must come here and we shall mix the dust with fresh curds and anoint you."

I saw Hild again the next day when we were all summoned to the church for its consecration and to witness Æthelflaed's betrothal. Hild, with all the other nuns of Wintanceaster, was in the side aisle, while Ragnar, Brida, and I, because we arrived late, had to stand at the very back of the church. I was taller than most men, but I could still see very little of the ceremony which seemed to last forever. Two bishops said prayers, priests scattered holy water, and a choir of monks chanted. Then the Archbishop of Contwaraburg preached a long sermon which, bizarrely, said nothing about the new church, nor about the betrothal, but instead berated the clergy of Wessex for wearing short tunics instead of long robes. This bestial practice, the archbishop thundered, had offended the holy father in Rome and must stop forthwith on pain of excommunication. A priest standing near us was wearing a short tunic and tried to crouch so that he looked like a dwarf in a long robe. The monks sang again and then my cousin, red-haired and cocksure, strutted to the altar and little Æthelflaed was led to his side by her father. The archbishop mumbled over them, they were sprinkled with holy water, then the newly betrothed couple were presented to the congregation and we all dutifully cheered.

Æthelflaed was hurried away as the men in the church congratulated Æthelred. He was twenty years old, eleven years older than Æthelflaed, and he was a short, red-haired, bumptious young man who was convinced of his own importance. That importance was that he was his father's son, and his father was the chief ealdorman in southern Mercia which was the region of that country least infested by Danes, and so one day Æthelred would become the leader of the free Mercian Saxons. Æthelred, in short, could deliver a large part of Mercia to Wessex's rule, which was why he had been promised Alfred's daughter in marriage. He made his way down the nave, greeting the lords of Wessex, then saw me and looked surprised. "I heard you were captured in the north," he said.

"I was."

"And here you are. And you're just the man I want." He smiled, certain that I liked him, in which certainty he could not have been more mistaken, but Æthelred assumed that everyone else in the whole world was envious of him and wanted nothing more than to be his friend. "The king," he said, "has honored me with the command of his household guard."

"Alfred has?" I asked, surprised.

"At least until I assume my father's duties."

"Your father's well, I trust?" I asked drily.

"He's sick," Æthelred said, sounding pleased, "so who knows how long I shall command Alfred's guard. But you'd be of great use to me if you would serve in the household troops."

"I'd rather shovel shit," I said, then held a hand toward Brida. "Do you remember Brida?" I asked. "You tried to rape her ten years ago."

He went bright red, said nothing, but just hurried away. Brida laughed as he retreated, then gave a very small bow because Ælswith, Alfred's wife, was walking past us. Ælswith ignored us, for she had never liked Brida or me, but Eanflæd smiled. She was Ælswith's closest companion and I kissed my hand toward her. "She was a tavern whore," I told Brida, "and now she rules the king's household."

"Good for her," Brida said.

"Does Alfred know she was a whore?" Ragnar asked.

"He pretends not to know," I said.

Alfred came last. He looked sick, but that was nothing unusual. He half inclined his head to me, but said nothing, though Beocca scuttled over to me as we waited for the crowd at the door to thin. "You're to see the king after midday prayers," he told me, "and you too, Lord Ragnar. I shall summon you."

"We'll be in the Two Cranes," I told him.

"I don't know why you like that tavern."

"Because it's a brothel too, of course," I said. "And if you go there, father, make sure you carve a notch in one of the beams to show you humped one of the ladies. I'd recommend Ethel. She's only got one hand, but it's a miracle what she can do with it."

"Oh dear God, Uhtred, dear God. What an ugly cesspit you have for a mind. If I ever marry, and I pray God for that dear happiness, I shall go unstained to my bride."

"I pray you do too, father," I said, and I meant it. Poor Beocca. He was so ugly and he dreamed of a wife, but he had never found one and I doubted he ever would. There were plenty of women willing to marry him, squint and all, for he was, after all, a privileged priest high in Alfred's estimation, but Beocca was waiting for love to strike him like a lightning bolt. He would stare at beautiful women, dream his hopeless dreams, and say his prayers. Perhaps, I thought, his heaven would reward him with a glorious bride, but nothing I had ever heard about the Christian heaven suggested that such joys were available.

Beocca fetched us from the Two Cranes that afternoon. I noted that he glanced at the beams and looked shocked at the number of notches, but he said nothing of them, leading us instead to the palace where we surrendered our swords at the gatehouse. Ragnar was commanded to wait in the courtyard while Beocca took me to Alfred who was in his study, a small room that had been part of the Roman building that was the heart of Wintanceaster's palace. I had been in the room before, so I was not surprised by the scant furniture, nor by the piles of parchments that spilled from the wide window ledge. The walls were of stone, and whitewashed, so it was a well-lit room, though for some reason Alfred had a score of candles burning in one corner. Each candle had been scored with deep lines about a thumb's width apart. The candles were certainly not there for illumination because an autumnal sun streamed through the big window, and I did not want to ask what purpose the candles served in case he told me. I merely assumed there was a candle for every saint he had prayed to over the last few days and each of the scored lines was a sin that had to be burned away. Alfred had a very acute conscience for sins, especially mine.

Alfred was dressed in a brown robe so that he looked like a monk. His hands, like Beocca's, were ink-stained. He appeared pale and sick. I had heard his stomach troubles were bad again and every now and then he flinched as a pain stabbed at his belly. But he greeted me warmly enough. "Lord Uhtred. I trust you are in health?"

"I am, lord," I said, still kneeling, "and hope the same for you."

"God afflicts me. There is purpose in that, so I must be glad of it. Stand, please. Is Earl Ragnar with you?"

"He is outside, lord."

"Good," he said. I stood in the only space left in the small room. The mysterious candles took up a large area, and Beocca was standing against the wall next to Steapa who took up even more. I was surprised to see Steapa. Alfred favored clever men and Steapa was hardly clever. He had been born a slave, now he was a warrior, and in truth he was not much good for anything beyond consuming ale and slaughtering the king's enemies, two tasks he did with a brutal efficiency. Now he stood just beyond the king's high writing desk with an awkward expression as though he were unsure why he had been summoned.

I thought Alfred would ask about my ordeal, for he liked to hear stories of distant places and strange people, but he ignored it utterly, instead asking for my opinion of Guthred and I said I liked Guthred, which seemed to surprise the king. "You like him," Alfred asked, "despite what he did to you?"

"He had little choice, lord," I said. "I told him that a king must be ruthless in defense of his realm."

"Even so," Alfred watched me with a dubious face.

"If we mere men, lord, wanted gratitude from kings," I said with my most earnest expression, "then we should be forever disappointed."

He looked at me sternly then gave a rare burst of laughter. "I've missed you, Uhtred," he said. "You are the only man who is impertinent with me."

"He did not mean it, lord," Beocca said anxiously.

"Of course he meant it," Alfred said. He pushed some parchments aside on the window ledge and sat down. "What do you think of my candles?" he asked me.

"I find, lord," I said thoughtfully, "that they're more effective at night."

"I am trying to develop a clock," he said.

"A clock?"

"To mark the passing hours."

"You look at the sun, lord," I said, "and at night, the stars."

"Not all of us can see through clouds," he remarked tartly. "Each mark is supposed to represent one hour. I am endeavoring to find which markings are most accurate. If I can find a candle that burns twenty-four divisions between midday and midday then I shall always know the hour, won't I?"

"Yes, lord," I said.

"Our time must be properly spent," he said, "and to do that we must first know how much time we have."

"Yes, lord," I said again, my boredom obvious.

Alfred sighed, then looked through the parchments and found one embossed with a huge seal of sickly-green wax. "This is a message from King Guthred," he said. "He has asked for my advice and I am minded to offer it. To which end I am sending an embassy to Eoferwic. Father Beocca has agreed to speak for me."

"You do me a privilege, lord," Beocca said happily, "a great privilege."

"And Father Beocca will be carrying precious gifts for King Guthred," Alfred went on, "and those gifts must be protected, which means an escort of warriors. I thought, perhaps, you would provide that protection, Lord Uhtred? You and Steapa?"

"Yes, lord," I said, enthusiastically this time, for all I dreamed of was Gisela and she was in Eoferwic.

"But you are to understand," Alfred said, "that Father Beocca is in charge. He is my ambassador and you will take his orders. Is that understood?"

"Indeed, lord," I said, though in truth I had no need to accept

Alfred's instructions. I was no longer sworn to him, I was not a West Saxon, but he was asking me to go where I wanted to go and so I did not remind him that he lacked my oath.

He did not need reminding. "You will all three return before Christmas to report on your embassy," he said, "and if you do not swear to that," he was looking at me now, "and swear to be my man, then I shall not let you go."

"You want my oath?" I asked him.

"I insist on it, Lord Uhtred," he said.

I hesitated. I did not want to be Alfred's man again, but I sensed there was far more behind this so-called embassy than the provision of advice. If Alfred wanted to advise Guthred why not do it in a letter? Or send a half-dozen priests to weary Guthred's ears? But Alfred was sending Steapa and myself and, in truth, the two of us were only fit for one thing, fighting. And Beocca, though undoubtedly a good man, was hardly an impressive ambassador. Alfred, I thought, wanted Steapa and me in the north, which meant he wanted violence done, and that was encouraging, but still I hesitated and that annoyed the king.

"Must I remind you," Alfred asked with some asperity, "that I went to a deal of trouble to free you from your slavery?"

"Why did you do that, lord?" I asked.

Beocca hissed, angry that I had not yielded immediately to the king's wishes, and Alfred looked affronted, but then he seemed to accept that my question deserved an answer. He motioned Beocca to silence, then fidgeted with the seal on Guthred's letter, shredding scraps of green wax. "The Abbess Hildegyth convinced me," he said at last. I waited. Alfred glanced at me and saw I thought there was more to the answer than Hild's entreaties. He shrugged. "And it seemed to me," he said awkwardly, "that I owed you more than I repaid you for your services at Æthelingæg."

It was hardly an apology, but it was an acknowledgment that five hides were no reward for a kingdom. I bowed my head. "Thank you, lord," I said, "and you shall have my oath." I did not want to give it to him, but what choice did I have? Thus are our lives decided. For years I had swayed between love of the Danes and loyalty to the Saxons and there, beside the guttering candle-clocks, I gave my services to a king I disliked. "But might I ask, lord," I went on, "why Guthred needs advice?"

"Because Ivarr Ivarson tires of him," Alfred said, "and Ivarr would have another, more compliant, man on Northumbria's throne."

"Or take the throne for himself?" I suggested.

"Ivarr, I think, does not want a king's heavy responsibilities," Alfred said. "He wants power, he wants money, he wants warriors, and he wants another man to do the hard work of enforcing the laws on the Saxons and raising taxes from the Saxons. And he will choose a Saxon to do that." That made sense. It was how the Danes usually governed their conquered Saxons. "And Ivarr," Alfred went on, "no longer wants Guthred."

"Why not, lord?"

"Because King Guthred," Alfred said, "attempts to impose his law equally on Danes and Saxons alike."

I remembered Guthred's hope that he would be a just king. "Is that bad?" I asked.

"It is foolishness," Alfred said, "when he decrees that every man, whether pagan or Christian, must donate his tithe to the church."

Offa had mentioned that church tax and it was, indeed, a foolish imposition. The tithe was a tenth of everything a man grew, reared or made, and the pagan Danes would never accept such a law. "I thought you would approve, lord," I said mischievously.

"I approve of tithing, of course," Alfred said wearily, "but a tithe should be given with a willing heart."

"*Hilarem datorem diligit Deus*," Beocca put in unhelpfully. "It says so in the gospel book."

"'God approves a cheerful giver,'" Alfred provided the translation, "but when a land is half pagan and half Christian you do not encourage unity by offending the more powerful half. Guthred must be a Dane to the Danes and a Christian to the Christians. That is my advice to him."

"If the Danes rebel," I asked, "does Guthred have the power to defeat them?"

"He has the Saxon fyrd, what's left of it, and some Danish Christians, but too few of those, alas. My estimate is that he can raise six hundred spears, but fewer than half of those will be reliable in battle."

"And Ivarr?" I asked.

"Nearer a thousand. And if Kjartan joins him then he will have far more. And Kjartan is encouraging Ivarr."

"Kjartan," I said "doesn't leave Dunholm."

"He doesn't need to leave Dunholm," Alfred said, "he needs only to send two hundred men to assist Ivarr. And Kjartan, I am told, has a particular hatred of Guthred."

"That's because Guthred pissed all over his son," I said.

"He did what?" The king stared at me.

"Washed his hair with piss," I said. "I was there."

"Dear God," Alfred said, plainly thinking that every man north of the Humber was a barbarian.

"So what Guthred must do now," I said, "is destroy Ivarr and Kjartan?"

"That is Guthred's business," Alfred said distantly.

"He must make peace with them," Beocca said, frowning at me.

"Peace is always desirable," Alfred said, though without much enthusiasm.

"If we are to send missionaries to the Northumbrian Danes, lord," Beocca urged, "then we must have peace."

"As I said," Alfred retorted, "peace is desirable." Again he spoke without fervor and that, I thought, was his real message. He knew there could not be peace.

I remembered what Offa, the dog-dancing man, had told me about marrying Gisela to my uncle. "Guthred could persuade my uncle to support him," I suggested.

Alfred gave me a speculative look. "Would you approve of that, Lord Uhtred?"

"Ælfric is a usurper," I said. "He swore to recognize me as heir to Bebbanburg and broke that oath. No, lord, I would not approve."

Alfred peered at his candles that guttered away, smearing the whitewashed wall with their smoke. "This one," he said, "burns too fast." He licked his fingers, pinched out the flame, and put the dead candle in a basket with a dozen other rejects. "It is greatly to be wished," he said, still examining his candles, "that a Christian king reigns in Northumbria. It is even desirable that it should be Guthred. He is a Dane, and if we are to win the Danes to a knowledge and love of Christ then we need Danish kings who are Christians. What we do not need is Kjartan and Ivarr making war on the Christians. They would destroy the church if they could."

"Kjartan certainly would," I said.

"And I doubt your uncle is strong enough to defeat Kjartan and Ivarr," Alfred said, "even if he were willing to ally himself with Guthred. No," he paused, thinking, "the only solution is for Guthred to make his peace with the pagans. That is my advice to him." He spoke the last few words directly to Beocca.

Beocca looked pleased. "Wise advice, lord," he said, "praise be to God."

"And speaking of pagans," Alfred glanced at me, "what will the Earl Ragnar do if I release him?"

"He won't fight for Ivarr," I said firmly.

"You can be sure of that?"

"Ragnar hates Kjartan," I said, "and if Kjartan is allied to Ivarr then Ragnar will hate both men. Yes, lord, I can be sure of that."

"So if I release Ragnar," Alfred asked, "and allow him to go north with you, he will not turn against Guthred?"

"He'll fight Kjartan," I said, "but what he will think of Guthred I don't know."

Alfred considered that answer, then nodded. "If he is opposed to Kjartan," he said, "that should be sufficient." He turned and smiled at Beocca. "Your embassy, father, is to preach peace to Guthred. You will advise him to be a Dane among the Danes and a Christian among the Saxons."

"Yes, of course, lord," Beocca said, but it was plain he was thoroughly confused. Alfred talked peace, but was sending warriors, for he knew there could not be peace while Ivarr and Kjartan lived. He dared not make such a pronouncement publicly, or else the northern Danes would accuse Wessex of interfering in Northumbrian affairs. They would resent that, and their resentment would add strength to Ivarr's cause. And Alfred wanted Guthred on Northumbria's throne because Guthred was a Christian, and a Christian Northumbria was more likely to welcome a Saxon army when it came, if it came. Ivarr and Kjartan would make Northumbria into a pagan stronghold if they could, and Alfred wanted to prevent that. Beocca, therefore, was to preach peace and conciliation, but Steapa, Ragnar, and I would carry swords. We were his dogs of war and Alfred knew full well that Beocca could not control us.

He dreamed, Alfred did, and his dreams encompassed all the isle of Britain.

And I was once again to be his sworn man, and that was not what I had wanted, but he was sending me north, to Gisela, and that I did want and so I knelt to him, placed my hands between his, swore the oath and thus lost my freedom. Then Ragnar was summoned and he also knelt and was granted his freedom.

And next day we all rode north.

Gisela was already married.

I heard that from Wulfhere, Archbishop of Eoferwic, and he should have known because he had performed the ceremony in his big church. It seemed I had arrived five days too late and when I heard the news I felt a despair like that which had caused my tears in Haithabu. Gisela was married.

It was autumn when we reached Northumbria. Peregrine falcons patrolled the sky, stooping on the newly arrived woodcock or on the gulls that flocked in the rain-drowned furrows. It had been a fine autumn so far, but the rains arrived from the west as we traveled north through Mercia. There were ten of us; Ragnar and Brida, Steapa and myself, and Father Beocca who had charge of three servants who led the packhorses carrying our shields, armor, changes of clothing, and the gifts Alfred was sending to Guthred. Ragnar led two men who had shared his exile. All of us were mounted on fine horses that Alfred had given us and we should have made good time, but Beocca slowed us. He hated being on horseback and even though we padded his mare's saddle with two thick fleeces he was still crippled by soreness. He had spent the journey rehearsing the speech with which he would greet Guthred, practicing and practicing the words until we were all bored by them. We had encountered no trouble in Mercia, for Ragnar's presence ensured that we were welcome in Danish halls. There was still a Saxon king in northern Mercia, Ceolwulf was his name, but we did not meet him and it was plain that the real power lay with the great Danish lords. We crossed the border into Northumbria under a pelting rainstorm and it was still raining as we rode into Eoferwic.

And there I learned that Gisela was married. Not only married, but gone from Eoferwic with her brother. "I solemnized the marriage," Wulfhere, the archbishop, told us. He was spooning barley soup into his mouth and long dribbles hung in glutinous loops in his white beard. "The silly girl wept all through the ceremony, and she wouldn't take the mass, but it makes no difference. She's still married."

I was horrified. Five days, that was all. Fate is inexorable. "I thought she'd gone to a nunnery," I said, as if that made any difference.

"She lived in a nunnery," Wulfhere said, "but putting a cat into a stable doesn't make it a horse, does it? She was hiding herself away! It was a waste of a perfectly good womb! She's been spoiled, that's her trouble. Allowed to live in a nunnery where she never said a prayer. She needed the strap, that one. A good thrashing, that's what I'd have given her. Still, she's not in the nunnery now. Guthred pulled her out and married her off."

"To whom?" Beocca asked.

"Lord Ælfric, of course."

"Ælfric came to Eoferwic?" I asked, astonished, for my uncle was as reluctant to leave Bebbanburg as Kjartan was to quit the safety of Dunholm.

"He didn't come," Wulfhere said. "He sent a score of men and one of those stood in for Lord Ælfric. It was a proxy wedding. Quite legal."

"It is," Beocca said.

"So where is she?" I asked.

"Gone north," Wulfhere waved his horn spoon. "They've all gone. Her brother's taken her to Bebbanburg. Abbot Eadred's with them, and he's taken Saint Cuthbert's corpse, of course. And that awful man Hrothweard went as well. Can't stand Hrothweard. He was the idiot who persuaded Guthred to impose the tithe on the Danes. I told Guthred it was foolishness, but Hrothweard claimed to have got his orders directly from Saint Cuthbert, so nothing I could say had the slightest effect. Now the Danes are probably gathering their forces, so it's going to be war."

"War?" I asked. "Has Guthred declared war on the Danes?" It sounded unlikely.

"Of course not! But they've got to stop him." Wulfhere used the sleeve of his robe to mop up his beard.

"Stop him from doing what?" Ragnar asked.

"Reaching Bebbanburg, of course, what else? The day Guthred delivers his sister and Saint Cuthbert to Bebbanburg is the day Ælfric gives him two hundred spearmen. But the Danes aren't going to stand for that! They more or less put up with Guthred, but only because he's too weak to order them about, but if he gets a couple of hundred prime spearmen from Ælfric, the Danes will squash him like a louse. I should think Ivarr is already gathering troops to stop the nonsense."

"They've taken the blessed Saint Cuthbert with them?" Beocca asked.

The archbishop frowned at Beocca. "You're an odd ambassador," he said.

"Odd, lord?"

"Can't look straight, can you? Alfred must be hard up for men if he sends an ugly thing like you. There used to be a priest in Bebbanburg with a squint. That was years ago, back in old Lord Uhtred's day."

"That was me," Beocca said eagerly.

"Don't be a fool, of course it wasn't. The fellow I'm talking about was young and red-haired. Take all the chairs, you brainless idiot!" he turned on a servant, "all six of them. And bring me more bread." Wulfhere was planning to escape before war broke out between Guthred and the Danes and his courtyard was busy with wagons, oxen, and packhorses because the treasures of his big church were being packed up so they could be taken to someplace that offered safety. "King Guthred took Saint Cuthbert," the archbishop said, "because that's Ælfric's price. He wants the corpse as well as the womb. I just hope he remembers which one to poke."

My uncle, I realized, was making his bid for power. Guthred was weak, but he did possess the great treasure of Cuthbert's corpse and if Ælfric could gain possession of the saint then he would become the guardian of all Northumbria's Christians. He would also make a small fortune from the pennies of pilgrims. "What he's doing," I said, "is remaking Bernicia. He'll call himself king before too long."

Wulfhere looked at me as though I was not a complete fool. "You're right," he said, "and his two hundred spearmen will stay with Guthred for a month, that's all. Then they'll go home and the Danes will roast Guthred over a fire. I warned him! I told him a dead saint was worth more than two hundred spearmen, but he's desperate. And if you want to see him, you'd best go north." Wulfhere had received us because we were Alfred's ambassadors, but he had offered us neither food nor shelter and he plainly wanted to see the back of us as soon as decently possible. "Go north," he reiterated, "and you might find the silly man alive."

We went back to the tavern where Steapa and Brida waited and I cursed the three spinners who had let me come so close, and then denied me. Gisela had been gone four days, which was more than enough time to reach Bebbanburg, and her brother's desperate bid for Ælfric's support had probably stirred the Danes to revolt. Not that I cared about the anger of the Danes. I was only thinking of Gisela.

"We have to go north," Beocca said, "and find the king."

"You step inside Bebbanburg," I told him, "and Ælfric will kill you." Beocca, when he fled Bebbanburg, had taken all the parchments that proved I was the rightful lord, and Ælfric knew and resented that.

"Ælfric won't kill a priest," Beocca said, "not if he cares for his soul. And I'm an ambassador! He can't kill an ambassador."

"So long as he's safe inside Bebbanburg," Ragnar put in, "he can do whatever he likes."

"Maybe Guthred didn't reach Bebbanburg," Steapa said, and I was so surprised that he had spoken at all that I did not really pay attention. Nor, it seemed, did anyone else, for none of us responded. "If they don't want the girl married," Steapa went on, "they'll stop him."

"They?" Ragnar asked.

"The Danes, lord," Steapa said.

"And Guthred will be traveling slowly," Brida added.

"He will?" I asked.

"You said he's taken Cuthbert's corpse with him."

Hope stirred in me. Steapa and Brida were right. Guthred might be intent on reaching Bebbanburg, but he could travel no faster than the corpse could be carried, and the Danes would want to stop him. "He could be dead by now," I said.

"Only one way to find out," Ragnar said.

We rode next dawn, taking the Roman road north, and we rode as fast we could. So far we had coddled Alfred's horses, but now we drove them hard, though we were still slowed by Beocca. Then, as the morning wore on, the rains came again. Gentle at first, but soon hard enough to make the ground treacherous. The wind rose, and it was in our faces. Thunder sounded far off and the rain fell with a new intensity and we were all spattered by mud, we were all cold and all soaked. The trees thrashed, shedding their last leaves into the bitter wind. It was a day to be inside a hall, beside a vast fire.

We found the first bodies beside the road. They were two men who lay naked with their wounds washed bloodless by the rain. One of the dead men had a broken sickle beside him. Another three corpses were a half-mile to the north, and two of them had wooden crosses about their necks which meant they were Saxons. Beocca made the sign of the cross over their bodies. Lightning whipped the hills to the west, then Ragnar pointed ahead and I saw, through the hammering rain, a settlement beside the road. There were a few low houses, what might have been a church, and a high-ridged hall within a wooden palisade.

There was a score of horses tied to the hall's palisade and, as we appeared from the storm, a dozen men ran from the gate with swords and spears. They mounted and galloped down the road toward us, but slowed when they saw the arm rings Ragnar and I wore. "Are you Danes?" Ragnar shouted.

"We're Danes!" They lowered their swords and turned their horses to escort us. "Have you seen any Saxons?" one of them asked Ragnar.

"Only dead ones."

We stabled the horses in one of the houses, pulling down part of the roof to enlarge the door so the horses could be taken inside. There was a Saxon family there and they shrank from us. The woman whimpered and held her hands toward us in mute prayer. "My daughter's ill," she said.

The girl lay in a dark corner, shivering. She did not look ill so much as terrified. "How old is she?" I asked.

"Eleven years, lord, I think," the girl's mother answered.

"She was raped?" I asked.

"By four men, lord," she said.

"She's safe now," I said, and I gave them coins to pay for the damage to the roof and we left Alfred's servants and Ragnar's two men to guard the horses, then joined the Danes in the big hall where a fire burned fierce in the central hearth. The men about the flames made room for us, though they were confused that we traveled with a Christian priest. They looked at the bedraggled Beocca suspiciously, but Ragnar was so obviously a Dane that they said nothing, and his arm rings, like mine, indicated that he was a Dane of the highest rank. The men's leader must have been impressed by Ragnar for he half bowed. "I am Hakon," he said, "of Onhripum."

"Ragnar Ragnarson," Ragnar introduced himself. He introduced neither Steapa nor myself, though he did nod toward Brida. "And this is my woman."

Hakon knew of Ragnar, which was not surprising for Ragnar's name was famous in the hills to the west of Onhripum. "You were a hostage in Wessex, lord?" he asked.

"No longer," Ragnar said shortly.

"Welcome home, lord," Hakon said.

Ale was brought to us, and bread and cheese and apples. "The dead we saw on the road," Ragnar asked, "that was your work?"

"Saxons, lord. We're to stop them gathering."

"You certainly stopped those men gathering," Ragnar said, provoking a smile from Hakon. "Whose orders?" Ragnar asked.

"The Earl Ivarr, lord. He's summoned us. And if we find Saxons with weapons we're to kill them."

Ragnar mischievously jerked his head at Steapa. "He's a Saxon, he's armed."

Hakon and his men looked at the huge, baleful Steapa. "He's with you, lord."

"So why has Ivarr summoned you?" Ragnar demanded.

And so the story emerged, or as much as Hakon knew. Guthred had traveled this same road north, but Kjartan had sent men to block his path. "Guthred has no more than a hundred and fifty spearmen," Hakon told us, "and Kjartan opposed him with two hundred or more. Guthred did not try to fight."

"So where is Guthred?"

"He ran away, lord."

"Where?" Ragnar asked sharply.

"We think west, lord, toward Cumbraland."

"Kjartan didn't follow?"

"Kjartan, lord, doesn't go far from Dunholm. He fears Ælfric of Bebbanburg will attack Dunholm if he goes far away, so he stays close."

"And you're summoned where?" Ragnar demanded.

"We're to meet the Lord Ivarr at Thresk," Hakon said.

"Thresk?" Ragnar was puzzled. Thresk was a settlement beside a lake some miles to the east. Guthred, it appeared, had gone west, but Ivarr was raising his banner to the east. Then Ragnar understood. "Ivarr will attack Eoferwic?"

Hakon nodded. "Take Guthred's home, lord," he said, "and where can he go?"

"Bebbanburg?" I suggested.

"There are horsemen shadowing Guthred," Hakon said, "and if he tries to go north Kjartan will march again." He touched his sword's hilt. "We shall finish the Saxons forever, lord. The Lord Ivarr will be glad of your return."

"My family," Ragnar said harshly, "does not fight alongside Kjartan."

"Not even for plunder?" Hakon asked. "I hear Eoferwic is full of plunder."

"It's been plundered before," I said, "how much can be left?"

"Enough," Hakon said flatly.

Ivarr, I thought, had devised a clever strategy. Guthred, accompanied by too few spearmen and cumbered with priests, monks, and a dead saint, was wandering in the wild Northumbrian weather, and meanwhile his enemies would capture his palace and his city, and with them the city's garrison that formed the heart of Guthred's forces. Kjartan, meanwhile, was keeping Guthred from reaching the safety of Bebbanburg.

"Whose hall is this?" Ragnar asked.

"It belonged to a Saxon, lord," Hakon said.

"Belonged?"

"He drew his sword," Hakon explained, "so he and all his folk are dead. Except two daughters." He jerked his head toward the back of the hall. "They're in a cattle byre if you want them."

More Danes arrived as evening fell. They were all going to Thresk and the hall was a good place to shelter from the weather that was now blowing a full storm. There was ale in the hall and inevitably men got drunk, but they were happily drunk because Guthred had made a terrible mistake. He had marched north with too few men in the belief that the Danes would not interfere with him, and now these Danes had the promise of an easy war and much plunder.

We took one of the sleeping platforms at the side of the hall for our own use. "What we have to do," Ragnar said, "is go to Synning-thwait."

"At dawn," I agreed.

"Why Synningthwait?" Beocca wanted to know.

"Because that's where my men are," Ragnar said, "and that's what we need now. Men."

"We need to find Guthred!" Beocca insisted.

"We need men to find him," I said, "and we need swords." Northumbria was falling into chaos and the best way to endure chaos was to be surrounded by swords and spears.

Three drunken Danes had watched us talking and they were intrigued, perhaps offended, that we included a Christian priest in our conversation. They crossed to the platform and demanded to know who Beocca was and why we were keeping him company.

"We're keeping him," I said, "in case we get hungry." That satisfied them, and the joke was passed about the hall to more laughter.

The storm passed in the night. Thunder growled ever more faintly, and the intensity of the rain on the wind-tossed thatch slowly diminished so that by dawn there was only a light drizzle and water dripping from the moss-covered roof. We dressed in mail and helmets and, as Hakon and the other Danes went east toward Thresk, we rode west into the hills.

I was thinking of Gisela, lost somewhere in the hills and a victim of her brother's desperation. Guthred must have thought that it was too late in the year for armies to assemble, and that he could slip past Dunholm to Bebbanburg without the Danes trying to oppose him. Now he was on the edge of losing everything. "If we find him," Beocca asked me as we rode, "can we take him south to Alfred?"

"Take him south to Alfred?" I asked. "Why would we do that?"

"To keep him alive. If he's a Christian then he'll be welcome in Wessex."

"Alfred wants him to be king here," I said.

"It's too late," Beocca said gloomily.

"No," I said, "it's not too late." Beocca stared at me as though I were mad, and perhaps I was, but in the chaos that darkened Northumbria there was one thing Ivarr had not thought of. He must have believed he had already won. His forces were assembling and Kjartan was driving Guthred into the wild center of the country where no army could survive for long in cold and wind and rain. But Ivarr had forgotten Ragnar. Ragnar had been away so long, yet he held a stretch of land in the hills and that land supported men, and those men were sworn to Ragnar's service.

And so we rode to Synningthwait and I had a lump in my throat as we cantered into the valley for it had been near Synningthwait that I had lived as a child, where I had been raised by Ragnar's father, where I had learned to fight, where I had been loved, where I had been happy, and where I had watched Kjartan burn Ragnar's hall and murder its inhabitants. This was the first time I had returned since that foul night.

Ragnar's men lived in the settlement or in the nearby hills, though the first person I saw was Ethne, the Scottish slave we had freed at Gyruum. She was carrying two pails of water and she did not recognize me till I called her name. Then she dropped the pails and ran toward the houses, shouting, and Finan emerged from a low doorway. He shouted with delight, and more folk appeared, and suddenly there was a crowd cheering because Ragnar had come back to his people.

Finan could not wait for me to dismount. He walked beside my horse, grinning. "You want to know how Sverri died?" he asked me.

"Slowly?" I guessed.

"And loudly." He grinned. "And we took his money."

"Much money?"

"More than you can dream of!" he said exultantly. "And we burned his house. Left his woman and children weeping."

"You let them live?"

He looked embarrassed. "Ethne felt sorry for them. But killing him was pleasure enough." He grinned up at me again. "So are we going to war?"

"We're going to war."

"We're to fight that bastard Guthred, eh?" Finan said.

"You want to do that?"

"He sent a priest to say we had to pay the church money! We chased him away."

"I thought you were a Christian," I said.

"I am," Finan said defensively, "but I'll be damned before I give a priest a tenth of my money."

The men of Synningthwait expected to fight for Ivarr. They were Danes, and they saw the imminent war as one between Danes and upstart Saxons, though none had much enthusiasm for the fight because Ivarr was not liked. Ivarr's summons had reached Synning-thwait five days before and Rollo, who commanded in Ragnar's absence, had deliberately dallied. Now the decision belonged to Rag-nar and that night, in front of his hall where a great fire burned beneath the clouds, he invited his men to speak their minds. Ragnar could have ordered them to do whatever he wanted, but he had not seen most of them in three years and he wanted to know their temper. "I'll let them speak," he told me, "then I'll tell them what we'll do."

"What will we do?" I asked.

Ragnar grinned. "I don't know yet."

Rollo spoke first. He did not dislike Guthred, he said, but he won-dered if Guthred was the best king for Northumbria. "A land needs a king," he said, "and that king should be fair and just and generous and strong. Guthred is neither just nor strong. He favors the Chris-tians." Men murmured support.

Beocca was sitting beside me and understood enough of what was being said to become upset. "Alfred supports Guthred!" he hissed to me.

"Be quiet," I warned him.

"Guthred," Rollo went on, "demanded that we pay a tax to the Christian priests."

"Did you?" Ragnar asked.

"No."

"If Guthred is not king," Ragnar demanded, "who should be?" No one spoke. "Ivarr?" Ragnar suggested, and a shudder went through the crowd. No one liked Ivarr, and no one spoke except Beocca and he only managed one word before I choked off his protest with a sharp dig into his bony ribs. "What about Earl Ulf?" Ragnar asked.

"Too old now," Rollo said. "Besides he's gone back to Cair Ligualid and wants to stay there."

"Is there a Saxon who would leave us Danes alone?" Ragnar asked, and again no one answered. "Another Dane, then?" Ragnar suggested.

"It must be Guthred!" Beocca snapped like a dog.

Rollo took a pace forward as if what he was about to say was important. "We would follow you, lord," he said to Ragnar, "for you are fair and just and generous and strong." That provoked wild applause from the crowd gathered about the fire.

"This is treason!" Beocca hissed.

"Be quiet," I told him.

"But Alfred told us . . ."

"Alfred is not here," I said, "and we are, so be quiet."

Ragnar gazed into the fire. He was such a good-looking man, so strong-faced, so open-faced and cheerful, yet at that moment he was troubled. He looked at me. "You could be king," he said.

"I could," I agreed.

"We are here to support Guthred!" Beocca yapped.

"Finan," I said, "beside me is a squint-eyed, club-footed, palsied priest who is irritating me. If he speaks again, cut his throat."

"Uhtred!" Beocca squeaked.

"I shall allow him that one utterance," I told Finan, "but the next time he speaks you will send him to his forefathers."

Finan grinned and drew his sword. Beocca went silent.

"You could be king," Ragnar said to me again, and I was aware of Brida's dark eyes resting on me.

"My ancestors were kings," I said, "and their blood is in me. It is the blood of Odin." My father, though a Christian, had always been proud that our family was descended from the god Odin.

"And you would be a good king," Ragnar said. "It is better that a Saxon rules, and you are a Saxon who loves the Danes. You could be King Uhtred of Northumbria, and why not?" Brida still watched me. I knew she was remembering the night when Ragnar's father had died, and when Kjartan and his yelling crew had cut down the men and women stumbling from the burning hall. "Well?" Ragnar prompted me.

I was tempted. I confess I was very tempted. In their day my family had been kings of Bernicia and now the throne of Northumbria was there for the taking. With Ragnar beside me I could be sure of Danish support, and the Saxons would do what they were told. Ivarr would resist, of course, as would Kjartan and my uncle, but that was nothing new and I was certain I was a better soldier than Guthred.

And yet I knew it was not my fate to be king. I have known many kings and their lives are not all silver, feasting, and women. Alfred looked worn out by his duties, though part of that was his constant sickness and another part an inability to take his duties lightly. Yet Alfred was right in that dedication to duty. A king has to rule, he has to keep a balance between the great thegns of his kingdom, he has to fend off rivals, he has to keep the treasury full, he has to maintain roads and fortresses and armies. I thought of all that while Ragnar and Brida stared at me and while Beocca held his breath beside me, and I knew I did not want the responsibility. I wanted the silver, the feasting, and the women, but those I could have without a throne. "It is not my fate," I said.

"Maybe you don't know your fate," Ragnar suggested.

The smoke whirled into the cold sky that was bright with sparks. "My fate," I said, "is to be the ruler of Bebbanburg. I know that. And I know Northumbria cannot be ruled from Bebbanburg. But perhaps it is your fate," I said to Ragnar.

He shook his head. "My father," he said, "and his father, and his father before him, were all Vikings. We sailed to where we could take wealth. We grew rich. We had laughter, ale, silver, and battle. If I were to be king then I would have to protect what I have from the men who would take it from me. Instead of being a Viking I would be a shepherd. I want to be free. I have been a hostage too long, and I want my freedom. I want my sails in the wind and my swords in the sun. I do not wish to be heaped with duties." He had been thinking what I had been thinking, though he had said it far more eloquently. He grinned suddenly, as if released from a burden. "I wish to be richer than any king," he declared to his men, "and I will make you all rich with me."

"So who is to be king?" Rollo asked.

"Guthred," Ragnar said.

"Praise God," Beocca said.

"Quiet," I hissed.

Ragnar's men were not happy with his choice. Rollo, gaunt and bearded and loyal, spoke for them. "Guthred favors the Christians," he said. "He is more Saxon than Dane. He would make us all worship their nailed god."

"He will do what he's told to do," I said firmly, "and the first thing we tell him is that no Dane will pay a tithe to their church. He will be a king like Egbert was king, obedient to Danish wishes." Beocca was spluttering, but I ignored him. "What matters," I went on, "is which Dane gives him his orders. Is it to be Ivarr? Kjartan? Or Ragnar?"

"Ragnar!" men shouted.

"And my wish," Ragnar had moved closer to the fire so that the flames illuminated him and made him look bigger and stronger, "my wish," he said again, "is to see Kjartan defeated. If Ivarr beats Guthred then Kjartan will grow stronger, and Kjartan is my enemy. He is our enemy. There is a bloodfeud between his family and mine, and I would end that feud now. We march to help Guthred, but if Guthred does not assist us in taking Dunholm then I swear to you that I shall kill Guthred and all his folk and take the throne. But I would rather stand in Kjartan's blood than be king of all the Danes. I would rather be the slayer of Kjartan than be king of all the earth. My quarrel is not with Guthred. It is not with the Saxons. It is not with the Christians. My quarrel is with Kjartan the Cruel."

"And in Dunholm," I said, "there is a hoard of silver worthy of the gods."

"So we will find Guthred," Ragnar announced, "and we shall fight for him!"

A moment before, the crowd had wanted Ragnar to lead them against Guthred, but now they cheered the news that they were to fight for the king. There were seventy warriors there, not many, but they were among the best in Northumbria and they thumped swords against shields and shouted Ragnar's name.

"You can speak now," I told Beocca.

But he had nothing to say.

And next dawn, under a clear sky, we rode to find Guthred.

And Gisela.

PART THREE

SHADOW-WALKER

EIGHT

We were seventy-six warriors, including Steapa and myself. All of us were on horseback and all had weapons, mail or good leather, and helmets. Two score of servants on smaller horses carried the shields and led our spare stallions, but those servants were not fighting men and were not counted among the seventy-six. There had been a time when Ragnar could raise over two hundred warriors, but many had died at Ethandun and others had found new lords in the long months while Ragnar was a hostage, but seventy-six was still a good number. "And they're formidable men," he told me proudly.

He rode under his banner of an eagle's wing. It was a real eagle's wing nailed to the top of a high pole, and his helmet was decorated with two more such wings. "I dreamed of this," he told me as we rode eastward, "I dreamed of riding to war. All that time I was a hostage I wanted to be riding to war. There's nothing in life like it, Uhtred, nothing!"

"Women?" I asked.

"Women and war!" he said, "women and war!" He whooped for joy and his stallion pricked back its ears and took a few short, high steps as if it shared its master's happiness. We rode at the front of the column, though Ragnar had a dozen men mounted on light ponies ranging far ahead of us. The dozen men signaled to each other and back to Ragnar, and they spoke to shepherds and listened to rumor and smelt the wind. They were like hounds seeking scent, and they looked for Guthred's trail, which we expected to find leading west toward Cumbraland, but as the morning wore on the scouts kept tending eastward. Our progress was slow, which frustrated Father Beocca, but before we could ride fast we had to know where we were going. Then, at last, the scouts seemed confident that the trail led east and spurred their ponies across the hills and we followed. "Guthred's trying to go back to Eoferwic," Ragnar guessed.

"He's too late for that," I said.

"Or else he's panicking," Ragnar suggested cheerfully, "and doesn't know what he's doing."

"That sounds more likely," I said.

Brida and some twenty other women rode with us. Brida was in leather armor and had a black cloak held at her neck with a fine brooch of silver and jet. Her hair was twisted high and held in place with a black ribbon, and at her side was a long sword. She had grown into an elegant woman who possessed an air of authority and that, I think, offended Father Beocca who had known her since she was a child. She had been raised a Christian, but had escaped the faith and Beocca was upset by that, though I think he found her beauty more disturbing. "She's a sorceress," Beocca hissed at me.

"If she's a sorceress," I said, "then she's a good person to have on your side."

"God will punish us," he warned.

"This isn't your god's country," I told him. "This is Thor's land."

He made the sign of the cross to protect himself from the evil of my words. "And what were you doing last night?" he asked indignantly. "How could you even think of being king here?"

"Easily," I said. "I am descended from kings. Unlike you, father. You're descended from swineherds, aren't you?"

He ignored that. "The king is the Lord's anointed," he insisted. "The king is chosen by God and by all the throng of holy saints. Saint Cuthbert led Northumbria to Guthred, so how could you even think of replacing him? How could you?"

"We can turn around and go home then," I said.

"Turn around and go home?" Beocca was appalled. "Why?"

"Because if Cuthbert chose him," I said, "then Cuthbert can defend him. Guthred doesn't need us. He can go into battle with his dead saint. Or maybe he already has," I said, "have you thought of that?"

"Thought of what?"

"That Guthred might already be defeated. He could be dead. Or he could be wearing Kjartan's chains."

"God preserve us," Beocca said, making the sign of the cross again.

"It hasn't happened," I assured him.

"How do you know?"

"Because we'd have met his fugitives by now," I said, though I could not be certain of that. Perhaps Guthred was fighting even as we spoke, but I had a feeling he was alive and not too far away. It is hard to describe that feeling. It is an instinct, as hard to read as a god's message in the fall of a wren's feather, but I had learned to trust the feeling.

And my instinct was right, for late in the morning one of the scouts came racing back across the moorland with his pony's mane tossing in the wind. He slewed around in a burst of turf and bracken to tell Ragnar that there was a large band of men and horses in the valley of the River Swale. "They're at Cetreht, lord," he said.

"On our side of the river?" Ragnar asked.

"On our side, lord," the scout said, "in the old fort. Trapped there."

"Trapped?"

"There's another war-band outside the fort, lord," the scout said. He had not ridden close enough to see any banners, but two other scouts had ridden down into the valley while this first galloped back to bring us the news that Guthred was probably very near.

We quickened our pace. Clouds raced in the wind and at midday a sharp rain fell briefly, and just after it ended we met the two scouts who had ridden down to the fields outside the fort and spoken to the war-band. "Guthred's in the fort," one of them reported.

"So who's outside?"

"Kjartan's men, lord," the man said. He grinned, knowing that if any of Kjartan's men were close then there would be a fight. "There are sixty of them, lord. Only sixty."

"Is Kjartan there? Or Sven?"

"No, lord. They're led by a man called Rolf."

"You spoke to him?"

"Spoke to him and drank his ale, lord. They're watching Guthred. Making sure he doesn't run away. They're keeping him there until Ivarr comes north."

"Till Ivarr comes?" Ragnar asked. "Not Kjartan?"

"Kjartan stays at Dunholm, lord," the man said, "that's what they said, and that Ivarr will come north once he's garrisoned Eoferwic."

"There are sixty of Kjartan's men in the valley," Ragnar shouted back to his warriors, and his hand instinctively went to the hilt of Heart-Breaker. That was his sword, given the same name as his father's blade as a reminder of his duty to revenge Ragnar the Elder's death. "There are sixty men to kill!" he added, then called for a servant to bring his shield. He looked back to the scouts. "Who did they think you were?"

"We claimed to serve Hakon, lord. We said we were looking for him."

Ragnar gave the men silver coins. "You did well," he said. "So how many men does Guthred have in the fort?"

"Rolf says he's got at least a hundred, lord."

"A hundred? And he hasn't tried to drive off sixty men?"

"No, lord."

"Some king," Ragnar said scornfully.

"If he fights them," I said, "then at the end of the day he'll have fewer than fifty men."

"So what's he doing instead?" Ragnar wanted to know.

"Praying, probably."

Guthred, as we later learned, had panicked. Thwarted in his efforts to reach Bebbanburg he had turned west toward Cumbraland, think-

ing that in that familiar country he would find friends, but the
weather had slowed him, and there were enemy horsemen always in
sight and he feared ambush in the steep hills ahead. So he had
changed his mind and decided to return to Eoferwic, but had got no
farther than the Roman fort that had once guarded the crossings of
the Swale at Cetreht. He was desperate by then. Some of his spearmen
had deserted, reckoning that only death waited for them if they
stayed with the king, so Guthred had sent messengers to summon
help from Northumbria's Christian thegns, but we had already seen
the corpses and knew no help would come. Now he was trapped. The
sixty men would hold him in Cetreht until Ivarr came to kill him.

"If Guthred is praying," Beocca said sternly, "then those prayers
are being answered."

"You mean the Christian god sent us?" I asked.

"Who else?" he responded indignantly as he brushed down his
black robe. "When we meet Guthred," he told me, "you will let me
speak first."

"You think this is a time for ceremony?"

"I'm an ambassador!" he protested, "you forget that." His indigna-
tion suddenly burst like a rain-sodden stream overflowing its banks.
"You have no conception of dignity! I am an ambassador! Last night,
Uhtred, when you told that Irish savage to cut my throat, what were
you thinking of?"

"I was thinking of keeping you quiet, father."

"I shall tell Alfred of your insolence. You can be sure of that. I shall
tell him!"

He went on complaining, but I was not listening for we had ridden
across the skyline and there was Cetreht and the curving River Swale
beneath us. The Roman fort was a short distance from the Swale's
southern bank and the old earth walls made a wide square which
enclosed a village which had a church at its center. Beyond the fort
was the stone bridge the Romans had made to carry their great road
which led from Eoferwic to the wild north, and half of the old arch
still stood.

As we rode closer I could see that the fort was full of horses and people. A standard flew from the church's gable and I assumed that must be Guthred's flag showing Saint Cuthbert. A few horsemen were north of the river, blocking Guthred's escape across the ford, while Rolf's sixty riders were in the fields south of the fort. They were like hounds stopping up a fox's earth.

Ragnar had checked his horse. His men were readying for a fight. They were pushing their arms into shield loops, loosening swords in scabbards, and waiting for Ragnar's orders. I gazed into the valley. The fort was a hopeless refuge. Its walls had long eroded into the ditch and there was no palisade, so that a man could stroll over the ramparts without even breaking stride. The sixty horsemen, if they had wished, could have ridden into the village, but they preferred to ride close to the old wall and shout insults. Guthred's men watched from the fort's edge. More men were clustered about the church. They had seen us on the hill and must have thought we were new enemies, for they were hurrying toward the remnants of the southern rampart. I stared at the village. Was Gisela there? I remembered the flick of her head and how her eyes had been shadowed by her black hair, and I unconsciously spurred my horse a few paces forward. I had spent over two years of hell at Sverri's oar, but this was the moment I had dreamed of through all that time, and so I did not wait for Ragnar. I touched spurs to my horse again and rode alone into the valley of the Swale.

Beocca, of course, followed me, squawking that as Alfred's ambassador he must lead the way into Guthred's presence, but I ignored him and, halfway down the hill he tumbled from his horse. He gave a despairing cry and I left him limping in the grass as he tried to retrieve his mare.

The late autumn sun was bright on the land that was still wet from rain. I carried a shield with a polished boss, I was in mail and helmet, my arm rings shone, I glittered like a lord of war. I twisted in my saddle to see that Ragnar had started down the hill, but he was slanting eastward, plainly intent on cutting off the retreat of Kjartan's men, whose best escape would lie in the eastern river meadows.

I reached the hill's foot and spurred across the flat river plain to join the Roman road. I passed a Christian cemetery, the ground lumpy and scattered with small wooden crosses looking toward the one larger cross which would show the resurrected dead the direction of Jerusalem on the day the Christians believed their corpses would rise from the earth. The road led straight past the graves to the fort's southern entrance, where a crowd of Guthred's men watched me. Kjartan's men spurred to intercept me, barring the road, but they showed no apprehension. Why should they? I appeared to be a Dane, I was one man and they were many, and my sword was still in its scabbard. "Which of you is Rolf?" I shouted as I drew near them.

"I am," a black-bearded man urged his horse toward me. "Who are you?"

"Your death, Rolf," I said, and I drew Serpent-Breath and touched my heels to the stallion's flanks and he went into the full gallop and Rolf was still drawing his sword when I pounded past him and swung Serpent-Breath and the blade sliced through his neck so that his head and helmet flew back, bounced on the road and rolled under my horse's hooves. I was laughing because the battle-joy had come. Three men were ahead of me and none had yet drawn a sword. They just stared at me, aghast, and at Rolf's headless trunk that swayed in the saddle. I charged the center man, letting my horse barge into his and striking him hard with Serpent-Breath, and then I was through Kjartan's horsemen and the fort was in front of me.

Fifty or sixty men were standing at the fort's entrance. Only a handful were mounted, but nearly all had swords or spears. And I could see Guthred there, his fair curly hair bright in the sun, and next to him was Gisela. I had tried so often to summon her face in those long months at Sverri's oar, and I had always failed, yet suddenly the wide mouth and the defiant eyes seemed so familiar. She was dressed in a white linen robe, belted at her waist with a silver chain, and she had a linen bonnet on her hair which, because she was married, was bound into a knot. She was holding her brother's arm, and Guthred was just staring at the strange events unfolding outside his refuge.

Two of Kjartan's men had followed me while the rest were milling around, torn between the shock of Rolf's death and the sudden appearance of Ragnar's war-band. I turned on the two men following me, wrenching the stallion about so sharply that his hooves scrabbled in the wet mud, but my sudden turn drove my pursuers back. I spurred after them. One was too fast, the second was on a lumbering horse and he heard my hoofbeats and swung his sword back in a desperate attempt to drive me off. I took the blade on my shield, then lunged Serpent-Breath into the man's spine so that his back arched and he screamed. I tugged Serpent-Breath free and back-swung her into the man's face. He fell from the saddle and I rode around him, sword red, and took off my helmet as I spurred again toward the fort.

I was showing off. Of course I was showing off. One man against sixty? But Gisela was watching. In truth I was in no real danger. The sixty men had not been ready for a fight, and if they pursued me now I could take refuge with Guthred's men. But Kjartan's men were not pursuing. They were too nervous of Ragnar's approach and so I ignored them, riding close to Guthred and his men instead.

"Have you forgotten how to fight?" I shouted at them. I ignored Guthred. I even ignored Gisela, though I had taken off my helmet so she would recognize me. I knew she was watching me. I could sense those dark eyes and sense her astonishment and I hoped it was a joyful astonishment. "They've all got to die!" I shouted, pointing my sword at Kjartan's men. "Every last one of the bastards has to die, so go out and kill them!"

Ragnar struck then and there was the hammer of shield on shield, the clangor of swords and the scream of men and horses. Kjartan's men were scattering and some, despairing of making an escape eastward, were galloping to the west. I looked at the men in the gateway, "Rypere! Clapa! I want those men stopped!"

Clapa and Rypere were staring at me as though I were a ghost, which I suppose I was in a way. I was glad Clapa was still with

Guthred, for Clapa was a Dane and that suggested Guthred could still command some Danish allegiance. "Clapa! You earsling!" I yelled. "Stop dawdling like a boiled egg. Get on a horse and fight!"

"Yes, lord!"

I rode closer still until I was staring down at Guthred. There was a fight going on behind me and Guthred's men, stirred from their torpor, were hurrying to join the slaughter, but Guthred had no eyes for the battle. He just stared up at me. There were priests behind him and Gisela was beside him, but I looked only into Guthred's eyes and saw the fear there. "Remember me?" I asked coldly.

He had no words.

"You would do well," I said, "to set a kingly example and kill a few men right now. You have a horse?"

He nodded and still could not speak.

"Then get on your horse," I said curtly, "and fight."

Guthred nodded and took one backward pace, but though his servant led a horse forward Guthred did not mount. I looked at Gisela then and she looked back and I thought her eyes could light a fire. I wanted to speak, but it was my turn to have no words. A priest plucked at her shoulder as if summoning her away from the fighting, but I twitched Serpent-Breath's bloody blade toward the man and he went very still. I looked back at Gisela and it seemed as if I had no breath, as if the world stood still. A gust of wind lifted a wisp of black hair showing beneath her bonnet. She brushed it away, then smiled. "Uhtred," she said, as though saying the name for the very first time.

"Gisela," I managed to speak.

"I knew you'd come back," she said.

"I thought you were going to fight," I snarled at Guthred and he ran off like a whipped dog.

"Do you have a horse?" I asked Gisela.

"No."

"You!" I shouted at a boy gawping at me. "Fetch me that horse!" I pointed to the stallion of the man I had injured in the face. That man was now dead, killed by Guthred's men as they joined the fight.

The boy brought me the stallion and Gisela scrambled into its saddle, hoisting her skirts inelegantly around her thighs. She pushed her muddy shoes into the stirrups then held out a hand to touch my cheek. "You're thinner," she said.

"So are you."

"I have not been happy," she said, "since the moment you left." She kept her hand on my cheek for a heartbeat, then impulsively took it away and tore off the linen bonnet and unpinned her black hair so that it fell around her shoulders like the hair of an unwed girl. "I'm not married," she said, "not properly married."

"Not yet," I said, and my heart was so full of joy. I could not take my eyes from her. I was with her again and the months of slavery dropped away as though they had never happened.

"Have you killed enough men yet?" she asked mischievously.

"No."

So we rode toward the slaughter.

You cannot kill everyone in an enemy army. Or rarely. Whenever the poets sing a tale of battle they always insist that no enemy escapes unless the poet himself happens to be part of the fight when he alone escapes. It is strange that. Poets always live while everyone else dies, but what do poets know? I have never seen a poet in a shield wall. Yet, outside Cetreht, we must have killed over fifty of Kjartan's men, and then everything became chaotic because Guthred's men could not tell the difference between Kjartan's followers and Ragnar's Danes, and so some of the enemy escaped as we pulled warriors apart. Finan, attacked by two of Guthred's household troops, had killed both of them and, when I found him, he was about to attack a third. "He's on our side," I shouted to Finan.

"He looks like a rat," Finan snarled.

"His name," I said, "is Sihtric, and he once swore me an oath of loyalty."

"Still looks like a rat, he does."

"Are you on our side?" I called to Sihtric, "or did you rejoin your father's troops?"

"Lord, lord!" Sihtric came running to me and fell to his knees in the trampled mud beside my horse. "I'm still your man, lord."

"You didn't take an oath to Guthred?"

"He never asked me, lord."

"But you served him? You didn't run back to Dunholm?"

"No, lord! I stayed with the king."

"He did," Gisela confirmed.

I gave Serpent-Breath to Gisela, then reached down and took Sihtric's hand. "So you're still my man?"

"Of course, lord." He was clutching my hand, gazing at me with disbelief.

"You're not much use, are you," I said, "if you can't beat a skinny Irishman like him?"

"He's quick, lord," Sihtric said.

"So teach him your tricks," I told Finan, then I patted Sihtric's cheek. "It's good to see you, Sihtric."

Ragnar had two prisoners and Sihtric recognized the taller of the two. "His name is Hogga," he told me.

"He's a dead Hogga now," I said. I knew Ragnar would not let any of Kjartan's men survive while Kjartan himself lived. This was the bloodfeud. This was hatred. This was the start of Ragnar's revenge for his father's death, but for the moment Hogga and his shorter companion evidently believed they would live. They were talking avidly, describing how Kjartan had close to two hundred men in Dunholm. They said Kjartan had sent a large war-band to support Ivarr, while the rest of his men had followed Rolf to this bloody field by Cetreht.

"Why didn't Kjartan bring all his men here?" Ragnar wanted to know.

"He won't leave Dunholm, lord, in case Ælfric of Bebbanburg attacks when he's gone."

"Has Ælfric threatened to do that?" I asked.

"I don't know, lord," Hogga said.

It would be unlike my uncle to risk an attack on Dunholm, though perhaps he would lead men to rescue Guthred if he knew where Guthred was. My uncle wanted the saint's corpse and he wanted Gisela, but my guess was that he would risk little to get those two things. He would certainly not risk Bebbanburg itself, any more than Kjartan would risk Dunholm.

"And Thyra Ragnarsdottir?" Ragnar resumed his questioning. "Does she live?"

"Yes, lord."

"Does she live happily?" Ragnar asked harshly.

They hesitated, then Hogga grimaced. "She is mad, lord." He spoke in a low voice. "She is quite mad."

Ragnar stared at the two men. They became uncomfortable under his gaze, but then Ragnar looked up at the sky where a buzzard floated down from the western hills. "Tell me," he said, and his voice was suddenly low, almost easy, "how long have you served Kjartan?"

"Eight years, lord," Hogga said.

"Seven years, lord," the other man said.

"So you both served him," Ragnar said, still speaking softly, "before he fortified Dunholm?"

"Yes, lord."

"And you both served him," Ragnar went on, his voice harsh now, "when he took men to Synningthwait and burned my father's hall. When he took my sister as his son's whore. When he killed my mother and my father."

Neither man answered. The shorter of the two was shaking. Hogga looked around as if to find a way to escape, but he was surrounded by mounted sword-Danes, then he flinched as Ragnar drew Heart-Breaker.

"No, lord," Hogga said.

"Yes," Ragnar said and his face twisted with anger as he chopped down. He had to dismount to finish the job. He killed both men, and he hacked at their fallen bodies in fury. I watched, then turned to see Gisela's face. It showed nothing, then she became conscious of my gaze and turned toward me with a small look of triumph as if she knew I had half expected her to be horrified by the sight of men being disembowelled. "They deserved it?" she asked.

"They deserved it," I said.

"Good."

Her brother, I noted, had not watched. He was nervous of me, for which I did not blame him, and doubtless terrified of Ragnar who was bloodied like a butcher, and so Guthred had gone back to the village, leaving us with the dead. Father Beocca had managed to find some of Guthred's priests and, after talking with them, he limped to us. "It is agreed," he said, "that we shall present ourselves to the king in the church." He suddenly became aware of the two severed heads and the sword-slashed bodies. "Dear God, who did that?"

"Ragnar."

Beocca made the sign of the cross. "The church," he said, "we're to meet in the church. Do try to wipe that blood off your mail, Uhtred. We're an embassy!"

I turned to see a handful of fugitives crossing the hilltops to the west. They would doubtless cross the river higher up and join the horsemen on the far bank, and those horsemen would be wary now. They would send word to Dunholm that enemies had come, and Kjartan would hear of the eagle-wing banner and know that Ragnar was returned from Wessex.

And perhaps, on his high crag, behind his high walls, he would be frightened.

I rode to the church, taking Gisela with me. Beocca hurried after on foot, but he was slow. "Wait for me!" he shouted, "wait for me!"

I did not wait. Instead I spurred the stallion faster and left Beocca far behind.

It was dark in the church. The only illumination came from a small window above the door and from some feeble rushlights burning on the altar that was a trestle table covered by a black cloth. Saint Cuthbert's coffin, together with the other two chests of relics, stood in front of the altar where Guthred sat on a milking stool flanked by two men and a woman. The Abbot Eadred was one of the men and Father Hrothweard was the other. The woman was young, had a plumply pretty face, and a pregnant belly. I learned later she was Osburh, Guthred's Saxon queen. She glanced from me to her husband, evidently expecting Guthred to speak, but he was silent. A score of warriors stood on the left side of the church and a larger number of priests and monks on the right. They had been arguing, but all went quiet when I entered.

Gisela held my left arm. Together we walked down the church until we faced Guthred, who seemed incapable of looking at me or speaking to me. He opened his mouth once, but no words came, and he looked past me as if hoping that someone less baleful would come through the church door. "I'm going to marry your sister," I told him.

He opened his mouth and closed it again.

A monk moved as if to protest my words and was pulled back by a companion and I saw that the gods had been especially good to me that day, for the pair were Jænberht and Ida, the monks who had negotiated my slavery. Then, from the other side of the church, a man did protest. "The Lady Gisela," he said, "is already married."

I saw that the speaker was an older man, gray-haired and stout. He was dressed in a short brown tunic with a silver chain about his neck and he jerked his head up belligerently as I walked toward him. "You're Aidan," I said. It had been fourteen years since I had been in Bebbanburg, but I recognized Aidan. He had been one of my father's doorkeepers, charged with keeping unwanted folk out of the great hall, but the silver chain made it clear that he had risen in rank since then. I flicked the chain with my hand. "What are you now, Aidan?" I demanded.

"Steward to the Lord of Bebbanburg," he said gruffly. He did not recognize me. How could he? I had been nine years old when he last saw me.

"So that makes you my steward," I said.

"Your steward?" he asked, then he realized who I was and he stepped back to join two young warriors. That step was involuntary, though Aidan was no coward. He had been a good soldier in his day, but meeting me had shocked him. He recovered though, and faced me defiantly. "The Lady Gisela," he said, "is married."

"Are you married?" I asked Gisela.

"No," she said.

"She's not married," I told Aidan.

Guthred cleared his throat as if to speak, but then fell silent as Ragnar and his men filed into the church.

"The lady is married," a voice called from among the priests and monks. I turned to see that it was Brother Jænberht who had spoken. "She is married to the Lord Ælfric," Jænberht insisted.

"She's married to Ælfric?" I asked as if I had not heard that news, "she's married to that whore-born piece of lice-shit?"

Aidan gave one of the warriors beside him a hard nudge, and the man drew his sword. The other did the same, and I smiled at them, then very slowly drew Serpent-Breath.

"This is a house of God!" Abbot Eadred protested. "Put your swords away!"

The two young men hesitated, but when I kept Serpent-Breath drawn they kept their own blades ready, though neither moved to attack me. They knew my reputation and, besides, Serpent-Breath was still sticky with the blood of Kjartan's men.

"Uhtred!" This time it was Beocca who interrupted me. He burst into the church and pushed past Ragnar's men. "Uhtred!" he called again.

I turned on him. "This is my business, father," I said, "and you will leave me to it. You remember Aidan?" Beocca looked confused, then he recognized the steward who had been at Bebbanburg during all the years that Beocca had been my father's priest. "Aidan wants these two boys to kill me," I said, "but before they oblige him," I was looking at the steward again, "tell me how Gisela can be married to a man she's never met?"

Aidan glanced across at Guthred as if expecting help from the king, but Guthred was still motionless, so Aidan had to confront me alone. "I stood beside her in Lord Ælfric's place," he said, "so in the eyes of the church she is married."

"Did you hump her as well?" I demanded, and the priests and monks hissed their disapproval.

"Of course not," Aidan said, offended.

"If no one's ridden her," I said, "then she's not married. A mare isn't broken until she's saddled and ridden. Have you been ridden?" I asked Gisela.

"Not yet," she said.

"She is married," Aidan insisted.

"You stood at the altar in my uncle's place," I said, "and you call that a marriage?"

"It is," Beocca said quietly.

"So if I kill you," I suggested to Aidan, ignoring Beocca, "she'll be a widow?"

Aidan pushed one of the warriors toward me and, like a fool, the man came, and Serpent-Breath slashed once, very hard, and his sword was knocked away and my blade was at his belly. "You want your guts strewn across the floor?" I asked him gently. "I am Uhtred," I said, my voice hard and boastful now, "I am the Lord of Bebbanburg and the man who killed Ubba Lothbrokson beside the sea." I prodded my blade, driving him back. "I have killed more men than I could count," I told him, "but don't let that stop you fighting me. You want to boast that you killed me? That piece of toad-snot, Ælfric, will be pleased if you did. He'll reward you." I jabbed again. "Go on," I said, my anger rising, "try." He did nothing of the sort. Instead he took another faltering backward step and the other warrior did the same. That was hardly surprising, for Ragnar and Steapa had joined me, and behind them was a bunch of war-Danes who were dressed in mail and carrying axes and swords. I looked at Aidan. "You can crawl back to my uncle," I said, "and tell him he has lost his bride."

"Uhtred!" Guthred had at last managed to speak.

I ignored him. Instead I walked across the church to where the priests and monks huddled. Gisela came with me, still holding my arm and I gave her Serpent-Breath to hold, then stopped in front of Jænberht. "You think Gisela is married?" I asked him.

"She is," he said defiantly. "The bride-price is paid and the union solemnized."

"Bride-price?" I looked at Gisela. "What did they pay you?"

"We paid them," she said. "They were given one thousand shillings and Saint Oswald's arm."

"Saint Oswald's arm?" I almost laughed.

"Abbot Fadred found it," Gisela said drily.

"Dug it out of a pauper's graveyard, more like," I said.

Jænberht bristled. "All has been done," he said, "according to the laws of man and of the holy church. The woman," he looked sneeringly at Gisela, "is married."

There was something about his narrow, supercilious face that irritated me, so I reached out and grasped his tonsured hair. He tried to resist, but he was feeble and I jerked his head forward and down, then brought my right knee up hard so that his face was smashed into the mail of my thigh.

I hauled him upright and looked into his bloody face. "Is she married?"

"She is married," he said, his voice thickened by the blood in his mouth, and I jerked his head down again and this time I felt his teeth break against my knee.

"Is she married?" I asked. He said nothing this time, so I yanked his head down again and felt his nose being crunched on my mail-clad knee. "I asked you a question," I said.

"She is married," Jænberht insisted. He was shaking with anger, wincing with pain, and the priests were protesting at what I was doing, but I was lost in my own abrupt rage. This was my uncle's tame monk, the man who had negotiated with Guthred to make me a slave. He had conspired against me. He had tried to destroy me and that realization made my fury ungovernable. It was a sudden blood-red anger, fed by the memory of the humiliations I had suffered on

Sverri's *Trader*, so I pulled Jænberht's head toward me again, but this time, instead of kneeing his face, I drew Wasp-Sting, my short-sword, and cut his throat. One slash. It took a heartbeat to draw the sword, and in that instant I saw the monk's eyes widen in disbelief, and I confess that I half disbelieved what I was doing myself. But I did it anyway. I cut his throat and Wasp-Sting's steel scraped against tendon and gristle, then sliced through their resistance so that blood sheeted down my mail coat. Jænberht, shuddering and bubbling, collapsed onto the wet rushes.

The monks and priests shrieked like women. They had been appalled when I had hammered Jænberht's face, but none had expected outright murder. Even I was surprised by what my anger had done, but I felt no regret, nor did I see it as murder. I saw it as revenge and there was an exquisite pleasure in it. Every pull on Sverri's oar and every blow I had taken from Sverri's crewmen had been in that sword-cut. I looked down at Jænberht's dying twitches, then up at his companion, Brother Ida. "Is Gisela married?" I demanded of him.

"Under church law," Ida began, stammering slightly, then he paused and looked at Wasp-Sting's blade. "She is not married, lord," he went on hurriedly, "until the marriage is consummated."

"Are you married?" I asked Gisela.

"Of course not," she said.

I stooped and wiped Wasp-Sting clean on the skirts of Jænberht's robe. He was dead now, his eyes still showing the surprise of it. One priest, braver than the rest, knelt to pray over the monk's corpse, but the other churchmen looked like sheep confronted by a wolf. They gaped at me, too horrified to protest. Beocca was opening and closing his mouth, saying nothing. I sheathed Wasp-Sting, took Serpent-Breath from Gisela and together we turned toward her brother. He was staring at Jænberht's corpse and at the blood that had splashed across the floor and onto his sister's skirts, and he must have thought I was about to do the same to him, for he put a hand to his own sword. But then I pointed Serpent-Breath at Ragnar. "This is the Earl Ragnar," I said to

Guthred, "and he's here to fight for you. You don't deserve his help. If it were up to me you'd go back to wearing slave shackles and emptying King Eochaid's shit-pail."

"He is the Lord's anointed!" Father Hrothweard protested. "Show respect!"

I hefted Wasp-Sting. "I never liked you either," I said.

Beocca, appalled at my behavior, thrust me aside and offered Guthred a bow. Beocca looked pale, and no wonder, for he had just seen a monk murdered, but not even that could put him off his glorious task of being the West Saxon ambassador. "I bring you greetings," he said, "from Alfred of Wessex who . . ."

"Later, father," I said.

"I bring you Christian greetings from . . ." Beocca tried again, then squealed because I dragged him backward. The priests and monks evidently thought I was going to kill him, for some of them covered their eyes.

"Later, father," I said, letting go of him, then I looked at Guthred. "So what do you do now?" I asked him.

"Do?"

"What do you do? We've taken away the men guarding you, so you're free to go. So what do you do?"

"What we do," it was Hrothweard who answered, "is punish you!" He pointed at me and the anger came on him. He shouted that I was a murderer, a pagan, and a sinner and that God would take his vengeance on Guthred if I were allowed to remain unpunished. Queen Osburh looked terrified as Hrothweard screamed his threats. He was all energy and wild hair and spluttering passion as he shouted that I had killed a holy brother. "The only hope for Haliwerfolkland," he ranted, "is our alliance with Ælfric of Bebbanburg. Send the Lady Gisela to Lord Ælfric and kill the pagan!" He pointed at me. Gisela was still beside me, her hand clutching mine. I said nothing.

Abbot Eadred, who now looked as old as the dead Saint Cuthbert, tried to bring calm to the church. He held his hands aloft till there was silence, then he thanked Ragnar for killing Kjartan's men. "What

we must do now, lord King," Eadred turned to Guthred, "is carry the
saint northward. To Bebbanburg."

"We must punish the murderer!" Hrothweard intervened.

"Nothing is more precious to our country than the body of the
holy Cuthbert," Eadred said, ignoring Hrothweard's anger, "and we
must take it to a place of safety. We should ride tomorrow, ride north,
ride to the sanctuary of Bebbanburg."

Aidan, Ælfric's steward, sought permission to speak. He had come
south, he said, at some risk and in good faith, and I had insulted him,
his master, and the peace of Northumbria, but he would ignore the
insults if Guthred were to take Saint Cuthbert and Gisela north to
Bebbanburg. "It is only in Bebbanburg," Aidan said, "that the saint
will be safe."

"He must die," Hrothweard insisted, thrusting a wooden cross
toward me.

Guthred was nervous. "If we ride north," he said, "Kjartan will
oppose us."

Eadred was ready for that objection. "If the Earl Ragnar will ride
with us, lord, then we shall survive. The church will pay Earl Ragnar
for that service."

"But there will be no safety for any of us," Hrothweard shouted, "if
a murderer is permitted to live." He pointed the wooden cross at me
again. "He is a murderer! A murderer! Brother Jænberht is a martyr!"
The monks and priests shouted their support, and Guthred only
stopped their clamor by remembering that Father Beocca was an
ambassador. Guthred demanded silence and then invited Beocca to
speak.

Poor Beocca. He had been practicing for days, polishing his words,
saying them aloud, changing them, and then changing them back.
He had asked advice on his speech, rejected the advice, declaimed the
words endlessly, and now he delivered his formal greeting from
Alfred and I doubt Guthred heard a word of it, for he was just looking
at me and at Gisela, while Hrothweard was still hissing poison in his
ear. But Beocca droned on, praising Guthred and Queen Osburh,

declaring that they were a godly light in the north and generally bor-
ing anyone who might have been listening. Some of Guthred's warriors mocked his speech by making faces or pretending to squint until
Steapa, tired of their cruelty, went to stand beside Beocca and put a
hand on his sword hilt. Steapa was a kind man, but he looked
implacably violent. He was huge, for a start, and his skin seemed to
have been stretched too tight across his skull, so leaving him incapable of making any expressions other than pure hatred and wolfish
hunger. He glared around the room, daring any man to belittle
Beocca, and they all stayed silent and awed.

Beocca, of course, believed it was his eloquence that stilled them. He
finished his speech with a low bow to Guthred, then presented the gifts
Alfred had sent. There was a book which Alfred claimed to have translated from Latin into English, and maybe he had. It was full of Christian homilies, Beocca said, and he bowed as he presented the heavy
volume that was enclosed in jeweled covers. Guthred turned the book
this way and that, worked out how to unclasp the cover and then
looked at a page upside down and declared it was the most valuable gift
he had ever received. He said the same of the second gift, which was a
sword. It was a Frankish blade and the hilt was of silver and the pommel was a chunk of bright crystal. The last gift was undoubtedly the
most precious, for it was a reliquary of the finest gold studded with
bright garnets, and inside were hairs from the beard of Saint Augustine
of Contwaraburg. Even Abbot Eadred, the guardian of Northumbria's
holiest corpse, was impressed and leaned forward to touch the glitter-
ing gold. "The king means a message by these gifts," Beocca said.

"Keep it short," I muttered, and Gisela pressed my hand.

"I would be delighted to hear his message," Guthred said politely.

"The book represents learning," Beocca said, "for without learning
a kingdom is a mere husk of ignorant barbarism. The sword is the
instrument by which we defend learning and protect God's earthly
kingdom, and its crystal stands for the inner eye which permits us to
discover our Savior's will. And the hairs of the holy Augustine's beard,
lord King, remind us that without God we are nothing, and that

without the holy church we are as chaff in the wind. And Alfred of Wessex wishes you a long and learned life, a Godly rule, and a safe kingdom." He bowed.

Guthred made a speech of thanks, but it ended plaintively. Would Alfred of Wessex send Northumbria help?

"Help?" Beocca asked, not sure how else to respond.

"I need spears," Guthred said, though how he thought he could last long enough for any West Saxon troops to reach him was a mystery.

"He sent me," I said in answer.

"Murderer!" Hrothweard spat. He would not give up.

"He sent me," I said again, and I let go of Gisela's hand and went to join Beocca and Steapa in the nave's center. Beocca was making small flapping motions as if to tell me to go away and keep quiet, but Guthred wanted to hear me. "Over two years ago," I reminded Guthred, "Ælfric became your ally and my freedom was the price for that alliance. He promised you he would destroy Dunholm, yet I hear Dunholm still stands and that Kjartan still lives. So much for Ælfric's promise. And yet you would put your faith in him again? You think that if you give him your sister and a dead saint that Ælfric will fight for you?"

"Murderer," Hrothweard hissed.

"Bebbanburg is still two days' march away," I said, "and to get there you need the Earl Ragnar's help. But the Earl Ragnar is my friend, not yours. He has never betrayed me."

Guthred's face jerked at the mention of betrayal.

"We don't need pagan Danes," Hrothweard hissed at Guthred. "We must rededicate ourselves to God, lord King, here in the River Jordan, and God will see us safe through Kjartan's land!"

"The Jordan?" Ragnar asked behind me. "Where's that?"

I thought the River Jordan was in the Christians' holy land, but it seemed it was here, in Northumbria. "The River Swale," Hrothweard was shouting as if he addressed a congregation of hundreds, "was where the blessed Saint Paulinus baptized Edwin, our country's first

Christian king. Thousands of folk were baptized here. This is our holy river! Our Jordan! If we dip our swords and spears in the Swale, then God will bless them. We cannot be defeated!"

"Without Earl Ragnar," I told Hrothweard scornfully, "Kjartan will tear you to pieces. And Earl Ragnar," I looked at Guthred again, "is my friend, not yours."

Guthred took his wife's hand, then summoned the courage to look me in the eye. "What would you do, Lord Uhtred?"

My enemies, and there were plenty of those in that church, noted that he called me Lord Uhtred and there was a shudder of distaste. I stepped forward. "It's easy, lord," I said, and I had not known what I was going to say, but suddenly it came to me. The three spinners were either playing a joke, or else they had given me a fate as golden as Guthred's, for suddenly it did all seem easy.

"Easy?" Guthred asked.

"Ivarr has gone to Eoferwic, lord," I said, "and Kjartan has sent men to stop you reaching Bebbanburg. What they are trying to do, lord, is to keep you a fugitive. They will take your fortresses, capture your palace, destroy your Saxon supporters, and when you have nowhere to hide they will take you and they will kill you."

"So?" Guthred asked plaintively. "What do we do?"

"We place ourselves, lord, in a fortress, of course. In a place of safety."

"Where?" he asked.

"Dunholm," I said, "where else?"

He just stared at me. No one else spoke. Even the churchmen, who only a moment before had been howling for my death, were silent. And I was thinking of Alfred, and how, in that dreadful winter when all Wessex seemed doomed, he had not thought of mere survival, but of victory.

"If we march at dawn," I said, "and march fast, then in two days we shall take Dunholm."

"You can do that?" Guthred asked.

"No, lord," I said, "we can do it." Though how, I had not the slightest idea. All I knew was that we were few and the enemy numerous, and that so far Guthred had been like a mouse in that enemy's paws, and it was time that we fought back. And Dunholm, because Kjartan had sent so many men to guard the Bebbanburg approaches, was as weak as it was ever likely to be.

"We can do it," Ragnar said. He came to stand beside me.

"Then we shall," Guthred said, and that was how it was decided.

The priests did not like the notion that I would live unpunished, and they liked it even less when Guthred brushed their complaints away and asked me to go with him to the small house that were his quarters. Gisela came too and she sat against the wall and watched the two of us. A small fire burned. It was cold that afternoon, the first cold of the coming winter.

Guthred was embarrassed to find himself with me. He half smiled. "I am sorry," he said haltingly.

"You're a bastard," I said.

"Uhtred," he began, but could find nothing more to say.

"You're a piece of weasel-shit," I said, "you're an earsling."

"I'm a king," he said, trying to regain his dignity.

"So you're a royal piece of weasel-shit. An earsling on a throne."

"I," he said and still could find nothing more to say, so instead he sat on the only chair in the room and gave a shrug.

"But you did the right thing," I told him.

"I did?" he brightened.

"But it didn't work, did it? You were supposed to sacrifice me to get Ælfric's troops on your side. You were supposed to crush Kjartan like a louse, but he's still there, and Ælfric calls himself Lord of Bernicia, and you've got a Danish rebellion on your hands. And for that I slaved at an oar for over two years?" He said nothing. I unbuckled my sword belt and then tugged the heavy mail coat over my head and let it collapse on the floor. Guthred was puzzled as he watched me pull the tunic off my left shoulder, then I showed him the slave scar that Hakka had carved into my upper arm. "You know what that is?" I asked. He shook his head. "A slave mark, lord King. You don't have one?"

"No," he said.

"I took it for you," I said. "I took it so you could be king here, but instead you're a priest-ridden fugitive. I told you to kill Ivarr long ago."

"I should have done," he admitted.

"And you let that miserable piece of hairy gristle, Hrothweard, impose a tithe on the Danes?"

"It was for the shrine," he said. "Hrothweard had a dream. He said Saint Cuthbert spoke to him."

"Cuthbert's talkative for a dead man, isn't he? Why don't you remember that you rule this land, not Saint Cuthbert?"

He looked miserable. "The Christian magic has always worked for me," he said.

"It hasn't worked," I said scornfully. "Kjartan lives, Ivarr lives, and you face a revolt of the Danes. Forget your Christian magic. You've got me now, and you've got Earl Ragnar. He's the best man in your kingdom. Look after him."

"And you," he said, "I shall look after you. I promise."

"I am," Gisela said.

"Because you're going to be my brother-in-law," I told Guthred.

He nodded at that, then gave me a wan smile. "She always said you'd come back."

"And you thought I was dead?"

"I hoped you were not," he said. Then he stood and smiled. "Would you believe me," he asked, "if I said I missed you?"

"Yes, lord," I said, "because I missed you."

"You did?" he asked in hope.

"Yes, lord," I said, "I did." And oddly enough, that was true. I had thought I would hate him when I saw him again, but I had forgotten his infectious charm. I liked him still. We embraced. Guthred picked up his helmet and went to the door that was a piece of cloth hooked onto nails. "I shall leave you my house tonight," he said, smiling. "The two of you," he added.

And he did.

Gisela. These days, when I am old, I sometimes see a girl who
reminds me of Gisela and there comes a catch into my throat. I see a
girl with a long stride, see the black hair, the slim waist, the grace of
her movements and the defiant upward tilt of her head. And when I
see such a girl I think I am seeing Gisela again, and often, because I
have become a sentimental fool in my dotage, I find myself with tears
in my eyes.

"I already have a wife," I told her that night.

"You're married?" Gisela asked me.

"Her name is Mildrith," I said, "and I married her a long time ago
because Alfred ordered it, and she hates me, and so she's gone into a
nunnery."

"All your women do that," Gisela said. "Mildrith, Hild, and me."

"That's true," I said, amused. I had not thought of it before.

"Hild told me to go into a nunnery if I was threatened," Gisela
told me.

"Hild did?"

"She said I'd be safe there. So when Kjartan said he wanted me to
marry his son, I went to the nunnery."

"Guthred would never have married you to Sven," I said.

"My brother thought about it," she said. "He needed money. He
needed help and I was all he had to offer."

"The peace cow."

"That's me," she said.

"Did you like the nunnery?"

"I hated it all the time you were away. Are you going to kill Kjartan?"

"Yes."

"How?"

"I don't know," I said. "Or perhaps Ragnar will kill him. Ragnar has
more cause than me."

"When I refused to marry Sven," Gisela said, "Kjartan said he'd
capture me and let his men rape me. He said he'd stake me on the

ground and let his men use me, and when they were done he'd let his dogs have me. Did you and Mildrith have children?"

"One," I said, "a son. He died."

"Mine won't die. My sons will be warriors, and my daughter will be the mother of warriors."

I smiled, then ran my hand down her long spine so that she shivered on top of me. We were covered by three cloaks and her hair was wet because the thatch was leaking. The floor-rushes were rotted and damp beneath me, but we were happy. "Did you become a Christian in your nunnery?" I asked her.

"Of course not," she said scornfully.

"They didn't mind?"

"I gave them silver."

"Then they didn't mind," I said.

"I don't think any Dane is a real Christian," she told me.

"Not even your brother?"

"We have many gods," she said, "and the Christian god is just another one. I'm sure that's what Guthred thinks. What's the Christian god's name? A nun did tell me, but I've forgotten."

"Jehovah."

"There you are, then. Odin, Thor, and Jehovah. Does he have a wife?"

"No."

"Poor Jehovah," she said.

Poor Jehovah, I thought, and was still thinking it when, in a persistent rain that slashed on the stony remnants of the Roman road and turned the fields to mud, we crossed the Swale and rode north to take the fortress that could not be taken. We rode to capture Dunholm.

NINE

I t seemed simple when I suggested it. We should ride to Dunholm, make a surprise attack, and thus provide Guthred with a safe refuge and Ragnar with revenge, but Hrothweard had been determined to thwart us and, before we rode, there had been another bitter argument. "What happens," Hrothweard had demanded of Guthred, "to the blessed saint? If you ride away, who guards Cuthbert?"

Hrothweard had passion. It was fed by anger, I suppose. I have known other men like him, men who could work themselves into a welter of fury over the smallest insult to the one thing they hold most dear. For Hrothweard that one thing was the church, and anyone who was not a Christian was an enemy to his church. He had become Guthred's chief counselor, and it was his passion that gained him that position. Guthred still saw Christianity as a superior kind of sorcery, and in Hrothweard he thought he had found a man capable of working the magic. Hrothweard certainly looked like a sorcerer. His hair was wild, his beard jutted, he had vivid eyes, and boasted the loudest voice of any man I have ever met. He was unmarried, devoted only to his beloved religion, and men reckoned he would become the archbishop in Eoferwic when Wulfhere died.

Guthred had no passion. He was reasonable, gentle mostly, wanting those about him to be happy, and Hrothweard bullied him. In

Eoferwic, where most of the citizens were Christians, Hrothweard had the power to summon a mob into the streets, and Guthred, to keep the city from riots, had deferred to Hrothweard. And Hrothweard had also learned to threaten Guthred with Saint Cuthbert's displeasure, and that was the weapon he used on the eve of our ride to Dunholm. Our only chance of capturing the fortress was surprise, and that meant moving fast, and in turn that required that Cuthbert's corpse and Oswald's head and the precious gospel book must be left in Cetreht along with all the priests, monks, and women. Father Hrothweard insisted that our first duty was to protect Saint Cuthbert. "If the saint falls into the hands of the pagans," he shouted at Guthred, "then he will be desecrated!" He was right, of course. Saint Cuthbert would be stripped of his pectoral cross and his fine ring, then fed to the pigs, while the precious gospel book from Lindisfarena would have its jeweled cover ripped off and its pages used to light fires or wipe Danish arses. "Your first duty is to protect the saint," Hrothweard bellowed at Guthred.

"Our first duty," I retorted, "is to preserve the king."

The priests, of course, supported Hrothweard, and once I intervened he turned his passion against me. I was a murderer, a pagan, a heretic, a sinner, a defiler, and all Guthred needed to do to preserve his throne was bring me to justice. Beocca alone among the churchmen tried to calm the wild-haired priest, but Beocca was shouted down. Priests and monks declared that Guthred would be cursed by God if he abandoned Cuthbert, and Guthred looked confused and it was Ragnar who ended the silliness. "Hide the saint," he suggested. He had to say it three times before anyone heard him.

"Hide him?" Abbot Eadred asked.

"Where?" Hrothweard demanded scornfully.

"There is a graveyard here," Ragnar said. "Bury him. Who would ever search for a corpse in a graveyard?" The clerics just stared at him. Abbot Eadred opened his mouth to protest, but the suggestion was so sensible that the words died on his lips. "Bury him," Ragnar went on, "then go west into the hills and wait for us."

Hrothweard tried to protest, but Guthred supported Ragnar. He named ten warriors who would stay to protect the priests, and in the morning, as we rode, those men were digging a temporary grave in the cemetery where the saint's corpse and the other relics would be hidden. The men from Bebbanburg also stayed at Cetreht. That was on my insistence. Aidan wanted to ride with us, but I did not trust him. He could easily cause my death by riding ahead and betraying our approach to Kjartan and so we took all his horses, which forced Aidan and his men to stay with the churchmen. Osburh, Guthred's pregnant queen, also remained. Abbot Eadred saw her as a hostage against Guthred's return, and though Guthred made a great fuss of the girl I sensed that he had no great regrets at leaving her. Osburh was an anxious woman, as prone to tears as my wife Mildrith and, also like Mildrith, a great lover of priests. Hrothweard was her confessor and I supposed that she preached the wild man's message in Guthred's bed. Guthred assured her that no roving Danes would come near Cetreht once we had left, but he could not be certain of that. There was always a chance that we would return to find them all slaughtered or taken prisoner, but if we stood any hope of taking Dunholm then we had to move fast.

Was there any hope? Dunholm was a place where a man could grow old and defy his enemies in safety. And we were fewer than two hundred men, along with a score of women who insisted on coming. Gisela was one of those, and she, like the other women, wore breeches and a leather jerkin. Father Beocca also joined us. I told him he could not ride fast enough and that, if he fell behind, we would abandon him, but he would not hear of staying in Cetreht. "As ambassador," he announced grandly, "my place is with Guthred."

"Your place is with the other priests," I said.

"I shall come," he said stubbornly and would not be dissuaded. He made us tie his legs to his saddle-girth so he could not fall off and then he endured the hard pace. He was in agony, but he never complained. I suspect he really wanted to see the excitement. He might have been a squint-eyed cripple and a club-footed priest and an ink-spattered clerk and a pedantic scholar, but Beocca had the heart of a warrior.

We left Cetreht in a misted late autumn dawn that was laced with rain, and Kjartan's remaining riders, who had returned to the river's northern bank, closed in behind us. There were eighteen of them now, and we let them follow us and, to confuse them, we did not stay on the Roman road which led straight across the flatter land toward Dunholm, but after a few miles turned north and west onto a smaller track which climbed into gentle hills. The sun broke through the clouds before midday, but it was low in the sky so that the shadows were long. Redwings flocked beneath the falcon-haunted clouds. This was the time of year that men culled their livestock. Cattle were being pole-axed, and pigs, fattened on the autumn's plentiful acorns, were being slaughtered so their meat could be salted into barrels or hung to dry over smoky fires. The tanning pits stank of dung and urine. The sheep were coming down from the high pastures to be folded close to steadings, while in the valleys the trees rang with the noise of axes as men lay in their winter supply of firewood.

The few villages we passed were empty. Folk must have been warned that horsemen were coming and so they fled before we arrived. They hid in woodlands till we were past, and prayed we did not stay to plunder. We rode on, still climbing, and I had no doubt that the men following us would have sent messengers up the Roman road to tell Kjartan that we were slanting to the west in an attempt to circle Dunholm. Kjartan had to believe that Guthred was making a desperate attempt to reach Bebbanburg, and if we deceived him into that belief then I hoped he would send yet more men out of the fortress, men who would bar the crossings of the Wiire in the western hills.

We spent that night in those hills. It rained again. We had some small shelter from a wood which grew on a south-facing slope and there was a shepherd's hut where the women could sleep, but the rest of us crouched about fires. I knew Kjartan's scouts were watching us from across the valley, but I hoped they were now convinced we were going west. The rain hissed in the fire as Ragnar, Guthred, and I talked with Sihtric, making him remember everything about the place where he had been raised. I doubt I learned anything new. Sihtric had told me all he knew long before and I had often thought of it as I rowed Sverri's boat, but I listened again as he explained that Dunholm's palisade went clear around the crag's summit and was broken only at the southern end where the rock was too steep for a man to climb. The water came from a well on the eastern side. "The well is outside the palisade," he told us, "down the slope a bit."

"But the well has its own wall?"

"Yes, lord."

"How steep a slope?" Ragnar asked.

"Very steep, lord," Sihtric said. "I remember a boy falling down there and he hit his head on a tree and became stupid. And there's a second well to the west," he added, "but that's not used much. The water's murky."

"So he's got food and water," Guthred said bitterly.

"We can't besiege him," I said, "we don't have the men. The eastern well," I turned back to Sihtric, "is among trees. How many?"

"Thick trees, lord," he said, "hornbeams and sycamore."

"And there has to be a gate in the palisade to let men reach the well?"

"To let women go there, lord, yes."

"Can the river be crossed?"

"Not really, lord," Sihtric was trying to be helpful, but he sounded despondent as he described how the Wiire flowed fast as it circled Dunholm's crag. The river was shallow enough for a man to wade, he said, but it was treacherous with sudden deep pools, swirling currents and willow-braided fish traps. "A careful man can cross it in daytime, lord," he said, "but not at night."

I tried to recall what I had seen when, dressed as the dead swordsman, I had stood so long outside the fortress. The ground fell steeply to the east, I remembered, and it was ragged ground, full of tree stumps and boulders, but even at night a man should be able to clamber down that slope to the river's bank. But I also remembered a steep shoulder of rock hiding the view downriver, and I just hoped that shoulder was not so steep as the picture lingering in my head. "What we must do," I said, "is reach Dunholm tomorrow evening. Just before dark. Then attack in the dawn."

"If we arrive before dark," Ragnar pointed out, "they'll see us, and be ready for us."

"We can't get there after dark," I suggested, "because we'll never find the way. Besides, I want them to be ready for us."

"You do?" Guthred sounded surprised.

"If they see men to their north they'll pack their ramparts. They'll have the whole garrison guarding the gate. But that isn't where we'll attack." I looked across the fire at Steapa. "You're frightened of the dark, aren't you?"

The big face stared back at me across the flames. He did not want to admit that he was frightened of anything, but honesty overcame his reluctance. "Yes, lord."

"But tomorrow night," I said, "you'll trust me to lead you through the darkness?"

"I'll trust you, lord," he said.

"You and ten other men," I said, and I thought I knew how we could capture the impregnable Dunholm. Fate would have to be on our side, but I believed, as we sat in that wet cold darkness, that the three spinners had started weaving a new golden thread into my destiny. And I had always believed Guthred's fate was golden.

"Just a dozen men?" Ragnar asked.

"A dozen sceadugengan," I said, because it would be the shadow-walkers who would take Dunholm. It was time for the strange things that haunt the night, the shape-shifters and horrors of the dark, to come to our help.

And once Dunholm was taken, if it could be taken, we still had to kill Ivarr.

We knew Kjartan would have men guarding the Wiire's upstream crossings. He would also know that the farther west we went the

easier the crossing would be, and I hoped that belief would persuade him to send his troops a long way upriver. If he planned to
fight and stop us he had to send his warriors now, before we
reached the Wiire, and to make it seem even more likely that we
were going deep into the hills we did not head directly for the river
next morning, but instead rode north and west onto the moors.
Ragnar and I, pausing on a long windswept crest, saw six of Kjartan's scouts break from the pursuing group and spur hard eastward.
"They've gone to tell him where we're going," Ragnar said.

"Time to go somewhere else then," I suggested.

"Soon," Ragnar said, "but not yet."

Sihtric's horse had cast a shoe and we waited while he saddled one
of the spare horses, then we kept going northwest for another hour.
We went slowly, following sheep tracks down into a valley where
trees grew thick. Once in the valley we sent Guthred and most of the
riders ahead, still following the tracks west, while twenty of us waited
in the trees. Kjartan's scouts, seeing Guthred and the others climb
onto the farther moors, followed carelessly. Our pursuers were only
nine men now, the rest had been sent with messages to Dunholm,
and the nine who remained were mounted on light horses, ideal for
scrambling away from us if we turned on them, but they came unsus-
pecting into the trees. They were halfway through the wood when
they saw Ragnar waiting ahead and then they turned to spur away,
but we had four groups of men waiting to ambush them. Ragnar was
in front of them, I was moving to bar their retreat, Steapa was on
their left and Rollo on their right, and the nine men suddenly realized they were surrounded. They charged at my group in an attempt
to break free of the thick wood, but the five of us blocked their path
and our horses were heavier and two of the scouts died quickly, one
of them gutted by Serpent-Breath, and the other seven tried to scat-
ter, but they were obstructed by brambles and trees, and our men
closed on them. Steapa dismounted to pursue the last enemy into
a bramble thicket. I saw his ax rise and chop down, then heard a
scream that went on and on. I thought it must stop, but on it went

and Steapa paused to sneeze, then his ax rose and fell again and there was sudden silence.

"Are you catching a cold?" I asked him.

"No, lord," he said, forcing his way out of the brambles and dragging the corpse behind him. "His stink got up my nose."

Kjartan was blind now. He did not know it, but he had lost his scouts, and as soon as the nine men were dead we sounded a horn to summon Guthred back, and, as we waited for him, we stripped the corpses of anything valuable. We took their horses, arm rings, weapons, a few coins, some damp bread, and two flasks of birch ale. One of the dead men had been wearing a fine mail coat, so fine that I suspected it had been made in Frankia, but the man had been so thin that the coat fitted none of us until Gisela took it for herself. "You don't need mail," her brother said scornfully.

Gisela ignored him. She seemed astonished that so fine a coat of mail could weigh so much, but she pulled it over her head, freed her hair from the links at her neck and buckled one of the dead men's swords about her waist. She put on her black cloak and stared defiantly at Guthred. "Well?"

"You frighten me," he said with a smile.

"Good," she said, then pushed her horse against mine so the mare would stay still as she mounted, but she had not reckoned with the weight of the mail and had to struggle into the saddle.

"It suits you," I said, and it did. She looked like a Valkyrie, those warrior maidens of Odin who rode the sky in shining armor.

We turned east then, going faster now. We rode through the trees, ducking continually to keep the branches from whipping our eyes, and we went downhill, following a rain-swollen stream that must lead to the Wiire. By the early afternoon we were close to Dunholm, probably no more than five or six miles away, and Sihtric now led us, for he reckoned he knew a place where we could cross the river. The Wiire, he told us, turned south once it had passed Dunholm, and it widened as it flowed through pastureland and there were fords in those gentler valleys. He knew the country well for his mother's parents had lived there and as a child he had often driven cattle through the river. Better still those fords were on Dunholm's eastern side, the flank Kjartan would not be guarding, but there was a risk that the rain, which started to pour again in the afternoon, would so fill the Wiire that the fords would be impassable.

At least the rain hid us as we left the hills and rode into the river valley. We were now very close to Dunholm, that lay just to the north, but we were hidden by a wooded spur of high ground at the foot of which was a huddle of cottages. "Hocchale," Sihtric told me, nodding at the settlement, "it's where my mother was born."

"Your grandparents are still there?" I asked.

"Kjartan had them killed, lord, when he fed my mother to his dogs."

"How many dogs does he have?"

"There were forty or fifty when I was there, lord. Big things. They only obeyed Kjartan and his huntsmen. And the Lady Thyra."

"They obeyed her?" I asked.

"My father wanted to punish her once," Sihtric said, "and he set the dogs on her. I don't think he was going to let them eat her, I think he just wanted to frighten her, but she sang to them."

"She sang to them?" Ragnar asked. He had hardly mentioned Thyra in the last weeks. It was as if he felt guilty that he had left her so long in Kjartan's power. I knew he had tried to find her in the early days of her disappearance, he had even faced Kjartan once when another Dane had arranged a truce between them, but Kjartan had vehemently denied that Thyra was even at Dunholm, and after that Ragnar had joined the Great Army that had invaded Wessex and then he had become a hostage, and all that while Thyra had been in Kjartan's power. Now Ragnar looked at Sihtric. "She sang to them?" he asked again.

"She sang to them, lord," Sihtric confirmed, "and they just lay down. My father was angry with them." Ragnar frowned at Sihtric as though he did not believe what he heard. Sihtric shrugged. "They say she's a sorcerer, lord," he explained humbly.

"Thyra's no sorcerer," Ragnar said angrily. "All she ever wanted was to marry and have children."

"But she sang to the dogs, lord," Sihtric insisted, "and they lay down."

"They won't lie down when they see us," I said. "Kjartan will loose them on us as soon as he sees us."

"He will, lord," Sihtric said, and I could see his nervousness.

"So we'll just have to sing to them," I said cheerfully.

We followed a sodden track beside a flooded ditch to find the Wiire swirling fast and high. The ford looked impassable. The rain was getting harder, pounding the river that fretted at the top of its steep banks. There was a high hill on the far bank and the clouds were low enough to scrape the black, bare branches at its long summit. "We'll never cross here," Ragnar said. Father Beocca, tied to his saddle and with his priest's robes sodden, shivered. The horsemen milled in the mud, watching the river that threatened to spill over its banks, but then Steapa, who was mounted on a huge black stallion, gave a grunt and simply rode down the track into the water. His horse baulked at the river's hard current, but he forced it onward until the water was seething over his stirrups, and then he stopped and beckoned that I should follow.

His idea was that the biggest horses would make a barrier to break the river's force. I pushed my horse up against Steapa's, then more men came and we held onto each other, making a wall of horseflesh that slowly reached across the Wiire, that was some thirty or forty paces wide. We only needed to make our dam at the river's center where the current was strongest, and once we had a hundred men struggling to keep their horses still, Ragnar urged the rest through the calmer water provided by our makeshift dam. Beocca was terrified, poor man, but Gisela took his reins and spurred her own mare into the water. I hardly dared watch: If her horse had been swept away then the mail coat would have dragged her under, but she and Beocca made it safe to the far bank, and two by two the others followed. One woman and one warrior were swept away, but both scrambled safely across and their horses found footing downstream and reached the bank. Once the smaller horses were across we slowly unmade our wall and inched through the rising river to safety.

It was already getting dark. It was only midafternoon, but the clouds were thick. It was a black, wet, miserable day, and now we had to climb the escarpment through the dripping trees, and in places the slope was so steep that we were forced to dismount and lead the horses. Once at the summit we turned north, and I could see Dunholm when the low cloud allowed it. The fortress showed as a dark smear on its high rock and above it I could see the smoke from the garrison fires mingling with the rain clouds. It was possible that men on the southern ramparts could see us now, except that we were riding through trees and our mail was smeared with mud, but even if they could see us they would surely not suspect we were enemies. The last they had heard of Guthred was that he and his desperate men were riding westward, looking for a place to cross the Wiire, and now we were to the east of the fortress and already across the river.

Sihtric still led us. We dropped east off the hill's summit, hiding ourselves from the fortress, then rode into a valley where a stream foamed westward. We forded it easily enough, climbed again, and all the time we pounded past miserable hovels where frightened folk peered from low doorways. They were Kjartan's own slaves, Sihtric told me, their job to raise pigs and cut firewood and grow crops for Dunholm.

Our horses were tiring. They had been ridden hard across soft ground and they carried men in mail with heavy shields, but our journey was almost done. It did not matter now if the garrison saw us, because we had come to the hill on which the fortress stood and no one could leave Dunholm without fighting their way past us. If Kjartan had sent warriors west to find us then he could no longer send a messenger to summon those men back because we now controlled the only road that led to his fastness.

And so we came to the neck where the ridge dropped slightly and the road turned south before climbing to the massive gatehouse, and we stopped there and our horses spread along the higher ground and, to the men on Dunholm's wall, we must have looked like a dark army. All of us were muddy, our horses were filthy, but Kjartan's men could see our spears and shields and swords and axes. By now they would know we were the enemy and that we had cut their only road, and they probably laughed at us. We were so few and their fortress was so high and their wall was so big and the rain still crashed on us and the drenching dark crept along the valleys on either side of us as a slither of lightning crackled wicked and sharp across the northern sky.

We picketed the horses in a waterlogged field. We did our best to rid the beasts of mud and pick their hooves clean, then we made a score of fires in the lee of a blackthorn hedge. It took forever to light the first fire. Many of our men carried dry kindling in leather pouches, but as soon as the kindling was exposed to the rain it became soggy. Eventually two men made a crude tent with their cloaks and I heard the click of steel on flint and saw the first trace of smoke. They protected that small fire as though it were made of gold, and at last the flames took hold and we could pile the wet firewood on top. The logs seethed and hissed and crackled, but the flames gave us some small warmth and the fires told Kjartan that his enemies were still on the hill. I doubt he thought Guthred had the courage to make such an attack, but he must have known Ragnar was returned from Wessex and he knew I had come back from the dead and perhaps, in that long wet night of rain and thunder, he felt a shiver of fear.

And while he shivered, the sceadugengan slithered in the dark.

As night fell I stared at the route I had to take in the darkness, and it was not good. I would have to go down to the river, then southward along the water's edge, but just beneath the fortress wall, where the river vanished about Dunholm's crag, a massive boulder blocked the way. It was a monstrous boulder, bigger than Alfred's new church at Wintanceaster, and if I could not find a way around it then I would have to climb over its wide, flat top which lay less than a spear's throw from Kjartan's ramparts. I sheltered my eyes from the rain and stared hard, and decided there might be a way past the giant stone at the river's edge.

"Can it be done?" Ragnar asked me.

"It has to be done," I said.

I wanted Steapa with me, and I chose ten other men to accompany us. Both Guthred and Ragnar wanted to come, but I refused them. Ragnar was needed to lead the assault on the high gate, and Guthred was simply not warrior enough. Besides, he was one of the reasons we fought this battle and to leave him dead on Dunholm's slopes would make a nonsense of the whole gamble. I took Beocca to one side. "Do you remember," I asked him, "how my father made you stay by my side during the assault on Eoferwic?"

"Of course I do!" he said indignantly. "And you didn't stay with me, did you? You kept trying to join the fight! It was all your fault that you were captured." I had been ten years old and desperate to see a battle. "If you hadn't run away from me," he said, still sounding indignant, "you would never have been caught by the Danes! You'd be a Christian now. I blame myself. I should have tied your reins to mine."

"Then you'd have been captured as well," I said, "but I want you to do the same for Guthred tomorrow. Stay by him and don't let him risk his life."

Beocca looked alarmed. "He's a king! He's a grown man. I can't tell him what to do."

"Tell him Alfred wants him to live."

"Alfred might want him to live," he said gloomily, "but put a sword into a man's hand and he loses his wits. I've seen it happen!"

"Then tell him you had a dream and Saint Cuthbert says he's to stay out of trouble."

"He won't believe me!"

"He will," I promised.

"I'll try," Beocca said, then looked at me with his one good eye. "Can you do this thing, Uhtred?"

"I don't know," I told him honestly.

"I shall pray for you."

"Thank you, father," I said. I would be praying to every god I could think of, and adding another could not hurt. In the end, I decided, it was all up to fate. The spinners already knew what we planned and knew how those plans would turn out and I could only hope they were not readying the shears to cut my life's threads. Perhaps, above everything else, it was the madness of my idea that might give it wings and so let it succeed. There had been madness in Northumbria's air ever since I had first returned. There had been a slaughterous madness in Eoferwic, a holy insanity in Cair Ligualid, and now this desperate idea.

I had chosen Steapa, for he was worth three or four other men. I took Sihtric because, if we got inside Dunholm, he would know the ground. I took Finan because the Irishman had a fury in his soul that I reckoned would turn to savagery in battle. I took Clapa because he was strong and fearless, and Rypere because he was cunning and lithe. The other six were from Ragnar's men, all of them strong, all young, and all good with weapons, and I told them what we were going to do, and then made sure that each man had a black cloak that swathed him from head to foot. We smeared a mixture of mud and ash on our hands, faces, and helmets. "No shields," I told them. That was a hard decision to make, for a shield is a great comfort in battle, but shields were heavy and, if they banged on stones or trees, would make a noise like a drumbeat. "I go first," I told them, "and we'll be going slowly. Very slowly. We have all night."

We tied ourselves together with leather reins. I knew how easy it was for men to get lost in the dark, and on that night the darkness was absolute. If there was any moon it was hidden by thick clouds from which the rain fell steadily, but we had three things to guide us. First there was the slope itself. So long as I kept the uphill side to my right then I knew we were on the eastern side of Dunholm, and second there was the rushing hiss of the river as it curled about the crag, and last there were the fires of Dunholm itself. Kjartan feared an assault in the night and so he had his men hurl flaming logs from the high gate's rampart. Those logs lit the track, but to produce them he had to keep a great fire burning in his courtyard and that blaze outlined the top of the ramparts and glowed red on the belly of the low rushing clouds. That raw light did not illuminate the slope, but it was there, beyond the black shadows, a livid guide in our wet darkness.

I had Serpent-Breath and Wasp-Sting hanging from my belt and, like the others, I carried a spear with its blade wrapped in a scrap of cloth so that no stray light could reflect from the metal. The spears would serve as staffs on the uneven ground and as probes to feel the way. We did not leave until it was utterly dark, for I dared not risk a sharp-eyed sentry seeing us scramble toward the river, but even in the dark our journey was easy enough at first, for our own fires showed us a way down the slope. We headed away from the fortress so that no one on its ramparts would see us leave the firelit camp, and then we worked our way down to the river and there turned southward. Our route now led across the base of the slope where trees had been felled and I had to feel my way between the stumps. The ground was thick with brambles and with the litter of tree-felling. There were small branches left to rot and we made a lot of noise trampling them underfoot, but the sound of the rain was louder still and the river seethed and roared to our left. My cloak kept catching on twigs or stumps and I tore its hem ragged dragging it free. Every now and then a great crack of lightning whipped earthward and we froze each time and, in the blue-white dazzle, I could see the fort outlined high above me. I could even see the spears of the sentries like thorny sparks against the sky, and I thought those sentries must be cold, soaked, and miserable. The thunder came a heartbeat later and it was always close, banging above us as if Thor were beating his war hammer against a giant iron shield. The gods were watching us. I knew that. That is what the gods do in their sky-halls. They watch us and they reward us for our daring or punish us for our insolence, and I clutched Thor's hammer to tell him that I wanted his help, and Thor cracked the sky with his thunder and I took it as a sign of his approval.

The slope grew steeper. Rain was running off the soil which, in places, was nothing but slick mud. We all fell repeatedly as we edged southward. The tree stumps became sparser, but now there were boulders embedded in the slope and the wet stones were slick, so slick that in some places we were forced to crawl. It was getting darker too, for the slope bulged above us to hide the fire-edged ramparts and we slid and scrambled and cursed our way into a soul-scaring blackness. The river seemed very close and I feared sliding off a slab of rock and falling into the hurrying water.

Then my groping spear cracked against stone and I realized we had come to the huge boulder which, in the dark, felt like a monstrous cliff. I thought I had seen a way past on the river's edge and I explored that way, going slowly, always thrusting the spear shaft ahead, but if I had seen a route in the twilight I could not find it now. The boulder appeared to overhang the water and there was no choice but to climb back up the slope beside the great rock and then slither over its domed top, and so we inched our way upward, clinging to saplings and kicking footholds in the sopping earth, and every foot we climbed took us closer to the ramparts. The leather ropes joining us kept catching on snags and it seemed to take forever to reach a spot where the firelight glowing above the palisade showed a way onto the rock's summit.

That summit was a stretch of open stone, pitched like a shallow roof and about fifteen paces wide. The western end rose to the ramparts while the eastern edge ended in a sheer drop to the river, and all that I saw in a flicker of far-off lightning that ripped across the northern clouds. The center of the boulder's top, where we would have to cross, was no more than twenty paces from Kjartan's wall and there was a sentry there, his spear blade revealed by the lightning as a flash of white fire. We huddled beside the stone and I made every man untie the leather rope from his belt. We would retie the reins into one rope and I would crawl across first, letting the rope out behind me, and then each man must follow. "One at a time," I said, "and wait till I tug the rope. I'll tug it three times. That's the signal for the next man to cross." I had to half shout to make myself

heard over the pounding rain and gusting wind. "Crawl on your bellies,"
I told them. If lightning struck, then a prone man covered by a muddy
cloak would be far less visible than a crouching warrior. "Rypere goes
last," I said, "and he brings the rope with him."

It seemed to me that it took half the night just to cross that short
stretch of open rock. I went first, and I crawled blind in the dark and
had to grope with the spear to find a place where I could slither down
the boulder's far side. Then I tugged the rope and after an interminable wait I heard a man crawling on the stone. It was one of Ragnar's Danes who followed the rope to join me. Then one by one the
others came. I counted them in. We helped each man down, and I
prayed there would be no lightning, but then, just as Steapa was
halfway across, there was a crackling blue-white fork that slashed
clear across the hilltop and lit us like worms trapped by the fire of the
gods. In that moment of brightness I could see Steapa shaking, and
then the thunder bellowed over us and the rain seemed to grow even
more malevolent. "Steapa!" I called, "come on!" but he was so shaken
that he could not move and I had to wriggle back onto the boulder,
take his hand and coax him onward, and while doing that I somehow
lost count of the number of men who had already crossed so that,
when I thought the last had arrived I discovered Rypere was still on
the far side. He scrambled over quickly, coiling the rope as he came,
and then we untied the reins and again joined ourselves belt to belt.
We were all chilled and wet, but fate had been with us and no chal-
lenging shout had come from the ramparts.

We slid and half fell back down the slope, seeking the riverbank.
The hillside was much steeper here, but sycamores and hornbeams
grew thick and they made the journey easier. We went on south, the
ramparts high to our right and the river ominous and loud to our left.
There were more boulders, none the size of the giant that had
blocked us before, but all difficult to negotiate, and each one took
time, so much time, and then, as we skirted the uphill side of one
great rock, Clapa dropped his spear, and it clattered down the stone
and banged on a tree.

It did not seem possible that the noise could have been heard up at the ramparts. The rain was seething onto the trees and the wind was loud at the palisade, but someone in the fort heard something or suspected something, for suddenly a burning log was thrown over the wall to crash through the wet branches. It was thrown twenty paces north of us, and we happened to be stopped at the time while I found a way past yet another rock, and the light of the flames was feeble. We were nothing but black shadows among the shadows of the trees. The flickering fire was swiftly extinguished by the rain and I hissed at my men to crouch. I expected more fire to be thrown, and it was, this time a big twisted brand of oil-soaked straw that burned much brighter than the log. Again it was thrown in the wrong place, but its light reached us, and I prayed to Surtur, the god of fire, that he extinguish the flames. We huddled, still as death, just above the river, and then I heard what I feared to hear.

Dogs.

Kjartan, or whoever guarded this stretch of the wall, had sent the war dogs out through the small gate which led to the well. I could hear the huntsmen calling to them with the sing-song voices that drove hounds into undergrowth, and I could hear the dogs baying and I knew there was no escape from this steep, slippery slope. We had no chance of scrambling back up the hill and across the big boulder before the dogs would be on us. I pulled the cloth off the spearhead, thinking that at least I could drive the blade into one beast before the rest trapped, mauled, and savaged us, and just then another splinter of lightning slithered across the night and the thunder cracked like the sound of the world's ending. The noise pounded us and echoed like drumbeats in the river valley.

Hounds hate thunder, and thunder was Thor's gift to us. A second peal boomed in the sky and the hounds were whimpering now. The rain became vicious, driving at the slope like arrows, its sound suddenly drowning the noise of the frightened dogs. "They won't hunt," Finan shouted into my ear.

"No?"

"Not in this rain."

The huntsmen called again, more urgently, and as the rain slackened slightly I heard the dogs coming down the slope. They were not racing down, but slinking reluctantly. They were terrified by the thunder, dazzled by the lightning and bemused by the rain's malevolence. They had no appetite for prey. One beast came close to us and I thought I saw the glint of its eyes, though how that was possible in that darkness, when the hound was only a shape in the sodden blackness, I do not know. The beast turned back toward the hilltop and the rain still slashed down. There was silence now from the huntsmen. None of the hounds had given tongue so the huntsmen must have assumed no quarry had been found and still we waited, crouching in the awful rain, waiting and waiting, until at last I decided the hounds were back in the fortress and we stumbled on.

Now we had to find the well, and that proved the most difficult task of all. First we remade the rope from the reins and Finan held one end while I prowled uphill. I groped through trees, slipped on the mud, and continually mistook tree trunks for the well's palisade. The rope snagged on fallen branches, and twice I had to go back, move everyone some yards southward and start my search again. I was very close to despair when I tripped and my left hand slid down a lichen-covered timber. A splinter drove into my palm. I fell hard against the timber and discovered it was a wall, not some discarded branch, and then realized I had found the palisade protecting the well. I yanked on the rope so that the others could clamber up to join me.

Now we waited again. The thunder moved farther north and the rain subsided to a hard, steady fall. We crouched, shivering, waiting for the first gray hint of dawn, and I worried that Kjartan, in this rain, would not need to send anyone to the well, but could survive on the water collected in rain barrels. Yet everywhere, I assume in all the world, folk fetch water in the dawn. It is the way we greet the day. We need water to cook and shave and wash and brew, and in all the aching hours at Sverri's oar I had often remembered Sihtric telling me that Dunholm's wells were beyond its palisades, and that meant that

Kjartan must open a gate every morning. And if he opened a gate then we could get into the impregnable fortress. That was my plan, the only plan I had, and if it failed we would be dead. "How many women fetch water?" I asked Sihtric softly.

"Ten, lord?" he guessed.

I peered around the palisade's edge. I could just see the glow of fire-light above the ramparts and I guessed the well was twenty paces from the high wall. Not far, but twenty paces of steep uphill climbing. "There are guards on the gate?" I asked, knowing the answer because I had asked the question before, but in the dark and with the killing ahead, it was comforting to speak.

"There were only two or three guards when I was there, lord."

And those guards would be dozy, I thought, yawning after a night of broken sleep. They would open the gate, watch the women go through, then lean on the wall and dream of other women. Yet only one of the guards had to be alert, and even if the gate guards were dreaming, then one alert sentinel on the wall would be sufficient to thwart us. I knew the wall on this eastern side had no fighting plat-form, but it did have smaller ledges where a man could stand and keep watch. And so I worried, imagining all that could go wrong, and beside me Clapa snored in a moment's snatched sleep and I was amazed that he could sleep at all when he was so drenched and cold, and then he snored again and I nudged him awake.

It seemed as though dawn would never come, and if it did we would be so cold and wet that we would be unable to move, but at last, on the heights across the river, there was a hint of gray in the night. The gray spread like a stain. We huddled closer together so that the well's palisade would hide us from any sentry on the wall. The gray became lighter and cocks crowed in the fortress. The rain was still steady. Beneath me I could see white flurries where the river foamed on rocks. The trees below us were visible now, though still shadowed. A badger walked ten paces from us, then turned and hur-ried clumsily downhill. A rent of red showed in a thinner patch of the eastern clouds and it was suddenly daylight, though a gloomy day-

light that was shot through with the silver threads of rain. Ragnar
would be making his shield wall now, lining men on the path to keep
the defenders' attention. If the women were to come for water, I
thought, then it must be soon, and I eased my way down the slope so
I could see all of my men. "When we go," I hissed, "we go fast! Up to
the gate, kill the guard, then stay close to me! And once we're inside,
we go slowly. Just walk! Look as if you belong there."

Twelve of us could not hope to attack all Kjartan's men. If we were
to win this day we had to sneak into the fortress. Sihtric had told me
that behind the well's gate was a tangle of buildings. If we could kill
the guards quickly, and if no one saw their deaths, then I hoped we
could hide in that tangle and then, once we were certain that no one
had discovered us, just walk toward the north wall. We were all in
mail or leather, we all had helmets, and if the garrison was watching
Ragnar approach then they might not notice us at all, and if they did,
they would assume we were defenders. Once at the wall I wanted to
capture a part of the fighting platform. If we could reach that platform and kill the men guarding it, then we could hold a stretch of the
wall long enough for Ragnar to join us. His nimbler men would climb
the palisade by driving axes into the timbers and using the embedded
weapons as steps, and Rypere was carrying our leather rope to help
them up. As more men came we could fight our way down the wall to
the high gate and open it to the rest of Ragnar's force.

It had seemed a good idea when I described it to Ragnar and
Guthred, but in that cold wet dawn it seemed forlorn and desperate
and I was suddenly struck by a sense of hopelessness. I touched my
hammer amulet. "Pray to your gods," I said, "pray no one sees us.
Pray we can reach the wall." It was the wrong thing to say. I should
have sounded confident, but instead I had betrayed my fears and this
was no time to pray to any gods. We were already in their hands and
they would help us or hurt us according to how they liked what we
did. I remember blind Ravn, Ragnar's grandfather, telling me that the
gods like bravery, and they love defiance, and they hate cowardice
and loathe uncertainty. "We are here to amuse them," Ravn had said,

"that is all, and if we do it well then we feast with them till time ends." Ravn had been a warrior before his sight went, and afterward he became a skald, a maker of poems, and the poems he made celebrated battle and bravery. And if we did this right, I thought, then we would keep a dozen skalds busy.

A voice sounded up the slope and I held up a hand to say we should all be silent. Then I heard women's voices and the thump of a wooden pail against timber. The voices came closer. I could hear a woman complaining, but the words were indistinct, then another woman answered, much clearer. "They can't get in, that's all. They can't." They spoke English, so they were either slaves or the wives of Kjartan's men. I heard a splash as a bucket fell down the well. I still held up my hand, cautioning the eleven men to stay still. It would take time to fill the buckets and the more time the better because it would allow the guards to become bored. I looked along the dirty faces, looking for any sign of uncertainty that would offend the gods, and I suddenly realized we were not twelve men, but thirteen. The thirteenth man had his head bowed so I could not see his face, so I poked his booted leg with my spear and he looked up at me.

She looked up at me. It was Gisela.

She looked defiant and pleading, and I was horrified. There is no number so unlucky as thirteen. Once, in Valhalla, there was a feast for twelve gods, but Loki, the trickster god, went uninvited and he played his evil games, persuading Hod the Blind to throw a sprig of mistletoe at his brother, Baldur. Baldur was the favorite god, the good one, but he could be killed by mistletoe and so his blind brother threw the sprig and Baldur died and Loki laughed, and ever since we have known that thirteen is the evil number. Thirteen birds in the sky are an omen of disaster, thirteen pebbles in a cooking pot will poison any food placed in the pot, while thirteen at a meal is an invitation to death. Thirteen spears against a fortress could only mean defeat. Even the Christians know thirteen is unlucky. Father Beocca told me that was because there were thirteen men at Christ's last meal, and the thirteenth was Judas. So I just stared in horror at Gisela and, to show what she had done, I put down my spear and held up ten fingers, then two, then pointed at her and held up one more. She gave a shake of her head as if to deny what I was telling her, but I pointed at her a second time and then at the ground, telling her she must stay where she was. Twelve would go to Dunholm, not thirteen.

"If the babe won't suck," a woman was saying beyond the wall, "then rub its lips with cowslip juice. It always works."

"Rub your tits with it, too," another voice said.

"And put a mix of soot and honey on its back," a third woman advised.

"Two more buckets," the first voice said, "then we can get out of this rain."

It was time to go. I pointed at Gisela again, gesturing angrily that she must stay where she was, then I picked up the spear in my left hand and drew Serpent-Breath. I kissed her blade and stood. It felt unnatural to stand and move again, to be in the daylight, to start walking around the well's palisade. I felt naked under the ramparts and I waited for a shout from a watchful sentinel, but none came. Ahead, not far ahead, I could see the gate and there was no guard standing in the open doorway. Sihtric was on my left, hurrying. The path was made of rough stone, slick and wet. I heard a woman gasp behind us, but still no one shouted the alarm from the ramparts, then I was through the gate and I saw a man to my right and I swept Serpent-Breath and she bit into his throat and I sawed her backward so that the blood was bright in that gray morning. He fell back against the palisade and I drove the spear into his ruined throat. A second gate guard watched the killing from a dozen yards away. His armor was a blacksmith's long leather apron and his weapon a wood-cutter's ax which he seemed unable to raise. He was standing with astonishment on his face and did not move as Finan approached him. His eyes grew wider, then he understood the danger and turned to run and Finan's spear tangled his legs and then the Irishman was standing over him and the sword stabbed down into his spine. I held up my hand to keep everyone still and silent. We waited. No enemy shouted. Rain dripped from the thatch of the buildings. I counted my men and saw ten, then Steapa came through the gate, closing it behind him. We were twelve, not thirteen.

"The women will stay at the well," Steapa told me.

"You're sure?"

"They'll stay at the well," he growled. I had told Steapa to talk to the women drawing water, and doubtless his size alone had quelled any ideas they might have of sounding an alarm.

"And Gisela?"

"She'll stay at the well too," he said.

And thus we were inside Dunholm. We had come to a dark corner of the fortress, a place where two big dung-heaps lay beside a long, low building. "Stables," Sihtric told me in a whisper, though no one alive was in sight to hear us. The rain fell hard and steady. I edged about the end of the stables and could see nothing except for more wooden walls, great heaps of firewood, and thatched roofs thick with moss. A woman drove a goat between two of the huts, beating the animal to make it hurry through the rain.

I wiped Serpent-Breath clean on the threadbare cloak of the man I had killed, then gave Clapa my spear and picked up the dead man's shield. "Sheathe swords," I told everyone. If we walked through the fortress with drawn swords we would attract attention. We must look like men newly woken who were reluctantly going to a wet, cold duty. "Which way?" I asked Sihtric.

He led us alongside the palisade. Once past the stables I could see three large halls that blocked our view of the northern ramparts. "Kjartan's hall," Sihtric whispered, pointing to the right-hand building.

"Talk naturally," I told him.

He had pointed to the largest hall, the only one with smoke coming from the roof-hole. It was built with its long sides east and west, and one gable end was hard up against the ramparts so we would be forced to go deep into the fortress center to skirt the big hall. I could see folk now, and they could see us, but no one thought us strange. We were just armed men walking through the mud, and they were

wet and cold and hurrying between the buildings, much too intent
on reaching warmth and dryness to worry about a dozen bedraggled
warriors. An ash tree grew in front of Kjartan's hall and a lone sentry
guarding the hall door crouched under the ash's leafless branches in a
vain effort to shelter from the wind and rain. I could hear shouting
now. It was faint, but as we neared the gap between the halls I could
see men on the ramparts. They were gazing north, some of them
brandishing defiant spears. So Ragnar was coming. He would be visible even in the half-light for his men were carrying flaming torches.
Ragnar had ordered his attackers to carry the fire so that the defenders would watch him instead of guarding Dunholm's rear. So fire and
steel were coming to Dunholm, but the defenders were jeering Ragnar's men as they struggled up the slippery track. They jeered because
they knew their walls were high and the attackers few, but the sceadugengan were already behind them and none of them had noticed
us, and my fears of the cold dawn began to ebb away. I touched the
hammer amulet and said a silent thank-you to Thor.

We were just yards from the ash tree that grew a few paces from
the door to Kjartan's hall. The sapling had been planted as a symbol
of Yggdrasil, the Tree of Life about which fate writhes, though this
tree looked sickly, scarce more than a sapling that struggled to find
space for its roots in Dunholm's thin soil. The sentry glanced at us
once, noticed nothing odd about our appearance, then turned and
looked across Dunholm's flat summit toward the gatehouse. Men
were crowded on the gatehouse rampart, while other warriors stood
on the wall's fighting platforms built to left and right. A large group
of mounted men waited behind the gate, doubtless ready to pursue
the beaten attackers when they were repulsed from the palisade. I
tried to count the defenders, but they were too many, so I looked to
the right and saw a stout ladder climbing to the fighting platform on
the western stretch of ramparts. That, I thought, is where we should
go. Climb that ladder, capture the western wall and we could let Ragnar inside and so revenge his father and free Thyra and astonish all
Northumbria.

I grinned, suddenly elated at the realization that we were inside Dunholm. I thought of Hild and imagined her praying in her simple chapel with the beggars already huddled outside her nunnery's gate. Alfred would be working, ruining his eyes by reading manuscripts in the dawn's thin light. Men would be stirring on every fortification in Britain, yawning and stretching. Oxen were being harnessed. Hounds would be excited, knowing a day's hunting was ahead, and here we were, inside Kjartan's stronghold and no one suspected our presence. We were wet, we were cold, we were stiff, and we were outnumbered by at least twenty to one, but the gods were with us and I knew we were going to win and I felt a sudden exultation. The battle-joy was coming and I knew the skalds would have a great feat to celebrate.

Or perhaps the skalds would be making a lament. For then, quite suddenly, everything went disastrously wrong.

TEN

The sentry beneath the ash tree turned and spoke to us. "They're wasting their time," he said, obviously referring to Ragnar's forces. The sentry had no suspicions, he even yawned as we approached him, but then something alarmed him. Perhaps it was Steapa, for there could surely be no man in Dunholm who was as tall as the West Saxon. Whatever, the man suddenly realized we were strangers and he reacted quickly by backing away and drawing his sword. He was about to yell a warning when Steapa hurled his spear that struck hard in the sentry's right shoulder, pitching him backward and Rypere followed fast, running his spear into the man's belly with such force that he pinned the man to the feeble ash tree. Rypere silenced him with his sword, and just as that blood flowed, two men appeared around the corner of the smaller hall to our left and they immediately began shouting that enemies were in the compound. One turned and ran, the other drew his sword, and that was a mistake for Finan feinted low with his spear and the man lowered his blade to parry and the spear flashed up to take him in the soft flesh beneath his jaw. The man's mouth bubbled blood onto his beard as Finan stepped close and brought his short-sword up into the man's belly.

Two more corpses. It was raining harder again, the drops hammering onto the mud to dilute the fresh blood and I wondered if we had time to dash across the wide open space to reach the rampart ladder, and just then, to make things worse, the door to Kjartan's hall opened and three men jostled in the doorway and I shouted at Steapa to drive them back. He used his ax, killing the first with an upward blow of ghastly efficiency and thrusting the gutted man back into the second who took the ax-head straight in the face, then Steapa kicked the two men aside to pursue the third who was now inside the hall. I sent Clapa to help Steapa. "And get him out of there fast," I told Clapa because the horsemen by the gate had heard the commotion now and they could see the dead men and see our drawn swords and they were already turning their horses.

And I knew then that we had lost. Everything had depended on surprise, and now that we had been discovered we had no chance of reaching the northern wall. The men on the fighting platforms had turned to watch us and some had been ordered off the ramparts and they were making a shield wall just behind the gate. The horsemen, there were about thirty riders, were spurring toward us. Not only had we failed, but I knew we would be lucky to survive. "Back," I shouted, "back!" All we could hope now was to retreat into the narrow alleys and somehow hold the horsemen off and reach the well gate. Gisela must be rescued and then there would be a frantic retreat downhill in front of a vengeful pursuit. Maybe, I thought, we could cross the river. If we could just wade through the swollen Wiire we might be safe from pursuit, but it was a tremulous hope at best. "Steapa!" I shouted, "Steapa! Clapa!" and the two came from the hall, Steapa with a blood-soaked ax. "Stay together," I shouted. The horsemen were coming fast, but we ran back toward the stables and the horse-men seemed wary of the dark, shadowed spaces between the build-ings for they reined in beside the ash tree with its dead man still pinned to the trunk and I thought their caution would let us survive just long enough to get outside the fortress. Hope revived, not of vic-tory, but of life, and then I heard the noise.

It was the sound of hounds baying. The horsemen had not stopped for fear of attacking us, but because Kjartan had released his dogs and I stared, appalled, as the hounds poured around the side of the smaller hall and came toward us. How many? Fifty? At least fifty. They were impossible to count. A huntsman drove them on with yelping shouts and they were more like wolves than hounds. They were rough-pelted, huge, howling, and I involuntarily stepped backward. This was the hellish pack of the wild hunt, the ghost-hounds that harry the darkness and pursue their prey across the shadow world when night falls. There was no time now to reach the gate. The hounds would sur-round us, they would drag us down, they would savage us, and I thought this must be my punishment for killing the defenseless Brother Jænberht in Cetreht, and I felt the cold, unmanning shudder of abject fear. Die well, I told myself, die well, but how could one die well beneath the teeth of hounds? Our mail coats would slow their sav-agery for a moment, but not for long. And the hounds could smell our fear. They wanted blood and they came in a howling scrabble of mud and fangs, and I lowered Serpent-Breath to take the first snarling bitch in the face and just then a new voice called to them.

It was the voice of a huntress. It called clear and loud, saying no words, just chanting a weird, shrieking call that pierced the morning like a sounding horn, and the hounds stopped abruptly, twisted about and whined in distress. The closest was just three or four paces from me, a bitch with a mud-clotted pelt, and she writhed and howled as the unseen huntress called again. There was something sad in that wordless call that was a wavering, dying shriek, and the bitch whined in sympathy. The huntsman who had released the hounds tried to whip them back toward us, but again the weird, ululating voice came clear through the rain, but sharper this time, as if the huntress were yelping in sudden anger, and three of the hounds leaped at the hunts-man. He screamed, then was overwhelmed by a mass of pelts and teeth. The riders spurred at the dogs to drive them off the dying man, but the huntress was making a wild screeching now that drove the whole pack toward the horses, and the morning was filled with the seethe of rain and the unearthly cries and the howl of hounds, and the horsemen turned in panic and spurred back toward the gatehouse.

The huntress called again, gentler now, and the hounds obediently milled around the feeble ash tree, letting the riders go.

I had just stared. I still stared. The hounds were crouching, teeth bared, watching the door of Kjartan's hall and it was there that the huntress appeared. She stepped over the gutted corpse Steapa had left in the doorway and she crooned at the hounds and they flattened themselves as she stared at us.

It was Thyra.

I did not recognize her at first. It had been years since I saw Ragnar's sister, and I only remembered her as a fair child, happy and healthy, with her sensible mind set on marrying her Danish warrior. Then her father's hall had been burned, her Danish warrior was killed, and she had been taken by Kjartan and given to Sven. Now I saw her again and she had become a thing from nightmare.

She wore a long cloak of deerskin, held by a bone brooch at her throat, but beneath the cloak she was naked. As she walked among the hounds the cloak kept being dragged away from her body that was painfully thin and foully dirty. Her legs and arms were covered with scars as though someone had slashed her repeatedly with a knife, and where there were no scars there were sores. Her golden hair was lank, matted, and greasy, and she had woven strands of dead ivy into the tangle. The ivy hung about her shoulders. Finan, seeing her, made the sign of the cross. Steapa did the same and I clutched at my hammer amulet. Thyra's curled fingernails were as long as a gelder's knives, and she waved those sorceress's hands in the air and suddenly screamed at the hounds who whined and writhed as if in pain. She glanced toward us and I saw her mad eyes and I felt a pulse of fear because she was suddenly crouching and pointing directly at me, and those eyes were bright as lightning and filled with hate. "Ragnar!" she shouted, "Ragnar!" The name sounded like a curse and the hounds twisted to stare where she pointed and I knew they would leap at me as soon as Thyra spoke again.

"I'm Uhtred!" I called to her, "Uhtred!" I took off my helmet so she could see my face. "I'm Uhtred!"

"Uhtred?" she asked, still looking at me, and in that brief moment she looked sane, even confused. "Uhtred," she said again, this time as if she were trying to remember the name, but the tone turned the hounds away from us and then Thyra screamed. It was not a scream at the hounds, but a wailing, howling screech aimed at the clouds, and suddenly she turned her fury on the dogs. She stooped and clutched handfuls of mud that she hurled at them. She still used no words, but spoke some tongue that the hounds understood and they obeyed her, streaming across Dunholm's rocky summit to attack the newly made shield wall behind the gate. Thyra followed them, calling to them, spitting and shuddering, filling the hell pack with frenzy, and the fear that had rooted me to the cold ground passed and I shouted at my men to go with her.

They were terrible things, those hounds. They were beasts from the world's chaos, trained only to kill, and Thyra drove them on with her high, wailing cries, and the shield wall broke long before the dogs arrived. The men ran, scattering across Dunholm's wide summit and the dogs followed them. A handful, braver than the rest, stayed at the gate and that was where I now wanted to go. "The gate!" I shouted at Thyra, "Thyra! Take them to the gate!" She began to make a barking sound, shrill and quick, and the hounds obeyed her by running toward the gatehouse. I have seen other hunters direct hounds as deftly as a horseman guides a stallion with knees and reins, but it is not a skill I have ever learned. Thyra had it.

Kjartan's men guarding the gate died hard. The dogs swarmed over them, teeth ripping, and I heard screams. I had still not seen Kjartan or Sven, but nor did I look for them. I only wanted to reach the big gate and open it for Ragnar, and so we followed the hounds, but then one of the horsemen recovered his wits and shouted at the frightened men to circle behind us. The horseman was a big man, his mail half covered by a dirty white cloak. His helmet had gilt-bronze eyeholes that hid his face, but I was certain it was Kjartan. He spurred his stallion and a score of men followed him, but Thyra howled some short, falling cadences, and a score of hounds turned to head the horsemen off. One rider, desperate to avoid the beasts, turned his horse too quickly and it fell, sprawling and kicking in the mud and a half-dozen hounds attacked the fallen beast's belly while others leaped across to savage the unsaddled rider. I heard the man wail and saw a dog stagger away with a leg broken by a flailing hoof. The horse was screaming. I kept running through the streaming rain and saw a spear come flashing down from the ramparts. The men on the gatehouse roof were trying to stop us with their spears. They hurled them at the pack which still tore at the fallen shield wall remnant, but there were too many hounds. We were close to the gate now, only twenty or thirty paces away. Thyra and her hounds had brought us safe across Dunholm's summit, and the enemy was in utter confusion, but then the white-cloaked horseman, beard thick beneath his armored eyes, dismounted and shouted at his men to slaughter the dogs.

They made a shield wall and charged. They held their shields low to fend off the dogs and used spears and swords to kill them. "Steapa!" I shouted, and he understood what was wanted and bellowed at the other men to go with him. He and Clapa were first among the dogs and I saw Steapa's ax thud down into a helmeted face as Thyra hurled the dogs at the new shield wall. Men were clambering down from the fighting platforms to join the wild fight and I knew we had to move fast before Kjartan's men slaughtered the pack and then came to slaughter us. I saw a hound leap high and sink its teeth into a man's face, and the man screamed and the dog howled with a sword in its belly, and Thyra was screeching at the hounds and Steapa was holding the center of the enemy shield wall, but it was lengthening as men joined its flanks and in a heartbeat or two the wings of the wall would fold about men and dogs and cut them down. So I ran for the gatehouse archway. That archway was undefended on the ground, but the warriors on the rampart above still had spears. All I had was the dead man's shield and I prayed it was a good one. I hoisted it over my helmet, sheathed Serpent-Breath, and ran.

The heavy spears crashed down. They banged into the shield and splashed into the mud, and at least two pierced through the shield's limewood boards. I felt a blow on my left forearm, and the shield became heavier and heavier as the spears weighed it down, but then I was under the arch, and safe. The dogs were howling and fighting. Steapa was bellowing at the enemy to come and fight him, but men avoided him. I could see the wings of Kjartan's wall closing and knew we would die if I could not open the gate. I saw I would need two hands to lift the huge locking bar, but one of the spears hanging from the shield had penetrated the mail of my left forearm and I could not pull it free, so I had to use Wasp-Sting to cut the leather shield-handles away. Then I could wrench the spear-point out of my mail and arm. There was blood on the mail-sleeve, but the arm was not broken and I lifted the huge locking bar and dragged it away from the gates.

Then I pulled the gates inward and Ragnar and his men were fifty paces away and they shouted when they saw me and ran with raised shields to protect themselves from the spears and axes thrown from the ramparts, and they joined the shield wall, lengthening it and carrying their blades and fury against Kjartan's astonished men.

And that was how Dunholm, the rocky fortress in its river-loop, was taken. Years later I was flattered by a lord in Mercia whose skald chanted a song of how Uhtred of Bebbanburg scaled the fortress crag alone and fought his way through two hundred men to open the dragon-guarded high gate. It was a fine song, full of sword-work and courage, but it was all nonsense. There were twelve of us, not one, and the dogs did most of the fighting, and Steapa did much of the rest, and if Thyra had not come from the hall then Dunholm might be ruled by Kjartan's descendants to this day. Nor was the fight over when the gate was opened, for we were still outnumbered, but we had the remaining dogs and Kjartan did not, and Ragnar brought his shield wall into the compound and there we fought the defenders.

It was shield wall against shield wall. It was the horror of two shield walls fighting. It was the thunder of shields crashing together and the grunts of men stabbing with short-swords or twisting spears into enemy bellies. It was blood and shit and guts spilled in the mud. The shield wall is where men die and where men earn the praise of skalds. I joined Ragnar's wall and Steapa, who had taken a shield from a hound-ripped horseman, bulled in beside me with his great war ax.

We stepped over dead and dying dogs as we drove forward. The shield becomes a weapon, its great iron boss a club to drive men back, and when the enemy falters you close up fast and ram the blade forward, then step over the wounded and let the men behind you kill them. It rarely lasts long before one wall breaks, and Kjartan's line broke first. He had tried to outflank us and send men around our rear, but the surviving hounds guarded our flanks, and Steapa was flailing with his ax like a madman, and he was so huge and strong that he hacked into the enemy line and made it look easy. "Wessex!" he kept shouting, "Wessex!" as though he fought for Alfred, and I was on his right and Ragnar on his left and the rain crashed on us as we followed Steapa through Kjartan's shield wall. We went clean through so that there was no enemy in front of us, and the broken wall collapsed as men ran back toward the buildings.

Kjartan was the man in the dirty white cloak. He was a big man, almost as tall as Steapa, and he was strong, but he saw his fortress fall and he shouted at his men to make a new shield wall, but some of his warriors were already surrendering. Danes did not give up readily, but they had discovered they were fighting fellow Danes, and there was no shame in yielding to such an enemy. Others were fleeing, going through the well gate, and I had a terror that Gisela would be discovered there and taken, but the women who had gone to draw water protected her. They all huddled inside the well's small palisade and the panicked men fled past them toward the river.

Not all panicked or surrendered. A few gathered about Kjartan and locked their shields and waited for death. Kjartan might have been cruel, but he was brave. His son, Sven, was not brave. He had commanded the men on the gatehouse ramparts, and almost all those men fled northward, leaving Sven with just two companions. Guthred, Finan, and Rollo climbed to deal with them, but only Finan was needed. The Irishman hated fighting in the shield wall. He was too light, he reckoned, to be part of such weight-driven killing, but in the open he was a fiend. Finan the Agile, he had been called, and I watched, astonished, as he leaped ahead of both

Guthred and Rollo and took on the three men alone, and his two
swords were as fast as a viper's strike. He carried no shield. He dazzled Sven's defenders with feints, twisted past their attacks, and
killed them both with a grin on his face, and then turned on Sven,
but Sven was a coward. He had backed into a corner of the rampart
and was holding his sword and shield wide apart as if to show he
meant no mischief. Finan crouched, still grinning, ready to drive
his long sword into Sven's exposed belly.

"He's mine!" Thyra wailed. "He's mine!"

Finan glanced at her and Sven twitched his sword arm, as if to
strike, but Finan's blade whipped toward him and he froze. He was
whimpering for mercy.

"He's mine!" Thyra shrieked. She was writhing her ghastly fingernails
towards Sven and was sobbing with hatred. "He's mine!" she cried.

"You belong to her," Finan said, "so you do," and he feinted at
Sven's stomach and when Sven brought his shield down to protect
himself, Finan just rammed his body into the shield, using his light
weight to tip Sven backward over the rampart. Sven screamed as he
fell. It was not a long drop, no more than the height of two tall men,
but he thumped into the mud like a sack of grain. He scrabbled on his
back, trying to get up, but Thyra was standing over him and she had
given a long, wailing call, and the surviving hounds had come to her.
Even the crippled hounds hauled themselves through muck and
blood to reach her side.

"No," Sven said. He stared up at her with his one eye. "No!"

"Yes," she hissed, and she bent down and took the sword from his
unresisting hand, and then she gave one yelp and the hounds closed
on him. He twitched and screamed as the fangs took him. Some,
trained to kill quickly, went for his throat, but Thyra used Sven's
sword to fend them off, and so the hounds killed Sven by chewing
him from the groin upward. His screams pierced the rain like blades.
His father heard it all and Thyra watched it and just laughed.

And still Kjartan lived. Thirty-four men stood with him and they
knew they were dead men and they were ready to die as Danes, but

then Ragnar walked toward them, the eagle wings on his helmet broken and wet, and he mutely pointed his sword at Kjartan and Kjartan nodded and stepped out of the shield wall. His son's guts were being eaten by hounds and Thyra was dancing in Sven's blood and crooning a victory song.

"I killed your father," Kjartan sneered at Ragnar, "and I'll kill you."

Ragnar said nothing. The two men were six paces apart, judging each other.

"Your sister was a good whore," Kjartan said, "before she went mad." He darted forward, shield up, and Ragnar stepped right to let Kjartan go past him and Kjartan anticipated the move and swept his sword low to slice Ragnar's ankles, but Ragnar had stepped back. The two men watched each other again.

"She was a good whore even after she went mad," Kjartan said, "except we had to tie her down to stop her struggling. Made it easier, see?"

Ragnar attacked. Shield high, sword low, and the two shields cracked together and Kjartan's sword parried the low strike, and both men heaved, trying to topple the other, and then Ragnar stepped back again. He had learned that Kjartan was fast and skillful.

"She's not a good whore now, though," Kjartan said. "She's too raddled. Too filthy. Even a beggar won't hump her now. I know. I offered her to one last week and he wouldn't have her. Reckoned she was too dirty for him." And suddenly he came forward fast and hacked at Ragnar. There was no great skill in his attack, just sheer strength and speed, and Ragnar retreated, letting his shield take the fury, and I feared for him and took a pace forward, but Steapa held me back.

"It's his fight," Steapa said.

"I killed your father," Kjartan said, and his sword drove a splinter of wood from Ragnar's shield. "I burned your mother," he boasted, and another blow rang on the shield boss, "and I whored your sister," he said, and the next sword blow drove Ragnar back two paces. "And I shall piss on your gutted body," Kjartan shouted and he reversed a swing, took his blade low and swept it at Ragnar's ankles again. This time he struck and Ragnar staggered. His crippled hand had instinctively dropped his shield low and Kjartan brought his own shield over the top to drive his enemy down, and Ragnar, who had said nothing throughout the fight, suddenly screamed. For a heartbeat I thought it was a doomed man's scream, but instead it was rage. He drove his body under Kjartan's shield, pushing the bigger man back by sheer strength, and then he stepped nimbly aside. I thought he had been lamed by the blow to his ankle, but he had iron strips on his boot and, though one strip was almost cut in two, and though he was bruised, he had not been injured and suddenly he was all anger and movement. It was as though he had woken up. He began to dance around Kjartan, and that was the secret of a duel. Keep moving. Ragnar moved, and he was filled with rage, and his speed almost matched Finan's swiftness, and Kjartan, who thought he had found his enemy's measure, was suddenly desperate. He had no more breath for insults, only enough to defend himself, and Ragnar was all ferocity and quickness. He hacked at Kjartan, turned him, hacked again, lunged, twisted away, feinted low, used his shield to knock away a parry and swept his sword, Heart-Breaker, to strike Kjartan's helmet. He dented the iron, but did not pierce it, and Kjartan shook his head and Ragnar banged shield on shield to drive the big man back. His next blow shattered one of the limewood boards of Kjartan's shield, the next took the shield's edge, splitting the iron rim, and Kjartan stepped back and Ragnar was keening, a sound so horrible that the hounds around Thyra began yelping in sympathy.

Over two hundred men watched. We all knew what would happen now for the battle-fever had come to Ragnar. It was the rage of a sword-Dane. No man could resist such anger, and Kjartan did well to survive as long as he did, but at last he was driven back and he tripped on a hound's corpse and fell on his back and Ragnar stepped over the frantic sweep of his enemy's heavy sword and thrust down hard with Heart-Breaker. The blow broke through the mail-sleeve of Kjartan's coat and severed the tendons of his sword arm. Kjartan tried to get up, but Ragnar kicked him in the face, then brought his heel hard down on Kjartan's throat. Kjartan choked. Ragnar stepped back and let his battered shield slide off his left arm. Then he used his crippled left hand to take away Kjartan's sword. He used his two good fingers to pull it from Kjartan's nerveless hand and he threw it into the mud and then he killed his enemy.

It was a slow death, but Kjartan did not scream once. He tried to resist at first, using his shield to fend off Ragnar's sword, but Ragnar bled him to death cut by cut. Kjartan said one thing as he died, a plea to be given back his sword so he could go to the corpse-hall with honor, but Ragnar shook his head. "No," he said, and never spoke another word until the last blow. That blow was a two-handed downward thrust into Kjartan's belly, a thrust that burst through the mail links and pierced Kjartan's body, and went through the mail beneath Kjartan's spine to stab the ground beneath, and Ragnar left Heart-Breaker there and stepped back as Kjartan writhed in his death pain. It was then that Ragnar looked up into the rain, his abandoned sword swaying where it pinned his enemy to the ground, and he shouted at the clouds. "Father!" he shouted, "Father!" He was telling Ragnar the Elder that his murder was avenged.

Thyra wanted vengeance as well. She had been crouching with her hounds to watch Kjartan's death, but now she stood and called to the hounds who ran toward Ragnar. My first thought was that she was sending the beasts to eat Kjartan's corpse, but instead they surrounded Ragnar. There were still twenty or more of the wolf-like beasts and they snarled at Ragnar, ringing him, and Thyra screamed at him. "You should have come before! Why didn't you come before?"

He stared at her, astonished at her anger. "I came as soon . . ." he began.

"You went viking!" she screamed at him. "You left me here!" The dogs were anguished by her grief and they writhed around Ragnar, their hides blood-matted and their tongues lolling over blood-streaked fangs, just waiting for the word that would let them tear him to red ruin. "You left me here!" Thyra wailed, and she walked into the dogs to face her brother. Then she dropped to her knees and began to weep. I tried to reach her, but the dogs turned on me, teeth bared and eyes wild, and I stepped hurriedly away. Thyra wept on, her grief as great as the storm which raged over Dunholm. "I shall kill you!" she screamed at Ragnar.

"Thyra," he said.

"You left me here!" she accused him. "You left me here!" She stood again, and suddenly her face looked sane once more, and I could see she was still a beauty beneath the filth and the scars. "The price of my life," she said to her brother in a calm voice, "is your death."

"No," a new voice said, "no, it is not."

It was Father Beocca who had spoken. He had been waiting under the high gate's arch and now he limped through the carnage and spoke with a stern authority. Thyra snarled at him. "You're dead, priest!" she said, and she gave one of her wordless yelps and the dogs turned on Beocca as Thyra began to twitch like a madwoman again. "Kill the priest!" she screamed at the dogs. "Kill him! Kill him! Kill him!"

I ran forward, then saw I had nothing to do.

The Christians often talk of miracles and I have always wanted to witness one such piece of magic. They claim the blind can be given their sight, the cripple made to walk, and the leper healed. I have heard them tell stories of men walking on water, and even of dead men raised alive from their graves, but I have never seen such things. If I had seen that great magic then I would be a Christian today, but the priests tell me we must have faith instead. But that day, in the relentless rain, I saw a thing which was as close to a miracle as ever I witnessed.

Father Beocca, the skirts of his priest's robes filthy with mud, limped into the press of vicious hounds. They had been sent to attack him, and Thyra was screaming at them to kill, but he ignored the beasts and they simply shrank away from him. They whimpered as though they feared this squint-eyed cripple and he hobbled calmly through their fangs and did not take his eyes off Thyra whose screeching voice faded to a whimper and then to great sobs. Her cloak was open, showing her scarred nakedness, and Beocca took off his own rain-sodden cloak and draped it about her shoulders. She had her hands at her face. She was still weeping, and the hounds bayed in sympathy, and Ragnar just watched. I thought Beocca would lead Thyra away, but instead he took her head in his two hands and he suddenly shook her. He shook her hard, and as he did he cried to the clouds. "Lord," he shouted, "take this demon from her! Take the evil one away! Spare her from Abaddon's grip!" She screamed then and the hounds put their heads back and howled at the rain. Ragnar was motionless. Beocca shook Thyra's head again, shook it so hard that I thought he might break her neck. "Take the fiend from her, Lord!" he called. "Release her to your love and to your great mercy!" He stared upward. His crippled hand was gripping Thyra's hair with its dead ivy strands, and he pushed her head backward and forward as he chanted in a voice as loud as a warrior lord on a field of slaughter. "In the name of the Father," he shouted, "and of the Son, and of the Holy Ghost, I command you, foul demons, to come from this girl. I cast you into the pit! I banish you! I send you to hell for evermore and a day, and I do it in the name of the Father, and of the Son, and of the Holy Ghost! Be gone!"

And Thyra suddenly began to cry. Not to scream and sob and gasp and struggle for breath, but just a gentle weeping, and she laid her head on Beocca's shoulder and he put his arms about her and cradled her and looked at us with resentment as if we, blood-stained and armed and fierce, were the allies of the demons he had banished. "She's all right now," he said awkwardly, "she's all right now. Oh, go away!" This peevish command was to the hounds and, astonishingly, they obeyed him, slinking away and leaving Ragnar unthreatened. "We must get her warm," Beocca said, "and we must get her dressed properly."

"Yes," I said, "we must."

"Well, if you won't do it," Beocca said indignantly, because I had not moved, "then I shall." And he led Thyra toward Kjartan's hall where the smoke still sifted from the roof-hole. Ragnar made to go after them, but I shook my head and he stopped. I put my right foot on Kjartan's dead belly and yanked Heart-Breaker free. I gave the sword to Ragnar and he embraced me, but there was little elation in either of us. We had done the impossible, we had taken Dunholm, but Ivarr still lived and Ivarr was the greater enemy.

"What do I say to Thyra?" Ragnar asked me.

"You tell her the truth," I said, because I did not know what else to say, and then I went to find Gisela.

Gisela and Brida washed Thyra. They washed her body and her hair, and they took the dead ivy away and they combed her golden hair, and then they dried it before the great fire in Kjartan's hall, and afterward they dressed her in a simple woolen robe and a cloak of otter fur. Ragnar then talked with her beside the fire. They talked alone and I walked with Father Beocca outside the hall. It had stopped raining. "Who is Abaddon?" I asked him.

"I was responsible for your education," he said, "and I am ashamed of myself. How could you not know that?"

"Well I don't," I said, "so who is he?"

"The dark angel of the bottomless pit, of course. I'm sure I told you that. He's the first demon who will torment you if you don't repent and become a Christian."

"You're a brave man, father," I told him.

"Nonsense."

"I tried to reach her," I said, "but I was scared of the hounds. They killed thirty or more men today and you just walked into them."

"They're only dogs," he said dismissively. "If God and Saint Cuthbert can't protect me from dogs, what can they do?"

I stopped him, put both my hands on his shoulders and squeezed. "You were very brave, father," I insisted, "and I salute you."

Beocca was enormously pleased with the compliment, but tried to look modest. "I just prayed," he said, "and God did the rest." I let him go and he walked on, kicking at a fallen spear with his club foot. "I didn't think the dogs would hurt me," he said, "because I've always liked dogs. I had one as a child."

"You should get yourself another one," I said. "A dog would be company for you."

"I couldn't work as a small boy," he went on as though I had not spoken. "Well, I could pick stones and scare birds off newly scattered seed, but I couldn't do proper work. The dog was my friend, but he died. Some other boys killed it." He blinked a few times. "Thyra's a pretty woman, isn't she?" he said, sounding wistful.

"She is now," I agreed.

"Those scars on her arms and legs," he said, "I thought Kjartan or Sven had cut her. But it wasn't them. She did it to herself."

"She cut herself?" I asked.

"Slashed herself with knives, she told me. Why would she do that?"

"To make herself ugly?" I suggested.

"But she isn't," Beocca said, puzzled. "She's beautiful."

"Yes," I said, "she is," and again I felt sorry for Beocca. He was getting old and he had always been crippled and ugly, and he had always wanted to marry, and no woman had ever come to him. He should have been a monk and thus forbidden to marry. Instead he was a priest, and he had a priest's mind for he looked at me sternly.

"Alfred sent me to preach peace," he said, "and I have watched you murder a holy brother, and now this." He grimaced at the dead.

"Alfred sent us to make Guthred safe," I reminded him.

"And we have to make certain Saint Cuthbert is safe," he insisted.

"We will."

"We can't stay here, Uhtred, we have to go back to Cetreht." He looked up at me with alarm in his one good eye. "We have to defeat Ivarr!"

"We will, father," I said.

"He has the biggest army in Northumbria!"

"But he will die alone, father," I said, and I was not sure why I said that. The words just came from my tongue, and I thought a god must have spoken through me. "He will die alone," I said again, "I promise it."

But there were things to do first. There was Kjartan's hoard to uncover from the hall where the dogs were kenneled, and we put Kjartan's slaves to work, digging into the shit-stinking floor, and beneath it were barrels of silver and vats of gold and crosses from churches and arm rings and leather bags of amber, jet, and garnets, and even bolts of precious imported silk that had half rotted away in the damp earth. Kjartan's defeated warriors made a pyre for their dead, though Ragnar insisted that neither Kjartan nor what was left of Sven should be given such a funeral. Instead they were stripped of their armor and their clothes and then their naked corpses were given to those pigs which had been spared the autumn slaughter and lived in the northwest corner of the compound.

Rollo was given charge of the fortress. Guthred, in the excitement of victory, had announced that the fort was now his property and that it would become a royal fortress of Northumbria, but I took him aside and told him to give it to Ragnar. "Ragnar will be your friend," I told him, "and you can trust him to hold Dunholm." I could trust Ragnar, too, to raid Bebbanburg's lands and to keep my treacherous uncle in fear.

So Guthred gave Dunholm to Ragnar, and Ragnar entrusted its keeping to Rollo and he left him just thirty men to hold the walls while we went south. Over fifty of Kjartan's defeated men swore their loyalty to Ragnar, but only after he had determined that none of them had taken part in the hall-burning that had killed his parents. Any man who had helped with that murder was killed. The rest would ride with us, first to Cetreht, and then to confront Ivarr.

So half our job was done. Kjartan the Cruel and Sven the One-Eyed were dead, but Ivarr lived and Alfred of Wessex, though he had never said as much, wanted him dead too.

So we rode south.

ELEVEN

We left next morning. The rain had gone southward, leaving a
rinsed sky ragged with small hurrying clouds beneath which
we rode from Dunholm's high gate. We left the treasure in Rollo's keeping. We were all wealthy men for we had taken Kjartan's fortune, and if
we survived our meeting with Ivarr then we would share those riches. I
had more than replaced the hoard I had left at Fifhaden and I would go
back to Alfred as a rich man, one of the richest in his kingdom, and that
was a cheering thought as we followed Ragnar's eagle-wing standard
toward the nearest ford across the Wiire.

Brida rode with Ragnar, Gisela was beside me, and Thyra would not
leave Beocca's side. I never did discover what Ragnar had said to her in
Kjartan's hall, but she was calm with him now. The madness was gone.
Her fingernails were trimmed, her hair was tidy beneath a white bonnet and that morning she had greeted her brother with a kiss. She still
looked unhappy, but Beocca had the words to comfort her and she
drew on those words as if they were water and she were dying of thirst.
They both rode mares and Beocca, for once, had forgotten his discom-
fort in the saddle as he talked with Thyra. I could see his good hand
gesturing as he spoke. Behind him a servant led a packhorse which carried four big altar crosses taken from Kjartan's hoard. Beocca had
demanded they be returned to the church, and none of us could deny

him for he had proved himself as great a hero as any of us, and now he leaned toward Thyra, spoke urgently, and she listened.

"She'll be a Christian within a week," Gisela said to me.

"Sooner," I said.

"So what happens to her?" she asked.

I shrugged. "He'll talk her into a nunnery, I suppose."

"Poor woman."

"At least she'll learn obedience there," I said. "She won't make twelve into thirteen."

Gisela punched my arm, thus hurting herself instead of me. "I swore," she said, rubbing her knuckles where they had scraped against my mail, "that once I found you again I would not leave you. Not ever."

"But thirteen?" I asked her. "How could you do that?"

"Because I knew the gods were with us," she said simply. "I cast the runesticks."

"And what do the runesticks say of Ivarr?" I asked.

"That he will die like a snake under a hoe," she said grimly, then flinched as a gobbet of mud, thrown up by a hoof of Steapa's horse, spattered onto her face. She wiped it off, then frowned at me. "Must we go to Wessex?"

"I swore as much to Alfred."

"You swore?"

"I gave him my oath."

"Then we must go to Wessex," she said without enthusiasm. "Do you like Wessex?"

"No."

"Alfred?"

"No."

"Why not?"

"He's too pious," I said, "and he's too earnest. And he stinks."

"All Saxons stink," she said.

"He stinks worse than most. It's his illness. It makes him shit all the time."

She grimaced. "Doesn't he wash?"

"At least once a month," I said, "and probably more often. He's very fastidious about washing, but he still stinks. Do I stink?"

"Like a boar," she said, grinning. "Will I like Alfred?"

"No. He won't approve of you because you're not a Christian."

She laughed at that. "What will he do with you?"

"He'll give me land," I said, "and expect me to fight for him."

"Which means you'll fight the Danes?"

"The Danes are Alfred's enemies," I said, "so yes. I'll fight the Danes."

"But they're my people," she said.

"And I've given Alfred my oath," I said, "so I must do what he wants." I leaned back as the stallion picked its way down a steep hill. "I love the Danes," I said, "love them far more than I do the West Saxons, but it's my fate to fight for Wessex. Wyrd bið ful aræd."

"Which means?"

"That fate is fate. That it rules us."

She thought about that. She was dressed in her mail again, but around her neck was a golden torc taken from Kjartan's treasures. It was made from seven strands twisted into one and I had seen similar things dug from the graves of ancient British chieftains. It gave her a wild look, which suited her. Her black hair was pinned under a woolen cap and she had a faraway look on her long face, and I thought I could look at that face forever. "So how long must you be Alfred's man?"

"Until he releases me," I said, "or until either he or I die."

"But you say he's sick. So how long can he live?"

"Probably not very long."

"So who becomes king then?"

"I don't know," I said, and I wished I did. Alfred's son, Edward, was a mewling child, much too young to rule, and his nephew, Æthelwold, from whom Alfred had usurped the throne, was a drunken fool. The drunken fool had the better claim to the throne, and I suddenly found myself hoping that Alfred would live long. That did surprise me. I had told Gisela the truth, that I did not like Alfred, but I recognized that he was the true power in the island of Britain. No one else had his vision, no one else had his determination, and Kjartan's death was not so much our doing, but Alfred's. He had sent us north, knowing we would do what he wanted even though he had not explicitly told us what that was, and I was struck by the thought that life as his oath-man might not be as dull as I had feared. But if he died soon, I thought, then that would be the end of Wessex. The thegns would fight for his crown and the Danes would scent the weakness and come like ravens to pluck the corpse-meat.

"If you're Alfred's sworn man," Gisela asked carefully, and her question revealed that she must have been thinking the same thoughts, "why did he let you come here?"

"Because he wants your brother to rule in Northumbria."

She thought about that. "Because Guthred is a Christian of sorts?"

"That's important to Alfred," I said.

"Or because Guthred's weak?" she suggested.

"Is he weak?"

"You know he is," she said scornfully. "He's a kind man, and folk have always liked him, but he doesn't know how to be ruthless. He should have killed Ivarr when he first met him, and he should have banished Hrothweard a long time ago, but he didn't dare. He's too frightened of Saint Cuthbert."

"And why would Alfred want a weak king on Northumbria's throne?" I asked blandly.

"So Northumbria will be weak," she said, "when the Saxons try to take back their land."

"Is that what your runesticks say will happen?" I asked.

"They say," she said, "that we will have two sons and a daughter, and that one son will break your heart, the other will make you proud, and that your daughter will be the mother of kings."

I laughed at that prophecy, not with scorn, but because of the certainty in Gisela's voice. "And does that mean," I asked, "that you will come to Wessex, even though I fight the Danes?"

"It means," she said, "that I'm not leaving your side. That's my oath."

Ragnar had sent scouts ahead and as the long day passed some of those men came back on tired horses. Ivarr, they had heard, had taken Eoferwic. It had been easy for him. Guthred's diminished garrison had surrendered the city rather than be slaughtered in its streets. Ivarr had taken what plunder he could find, placed a new garrison on the walls, and was already marching back north. He would not have heard of the fall of Dunholm yet, so he was plainly hoping to catch Guthred who, he must assume, either lingered at Cetreht or was wandering disconsolately toward the wastes of Cumbraland. Ivarr's army, the scouts had heard, was a horde. Some men said Ivarr led two thousand spears, a figure that Ragnar and I dismissed. It was certain, though, that Ivarr's men far outnumbered ours and probable that he was marching north on the same Roman road down which we traveled south. "Can we fight him?" Guthred asked me.

"We can fight him," Ragnar answered for me, "but we can't beat his army."

"So why are we marching south?"

"To rescue Cuthbert," I said, "and to kill Ivarr."

"But if we can't beat him?" Guthred was puzzled.

"We fight him," I said, adding to his confusion, "and if we can't beat him then we retreat to Dunholm. That's why we captured it, as a refuge."

"We're letting the gods decide what happens," Ragnar explained and, because we were confident, Guthred pressed us no further.

We reached Cetreht that evening. Our journey had been fast because we had no need to leave the Roman road, and we splashed through the Swale's ford as the sun reddened the western hills. The churchmen, rather than take refuge in those hills, had preferred to stay with Cetreht's meager comforts and no one had disturbed them while we had gone to Dunholm. They had seen mounted Danes on the southern hills, but none of those riders had approached the fort. The horsemen had watched, counted heads, and ridden away, and I assumed those men were Ivarr's scouts.

Father Hrothweard and Abbot Eadred seemed unimpressed that we had captured Dunholm. All they cared about was the corpse of the saint and the other precious relics which they dug up from the graveyard that same evening and carried in solemn procession to the church. It was there that I confronted Aidan, the steward of Bebbanburg, and his score of men who had stayed in the village. "It's safe for you to ride home now," I told them, "because Kjartan is dead."

I do not think Aidan believed me at first. Then he understood what we had achieved and he must have feared that the men who had captured Dunholm would march on Bebbanburg next. I wanted to do that, but I was sworn to return to Alfred before Christmas and that left me no time to confront my uncle.

"We shall leave in the morning," Aidan said.

"You will," I agreed, "and when you reach Bebbanburg you will tell my uncle that he is never far from my thoughts. You will tell him I have taken his bride. You will promise him that one day I shall slit his belly, and if he dies before I can fulfill that oath then promise him I shall slice the guts out of his sons instead, and if his sons have sons I shall kill them too. Tell him those things, and tell him that folk thought Dunholm was like Bebbanburg, impregnable, and that Dunholm fell to my sword."

"Ivarr will kill you," Aidan said defiantly.

"You had better pray as much," I said.

All the Christians prayed that night. They gathered in the church and I thought they might be asking their god to give us victory over the approaching forces of Ivarr, but instead they were giving thanks that the precious relics had survived. They placed Saint Cuthbert's body before the altar on which they put Saint Oswald's head, the gospel book, and the reliquary with the hairs of Saint Augustine's beard and they chanted, they prayed, they chanted again, and I thought they would never stop praying, but at last, in the night's dark heart, they fell silent.

I walked the fort's low wall, watching the Roman road stretch south through the fields beneath the waning moon. It was from there that

Ivarr would come and I could not be sure he would not send a band of picked horsemen to attack in the night and so I had a hundred men waiting in the village street. But no attack came, and in the darkness a small mist rose to blur the fields as Ragnar came to relieve me. "There'll be a frost by morning," he greeted me.

"There will," I agreed.

He stamped his feet to make them warm. "My sister," he said, "tells me she's going to Wessex. She says she'll be baptized."

"Are you surprised?"

"No," he said. He gazed down the long straight road. "It's for the best," he spoke bleakly, "and she likes your Father Beocca. So what will happen to her?"

"I suppose she'll become a nun," I said, for I could not think what other fate would wait for her in Alfred's Wessex.

"I let her down," he said, and I said nothing because it was true. "Must you go back to Wessex?" he asked.

"Yes. I'm sworn."

"Oaths can be broken," he said quietly, and that was true, but in a world where different gods ruled and fate is known only to the three spinners, oaths are our one certainty. If I broke an oath then I could not expect men to keep their oaths to me. That I had learned.

"I won't break my oath to Alfred," I said, "but I will make another oath to you. That I will never fight you, that what I have is yours to share, and that if you need help I will do all I can to bring it."

Ragnar said nothing for a while. He kicked at the turf on the wall's top and looked into the mist. "I swear the same," he said quietly and he, like me, was embarrassed and so he kicked at the turf again. "How many men will Ivarr bring?"

"Eight hundred?"

He nodded. "And we have fewer than three hundred."

"There won't be a fight," I said.

"No?"

"Ivarr will die," I said, "and that will be the end of it." I touched Serpent-Breath's hilt for luck and felt the slightly raised edges of

Hild's cross. "He will die," I said, still touching the cross, "and Guthred will rule, and he will do what you tell him to do."

"You want me to tell him to attack Ælfric?" he asked.

I thought about it. "No," I said.

"No?"

"Bebbanburg's too strong," I said, "and there's no back gate as there was at Dunholm. Besides, I want to kill Ælfric myself."

"Will Alfred let you do that?"

"He will," I said, though in truth I doubted Alfred ever would allow me such a luxury, but I was certain that my fate was to go back to Bebbanburg and I had faith in that destiny. I turned and stared at the village. "All quiet there?"

"All quiet," he said. "They've given up praying and are sleeping instead. You should sleep too."

I walked back up the street, but before joining Gisela I quietly opened the church door and saw priests and monks sleeping in the small light of the few candles guttering on the altar. One of them snored and I closed the door as silently as I had opened it.

I was woken in the dawn by Sihtric who banged on the door lintel. "They're here, lord!" he shouted. "They're here!"

"Who's here?"

"Ivarr's men, lord."

"Where?"

"Horsemen, lord, across the river!"

There were only a hundred or so riders, and they made no attempt to cross the ford and I guessed they had only been sent to the Swale's northern bank to cut off our escape. Ivarr's main force would appear to the south, though that prospect was not the chief excitement in that misted dawn. Men were shouting in the village. "What is it?" I asked Sihtric.

"Christians are upset, lord," he said.

I walked to the church to discover that the golden reliquary of Saint Augustine's beard, the precious gift from Alfred to Guthred, had been stolen. It had been on the altar with the other relics, but during the night it had vanished, and Father Hrothweard was wailing beside a hole scratched and torn into the wall of wattle and daub behind the altar. Guthred was there, listening to Abbot Eadred who was declaring the theft a sign of God's disapproval.

"Disapproval of what?" Guthred asked.

"The pagans, of course," Eadred spat.

Father Hrothweard was rocking back and forth, wringing his hands and shouting at his god to bring vengeance on the heathens who had desecrated the church and stolen the holy treasure. "Reveal the culprits, lord!" he shouted, then he saw me and evidently decided the revelation had come, for he pointed at me. "It was him!" he spat.

"Was it you?" Guthred asked.

"No, lord," I said.

"It was him!" Hrothweard said again.

"You must search all the pagans," Eadred told Guthred, "for if the relic isn't found, lord, then our defeat is certain. Ivarr will crush us for this sin. It will be God's chastisement on us."

It seemed a strange punishment, to allow a pagan Dane to defeat a Christian king because a relic had been stolen, but as a prophecy it seemed safe enough, for in the mid-morning, while the church was still being searched in a vain attempt to find the reliquary, one of Ragnar's men brought word that Ivarr's army had appeared. They were marching from the south and already forming their shield wall a half-mile from Ragnar's small force.

It was time, then, for us to go. Guthred and I were already in mail, our horses were saddled, and all we needed to do was ride south to join Ragnar's shield wall, but Guthred had been unnerved by the loss of the relic. As we left the church he took me aside. "Will you ask Ragnar if he took it?" he begged me. "Or ask if perhaps one of his men did?"

"Ragnar didn't take it," I said scornfully. "If you want to find the culprit," I went on, "search them." I pointed to Aidan and his horsemen who, now that Ivarr was close, were eager to start on their journey north, though they dared not leave so long as Ivarr's men barred the ford across the Swale. Guthred had asked them to join our shield wall, but they had refused, and now they waited for a chance to escape.

"No Christian would steal the relic!" Hrothweard shouted. "It's a pagan crime!"

Guthred was terrified. He still believed in Christian magic and he saw the theft as an omen of disaster. He plainly did not suspect Aidan, but then he did not know who to suspect and so I made it easy for him.

I summoned Finan and Sihtric who were waiting to accompany me to the shield wall. "This man," I told Guthred, pointing at Finan, "is a Christian. Aren't you a Christian, Finan?"

"I am, lord."

"And he's Irish," I said, "and everyone knows the Irish have the power of scrying." Finan, who had no more powers of scrying than I did, tried to look mysterious. "He will find your relic," I promised.

"You will?" Guthred asked Finan eagerly.

"Yes, lord," Finan said confidently.

"Do it, Finan," I said, "while I kill Ivarr. And bring the culprit to us as soon as you find him."

"I will, lord," he said.

A servant brought my horse. "Can your Irishman really find it?" Guthred asked me.

"I will give the church all my silver, lord," I said loudly enough for a dozen men to hear, "and I will give it my mail, my helmet, my arm rings and my swords, if Finan does not bring you both the relic and the thief. He's Irish and the Irish have strange powers." I looked at Hrothweard. "You hear that, priest? I promise all my wealth to your church if Finan does not find the thief!"

Hrothweard had nothing to say to that. He glared at me, but my promise had been made publicly and it was testimony to my innocence, so he contented himself by spitting at my horse's feet. Gisela, who had come to take the stallion's reins, had to skip aside to avoid the spittle. She touched my arm as I straightened the stirrup. "Can Finan find it?" she asked in a low voice.

"He can find it," I promised her.

"Because he has strange powers?"

"Because he stole it, my love," I said quietly, "on my orders. It's probably hidden in a dung-heap." I grinned at her, and she laughed softly.

I put my foot in the stirrup and readied to heave myself up, but again Gisela checked me. "Be careful," she said. "Men fear to fight Ivarr," she warned me.

"He's a Lothbrok," I said, "and all Lothbroks fight well. They love it. But they fight like mad dogs, all fury and savagery, and in the end they die like mad dogs." I mounted the stallion, settled my right foot in its stirrup, then took my helmet and shield from Gisela. I touched her hand for farewell, then pulled the reins and followed Guthred south.

We rode to join the shield wall. It was a short wall, easily outflanked by the much larger wall that Ivarr was forming to the south. His wall was over twice as long as ours which meant his men could wrap themselves about our line and kill us from the edges inward. If it came to battle we would be slaughtered, and Ivarr's men knew it. Their shield wall was bright with spears and ax-heads, and noisy with anticipation of victory. They were beating their weapons against their shields, making a dull drumbeat that filled the Swale's wide valley, and the drumbeat rose to a great clattering thunder when Ivarr's standard of the two ravens was lifted in the center of their line. Beneath the banner was a knot of horsemen who now broke free of the shield wall to ride toward us. Ivarr was among them, as was his rat-like son.

Guthred, Steapa, Ragnar, and I rode a few paces toward Ivarr and then waited. Ten men were in the approaching party, but it was Ivarr I watched. He was mounted on Witnere, which I had hoped he would be, for that gave me cause to quarrel with him, but I hung back, letting Guthred take his horse a few steps forward. Ivarr was staring at us one by one. He looked momentarily surprised to see me, but said nothing, and he seemed irritated when he saw Ragnar and he was duly impressed by Steapa's huge size, but he ignored the three of us, nodding instead at Guthred. "Worm-shit," he greeted the king.

"Lord Ivarr," Guthred replied.

"I am in a strangely merciful mood," Ivarr said. "If you ride away, then I shall spare your men's lives."

"We have no quarrel," Guthred said, "that cannot be settled by words."

"Words!" Ivarr spat, then shook his head. "Go beyond Northumbria," he said, "go far away, worm-shit. Run to your friend in Wessex, but leave your sister here as a hostage. If you do that I shall be merciful." He was not being merciful, but practical. The Danes were ferocious warriors, but far more cautious than their reputation suggested. Ivarr was willing to fight, but he was more willing to arrange a surrender, for then he would lose no men. He would win this fight, he knew that, but in gaining the victory he would lose sixty or seventy warriors and that was a whole ship's crew and a high price to pay. It was better to let Guthred live and pay nothing. Ivarr moved Witnere sideways so he could look past Guthred at Ragnar. "You keep strange company, Lord Ragnar."

"Two days ago," Ragnar said, "I killed Kjartan the Cruel. Dunholm is mine now. I think, perhaps, I should kill you, Lord Ivarr, so that you cannot try to take it from me."

Ivarr looked startled, as well he might. He glanced at Guthred, then at me, as if seeking confirmation of Kjartan's death, but our faces betrayed nothing. Ivarr shrugged. "You had a quarrel with Kjartan," he told Ragnar, "and that was your affair, not mine. I would welcome you as a friend. Our fathers were friends, were they not?"

"They were," Ragnar said.

"Then we should remake their friendship," Ivarr said.

"Why should he befriend a thief?" I asked.

Ivarr looked at me, his serpent eyes unreadable. "I watched a goat vomit yesterday," he said, "and what it threw up reminded me of you."

"I watched a goat shit yesterday," I retorted, "and what it dropped reminded me of you."

Ivarr sneered at that, but decided not to go on trading insults. His son, though, drew his sword and Ivarr held out a warning hand to tell the youngster that the killing time had not yet come. "Go away," he said to Guthred, "go far away and I will forget I ever knew you."

"The goat-turd reminded me of you," I said, "but its smell reminded me of your mother. It was a rancid smell, but what would you expect of a whore who gives birth to a thief?"

One of the warriors held Ivarr's son back. Ivarr himself just looked at me in silence for a while. "I can make your death stretch through three sunsets," he said at last.

"But if you return the stolen goods, thief," I said, "and then accept good King Guthred's judgment on your crime, then perhaps we will show mercy."

Ivarr looked amused rather than offended. "What have I stolen?" he asked.

"You're riding my horse," I said, "and I want it back now."

He patted Witnere's neck. "When you are dead," he said to me, "I shall have your skin tanned and made into a saddle so I can spend the rest of my life farting on you." He looked at Guthred. "Go away," he said, "go far away. Leave your sister as hostage. I shall give you a few moments to find your senses, and if you don't, then we shall kill you." He turned his horse away.

"Coward," I called to him. He ignored me, pushing Witnere through his men to lead them back to their shield wall. "All the Lothbroks are cowards," I said. "They run away. What have you done, Ivarr? Pissed your breeches for fear of my sword? You ran away from the Scots and now you run away from me!"

I think it was the mention of the Scots that did it. That huge defeat was still raw in Ivarr's memory, and I had scraped scorn on the rawness and suddenly the Lothbrok temper, that so far he had managed to control, took over. He hurt Witnere with the savage pull he gave on the bit, but Witnere turned obediently as Ivarr drew his long sword. He spurred toward me, but I angled past him, going toward the wide space in front of his army. That was where I wanted Ivarr to die, in sight of all his men, and there I turned my stallion back. Ivarr had followed me, but had checked Witnere, who was thumping the soft turf with his front right hoof.

I think Ivarr wished he had not lost his temper, but it was too late. Every man in both shield walls could see that he had drawn his sword and pursued me into the open meadow and he could not just ride away from that challenge. He had to kill me now, and he was not sure he could do it. He was good, but he had suffered injury, his joints were aching, and he knew my reputation.

His advantage was Witnere. I knew that horse, and knew it fought as well as most warriors. Witnere would savage my horse if he could, and he would savage me too, and my first aim was to get Ivarr out of the saddle. Ivarr watched me. I think he had decided to let me attack, for he did not release Witnere to the charge, but instead of riding at him, I turned my stallion toward Ivarr's shield wall. "Ivarr is a thief!" I shouted at his army. I let Serpent-Breath hang by my side. "He is a common thief," I shouted, "who ran from the Scots! He ran like a whipped puppy! He was weeping like a child when we found him!" I laughed and kept my eyes on Ivarr's shield wall. "He was crying because he was hurt," I said, "and in Scotland they call him Ivarr the Feeble." I saw, at the edge of my vision, that the goading had worked and that Ivarr was wheeling Witnere toward me. "He is a thief," I shouted, "and a coward!" And as I screamed the last derisive insult I touched my knee to my horse so he turned and I raised my shield. Witnere was all white eyes and white teeth, big hooves flailing up sodden turf, and as he closed I shouted his name. "Witnere! Witnere!" I knew that was probably not the name Ivarr had given the stallion, but perhaps Witnere remembered the name, or remembered me, for his ears pricked and his head came up and his pace faltered as I spurred my own horse straight at him.

I used the shield as a weapon. I just thrust it hard at Ivarr and, at the same moment, pushed up on my right stirrup, and Ivarr was trying to turn Witnere away, but the big stallion was confused and off balance. My shield slammed into Ivarr's and I threw myself at him, using my weight to force him backward. The risk was that I would fall and he would stay saddled, but I dared not let go of shield or sword to grip him. I just had to hope that my weight would drive him to the ground. "Witnere!" I shouted again, and the stallion half turned toward me and that small motion, along with my weight, was enough to topple Ivarr. He fell to his right and I collapsed between the two horses. I fell hard, and my own stallion gave me an inadvertent kick that pushed me against Witnere's hind legs. I scrambled up, slapped Witnere's rump with Serpent-Breath to drive him away and immediately ducked beneath my shield as Ivarr attacked. He had recovered faster than me, and his sword slammed against my shield, and he must have expected me to recoil from that blow, but I stopped it dead. My left arm, wounded by the thrown spear at Dunholm, throbbed from the force of his sword, but I was taller, heavier, and stronger than Ivarr and I shoved the shield hard to push him back.

He knew he was going to lose. He was old enough to be my father and he was slowed by old wounds, but he was still a Lothbrok and they learn fighting from the moment they are whelped. He came at me snarling, sword feinting high then thrusting low, and I kept moving, parrying him, taking his blows on my shield, and not even trying to fight back. I mocked him instead. I told him he was a pathetic old man. "I killed your uncle," I taunted him, "and he was not much better than you. And when you're dead, old man, I'll gut the rat you call a son. I'll feed his corpse to the ravens. Is that the best you can do?"

He had tried to turn me, but tried too hard and his foot had slipped on the wet grass and he had gone down onto one knee. He was open to death then, off balance and with his sword hand in the grass, but I walked away from him, letting him rise, and every Dane saw that I did that, and then they saw me throw away my shield. "I'll give him a chance," I called to them. "He's a miserable little thief, but I'll give him a chance!"

"You whore-born Saxon bastard," Ivarr snarled, and rushed me again. That was how he liked to fight. Attack, attack, attack, and he tried to use his shield to hurl me back, but I stepped away and clouted him over the back of his helmet with the flat of Serpent-Breath's blade. The blow made him stumble a second time, and again I walked away. I wanted to humiliate him.

That second stumble gave him caution, so that he circled me warily. "You made me a slave," I said, "and you couldn't even do that properly. You want to give me your sword?"

"Goat-turd," he said. He came in fast, lunging at my throat, dropping the sword to rake my left leg at the last moment, and I just moved aside and slapped Serpent-Breath across his rump to drive him away.

"Give me your sword," I said, "and I'll let you live. We'll put you in a cage and I'll take you around Wessex. Here is Ivarr Ivarson, a Lothbrok, I'll tell folk. A thief who ran away from the Scots."

"Bastard," he rushed again, this time trying to disembowel me with a savage sweep of the sword, but I stepped back and his long blade hissed past me and he grunted as he brought the blade back, all fury and desperation now, and I rammed Serpent-Breath forward so that she went past his shield and struck his breast and the force of the lunge drove him back. He staggered as my next stroke came, a fast one that rang on the side of his helmet and again he staggered, dizzied by the blow, and my third blow cracked into his blade with such force that his sword arm flew back and Serpent-Breath's tip was at his throat.

"Coward," I said, "thief."

He screamed in fury and brought his sword around in a savage stroke, but I stepped backward and let it pass. Then I slashed Serpent-Breath down hard to strike his right wrist. He gasped then, for the wrist bones were broken.

"It's hard to fight without a sword," I told him, and I struck again, this time hitting the sword so that the blade flew from his hand. There was terror in his eyes now. Not the terror of a man facing death, but of a warrior dying without a blade in his hand.

"You made me a slave," I said, and I rammed Serpent-Breath forward, striking him on one knee and he tried to back away, tried to reach his sword, and I slashed the knee again, much harder, sawing through leather to cut to the bone and he went down on one knee. I slapped his helmet with Serpent-Breath, then stood behind him. "He made me a slave," I shouted at his men, "and he stole my horse. But he is still a Lothbrok." I bent, picked up his sword by the blade, and held it to him. He took it.

"Thank you," he said.

Then I killed him. I took his head half off his shoulders. He made a gurgling noise, shuddered, and went down onto the grass, but he had kept hold of the sword. If I had let him die without the sword then many of the watching Danes would have thought me wantonly cruel. They understood he was my enemy, and understood I had cause to kill him, but none would think he deserved to be denied the corpse-hall. And one day, I thought, Ivarr and his uncle would welcome me there, for in the corpse-hall we feast with our enemies and remember our fights and fight them all over again.

Then there was a scream and I turned to see Ivar, his son, galloping toward me. He came as his father had come, all fury and mindless violence, and he leaned from the saddle to cut me in half with his blade and I met the blade with Serpent-Breath and she was by far the better sword. The blow jarred up my arm, but Ivar's blade broke. He galloped past me, holding a hand's breadth of sword, and two of his father's men caught up with him and forced him away before he could be killed. I called to Witnere.

He came to me. I patted his nose, took hold of the saddle and hauled myself onto his back. Then I turned him toward Ivarr's leaderless shield wall and gestured that Guthred and Ragnar should join me. We stopped twenty paces from the painted Danish shields. "Ivarr Ivarson has gone to Valhalla," I shouted, "and there was no disgrace in his death! I am Uhtred Ragnarson! I am the man who killed Ubba Lothbrokson and this is my friend, Earl Ragnar, who killed Kjartan the Cruel! We serve King Guthred."

"Are you a Christian?" a man shouted.

I showed him my hammer amulet. Men were passing the news of Kjartan's death down the long line of shields, axes, and swords. "I am no Christian!" I shouted when they were quiet again. "But I have seen Christian sorcery! And the Christians worked their magic on King Guthred! Have none of you been victims of sorcerers? Have none of you known your cattle to die or your wives to be sick? You all know sorcery, and the Christian sorcerers can work great magic! They have corpses and severed heads, and they use them to make magic, and they wove their spells about our king! But the sorcerer made a mistake. He became greedy, and last night he stole a treasure from King Guthred! But Odin has swept the spells away!" I twisted in the saddle and saw that Finan was at last coming from the fort.

He had been delayed by a scuffle at the fort's entrance. Some churchmen had tried to prevent Finan and Sihtric from leaving, but a score of Ragnar's Danes intervened and now the Irishman came riding across the pastureland. He was leading Father Hrothweard. Or rather Finan had a handful of Hrothweard's hair and so the priest had no choice but to stumble along beside the Irishman's horse.

"That is the Christian sorcerer, Hrothweard!" I shouted. "He attacked King Guthred with spells, with the magic of corpses, but we have found him out and we have taken the spells away from King Guthred! So now I ask you what we should do with the sorcerer!"

There was only one answer to that. The Danes, who knew well enough that Hrothweard had been Guthred's adviser, wanted him dead. Hrothweard, meanwhile, was kneeling on the grass, his hands clasped, staring up at Guthred. "No, lord!" He pleaded.

"You're the thief?" Guthred asked. He sounded disbelieving.

"I found the relic in his baggage, lord," Finan said, and held the golden pot toward Guthred. "It was wrapped in one of his shirts, lord."

"He lies!" Hrothweard protested.

"He's your thief, lord," Finan said respectfully, then made the sign of the cross, "I swear it on Christ's holy body."

"He's a sorcerer!" I shouted at Ivarr's Danes. "He will give your cattle the staggers, he will put a blight on your crops, he will make your women barren and your children sickly! Do you want him?"

They roared their need of Hrothweard, who was weeping uncontrollably.

"You may have him," I said, "if you acknowledge Guthred as your king."

They shouted their allegiance. They were beating swords and spears against their shields again, but this time in acclamation of Guthred, and so I leaned over and took his reins. "Time to greet them, lord," I told him. "Time to be generous with them."

"But," he looked down at Hrothweard.

"He is a thief, lord," I said, "and thieves must die. It is the law. It is what Alfred would do."

"Yes," Guthred said, and we left Father Hrothweard to the pagan Danes and we listened to his dying for a long time. I do not know what they did to him, for there was little left of his corpse, though his blood darkened the grass for yards around the place he died.

That night there was a poor feast. Poor because we had little enough food, though there was plenty of ale. The Danish thegns swore their allegiance to Guthred while the priests and monks huddled in the church, expecting murder. Hrothweard was dead and Jænberht had been murdered, and they all expected to become martyrs themselves, but a dozen sober men from Guthred's household troops were enough to keep them safe. "I shall let them build their shrine for Saint Cuthbert," Guthred told me.

"Alfred would approve of that," I said.

He stared across the fire that burned in Cetreht's street. Ragnar, despite his crippled hand, was wrestling with a huge Dane who had served Ivarr. Both men were drunk and more drunk men cheered them on and made wagers on who would win. Guthred stared, but did not see the contest. He was thinking. "I would never have believed," he said at last, puzzled, "that Father Hrothweard was a thief."

Gisela, sheltering under my cloak and leaning on my shoulder, giggled. "No man would ever believe that you and I were slaves, lord," I answered, "but so we were."

"Yes," he said in wonderment, "we were."

It is the three spinners who make our lives. They sit at the foot of
Yggdrasil and there they have their jests. It pleased them to make
Guthred the slave into King Guthred, just as it pleased them to send
me south again to Wessex.

While at Bebbanburg, where the gray sea never ceases to beat upon
the long pale sands and the cold wind frets the wolf's head flag above
the hall, they dreaded my return.

Because fate cannot be cheated, it governs us, and we are all its
slaves.

HISTORICAL NOTE

*L**ords of the North** opens a month or so after Alfred's astonishing victory over the Danes at Ethandun, a tale told in *The Pale Horseman*. Guthrum, the leader of the defeated army, retreated to Chippenham where Alfred laid siege to him, but hostilities came to a swift end when Alfred and Guthrum agreed to a peace. The Danes withdrew from Wessex and Guthrum and his leading earls all became Christians. Alfred, in turn, recognized Guthrum as the king of East Anglia.

Readers of the two previous novels in this series will know that Guthrum hardly had a sterling record for keeping peace agreements. He had broken the truce made at Wareham, and the subsequent truce negotiated at Exeter, but this last peace treaty held. Guthrum accepted Alfred as his godfather and took the baptismal name of Æthelstan. One tradition says he was baptized in the font still to be seen in the church at Aller, Somerset, and it seems that his conversion was genuine for, once back in East Anglia, he ruled as a Christian monarch. Negotiations between Guthrum and Alfred continued, for in 886 they signed the Treaty of Wedmore which divided England into two spheres of influence. Wessex and southern Mercia were to be Saxon, while East Anglia, northern Mercia, and Northumbria were to fall under Danish law. Thus the Danelaw was established, that northeastern half of England which, for a time, was to be ruled by Danish kings and which still bears, in place-names and dialects, the imprint of that era.

The treaty was a recognition by Alfred that he lacked the forces to drive the Danes out of England altogether, and it bought him time in which he could fortify his heartland of Wessex. The problem was that Guthrum was not the king of all the Danes, let alone the Norsemen, and he could not prevent further attacks on Wessex. Those would come in time, and will be described in future novels, but in large part the victory at Ethandun and the subsequent settlement with Guthrum secured the independence of Wessex and enabled Alfred and his successors to reconquer the Danelaw. One of Alfred's first steps in that long process was to marry his eldest daughter, Æthelflaed, to Æthelred of Mercia, an alliance intended to bind the Saxons of Mercia to those of Wessex. Æthelflaed, in time, was to prove a great heroine in the struggle against the Danes.

To move from the history of Wessex in the late ninth century to that of Northumbria is to pass from light into confusing darkness. Even the northern regnal lists, which provide the names of kings and the dates they ruled, do not agree, but soon after Ethandun a king named Guthred (some sources name him as Guthfrith) did take the throne at York (Eoferwic). He replaced a Saxon king, who was doubtless a puppet ruler, and he ruled into the 890s. Guthred is remarkable for two things; first, though Danish, he was a Christian, and second, there is a persistent story that he was once a slave, and on those slender foundations I have concocted this story. He was certainly associated with Abbot Eadred who was the guardian of Cuthbert's corpse (and of both the head of Saint Oswald and the Lindisfarne Gospels), and Eadred was eventually to build his great shrine for Cuthbert at Cuncacester, now Chester-le-Street in County Durham. In 995 the saint's body was finally laid to rest at Durham (Dunholm) where it remains.

Kjartan, Ragnar, and Gisela are fictional characters. There was an Ivarr, but I have taken vast liberties with his life. He is chiefly notable for his successors who will cause much trouble in the north. There is no record of a ninth-century fortress at Durham, though it seems to me unlikely that such an easily defensible site would have been ignored, and more than possible that any remnants of such a fort would have been destroyed during the construction of the cathedral and castle which have now occupied the summit for almost a thousand years. There was a fortress at Bebbanburg, transmuted over time into the present glories of Bamburgh Castle, and in the eleventh century it was ruled by a family with the name Uhtred, who are my ancestors, but we know almost nothing of the family's activities in the late ninth century.

The story of England in the late ninth and early tenth centuries is a tale which moves from Wessex northward. Uhtred's fate, which he is just beginning to recognize, is to be at the heart of that West Saxon reconquest of the land that will become known as England and so his wars are far from over. He will need Serpent-Breath again.

*Read on for an excerpt from the next book
in the Saxon Tales series*

SWORD
SONG

Bernard Cornwell

*Available in hardcover in
January 2008 from*

HARPER

An Imprint of HarperCollins*Publishers*
www.harpercollins.com

Darkness. Winter. A night of frost and no moon.

We floated on the River Temes, and beyond the boat's high bow I could see the stars reflected on the shimmering water. The river was in spate as melted snow fed it from countless hills. The winterbournes were flowing from the chalk uplands of Wessex. In summer those streams would be dry, but now they foamed down the long green hills and filled the river and flowed to the distant sea.

Our boat, which had no name, lay close to the Wessex bank. North across the river lay Mercia. Our bows pointed upstream. We were hidden beneath the leafless, bending branches of three willow trees, held there against the current by a leather mooring rope tied to one of those branches.

There were thirty-eight of us in that nameless boat, which was a trading ship that worked the upper reaches of the Temes. The ship's master was called Ralla, and he stood beside me with one hand on the steering oar. I could hardly see him in the darkness, but knew he wore a leather jerkin and had a sword at his side. The rest of us were in leather and mail, had helmets and carried shields, axes, swords or spears. Tonight we would kill.

Sihtric, my servant, squatted beside me and stroked a whetstone along the blade of his short sword. "She says she loves me," he told me.

"Of course she says that," I said.

He paused, and when he spoke again his voice had brightened, as though he had been encouraged by my words. "And I must be nineteen by now, lord! Maybe even twenty?"

"Eighteen?" I suggested.

"I could have been married four years ago, lord!"

"But why marry a whore?" I asked him harshly.

"She's . . ." Sihtric began.

"She's old," I snarled, "maybe thirty? And she's addled. Ealhswith only has to see a man and her thighs fly apart! If you lined up every man who'd tupped that whore, you'd have an army big enough to conquer all Britain." Beside me Ralla sniggered. "You'd be in that army, Ralla?" I asked.

"Twenty times over, lord," the shipmaster said.

"She loves me," Sihtric spoke sullenly.

"She loves your silver," I said, "and besides, why put a new sword in an old scabbard?"

We spoke almost in whispers. The night was full of noises. The water rippled, the bare branches clattered in the wind, a night creature splashed into the river, a vixen howled like a dying soul, and somewhere an owl hooted. The boat creaked. Sihtric's stone hissed and scraped on the steel. A shield thumped against a rower's bench. I dared not speak louder, despite the night's noises, because the enemy ship was upstream of us and the men who had gone ashore from that ship would have left sentries on board. Those sentries might have seen us as we slipped downstream on the Mercian bank, but by now they would surely have thought we were long gone towards Lundene.

"Look for something ripe and young," I advised Sihtric. "That potter's daughter is ready to wed. She must be thirteen."

"She's stupid," Sihtric objected.

"And what are you, then?" I demanded. "I give you silver, and you pour it into the nearest open hole! Last time I saw her she was wearing an arm band I gave you."

He sniffed, said nothing. His father had been Kjartan the Cruel, a Dane who had whelped Sihtric on one of his Saxon slaves. Yet Sihtric was a good boy, though in truth he was no longer a boy. He was a man who had stood in the shield wall. A man who had killed. A man who would kill again tonight. "I'll find you a wife," I promised him.

It was then we heard the screaming. It was faint because it came from very far off, a mere scratching noise in the darkness that told of pain and death to our south. There were screams and shouting. Women were screaming and doubtless men were dying.

"God damn them," Ralla said bitterly.

"That's our job," I said curtly.

"We should . . ." Ralla started, then thought better of speaking. I knew what he was going to say, that we should have gone to the village and protected it, but he knew what I would have answered.

I would have told him that we did not know which village the Danes were going to attack, and even if I had known I would not have protected it. We might have shielded the place if we had known where the attackers were going. I could have placed all my household troops in the small houses and, the moment the raiders came, erupted into the street with sword, axe, and spear, and we would have killed some of them, but in the dark many more would have escaped, and I did not want one to escape. I wanted every Dane, every Norseman, every raider dead. All of them, except one, and that one I would send eastward to tell the Viking camps on the banks of the Temes that Uhtred of Bebbanburg was waiting for them.

"Poor souls," Ralla muttered. To the south, through the tangle of black branches, I could see a red glow that betrayed burning thatch. The glow spread and grew brighter to lighten the winter sky beyond a row of coppiced trees. The glow reflected off my men's helmets, giving their metal a sheen of red, and I called for them to take the helmets off in case the enemy sentries in the large ship ahead saw the reflected glimmer.

I took off my own helmet with its silver wolf crest.

I am Uhtred, Lord of Bebbanburg, and in those days I was a lord of war. I stood there in mail and leather, cloaked and armed, young and strong. I had half my household troops in Ralla's ship while the other half were somewhere to the west, mounted on horses and under Finan's command.

Or I hoped they were waiting in the night-shrouded west. We in the ship had enjoyed the easier task, for we had slid down the dark river to find the enemy while Finan had been forced to lead his men across night-black country. But I trusted Finan. He would be there, fidgeting, grimacing, waiting to unleash his sword.

This was not our first attempt in that long wet winter to set an ambush on the Temes, but it was the first that promised success. Twice before I had been told that Vikings had come through the gap in Lundene's broken bridge to raid the soft, plump villages of Wessex, and both times we had come down river and found nothing. But this time we had trapped the wolves. I touched the hilt of Serpent-Breath, my sword, then touched the amulet of Thor's hammer that hung around my neck.

Kill them all, I prayed to Thor, kill them all but one.

It must have been cold in that long night. Ice skimmed the dips in the fields where the river had flooded, but I do not remember the cold. I remember the anticipation. I touched Serpent-Breath continually, and it seemed to me that she quivered. I sometimes thought that blade sang. It was a thin, half-heard song, a keening noise, the song of the blade wanting blood: the sword song.

We waited, and afterward, when it was all over, Ralla told me I had never stopped smiling.

*   *   *

I thought our ambush would fail for the raiders did not return to their ship till dawn blazed light across the east. Their sentries, I thought, must surely see us, but they did not. The drooping willow boughs served as a flimsy screen, or perhaps the rising winter sun dazzled them because no one saw us.

We saw them. We saw the mail-clad men herding a crowd of women and children across a rain-flooded pasture. I guessed there were fifty raiders and they had as many captives. The women would be the young ones from the burned village, and they had been taken for the raiders' pleasure. The children would go to the slave market in London and from there across the sea to Frankia or even beyond. The women, once they had been used, would also be sold. We were not so close that we could hear the prisoners sobbing, but I imagined it. To the south, where low green hills swelled from the river's plain, a great drift of smoke dirtied the clear winter sky to mark where the raiders had burned the village.

Ralla stirred. "Wait," I murmured, and Ralla went still. He was a grizzled man, ten years older than I, with eyes reduced to slits from the long years of staring across sun-reflecting seas. He was a shipmaster, soldier and friend. "Not yet," I said softly, and touched Serpent-Breath and felt the quiver in the steel.

Men's voices were loud, relaxed, and laughing. They shouted as they pushed their prisoners into the ship where they forced them to crouch in the cold-flooded bilge so that the overloaded craft would be stable for its voyage through the downriver shallows where the Temes raced across stone ledges and only the best and bravest shipmasters knew the channel. Then the warriors clambered aboard themselves. They took their plunder with them, the spits and cauldrons and ard-blades and knives and whatever else could be sold or melted or used. Their laughter was raucous. They were men who had slaughtered, and who would become rich on their prisoners, and they were in a cheerful, careless mood.

And Serpent-Breath sang soft in her scabbard.

I heard the clatter from the other ship as the oars were thrust into their rowlocks. A voice called out a command. "Push off!"

The great beak of the enemy ship, crowned with a monster's painted head, turned out into the river. Men shoved oar blades against the bank, pushing the boat farther out. The ship was already moving, carried towards us by the spate-driven current. Ralla looked at me.

"Now," I said. "Cut the line!" I called, and Cerdic, in our bows, slashed through the leather rope tethering us to the willow. We were only using twelve oars and those now bit into the river as I pushed my way forward between the rowers' benches. "We kill them all!" I shouted. "We kill them all!"

"Pull!" Ralla roared, and the twelve men heaved on their oars to fight the river's power.

"We kill every last bastard!" I shouted as I climbed onto the small bow platform where my shield waited. "Kill them all! Kill them all!" I put on my helmet, then pushed my left forearm through the shield loops, hefted the heavy wood, and slid Serpent-Breath from her fleece lined scabbard. She did not sing now. She screamed.

"Kill!" I shouted, "kill, kill, kill!" and the oars bit in time to my shouting. Ahead of us the enemy ship slewed in the river as panicked men missed their stroke. They were shouting, looking for shields, scrambling over the benches where a few men still tried to row. Women screamed, and men tripped each other.

"Pull!" Ralla shouted. Our nameless ship surged into the current as the enemy was swept towards us. Her monster's head had a tongue painted red, white eyes, teeth like daggers.

"Now!" I called to Cerdic, and he threw the grapnel with its chain so that it caught on the enemy ship's bow, and he hauled on the chain to sink the grapnel's teeth into the ship's timber and so draw her closer.

"Now kill!" I shouted, and leaped across the gap.

Oh the joy of being young. Of being twenty-eight years old, of being strong, of being a lord of war. All gone now, just memory is left, and memories fade. But the joy is bedded in the memory.

Serpent-Breath's first stroke was a back-cut. I made it as I landed on the enemy's bow platform where a man was trying to tug the grapnel free, and Serpent-Breath took him in the throat with a cut so fast and hard that it half severed his head. His whole skull flopped backwards as blood brightened the winter day. Blood splashed on my face. I was death come from the morning, blood-spattered death in mail and black cloak and wolf-crested helmet.

I am old now. So old. My sight fades, my muscles are weak, my piss dribbles, my bones ache, and I sit in the sun and fall asleep to wake tired. But I remember those fights, those old fights. My newest wife, as pious a piece of stupid woman who ever whined, flinches when I tell the stories, but what else do the old have but stories? She protested once, saying she did not want to know about heads flopping backwards in bright spraying blood, but how else are we to prepare our young for the wars they must fight? I have fought all my life. That was my fate, the fate of all of us. Alfred wanted peace, but peace fled from him, and the Danes came and the Norsemen came, and he had no choice but to fight. And when Alfred was dead and his kingdom was powerful, more Danes came, and more Norsemen, and the Britons came from Wales, and the Scots howled down from the north, and what can a man do but fight for his land, his family, his home, and his country? I look at my children and at their children and at their children's children, and I know they will have to fight, and that so long as there is a family named Uhtred, and so long as there is a kingdom on this windswept island, there will be war. So we cannot flinch from war. We cannot hide from its cruelty, its blood, its stench, its vileness, or its joy, because war will come to us whether we want it or not. War is fate, and wyrd bið ful ræd. Fate is inescapable.

So I tell these stories so that my children's children will know their fate. My wife whimpers, but I make her listen. I tell her how our ship crashed into the enemy's outside flank, and how the impact drove that other ship's bows toward the bank. That was what I had wanted, and Ralla had achieved it perfectly. Now he scraped his ship down the enemy's flank, our impetus snapping the Dane's forward oars as my men jumped aboard, swords and axes swinging. I had staggered after that first cut, but the dead man had fallen off the platform to impede two others trying to reach me, and I shouted a challenge as I leaped down to face them. Serpent-Breath was lethal. She was, she is, a lovely blade, forged in the north by a Saxon smith who had known his trade. He had taken seven rods, four of iron and three of steel, and he had heated them and hammered them into one long two-edged blade with a leaf-shaped point. The four softer iron rods had been twisted in the fire and those twists survived in the blade as ghostly wisps of pattern that looked like the curling flame-breath of a dragon, and that was how Serpent-Breath had gained her name.

A bristle-bearded man swung an axe at me that I met with my outthrust shield and slid the dragon-wisps into his belly. I gave a fierce twist with my right hand so that his dying flesh and guts did not grip the blade, then I yanked her out, more blood flying, and dragged the axe-impaled shield across my body to parry a sword cut. Sihtric was beside me, driving his short sword up into my newest attacker's groin. The man screamed. I think I was shouting. More and more of my men were aboard now, swords and axes glinting. Children cried, women screamed, raiders died.

The bows of the enemy ship thumped onto the bank's mud while her stern began to swing outwards in the river's grip. Some of the raiders, sensing death if they stayed aboard, jumped ashore, and that started a panic. More and more leaped for the bank, and it was then Finan came from the west. There was a small mist on the river meadows, just a pearly skein drifting over the iced puddles, and through it came Finan's bright horsemen. They came in two lines, swords held like spears, and Finan, my deadly Irishman, knew his business and galloped the first line past the escaping men to cut off their retreat and let his second line crash into the enemy before he turned and led his own men back to the kill.

"Kill them all!" I shouted to him. "Kill every last one!"

A wave of a blood-reddened sword was his reply. I saw Clapa, my big Dane, spearing an enemy in the river's shallows. Rypere was hacking his sword at a cowering man. Sihtric's sword hand was red. Cerdic was swinging an axe, shouting incomprehensibly as the blade crushed and pierced a Dane's helmet to spill blood and brains on the cowering prisoners. I think I killed two more, though my memory is not certain, though I do remember pushing a man down onto the deck and, as he twisted round to face me, sliding Serpent-Breath into his gullet and watching his face distort and his tongue protrude from the blood welling past his blackened teeth. I leaned on the blade as the man died and watched as Finan's men wheeled their horses to come back at the trapped enemy. The horsemen cut and slashed, Vikings screamed, and some tried to surrender. One young man knelt on a rower's bench, axe and shield discarded, and held his hands to me in supplication. "Pick up the axe," I told him, speaking Danish.

"Lord . . ." he began.

"Pick it up," I interrupted him, "and watch for me in the Corpse Hall." I waited till he was armed, then let Serpent-Breath take his life. I did it fast, showing mercy by slicing his throat with one quick-scraping drag. I looked into his eyes as I killed him, saw his soul fly, then stepped over his twitching body that slipped off the rower's bench to collapse bloodily in the lap of a young woman who began to scream hysterically. "Quiet!" I shouted at her. I scowled at all the other women and children screaming or weeping as they cowered in the bilge. I put Serpent-Breath into my shield hand, took hold of the mail collar of the dying man, and heaved him back onto the bench.

One child was not crying. He was a boy, perhaps nine or ten years old, and he was just staring at me, mouth agape, and I remembered myself at that age. What did that boy see? He saw a man of metal, for I had fought with the face plates of my helmet closed. You see less with the plates hinged across the cheeks, but the appearance is more frightening. That boy saw a tall man, mail-clad, sword bloody, steel-faced, stalking a boat of death. I eased off my helmet and shook my hair loose, then tossed him the wolf-crested metal. "Look after it, boy," I told him, then I gave Serpent-Breath to the girl who had been screaming. "Wash the blade in river water," I ordered her, "and dry it on a dead man's cloak." I gave my shield to Sihtric, then stretched my arms wide and lifted my face to the morning sun.

There had been fifty four raiders and sixteen still lived. They were prisoners. None had escaped past Finan's men. I drew Wasp Sting, my short sword that was so lethal in a shield wall fight when men are pressed close as lovers. "Any of you!" I looked at the women. "Who wants to kill the man who raped you, then do it now!"

Two women wanted revenge, and I let them use Wasp Sting. Both of them butchered their victim. One stabbed repeatedly, the other hacked, and both men died slowly. Of the remaining fourteen men, one was not in mail. He was the enemy's shipmaster. He was grey-haired with a scanty beard and brown eyes that looked at me belligerently. "Where did you come from?" I asked him.

He thought about refusing to answer, then thought better. "Beamfleot," he said.

"And Lundene?" I asked him. "The old city is still in Danish hands?"

"Yes."

"Yes, lord," I corrected him

"Yes, lord," he conceded.

"Then you will go to Lundene," I told him, "and then to Beamfleot, and then to anywhere you wish, and you will tell the northmen that Uhtred of Bebbanburg guards the River Temes. And you will tell them they are welcome to come here whenever they wish."

That one man lived. I hacked off his right hand before letting him go. I did it so he could never wield a sword again. By then we had lit a fire, and I thrust his bleeding stump into the red hot embers to seal the wound. He was a brave man. He flinched when we cauterized his stump, but he did not scream as his blood bubbled and his flesh sizzled. I wrapped his shortened arm in a piece of cloth taken from a dead man's shirt. "Go," I ordered him, pointing downriver. "Just go." He walked eastwards. If he was lucky he would survive the journey to spread the news of my savagery.

We killed the others, all of them.

"Why did you kill them?" My new wife asked once, distaste for my thoroughness evident in her voice.

"So they would learn to fear," I answered her, "of course."

"Dead men can't fear," she said.

I try to be patient with her. "A ship left Beamfleot," I explained, "and it never went back. And other men who wanted to raid Wessex heard of that ship's fate. And those men decided to take their swords somewhere else. I killed that ship's crew to save myself having to kill hundreds of other Danes."

"The Lord Jesus would have wanted you to show mercy," she said, her eyes wide.

She is an idiot.

Finan took some of the villagers back to their burned homes where they dug graves for their dead while my men hanged the corpses of our enemies from trees beside the river. We made ropes from strips torn from their clothes. We took their mail, their weapons, and their arm-rings. We cut off their long hair, for I liked to caulk my ships' planks with the hair of slain enemies, and then we hanged them and their pale naked bodies twisted in the small wind as the ravens came to take their dead eyes.

Fifty three bodies hung by the river. A warning to those who might follow. Fifty three signals that other raiders were risking death by rowing up the Temes.

Then we went home, taking the enemy ship with us.

And Serpent-Breath slept in her scabbard.

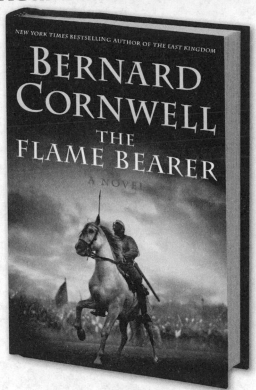